HENRY EVERY

HENRY EVERY

TALES OF PYRACY & MEMOIRS OF THE SOUL

WILL RITTWEGER

Henry Every: Tales of Pyracy & Memoirs of the Soul
Published 2024 by Sage & Taurus

Library of Congress Control Number: 2024906631

ISBN (paperback): 979-8-9902760-0-0
ISBN (hardcover): 979-8-9902760-1-7
eISBN: 979-8-9902760-2-4

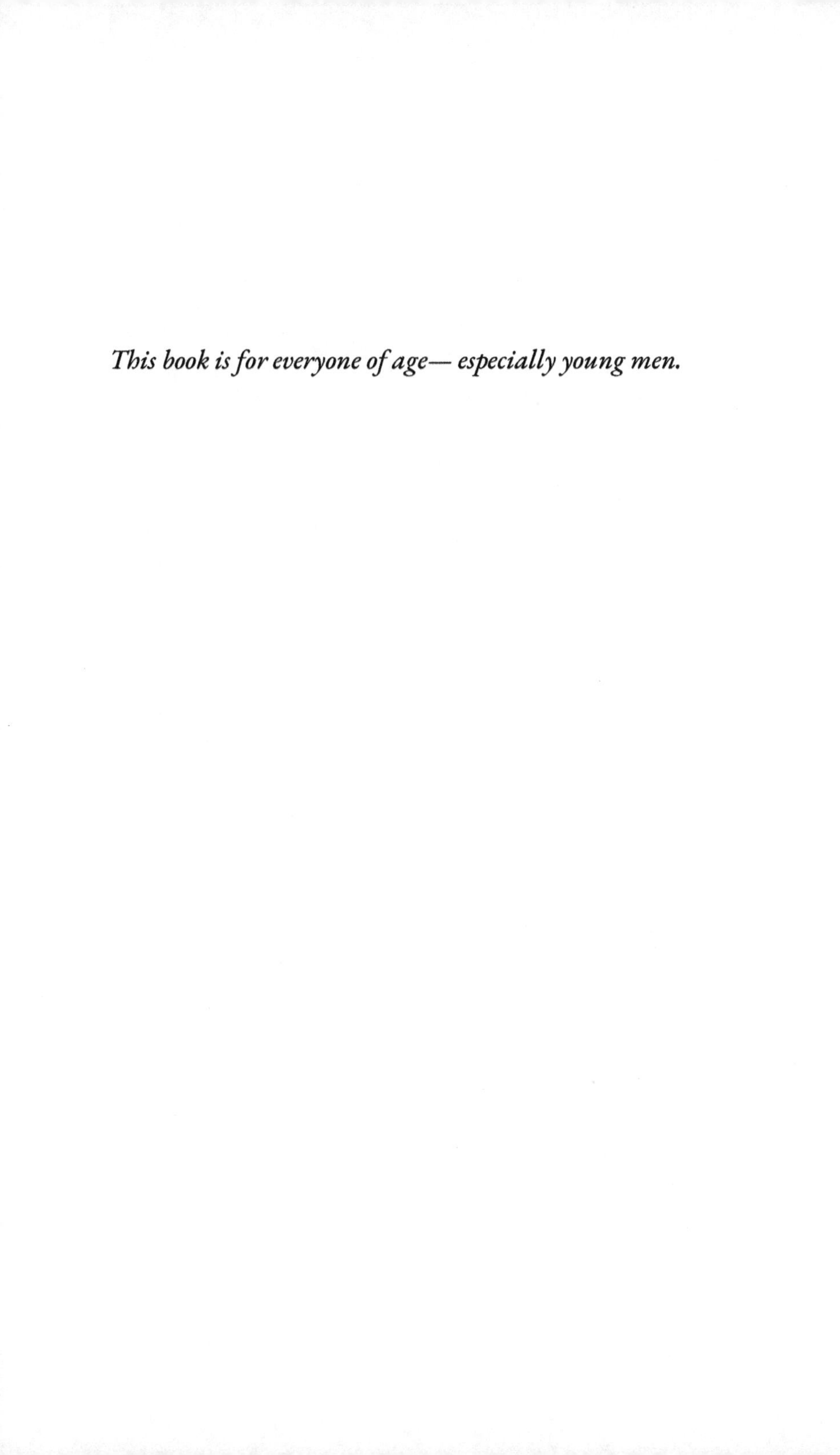

This book is for everyone of age— especially young men.

CONTENTS

HENRY EVERY

It began in early May, during the Year of our Lord 1694. It was the wildest ride of my life. And I miss every second of it. The smell of the salt. Breathing the ocean wind.

The *Fancy* cut through the sea like an everlasting cleaver as we ripped through eternity those two years we lasted.

Captain Henry Every was once a cosmic commodore of those high seas. He gave piracy flair, he gave it a sense of class for a short time, and, most of all, he instilled the honour in thievery. He did all of this through his charisma. We trusted him with our lives, surrendering over everything to the Captain and his ship.

He took me in. Out of the vast desert of goodness exempt from his heart, enveloped in hunger, he took me in. He took me in and protected me and taught me everything he knew. What was it worth? I attempt to account for it to this day.

My name is Rollins Cole. I grew up in the same town as Captain Henry Every. And he didn't find that out until the last day I ever knew him.

Chapter I

MUTINOUS BEGINNING

I wanted better— the crew, the captain, the career. But the options were so goddamn limited and not made for modern man. The only places made for man are the arena, the frontier, and the open sea— that is all. I wanted duty, peril, honour, and all that came with being a great man in this world, but there was no more honour to be had. Even battles or duels that challenged the grain of manhood in those who chose to fight were not what they used to be. Gunpowder, distance— they took away the intimate viciousness of the fight, the thumos. It was 1694 and I was reflecting on the days of the sword, where respect was keen in squabble. While those glorious days were long gone, my musings and self-pity persisted. Employed as a privateer, I was charged with manning cannons full of gunpowder and metal made to maim from afar. I rarely saw their faces, those enemies on the high seas, never directly fighting another man during my brief time in the King & Queen's Navy. Never faced a Frenchman with swords like it should have been. My time was characterised by cannon during the War of the Grand Alliance. I'd only fought ships, far off ideas. While I did believe I had the stomach for head-on brutality, I knew Gibson didn't.

As I swabbed the deck, Gibson walked by me and I looked at him like any other crewmate. Captain Gibson was made captain of our ship, the *Charles II*, shortly before I joined up. He was too bloody pale to command us and earn our respect. He was a meek lad, afflicted with a dull complexion and carelessly groomed black hair. It was said that his predecessor, Captain Strong, was a good skipper, but I hadn't had the chance to observe him much, for he died still in England's port. Gibson did not give a damn about the well-being of his crew, like any good captain should. He was self-centred and overly cautious. I could not trust his leadership, for he lacked the quality altogether. Had he the courage to lead us from this Spanish abyss, I would surely have followed him to the Locker. But he did no such thing. And I knew his obedience was not because he believed in the status of our contracts or lack of pay, but he simply lacked the stomach to defy anything or anyone. He had no guts. A man's got to have guts in this world, and the world must know he does.

I then watched our admiral, Admiral Sir O'Byrne, the Irishman, follow Captain Gibson down the stairs into the ship's upper deck shortly after Gibson passed me by. O'Byrne served as a Spanish Navy Marine. He knew what it was like to risk his skin every day in the line of fire. That was what I'd heard. He commanded all four ships of our expedition and was the only leader, besides Every, in the entire privateer convoy worth his salt, according to the fellas.

It was May the sixth, and we had been stuck at port in beautiful Corunna, Spain since January. The port's beauty faded as our spirit for movement halted. There is nothing that makes a man feel more stagnant than a ship stuck at port. And there is nothing that makes a man brew on his vexations more than swabbing with other disenfranchised lads. My shipmates were brooding. We did wonder and grow frustrated about the ennui. I got angry sometimes. I took my anger out on the deck swabbing at that moment, pressing my fingers nearly through the sponge, trying to let go of it. But a man must get good and angry when he is promised something and the agreement is severed. Such was the case with our wages. Our contracts had been violated and some of my crewmate's wives went as far as corresponding via letter with Sir James Houblon, the wealthy investor who paid our wages, in order to redeem our pay. It was to no avail. Luckily, I didn't have a family who needed me to send money home. Nor a wife. As the youngest crew member on the ship, at only twenty-two years, none of my older shipmates gave a damn about me, my young man quandaries, or the grim prospect of becoming a slave.

"What becomes of us, lads?" I asked my fellow swabbies.

"Ye saw the food inventory. It's meagre," One older swabbie said.

Another sailor brashly remarked, "We won't get paid. But even if we were being hoodwinked and we're not stagnant after all, we'd be sold into slavery. Don't fret yerself, Cole, ye could still find yer way out of it and live a full life, untouched and unharmed, for ye're a junior lad."

"Maybe," I said.

I exhibited a thick-skinned smirk and looked back at my swabbing. A sailor condemned to become a slave? There is no worse fate. Whenever I'd ask my crewmates about our situation, I was first answered with their pessimism about absent wages and lack of food, then followed-up with conspiratorial prospects of slavery, and finished off with snide remarks about the privilege of my youth. To them, the tormenting realities of slavery were comparably diminished because of my youth. They thought they had it worse than me. Pity became a competition aboard the ship.

Everybody thinks they've amassed the worst of fortunes, when often, fortune only becomes misfortune voluntarily. Privateers are odd. Whilst they go to any lengths to acquire fortune, they do not want to be free of their misfortunes— especially when their ship is at port. They love problems. Know this— sailors love the weight of their problems as if they are gold badges of achievement upon their dainty, shaggy, unofficial uniforms. The heft of their problems weighs them down not with burden, but with supposed blessing. I hated most sailors, for they carried such burdensome weight with them. When I came across a good one, a sailor who was as light as a feather and free of the damning forces of self-pity, I did my best to keep close. I thought of First Mate Every as a good one.

Every walked by us swabbies and went down into the upper deck. Shortly after, he, Captain Gibson, and Admiral O'Byrne reappeared on the main deck in our plain view. I tensed up at the likely incoming conflict and looked toward Every. The man had a fire in his eyes. He was the only sailor aboard man enough to go over Gibson's head and argue directly with Admiral O'Byrne, one of the few virtuous heads of this mostly unvirtuous convoy of snakes. O'Byrne was a thin, narrow-faced man, covered in Irish freckles. His red hair sharply contrasted his pale face. O'Byrne was a good man, patient, but he was caught up in our maelstrom. With authority, O'Byrne walked ahead of Gibson and Every, then turned around to face Every.

"Listen, Every, I know ye. And I know the whole crew of this frigate and other three ships in the expedition are on edge about the pay and the contracts. But ye have to give me some more time. Ye're tying my hands and cutting off my legs here," O'Byrne said in front of the entire crew.

Every stared and smirked at O'Byrne. By all measures of appearance and manner, Henry Every was a wolf. However, his position as first mate confined him to sheep's clothing. Overqualified for that position, his aspect evidently outgrew the restraint required of a first mate. Every had the look of great Jupiter about him, retaining all of the sharp, hard tenor of the framed, scowling expressions and frozen, frightening grimaces conjured from the stone busts of bearded Zeus, Poseidon, Hades, and their equivalents.

Every replied:

"And what should we do? Eat our hair and send home our earrings' gold for the family? That is going too far whilst we haven't left Corunna. I have a family like most of the older lads on this crew. We're English privateers under Spanish commission paid by English noblemen. English noblemen— the wealthiest under the Crown? We've got no wages, we're stuck, and we're quite salty now. Too damn salty to keep waiting like we've been. Gibson and ye keep saying the same bloody things, O'Byrne, tellin' us— 'we're all doing the best we can, and we've all made sacrifices, whether it be captain or crew.' For how long must a ship's crew, a ship's blood, be sacrificed?" Every asked gravely.

Every found a way to cut into a man's heart when he spoke if he wanted. He'd do it in a most elegant, calm manner. Whenever Every got passionately heated, if ever, someone had truly crossed a line. Houblon, O'Byrne, and Gibson seemed to be dancing that line.

"Ye must wait," O'Byrne said, turned around, and then left the ship with Gibson.

Although his rank was below those men, Every was mature and looked it. He had the age of thirty-five to him. An assortment of light and dark brown hairs encompassed his shallow mane and facial hair, with small greys unveiling themselves throughout. His beard concluded at the length of a thumb. Covering his seasoned hairs and headscarf postured a triple-cocked hat, black as ink with a silver stripe.

Every put his hands on his hips, standing in the middle of the deck, silently like a lone statue. He was a burly man, with a wide chest and broad stance, whose imposing physicality took up every measure of space around him. His height barely surpassed the average man, but his nonphysical stature dwarfed any man. Subdued fury catapulted his every gesture in that moment. The tails of his blood-red justacorps coat, with a black, high collar enchanted with golden buttons and hem, flapped in the soft breeze. The smoothly swaying jacket enveloped a dark long vest. His over-garments were fastened by a scarlet sash belt.

Every then altered his posture. Something was brewing within him. As he shifted his weight from one leg to the other, his sheathed cutlass and two dusky-brown pistols holstered in his sash, further extending the width of his imposing person, rattled slightly. Every then fiddled briefly with his white cravat burgeoning from his neck, and readjusted the small, white ruffled sleeves poking out on each wrist. His attire reflected his nature— miniscule blossoms of pale innocence swallowed by the deluging sea of a black and crimson garb. The apparel only seemed to make the demigod blend into the times and among the crew. Beneath the exterior of his proper, veiled garb, poking out via the skin of his head, neck, and hands, the body of his true, masculine complexion intimidated henceforth. All around us and him was silence, other than the wind and footsteps of the departing Gibson and O'Byrne.

Every was the first mate of our man-o'-war vessel and usually remained quiet in matters of crew vs. captainship. I think he saw it as politics, which he preferred to abstain from, as most honourable men do. But undoubtedly, he bit his tongue no longer. Every garnered our crew's respect and Gibson's respect by being a bridge between them in practical matters, when needed. He truly spoke with the heart of the crew that day. But it was for naught.

My eyes traced back toward Every's face. His eyelids faintly shuddered and lip quivered once in anger. It was unusual for him to get mad, however, the plight of our stagnation and wages affected not only Every's livelihood. It was affecting his family's, which was too beneath his standards to turn a blind eye toward. The integrity of the *Charles II*'s leadership had already been crumbling. Right then, from the small shifts in face and posture of Every, the man who was the binding of our ship and crew, the crumbling disintegrated.

Every walked away. I looked to my crewmates for their reactions after the exchange. There were no telltales. Their faces were blank, like mine. I wondered how the men reckoned with the quiet storm speedily approaching. Were we supposed to draw swords at one another in anguish toward our lot? Were we meant to see the worst of ourselves in one another over delayed wages? Should we have praised the admiral's forthcomingness? The captain's authority? The first mate's uprightness? The crew's patience? The vessel's integrity? The Almighty's mystery? Every wasn't a religious man but he had the grace and restraint of a biblical man. O'Byrne and Gibson were certainly an irreverent lot. What were us seamen to do to find a centre, to find a hearth and home amidst the overbearing yet voluntary wilderness of privateering on the high seas? Were our nobilities and determinations reliant upon a man on the chair who signed our wages or a man with his hands on the helm pointing the way? Were our lowest of lows reflected by the poop-deck scrubber and barnacle cleaner alike? Why did we have the desire to look at man as problem and solution, the end and the beginning of our joys and woes?

I was stuck in my mind. The swabbing was nothing to me. I had lived too long upon the world of flesh, duty, of brotherhood and tribes, and I felt dead. I came to the seas for the spirithood of saintliness, known predominantly by the monks and the holy ones who hid away, untouched by the vehement enclosures of duty to a rambunctious, undeserving neighbour. Yet I found myself absolutely reliant upon and servant to my sordid neighbour. I did not want to care for my neighbour anymore. I only wanted to be responsible for myself and my duty to the ship. I thought that our ship and leadership itself must be reformed. But men cannot be reformed if they are stagnant, if they lay around, waiting for progress, pay, and plans among a group of similarly disheartened men. Mutiny. Oh, fantastical mutiny. Her inevitability was in our foresights.

I was sick of having endless conversations with myself. Some excitement lay ahead. It was to happen. It was still the day before the incoming mutiny. After my swabbing ceased, I was staring out at the edge of where the port met the Atlantic, as I had done for countless days. The face of cowardice and colden fear reflected toward me from a crewmate, Oliver Rossi. He approached. Uncertainty possessed some of the men despite the obvious direction of our incoming second wind. Rossi, the Mediterranean lad, struck up a conversation with me and we found ourselves talking of mutiny.

"Rollins, ye must care about the captain's dealings. The crew lives and dies at its captain's mercy. The captain controls everything. Whosoever is captain hath the stakes of all our well-beings in his palms. This must be uncertain for ye, and ye must stick with Gibson, should Every attempt mutiny, for he is likely to fail. Gibson hath the rank and the weight of the fleet. Every only hath the love of the crew, and love is a fickle emotion," he said to me.

"Mutiny shall happen, I see it in Every's eyes. Oliver, each man is at the captain's mercy, but we can only observe and obey the captain. Whether I'm an observative obedient or a plain ol' disobedient, neither grant a captain power over my entire soul... only my aquatic services. I have watched a captain, loathed a captain, and praised a captain before. It is like chasing the wind. But. Sailing downwind and chasing the wind are two different things. No matter who is captain, Every or Gibson, I shall be sailing with the breeze that blows the hair out of my face. I shall be at peace. All the while, ye and the crew are whining and dying with each step of this ugly saga of who thinks they run the *Charles II*. The crew runs the boat, Rossi. Count me out of your bets. It is all a fad. A show of how little and puny man is in the current. How much he surrenders his belief and soul to a captain's mercy. I am indifferent to captainship. I have my wishes but a captain is only a captain, simply a position," I told him.

"Ye're lost. What the hell do ye mean?" he asked.

"What I mean is remember ye're guided from within, not without. And know who shall win the showdown but cease yer caring. The numbers, not the ranks or titles, steer the wheel when ye're at port or down on yer luck."

"Ye fool, ye have no place on this ship if ye lack a stake in what happens. Ye keep unfounded hopes. We should find ye a replacement," Rossi scorned me.

"Ah, but ye won't, and ye can't. For ye grant no power to yerself, only the captain, and my replacement is a captain's concern, not yers. Ye still think, live, and die at his token, ye lily-livered fool," I said, looking at Rossi's grimace.

Rossi walked away. Little did Rossi know, I relished at the direction Every would lead the ship. But I was careful, should our rebellious attempt to usurp the witless Gibson fail. I played both sides. I had a stake in what was happening, but Rossi was not to know. I did not want him to see that while I was above it all, I still kept one foot deeply entrenched in the matter. Why? I did not like that man. I did not trust him. I must outwit him, I thought, for Rossi was an ignorant lad. He was undoubtedly asleep, undoubtedly simple. A dull blade is far more dangerous than a sharpened blade. And Rossi was amongst the dullest. Rossi only saw us vs. them. He only saw Gibson and the status quo vs. Every and the tides of fate. Rossi was afraid of whatever potential Every could offer us disenfranchised, remaining a non-conspirator. All non-conspirators had to perish and be purged from our ship.

Nearby crewmates overheard our conversation, thus bringing the incoming mutiny and my indifference to their ears. I watched their reactions. Some of the listeners smirked, some frowned, and some were hard to read. I stuck by my beliefs. One should keep some roots of tradition. Furthermore, one must also see the direction of changing wind. I had a stake in Gibson, the familiar, and also in Every, the future. I occasionally sunk my teeth into the world's forbidden fruit of rebellion, yet always retained my inner fortress, away and above it all. I am averse to the malignancy of so-called "worldly progress" but I am a tender friend of moving forward. This practical stance was my temperament and my philosophy. My spirit was solidified and sturdy despite Rossi's fickle debate, but my hands and brain, in dealing with the world, must always be rough-and-tumble.

I noticed Every looking on, as well. In Every, I saw the altruistic heart of Jesus and the cunning mind of Satan. He was a duality, but which one was to be his dominant ruler— submission or rebellion? I may be God-fearing, and Every likely was, but I never heard him remark of the Almighty. Those last words he spoke to O'Byrne were not those of a man with blind faith, but of a man who sought to take matters into his own hands. It appeared his priorities relied upon the integrity of rank and a man's word, bedrocks of what had worked in the past for the good of the crew, not the hogwash which his superiors told him in order to save their own skin and preserve their position. Tradition and competence should prevail, not faith and meekness. But our superiors prescribed us a diet of submission and unfounded trust. Regardless of how the crew felt or who they chose to stick with, sailing the ship the proper way would maintain our divine providence, no matter the captain. Sailing with men of probity and honour, fitting for their rank, was paramount.

This world I lived in was going places I did not want it to. The crew was being strung along, believing they had agency over themselves. They gave advice as if they actually knew well what they spoke of. I looked at us all. We were a band of mostly illiterate sailors, who knew little about anything— and less of ourselves. But I knew my spirit. The world, evidenced by the crew, were all lost at sea, trying to find grounding on the wood planks of our ship. They failed to realise that the only safety from cannon fire and the blade came from the world of the spirit, not the luck of a proper captain on the right side of a mutiny. I sensed Every had a similar inner resolve, and that is why he had my favour, deep down, for he could handle himself in this chaos. I trusted him and his indifference. He had the courage to act in defiance of mortality or law, keep within the confines of the calm, invincibility of his spirit, try to improve the lot of babbling sailors who think themselves competent, and make our environment flourish through his own example— these qualities surely make a great sailor and a great man. I believed that fully, and I believed Every possessed these traits. He had proven it to me countless times in his dealings with the crew and his superiors.

Later that evening, Every bandied his mutiny recruiting throughout the convoy. He was the chief orchestrator, having consulted with other disgruntled officers, sailors on our ship, and those of a fellow convoy frigate, the *Dove*. Some crewmates didn't believe he would do it. I heard one sailor say, "Every won't intervene, he'll only speak and stand a-by" when we were sitting in a cluster at the mess that night, dipping our small shares of sea biscuits into beer. I myself originally wanted to abstain from any physical involvement in the conflict, but I could not resist fate. Blood was on the horizon. It was agreed that the next night, May the seventh, we were to take the *Charles II*. Every doubtlessly did not know who I truly was at the time. He would.

That next day of reckoning came, that fateful, self-interested day which made my mind fret and my blood boil. The hearty waters of mutiny were stirred in the depths of our crew. It was what I came to sea for at last— a real show, a real breaking free. How we waited for nightfall, like sharks on that seventh day in sunny May.

When the sun exited the sky, O'Byrne left the ship for the evening, and we all gathered at an inn two streets from the dock. We talked over and prioritised the order of the operation, squatting together like a mob of boys planning some mischief. The approach was straightforward— ally with the co-conspirators, round up the neutral, expel the opposition, and get on the open water as fast as possible. Shortly after the discussion, we walked out of the inn. The night was dark. Outside of the pub, that pivotal evening, my heart dropped when I spoke my only words to Every and the group of mutineers. We were taking our first steps toward the direction of the dock.

"Are we truly about to do this, lads?" I asked.

Many of them turned to look at Every, who, in turn, stopped and looked me dead in the eyes. Every's gaze scorched me back into line, thus out of my own fearful hesitations. He did not say a word, nor did he tolerate a moment of second thought, thus wielding the sword of providence in this duel. His message was sent. I didn't know if he would ever remember the stare after that night, but I never forgot it.

We continued, the gang of us moving forward inconspicuously. I looked around and saw the men's hands upon their sword handles, prematurely. Our faces shone with resolve, mirroring our leader. Boots clanked first on the streets and then onto the dock. Our swords were not yet drawn as we eventually stepped onto the dock. I could see the moonlight reflecting off the water beside the *Charles II*— white light on a black obsidian sea. There lay our wooden homeland ahead of us, to be taken back, to be taken into our hands. The ship looked quiet and destined for our taking, waiting to be removed from the sleepy port.

We all had a silent agreement for we did not know what the result of our efforts would be, likely failure, but we didn't look back or question any step we were about to take in our leap of faith. I ran about and removed our vessel's ropes from the cleats on the dock.

The speed of the moment slowed as we stepped off of the dock, across the gangway, then onto the main deck of our resting ship, separated from Corunna's dock for the first time since arriving months ago. The sound of water hitting the boat drowned out any noise of speech and rumbling boots in those moments. No more filibustering. Only moving up and forward.

We rushed aboard our man-o'-war, enveloping and reminding the watchmen of the mutiny with whispers and the unsheathing of our swords. Captain Gibson was incapacitated and bedridden with feverish drunkenness down below, not that he would have been much of an obstacle anyways. We scattered through the ship, like blood entering water. With drawn swords, we scanned the decks, top to bottom, for all of the men. We kept quiet until we were able to leave the dock and free ourselves from the nightmare port.

I loved the sight of determined sailors storming a ship in the pale moonlight. One has not felt the fumes of a fiery momentum so strong as that of a quiet mutiny. A pair of men stayed behind, at the ready, manning the pilot ladder and gangway. Nobody else in the harbour knew yet that we were taking the vessel. This surprise we yearned for was a flavour that caused men to drool from their clenching bruxism mouths. And mine. The time was finally ours. The anticipation stuffed and stifled within us for months was unleashed. At last, we would have at our hunger. It was in the air around us, circling, this satisfactory surprise.

Then down into the heart of the ship, we encroached. Men scattered everywhere, swirling throughout the corridors. The main lanes of the sleeping quarters housed about seventy men. Plenty of sailors remained at the ready down below. I saw many rising from their hammocks to grab their swords, showing loyalty to the movement when push came to shove, showing loyalty to Every. But a few men, a few small men, all mollycoddles, stayed in their hammocks frozen in fear or ran out of the ship's inner deck to desert the movement, when the moment of truth presented itself. The deserters were too afraid to fight back and defend the cause of our employment, too afraid to face the imminent challenges required of the direction mutiny was to take us. Those runners were boys amongst us men and they could not handle their own fear, the danger of mutiny, and the life of piracy imminently awaiting us.

I saw a sight I wished every man could see— his cowardly enemy running in the opposite direction. We let them all go. We had the power to do so. Every man on the boat knew mutiny would happen that night and still some could not stomach it. All deserters, waking up, nearly defecating all over themselves, and ditching all of their possessions, ran based purely on fear of the tremendous unknown and its mandated savageness to traverse it. We surrounded every nook of the vessel, with swords ready to slice. But all were spared, whether they joined, surrendered, or escaped. Miraculously, no blood was shed.

I sneaked away from the scene of pandemonium and made my way to the captain's quarters. Every was nowhere in sight since we got aboard and commenced the rounding up, therefore he must have been in the captain's quarters, I deduced. It was where the important business was conducted. I walked toward the quarters. Upon entering, I saw Every and Second Mate Joseph Dawson in Gibson's quarters, both lounging against the wall. They stood relaxed as the boat rumbled with lively boots. Gibson, likely laying on his bed, was blocked from my view by the wall next to the open door. Every and Dawson stared into that invisible place, beyond my sight.

There had not been this much going on aboard the ship since we arrived at Corunna months ago. Mutiny had brought life back aboard the *Charles II*. Sixty-four guns needed to be used, and they needed to be brandished by lively men, not the meek. I saw Every get off the wall, as I stood outside the door, frozen, watching the unfolding. I feared he would kill the bedridden Gibson, who was a weakened spectator. Every moved to the right. Was he to use force?

Every was once in the King & Queen's Navy. He fought in, and somehow survived, the Battle of Beachy Head. We'd both fought in that same war, but in different battles on different vessels. I fought aboard the *Romulus* ship of the line at Barfleur and La Hougue. Many Englishmen were slain that day at Beachy Head. Every must have known violence and death and war. He contained it. He walked toward Gibson's chair behind a desk, and sat in it. He then looked to the outside of the open door, toward me, and noticed my spectating.

"Come in," Every surprised me.

He saw me and I was embarrassed at my watching. I was a man of action, goddamnit, I should not have been a spectator. I walked into the captain's quarters and sheathed my sword. I looked at Dawson posturing against the wall, the candlelight brightening his pale, dirty face. I looked at Gibson. Gibson was captivated and rendered captive by both the sickness of rum and Every's firm control over his former chair, his former quarters, and his soon-to-be former captainship. Then Every asked me the question we were all asking ourselves in this plain, small, blue painted room with gold accents and one authoritative desk. Despite the varying positions and postures of us four men in that room, we were all wondering the same thing.

"Well, Cole," he looked away from me, coldly, and then gazed back to Gibson with the stare of a he-devil. "Should we kill him?"

Every asked as if the man he served under the past few months of our contract did not mean a damn thing, as if Gibson was a stepping stone. Gibson's command— forgotten, his life— collateral damage.

"I don't know, sir," I said.

"She's a big ship. But she doesn't fit two captains," Every said.

Every stopped talking and we all stared at Gibson, bedridden and mute from nausea. My eyes darted between Every and Dawson.

"There's no need for killing tonight," Every said.

Every sat up in the chair, opened the drawer, grabbed the captain's keys, stood up, then walked toward me. Second Mate Dawson followed behind, uncrossing his arms and giving Gibson a dirty look as they exited.

"What, we're going to leave the man, sir?" I asked Every.

"He can't do a thing. Come," Every confirmed and we departed the man and his bed.

Every locked the captain's cabin door behind us and continued walking. I fell in line with him and Dawson. We walked out of the captain's quarters to the stairs and I bolted past the pair onto the main deck. I saw more and more men running past either way, going below deck to secure the crew or running past me going upward to man the sails. Then I heard a tender bumping against the side of the ship. It must have been a more coordinated effort than I thought. They must have been men of the *James*, approaching from the frigate's direction. I ran to the rail to see who from the rest of our convoy had joined our cause. The tender was filled with a few more men, having rowed to join our mutiny. It was written.

"Our drunken bos'n is aboard," a man of the *James'* tender said to one of our watchmen, speaking in a code.

"Aye," our man responded, and they joined us.

By that time, all of the men aboard were either rounded up in surrender or grasping swords, looking for orders and readying the ship for an escape, as plenty more of our cause filed onto the main deck of our man-o'-war. I looked back to see Every and Dawson enter the wide open of the main deck. Every was calm. He moved about much slower than his initial, inspired charge of the *Charles II*. It was time to sail, and sail fast. The ropes called us and we whispered to one another. The sails and posts we manned called upon us to take the ship once and for all. Every pointed his finger east, the only logical way out of port which we all knew. Then we scattered about to our respective places.

The men commenced their business, unfurling the gaff sails, fore sails, and main sails. A helmsman grabbed the vessel by her throat, the wheel, and slammed it starboard to catch the soft residue of the westerly winds and generous tidal currents, setting us eastward toward the northern exit of the port. She soon started moving. We floated silently for a while and made it an impressive distance. I snuck to the head of the ship, looking starboard toward the *James*, one of the other frigates in the venture whose lanterns lit up a crew of onlookers on their deck. As we drifted, we were passing them on their starboard side. We had nearly coasted entirely past them but it was not far enough. A man yelled out from their deck. It was Captain Humphreys yelling, next to one of his men, that alerted us. I recognized his voice.

"Is that Every? Sir, the men are deserting," the figure of the *James* yelled toward us.

Then Every spoke the infamous words which all sailors remember him for.

"Of course."

Every shifted to the helm and took control of the *Charles II*'s steering. Then the statue-like man of the *James* became many men. Their sailors quickly busied their deck and armed their cannons. I ran for cover as our ship made an about-face. We turned hard to starboard, and moved forward and eastward. Then the *James* fired at us. What wanton monsters. Unless he wasn't a captain, Humphreys should have joined us. Men fire quickest upon those they envy the most. A captain, firing upon a first mate's mutiny? It must spell envy. What man shoots downward? The *James*' Captain Humphreys was a lowly captain.

A small Spanish fort, the Castle of San Antón, which overlooked the league of moored and docked ships in the port, was alerted and joined in the firing upon us. They were on our port side as the *James* was on our starboard. The wood chipped and ripped from the twelve-pounder balls of iron flying our way, coming for my head, on both sides of our vessel from the fort and from the *James*. I ducked and crawled. The hollering intensified, and the mutiny became loud. No more running— the chaos was created by men yelling. I rolled from the side of the vessel to the mast. Men ran around me all about our craft. I glanced back at the *James* and fort, which were eventually out of range as we slowly drifted away. We escaped by the thinnest of measures, the slightest amount of time, with miniscule damage inflicted.

Away we went, northward out of the port, away from the commands of any more English under Spanish contract in that hellish port. The *Charles II* was ours, as was the infamy of its grand swindle. We passed a Spanish Basque whaling vessel on our starboard side, coming into port. The whaling ship's stench, likely after she returned from the heart of the Bay of Biscay, permeated through the air around it, entering our nostrils. The combined smell of the sea and scent of dead fish one eventually became used to. But I had not smelled a dead whale before. It was unforgivable. That night, the dead whale was our smell of victory.

"On yer feet, Cole. This isn't a fucking exhibition," Third Mate Archibald Jamison yelled me up into action.

I went to my post, climbing to handle the fore-and-aft sails, but I did not pay attention. I looked back over our port side. I saw the distant whaling vessel and the entrance to the port where the ships of our old expedition remained. We continued westward, toward the Atlantic, and my eyesight fell upon the tall, towering Farum Brigantium, an old lighthouse supposedly built upon the body and arms of a mythological creature. What I didn't see beyond our previous path was my past itself— my family, those distant figures, my livelihood; and who I was— all henceforth left behind. Rollins Cole was no longer a privateer, no longer a lawful privateer. I was a pirate.

Whatever men tell in tales or in discourse, there is immense fear in piracy. But fear is the mother of all exhilaration. Once the excitement of mutiny dissipates, fear grabs hold of a pirate. And it never lets go. One can only get stronger or more arrogant in its grasp. He must be a ferocious dog toward the terror of cowardice or it shall own him forever.

I felt I played a role in the mutiny and had my intentions, but ultimately the infamy was out of my hands. I only chose my side and joined it with enthusiasm. Such was the life of a seaman. An individual seaman means little on a ship. Officers and crews were the puppeteers. I saw in Every a benevolent type of puppeteer, and I hoped he would someday see himself in me. I did not know what to feel in those moments as I manoeuvred the rigging. Maybe a hybrid of fear and ecstatic wonder. It was new territory for all of us.

These revelations dawned on me after the violence had settled down and the ship was silenced to the dull ordering of our *Charles II*'s westward manoeuvrings.

There is a grey area on the spectrum of dutiful submission. Follow God and His rules or trek with passionate overtaking found on the path of Luciferian freedom. The ship started to sail this in between. I'd heard many tales of freshly christened pirates going either way, toward virtue and brotherhood or toward vice, unrelenting rebelliousness, and unending hunger. Regardless of the manner in which either path began for them, vice had always won out in the end for pirates. There were no noble pirates I knew of to date. Even the most virtuous among them were still criminals and murderers. I hoped Every, our crew, and myself were going to be different. Self-preservation and cold slaughter are different animals. But desire is an all-encompassing predator, which stalks and haunts you at every corner of pirate life. Learning to navigate its twists and turns, for desire isn't wholly good or wholly evil, is a lifetime occupation.

Like the stories of many famed brilliant men, we had mostly improvised our path along the way. The remains of our former venture were in God's hands. We were in our own hands. We had to take our fortunes, not earn them by being compliant. Men in this world have no rite of passage, no grand initiation. No. There are plenty of mockeries made at this primitive notion— sacraments, courtship. But as a sailor, the only initiation into true selfhood, manhood, and independence is the route of piracy. It is a symbolic initiation of forging one's own destiny instead of following a country.

Outside, and to this world, I was a pirate. But inside, I was still Rollins Cole, a young man on a search. All men are searching. And we all choose whether we continue our search or give up whatever we're looking for somewhere along the way. I wondered what Every was searching for. I wondered what my father would think of my search and what he had searched for at my age. Did he stop searching when he became a husband and a father? Is my search hindered because of my new legal standing in the Empire, in the world?

These fundamental questions, all necessary, pertinent questions, occupy a sailor's mind when he is marooned or when he turns to piracy. Freedom audits a man. Right then, I felt I had lost God and lost my easy answers. The audience and steady, firm hand of a nation behind me had gone to the wayside in our rebellion. How must we contend with this world without these answers, without these sanctified paths? There was no more country or fathers' blessings. We had only our freedom, blinding freedom, blanketing us.

I can look to my superiors on how to conduct myself on ships. I can look to the poets for how I can allow my infatuations to dictate my decisions. I can look to good commanders and shifty politicians for how to rule others, even in their contrasting methods. But where do I look if I don't know what I'm looking for? And how was I to know what I had if I ever were to grasp it? I lose myself in this mind. It is the long-standing damnation which provoked in me the longing and constitution to be a sailor in the first place. I needed space to roam. I already had a permanent residence in my mind. My mind is an ocean of a never-ending series of waves tossing about, with only rare leaves. The same can be said for life on a ship. You're told to handle and rule a ship, but after spending enough time on her, you realise it is the vessel that handles and rules you. You attempt to control, pressure, and cajole the current of your own mind, but ultimately, it controls, pressures, and cajoles you. As above, so below. I was a sailor, through and through.

We handled minor affairs that first night, the late evening of our mutiny. Then we rested. On to a new day. The sun emerged and cast light upon a ship no longer sailed by men with loyalties to any empire, but by those with loyalties to seamanship, liberty, and themselves. We all gathered on deck, sailing as the Spanish sun claimed our formerly pale English skin.

"Doth any man here claim loyalty to the Crown or to the ol' captain? Any man who steps forward shall be spared. I give ye my word. All of ye know I am good for it," Every asked us boys and men, as he held his pistol pointing downward toward the deck.

A few men then stepped forward, going to the bow, where Gibson sat in his daze. I saw them and their weakling shadows walk away from life. But which one was the wiser? Me or them? Every came back to us men, stepping in to stop one bloke who was switching sides.

"I don't think so, Fitz. We need ye," Every said as he placed his hand on the man's chest, halting him.

It was Preston Fitzgerald, our chief and only surgeon. Every shot Fitz a deep stare, backing him into line. The surgeon retreated to us mutineers, despite his will. Fitzgerald's skills were too irreplaceably valuable to dismiss. Once the chess pieces were in place, with Every and Gibson as separate kings and us men as pawns, he commenced his rhetoric.

"So, Gibson, we seized our chance last night. Shall ye seize yer opportunity now? I give ye now liberty to sway us crew with words. Can ye win us back and command us, should I relieve meself of the wayward captainship? Let truth decide," he exalted and stood swaggeringly with his hands folded over one another at the belt, toting an eloquent pistol. "If ye do choose to speak, of course," he said mockingly, to Gibson.

"No," Gibson raised his heavy head and said before lowering it back to the ground.

"Oh, Mr. Gibson, is it the boozery that the captainship of an English-funded vessel permits ye? Or is it yer lack of stomach preventing ye from the call? Which is it? I can even extend ye a second mate position. Can ye handle it? Or is the bottle with discipline of a superior too restraining to keep ye happy?" Every asked.

"It is the inescapable fate of all pyrates that prohibits me— ye shall all hang," Gibson said with chilling confidence as his head remained drooped in the hot sun.

The deck fell silent, as two more men walked back to Gibson's side, leaving us. Every grinned at their side-switching.

"So. Ye shall be cast off, back to yer bosom of yer slavery and yer contracts. It is not for me," Every exclaimed and he turned around, outstretching his arms like Christ. "And anyone else? This is yer chance to go home, to be defined by what ye were and always shall be. But if ye stay with me, ye shall have somethin' better." His charisma returned the morale to the rag-tag pirates as we stiffened upright and nobody else shifted. "Our court is now adjourned," Every said.

The tender was prepared, the deserters entered, and two of our lads rowed off with them, bringing the deserters to the Spanish coast, then the pair returned. Considering he led the mutiny, confronted the old captain himself, and took the lead ever since, Every was unanimously elected captain of the vessel. Nevertheless, he mustered another court together shortly after Gibson and his loyalists were discarded, finalising the new crew of this *Charles II*.

"Now that we are alone, gentle pyrates of the *Charles II*, a ship which shall be rechristened, I must ask a question. Who shall be our captain? I'll let you decide. I suggest we nominate an upper rank and replace him, considering we ranked men have the most experience," he orchestrated then went silent. "So, please, who takes us to the Round?"

Every waved his hand and gestured to eight other men to come forward and be voted upon. They were all distinguished by high position and merited respect among the crew and in the eyes of the English and Spanish— the former first mate, second mate, third mate, quartermaster, bos'n, navigator, master-at-arms, and master gunner of the *Charles II*. Every, formerly the first mate, stepped forward to commence the voting. It was there that Every officially earned his rank above the master of ceremonies and leader of the mutiny. We unanimously voted to solidify his captainship of the vessel and crew. The other eight men voted for him, as well. All hands raised for Every.

"Well then. Is there any rebuttal? Good. To Madagascar, me boys," Captain Every said.

All men trusted his hand. A disgruntled and disheartened crew, once so divided, were unified under a single man's command. With his trusted council of the other eight most experienced comrades, Every henceforth became Caesar. The typical democracy aboard any other pirate vessel did not exist there. For us, one man led and a few wise ones advised, but everyone absolutely followed the Captain. Else, stagnation would come again. The difference was, despite retaining the custom of endowing some authority to the experienced and ranked men, the structure we maintained as privateers, one of our own commanded us, not a Houblon, O'Byrne, or Gibson. Every was common to all. Our sacred oath was between a captain and crew, not between a contract and crew or country and crew.

Before we permanently crossed our Rubicon by rechristening the vessel, Every became the sole sovereign of the *Charles II*, under God and fortune. It was then, May eighth, 1694, on bended knee, we looked upon our captain and adopted his spirit as our own— to take our wealth and to preserve the crew above all else. We enacted only two pirate articles. The first article stated that all sailors, including the ranked ones, were formally entitled to one share of all treasures collected— and Every was granted two. The second article stated that all men must obey the Captain's command, thus officially solidifying Captain Henry Every as the king of our man-o'-war. All agreed to the rules. Captain Every then set our course for the Pirate Round and we continued southward down the Atlantic Ocean.

<u>*Chapter II*</u>

SAME ORDERS, DIFFERENT FLAGS

Alongside our chief vocalist and troubadour, Clancy Williams, a lad only two years my senior, we sang our shanties with heavy rope in hand:

> *"We left our country, forget her!*
> *For Madagascar and treasure!*
> *We left our country, forget her!*
> *For Madagascar and treasure!"*

> *"Well, in stormy weather we go below deck!*
> *The mermaids all pine for our necks!*
> *A sperm whale blows a big, fat squall!*
> *To Davy Jones' locker, should our Fancy fall!"*

> *"We left our country, forget her!*
> *For Madagascar and treasure!*
> *We left our country, forget her!*
> *For Madagascar and treasure!"*

> *"Oh, the Cape calls out our names at dusk!*
> *We catch a fatty walrus by the tusk!*
> *We toast to sailing then a-twiddle our thumbs!*
> *No matter the splinters stuck on our bums!"*

> *"We left our country, forget her!*
> *For Madagascar and treasure!*

We left our country, forget her!
For Madagascar and treasure!"

Off to the Cape of Good Hope, where the Atlantic met the Indian Ocean, the vessel sailed. We elected to rename the ship and rechristen her. Addressed to great Neptune, in his *Ledger of the Deep*, we crossed out and renamed our vessel the *Fancy*. Keeping in his deepest respect, we performed the rituals. Firstly, we dropped anchor and commenced the removal of all remnants containing any *Charles II* namesake on board. Then we invoked the sacred passages to Neptune himself and dropped the retired metal nameplate over the bow, into the abyss. We recited the sacred words again, pouring the champagne in the sea from east to west, whilst Every and his replaced quartermaster, formerly the second mate, Joseph Dawson, drank from fine glass. Every devoted the words to the four gods of the wind, dashing champagne in each direction, to protect us from their wrath. We drank the entirety of the champagne and celebrated. *Fancy* was painted and carved on the new metal tag, tattooed upon her body. We furled the anchor and kept moving as one ship, one crew, under the unified rule of Captain Every.

That was a month beforehand. I remembered that day well. It had been a dull voyage thus far, as we entered the youth of June. We had not encountered any Englishman, Spaniard, Frenchman, Dutchman, or pirate thus far. I hoped we would soon. The *Fancy* and her crew had to prove themselves. We were experiencing the barrenness of sailing alone, without friends or foe to be seen. For as much as I wanted to clash swords, I would have taken any cannon or musket fire at that point. 'Twas too damn quiet. The steady listlessness began to echo our dark times at Corunna, despite our ship's constant, unanchored movement on the water.

Tending to new yet traditional activities, I sculpted a wooden figurine with my dagger. I'd broken the handle off of a hammer I found on the floor near my sleeping quarters. It was a dark wood. I was not an artistic man, but boredom makes any sailor talented. Man must beware of the devil in him, for when a ship sails long without foreign foe nearby, the monster waits for him to slip into his own chasms. The waiting was a dance with Satan himself. Hence, why many captains drank themselves into oblivion. A captain's lack of worthy objectives, failure to meet his own ideals of plundering treasure, and absence of infamy when targets are void taunt him. Captain Every had not drowned too far down, I supposed. The staunchness in his voice when he commanded us and loftiness in which he held his head were undeniable pieces of evidence to me for such a conclusion. He was still too invested and serious about our pirate business for me to have thought him distracted with good old grog. I felt Captain wanted to deliver right on his unspoken promise to us all, to deliver us from a dangerous, poor privateer life to that of rags-to-riches piracy. Besides, if he reduced himself to drinking to nothing, mutiny would claim his head and his family would be in a worse position than if he had simply kept patience in Corunna.

An unambitious captain is worse than no captain at all. When we created our two articles, I thought of him as a loon. For what man could ponder and legislate the second steps of wealth distribution of booty yet captured? Especially before we swan dove into the wasteland of the Southeast Atlantic. We had not seen another vessel in a month. The man was driven. Maybe blind. And maybe mad. But the Captain was definitely driven. I hoped his drive would preserve us. His conviction held me over. He was finally free to gaze upon us all and the sea with a fury only the authority of a captainship allowed.

I laid with my back against the wooden wall of the rail, sitting my bottom down on the main deck. Two crewmates sat beside me. Whenever Captain Every walked near us, we would stand in obedience. The Captain's stern voice, upright posture, and eyes of certitude passed us by a short time ago, therefore we were sitting down. We were swapping stories in between watch duties. One of the lads, Elijah Gordon, a thin, moustached lad, went on with a tale.

"There was a privateer and he'd gone to become a rogue, prosperous pirate. Swathes of goddamn treasure. After their plundering, his crew abandoned ship for lands in New Spain. Crew found out what they left for wasn't freedom. Abandoned their ship all for a woman he saw walking up a dock at port that day."

"Fool. What happened to 'em?" My other shipmate asked.

"'Twas a tale. Who the hell knows. Dead or in love, probably."

Singular obsessions— whether 'tis fame, a prize of riches, a woman, rank, praise, love, or fear are not conditions bound to pirates alone. Fascination can seduce any man and derail him, and overcome him with the madness of exclusivity.

I wondered if Captain Every had a madness concerning the good of the crew within his heart. Or was it his own personal desires blazing the path to the Round under the guise of the crew's best interests? Was he altruistic or self-centred? He owed the crew nothing, yet at the same time, they had backed his mutiny and unanimously elected him to a captainship. Thus he needed to earn his keep as our captain for he was indebted to us, and was compelled to repay his debt before our fondness for his assertion wore off. There is no honour amongst thieves? Well, there is certainly civic redemption and fidelity. We would cut your throat, but not before protecting your arse in a fight. Moral courage is required to be a pirate. On any given day, sailing on the open sea, you find vagabond and scallywag alike. But be sure, you shall find some sense of fidelity amongst a band of newly bred pirates. Let Captain Every be your exception and your proof. I wagered he would pay his debts to us without a second thought, if only fortune provided him the opportunity.

I had ample time to think to myself on the voyage. Think myself in circles. As if I wasn't already in the habit of thinking to myself a great deal in the first place. I considered my ambivalence on the subject of God. As a loyal subservient of England with a contract to Spain, and a half-hearted believer in the way of life as a privateer, I acted with uncertainty, faith, obedience, and devotion— the path of following God— in this manner. I followed the rules.

And then as I became a free man riding the waves of wickedness, bending my knee to no book, prophet, nation, or man other than myself and my captain, I'd strayed from the compliant path of God and His Holy way. Was this fall the source of my never-ending self-enquiry? Was my relationship, or lack thereof, with the figure in the sky an afterbirth of my relationship with loyalty and obedience itself? Which came first? The way of life and behaviour or the moral feelings and reverences? Am I a flickering light? Or a young man on the sea route to ruin? Is it in man's nature to be religious because he lacks the conviction to live life as a free man? Is it in man's nature to be irreligious, wanting to stray from the crippling caste of dogmatic discipline?

I had concluded, for the time being, as all philosophers must never come to final conclusions, put a case to rest, or dig their heels in, that I was on a so-called middle path— the path of uncertainty and duality, oscillating between obediences. I couldn't imagine Captain Every to be a man of this depth of thought, being the practical seafarer he was, tending to matters of direct importance on a level of responsibility I didn't share. He may possess a great depth of spirit, but likely not thought, for he scarcely had the luxury to ponder. In essence, Captain is on the middle road as well, being a noble man and a pirate at the same time. It always takes one to know one, and I know one when I see one. I am allegiant to no absolute truth other than the search for truth itself, finding maxims on rare occasions. Captain Henry Every was a dispenser of maxims for the time being. Captain Every was searching for something different too, I supposed. As I have learnt dozens of times before, he is not the answer to my search or my questions. He is not my purpose. But I do trust him and his lead. The only answers for life are to return to the search. What shall I find along the way? Everything. The only constant is change. My mind is fixed on its continually chaotic sprints. Oh, philosophy, you long, heavy road.

I looked around, sitting next to my two shipmates, and wondered. Did any man on this boat with me think of anything other than our pillage or the next meal? These men become whatever it takes to get what they want. I am likely the same. But I am geared toward something other than these men. The gruff pirates surrounding me, dainty and honest or dishonest as they were, never shut their mouths. They had minds to ponder, but I feared they lacked the care to ponder.

I birthed a new type of philosopher. A sailor-philosopher. It sounded reputable. At least to men like me. It was a rarity. Nonetheless, the philosopher in me, the new type, was a philosopher belonging to no school. Let me be unclassified and speak plainly. Let me erect this new school of thought, with her maiden voyage of these words and those stated above, as the philosophical school of *Chaoticism*. I am a Chaotic. We are Chaotics. This new school of mine, devised in a tedious voyage aboard a man-o'-war, somewhere in the East Atlantic, within one man's contemplations amidst heavy boredom, let it be known to all. On the ship, all who knew of my mind and its merits— knew me informally as a Chaotic.

Chaoticism is more than scepticism, and is far less concerned with making claims on the nature of fundamental reality. It cares not for defining life's meaning. Even the religions and values of our time, for they are merely signposts to be continued past and later discarded, are transient. A Chaotic is born the moment he realises that all truth lying behind, before, or ahead of him is not given, but is simply a matter of circumstance. Change any quality of a man's existence— his class, religion, nationality, birth year— and the truths he dearly holds on to will change. I was only a God-fearing Protestant because I am English. What is real is that we hole ourselves up in beliefs and values which are temporary. What other alternative is there? Freedom.

Chaoticism was not only a philosophy I uncovered, but a type of man, a type of thinker, a sailor-contemplator. One who holds fast to his beliefs as fast as he dispenses with them. One who clings to nothing and arrives at nothing for too long. No organised, absolute truth, system, or creed other than the search itself, the malleability of life as a journeyman. A Chaotic's mind runs faster, and more continuously, than any razeed vessel. His companionship and loyalty to curiosity overrules any allegiance to God or the old gods of tradition, lifestyle, people, and ways of thinking. Most men, at least aboard the *Fancy*, likely held the same beliefs since boyhood. The sailors traversed with expired maps. There was and is only one way for me, though, one middle ground. It is Chaoticism. And it worships a new god— the active, thinking, ever-searching mind. The scriptures found along the way— observations, beliefs, thoughts, theories, and conclusions, are simple encampments to be departed and strayed from. They number infinity and nil at the same time. They grow and die as the times progress.

How does a philosophy for life develop for a man? Nature and experience. I'd lived it. A sailor keeps on, as does a Chaotic. Just as the seasons and the undertakings of a man's life change, so must his beliefs and virtues adapt, grow, form, and vanish alongside the man. Take this temporary truth as a guiding philosophy to build all other philosophies upon. Should one harbour a belief about any subject and hold to it without exception, life will speedily show them the hollowness and falsity of their conviction. Had I clung to my boyhood philosophies, I would not have handled life as an adult sailor. One's philosophies must not be snatched up and nailed to the wall, but should come and go as the clouds do shift. This is Chaoticism, my chaotic philosophy.

I saw the Captain standing near the helm and asked myself— why did I have an explicit fondness for the Captain? Was it only the parts of myself which I aspired toward that I saw in him that caused my trust in the man? Was he a braver man than I, yet we shared characteristics in common that are rare aboard a man-o'-war? Was it... what is it? Being a sailor on the Atlantic, with all of her blue mystique and draw, was a pensive undertaking for me. But there I was and here you read. And do you read these words, seeing a young man grappling with life as he sails not only in the chaos of the ocean but the chaos of his life? Or am I a madman in the making, as Captain Henry Every may well be? Do you think I worship the lesser gods? Nonetheless, sailing and pirating are, at their core, occupations for both men of thought and men of action. Now do you understand why the bottle is a sailor's best friend? It's an attempt to dull the freedom of a mind that runs rampant.

"Shipwreck dead ahead," a deckhand yelled out from the crow's nest.

It was the first sign of anything notable other than water since ditching Gibson and his old world conspirators. What looked like a mound of smoking dirt soon became a wooden obstruction. A sole Union Jack laid floating in the water amongst the wood, barrels, and crates scattered about— the flag of most of our crew's homeland. After dismissing our Spanish privateering flag of the *Charles II*, we donned new colours. One of our new flags flaunted the skull and crossbones, coloured white in a sea of strong red, and the other had four downward white chevrons amongst a sea of heavy crimson— Captain Every's flags of the *Fancy*. We sailed along past the old flag on our starboard side. Captain Every stepped up ahead to the front of the crowd lining the rail as we furled sails to slow and observe.

"How long do ye think it's been?" Captain Every asked Quartermaster Dawson.

"It couldn't be more than an hour. Look at the pace she's sinking, sir," Dawson replied.

"See any survivors?" Captain Every asked.

"Doubtful," Dawson closed the case as Captain Every turned to another pirate, a stranger in our crowd.

"What's 'er meanin' of the shipwreck?" Captain Every asked the unknown, no more than ten years my senior.

"The only enemies of the Royal Navy around here are pyrates... or the French," the man said.

The crew looked to Captain Every. If we were in waters amongst a fully stocked French man-o'-war, we would go down firing, but we would surely go down. Additionally, our vessel lacked the speed to outsail one. All of the men knew this. Captain looked back at the wreck with contempt. We came close to some action, to some loot, that day. The destroyer, if she were French, must have been within an hour of us. If it was a pirate vessel, it could have been our long-awaited loot, our godsend of a good omen. But for the time being, the sunken ship remained a bad omen, as a gravesite and grave sight of our former countrymen. Should we have searched for the destroyer and stumbled upon a French warship, it would have proven too risky of a move to make, as we were heading toward the Cape and its Pirate Round, possessing much more fruitful ventures. We came close to getting our hands on something, but it slipped away, an hour away. The frustration dripped from Captain Every's bearded face. He turned away, nearly grimacing, and walked away from us onlookers. I don't think he wanted to show the crew his frustration, as not to levy our spirits in his temper after these shared calculations. He grasped what his confidence meant to us. But I noticed his fret.

"To the Cape," Captain Every ordered, as he returned to his quarters.

How did I know where he would go below deck? Where would he go? Where else was he to go to hide his face? The men spurred back into action, disregarding the diminished pile of carnage and a flag of England— a flag of our roots, plummeting to the ocean floor, soon out of our sight as we sailed away. Full speed again.

I thought the missed opportunity got to the men. Were they fit for this life? The frustrations of it? Fit for long journeys without signs of promise? Did they need immediacy? The unrewarded patience from the shipwreck had caused a gust of desire to sweep over the *Fancy* and through the hearts of the crew. I felt we all had a tempting impulse to search for the warship in any direction other than that of the Cape. Captain Every likely felt the same. At that point, what did we have to lose? The boredom made me battle-hungry, lustful, and belligerent. It must have spread to the rest of the crew.

A man to kill, a woman to take, a fight to be had, a prize to be retrieved, or a life to be lost. Anything was better than boredom. I did not worry about myself as much as the other men. I had a wooden figurine to sculpt, ideas to ponder, fantasies of an inner kingdom to tend to. But most of the men lacked this despite their mature age. They were closed books. They needed their pleasures, their conquests. As I did, of course, but not nearly to the same extent.

We dispersed from the crowd on the main deck after putting the *Fancy* into high speed, continuing south. I walked over to the port side and leaned against a bag of potatoes. All I could think about was moving forward to new adventures and the Pirate Round. Real opportunities captivated me with their high fables. My mouth watered at the possibility of action, of living up to the ideals I'd heard of in stories that drew me to the sea. The shipwreck unearthed this old desire. I looked to the left, exiting out of my imagination. I saw Oliver Rossi again, rancorous as ever. He laid against another pile of potato sacks up against the tender on the centre of the ship. We locked eyes for a moment then dismissed one another, both looking at the southern horizon.

"Say, Cole, I'm surprised ye didn't jump into that shipwreck and swim around. Surely a true contrarian such as yerself would do anything to get Every's attention," Rossi said and must have wanted to get a rise out of me to contend with his unfulfilled plunderous desires.

"If ye despise Captain Every and meself so strongly, why don't ye leave? If I'm being honest, Oliver, I was shocked to see ye on the proper side of the mutiny. Ye feigned like a Gibson conspirator on the seventh, but on the eighth ye were nothin' of the sort. I didn't see ye that evening with a sword in hand," I said.

"Ye're the one who said it best. One must know which way the wind blows. The wind favoured Every," Rossi said, mockingly.

"Go to Hell. The wind guides the *Fancy* and the crew. But it doesn't guide me. Nor does methink it guides Captain Every. Doth the wind, so invisible in her steadfastness, show ye the path, blind man?" I was not an arrogant man, but when I argued with men, as rarely as it did happen, I exploited some mysterious edge, speaking in a strange language to confuse the violator and come off more intelligent than I was.

"Cole, don't act like ye're a prince of pyrates. Ye're just another able-bodied seaman." Unfortunately, Rossi understood me.

"I'm as new to this as ye, friend. But I am cut from a different cloth." I stood up. "And that's something ye'll never understand. Ye're just a pawn on this ship." I hated having to be vicious and condescending, but one loses all outside respect and self-respect when he submits.

If a man sacrifices his fangs for temporary admiration, he is not a man. But I walked away, not looking to fight my own crewmate that day. I wasn't giving in to his slander, for he wasn't worth it. Down below, I walked around the second deck, amongst a sea of men, further and further from the main deck. Holding onto my wooden figurine, fiddling with it in my pocket, I approached the open walled kitchen where our Chief Steward and Cook worked— Allston Pettyhouse. Pretty Al, as we called him, was cooking something. It wasn't important what he was cooking. He had something else for me.

"So, do ye have it?" I asked as he looked up, and side-eyed me, trying to put me down from his forty-year-old high horse.

The tall Pretty Al was bald, and not happy about it. Probably why he sided with Captain Every during the mutiny— he was a bitter, washed-up man. And not a pretty one at that.

"Rollins. Good day, yerself. I don't have yer opium and I told ye I sold my last at Corunna. When we get going in the Round, I'll get my hands on some more," he assured me, as a good provider would.

I felt bitter in my desperation for the sensation of opium. The temptation of poppy befell many men, even on board. Pretty Al had commerce aboard the *Fancy*, though I did not know who else partook. I thought Pettyhouse was lying to me about his lack of supply. But for what it was worth, I thought he was looking out for me. He saw something good in me worth salvaging, beyond the grips of an ivory flower's hand. Maybe. Many good men who consume it often become incapacitated and consumed by it. I didn't know how much longer I could withstand our dull voyage. I had thought my-self impervious to the necessity of immediate pleasures upon a boring venture. I slowly realised how inaccurate this belief was. The conviction that I possessed the grit for true pirate life seemed more like a mirage at that moment. I'd only done opium once and it was with Pretty Al back in Corunna. Boredom made me eat the black stuff, see things, and throw it up later. My motto was to "try everything once, for how can ye dislike something unless ye try it?" However, I felt nothing when I took it. Then, I craved to know. Maybe it was better I did not satisfy that itch that day. Maybe in that moment of weakness I was spared from going down an opium hole I had only ever heard about. Maybe someone had watched over me, Pretty Al or otherwise. I thought Captain Every would have been ashamed of me if he'd heard I'd become a poppy whore.

It was one of my darker hours there in the shade below deck during that sunny day. Conflicted by what I had pranced about believing the whole journey thus far, I thought to myself— 'God, please deliver us from this wasteland of open sea, and bring us to wherever destiny remains.' For any destiny was better than the one I was in. I moved through a corridor into an empty room and closed my eyes. Clasping my hands together, I prayed to the Almighty for deliverance and hope. Hope proved to be a comparable sedative to the seductive sloops of opium. Hope was all I had to keep myself occupied with, when thoughts and figurines failed to distract me.

There were about eighty to eighty-five men aboard the *Fancy* at that time, and none of them saw me in my crippled state. I was alone in a small room. I was doubly lucky to be spared the embarrassment and imminent harassment should I have been seen feeling sorry for myself in public. I was lost. I'd discovered that my Chaoticism school, which I had imaginarily founded, was more of a refuge, confession, and condition, rather than a school of philosophy. A ship is a place which acts as a confessional vessel for a man. In those hidden corridors, on watch, or in his hammock, many realisations and admissions come to mind. My philosophy was my confession. My revelations and findings about life were my penance.

Melancholy had been creeping in for a while, thus requiring me to reinvent myself and my mind to avoid a certain death in spirit. That is the path of Chaoticism, to sail and keep on sailing. To be blind, but not paralysed, even if hope for better days and better thoughts was the plan for the moment. Even in melancholy, I must keep sailing, I told myself. I wondered what I'd hoped and prayed for that day, other than simply an end to boredom. I didn't realise it, but what I truly prayed for, what I most deeply wanted, was freedom and perspective.

Chapter III

FIRST TASTES OF PYRACY

"I... I... I don't know Captain," a young lookout said.

"What'd ye see, goddamnit?" Captain interrogated

"I... I... thought I saw three ships ahead."

"And ye waited 'til nightfall to whisper of it, lad?"

"I wasn't sure, sir. Methought them just blips. But we're at Maio now sir, and it dawned on me that there'd be Dutch ships around here. And they might be stocking up at port."

"Aye, it dawned on ye?" Captain Every mocked the babbling lookout.

We'd been looking, seething for any plunderous opportunity since Corunna, and the kid nearly blew it. It was three brown blips on a horizon to him, but it was the resurrection we had all been waiting for. They could have been Dutch slavers— something that would have definitely gotten the blood going again. I'd had my head down for weeks, keeping my hopes up for something to change. I had the same senses, the same body, the same instincts as every man on the boat. But I was the most sensitive. One can talk to any seasoned sailor and they wouldn't realise that the most frightful danger at sea wasn't a Kraken, an infamous pirate, nor any weapon. It is the boredom, the squandering of time. It appeared the sun was rising on the *Fancy* again and the lookout came close to darkening our opportunity, our long-awaited quench.

Alas, to the swords, flintlocks, and that great masculine sense of threat. By default, we'd already been declared faceless public en-emies, with Captain Every as our gang-leader, since raising a pirate flag. But we had yet to bring our terror upon others. Nobody cared for us privateers turned pirates. They soon would. It felt Viking-like, Spartan-like, Hun-like to bring our weapons and ferocity to others. Those three supposed ships, which we did come to find out were Dutch merchant ships, made for smooth prizes.

A predator must always have at its prey, even if they outnumber him. Some said the men we'd face had it coming. Some said they were easy targets. I believe one can either be the hammer or the nail in this world. I'd been a nail too long. Captain Every had been a nail too long. Don't come to sea as a nail. The world we're from is not a black and white one. Cosmopolitan arrogance and decorum don't extend to the open sea and her laws. Out there, it was that simple. It was kill or be killed. In the realm of waves and tides, one is either dead or alive, captain or crew, good or evil... the hammer or the bloody nail.

Passivity aboard the vessel made villains of us all. And I liked it. I saw red. Plenty of blue on the open ocean. Let's give the sun-glaring sea what it needs— some red. Desperation makes a monster of men. Necessity strips a man's morals from him. We didn't wait for nightfall to take something again. Never again. It felt as if there was broken glass under my feet, propelling me to pounce on those pitiful Dutch merchantmen at the first opportunity. The waiting gave me stone feet but the prospect of raiding made me jackrabbit-like. And maybe some of those merchantmen, were they not to lay down their life for their Republic's goods, would make great nails.

We followed the three Dutch ships to port, caught up swiftly, and waited until they dropped anchor. Then we pulled our vessel alongside their fleet and took them, without a fight, in the water of the defenceless port. A man-o'-war against Dutch ships, even outnumbering us three-to-one, was child's play, as our man-o'-war was a great juggernaut. Captain Every was a true leader on that day, walking aboard their flagship vessel first. Half of our crew followed. There wasn't a Spanish Night Watch of Corunna to worry about that time around.

"Follow me boys. At last," Captain said with a sword drawn, swaggering across a plank-bridge to the merchant vessel.

I followed him third in line and then saw a young Dutch sailor staring at me. That used to be me. It could have still been me had I lacked the stomach to follow Captain Every into the infinite void of daringness. We'd landed. We were amongst the meek.

"Who is the captain of this vessel? Or this fleet? It makes no difference to me."

I'd been content with my drifting from the way of God, the Crown, the welcoming arms of King William, custom, and all pious chains since that breakdown next to the *Fancy*'s kitchen. I was thinking of it as I stood on the merchant ship. I felt freedom in that moment of reflection, even if I'd sacrificed the supposed salvation or honour that only the pompous could have. I could look at a man and see a friend or foe, not only a child of God. Life was undoubtedly too complex for a Holy Book, even life on the black and white sea. The laws of life and the mind were haywire, but the laws of the sea were direct, whether one liked them or disagreed with them. While God may have been at plenty of places across the world, trust me, He ain't on the water. The black and white sea is an untouched land devoid of cosmic, calculated order. Some seamen need Holy Bibles. Pirates don't. We saw behind the curtain. Or at least I did. I felt welcomed into the predatory land for the time being, far from my old life as prey.

"I am the captain," a slender, lean man wearing a navy blue coat relinquished his anonymity and approached Captain Every with dignity.

"Well... what's yer name?" Captain Every asked.

I did not know where the captain was going, outside of general plunder, but I hoped we'd get to pillage something soon. The last thing our crew wanted to take was mercy upon those merchants. We needed the thievery.

"I am Captain Van Beurden. Who are ye, pyrate?"

"What is more important to ye? Yer crew or yer supplies? We want both, but I'd like to see where yer loyalties lie first."

Both of the Captains fell silent.

"Use yer imagination," Captain Van Beurden said.

The Dutch captain either had guts greater than his anchor or he didn't want to be captain of a ship any longer. Either way, he was a bold lad. Captain Every smirked at the man, looking through him, then walked beside him toward the ship's defenceless crew. He looked upon all of them and then went to the side of the vessel and looked upon the other two ships' crews engaged in the spectacle, all likely waiting for orders but giving no quarrel to us. What kind of triple-ship merchant convoy had no escort? If they decided to fight us, it would have been a suicide mission, regardless of their overwhelming numbers. All of us pirates waited for Captain Every's signal to let us blow off the steam and relieve the pressure. In other words— we awaited the order to slaughter those sheep. But he permitted nothing of the sort. Captain Every walked back to their captain.

"Captain Van Beurden, if ye give us the supplies we ask for, we'll spare all yer men." Captain Every then walked back to the side of the ship and yelled out to all their weary men. "If any man is to join our crew, come now."

Over a dozen lads scattered across the three vessels. The morale of those Dutch merchantmen must have been devastatingly low. They were boys amongst us. It felt good to be a thief in thief's paradise, the Atlantic. I later overheard the crew grumbling about not letting us slay the men, but we'd added numbers and supplies to our vessel. We'd added a triple-ship merchant convoy piracy to our name. Still, bigger plunders and the war for them were what we all looked forward to. A war we were supposed to fight against the French in the Caribbean as privateers under contract. We needed a replacement war.

Instead of a slaughter, there were additions. We had increased to about one-hundred men aboard— more and more mouths to feed, more and more men to please. Besides the already heavy vessel, the new additions of personnel weighed down our vessel. However, the more men we had, the more of our 46 cannons we could operate. With our firepower, the *Fancy* could deface any ship on this earth yet could not outsail any. The boat's weight and load were too darn heavy. We were due for a razeeing.

Soon we would have to trim. We sailed further south, nearing the Cape and continued closer along the Round. We stopped some time later at an island near the Gulf of Guinea. By that time, I had lost track of the date. I assumed there were no more formal regulations or paperwork to be filed. No ship-log or captain's-log, thus spawning our apathetic attitude toward the calendar. The days melted into one another and the nights were the only separator of them. We had to keep busy. One thing I missed from the buzzing life of home were its activities. Out on the sea, you have your crew and your duties and your boredom. Luckily, I'd found means of escaping and making the bleakness more verdant. The fiery activeness of home contrasted the dull weather. One thing I did not miss from home was her cold.

The trip to the Cape of Good Hope is adorned with many beautiful features, one being the heat. It is said you give an Englishman a home and he shall build a kingdom. Well, I say you give an Englishman a hot sun and he shall build a paradise. The *Fancy* had become our mock paradise. The guts of the Pirate Round, our mystical route, so far only existent in speech, imagination, and some of the older crew's tales, was remaining a ways off. Her fruitfulness drew nearer the closer to Madagascar we got. The ship was our vessel, our most trusted friend, and our faux Heaven for the time being. Us crew were the voluntary captives to its pearly gates. Her sails, though requiring industry, were angels in themselves.

The boat meant more to me than any house could. In a house, you're a countryman, but with a ship, a ship like the *Fancy* no less, you're a citizen of the world. Do yourself a favour, any of you sailors— find yourself a way onto a ship someday. It is only then that you shall know great freedom without requiring an even greater fortune. And should you stay at sea longer and become a man of rank, you'd get a say in how the ship is steered. It is a freedom to die for.

We'd ventured into the Gulf of Guinea waters, and some of the lads said there were more sharks there than on any other coast of Africa. From the shores of Annobon to Sao Tome to Principe and finally to Bioko, our then incoming midterm destination, it was a swimmer's death sentence. An Englishman could catch a fever and die, a swimmer could meet his end in a fish's jaws, and an African could find himself on his way to the American Colonies in chains. The coast was a most terrible place indeed, bustling with unfavourable activity. The islands housed many small-time pirates there en route to the Cape.

"My breath smells and this ship is slow. Let us clean our tongues and sharpen our ship. And then we shall set off again for Madagascar," Captain Every said.

We neared closer to the shore of Bioko. This *Fancy* retained her merits in firepower and intimidation, but not in speed. Yet. Speed was the greatest currency in the ocean. And as we planned for our Madagascar destination, we certainly needed both to escape the foxes and scare away the wolves amidst the wild waters of the incoming, saturated, hostile Indian Ocean. Captain Every and our crew had not followed the traditional blueprint for pirate life. We were once loyal contractors, all of us with stains of honour and respect to and from our fellow countrymen. We were men of lower means. Some were poorer and hence naturally turned to the life, however, it was the freedom and opportunity which drew us all to that position. Like all men-turned-pirates, rich, poor, or somewhere in the middle, a lack of money forced our hands. I'd contemplated our tectonic shift as we soon aimed to beach the *Fancy* on the shore of Bioko, the easternmost island in the Bight of Bonny, the Gulf of Guinea.

After thinking of the life I had left behind and the means which propelled me to that position in life, I'd begun to feel at home on the boat, our wooden tub, further letting go of my past. If I had to live my life over again, I'd still take the struggle of adventure over the mildly greater prosperity of a predictable life. My mind was a wanderer, coming to a grounding as our ship did the same. The wanderings of a philosophical mind amidst the gargantuan theatres of a ship were endless. I was a thinker and an outcast, fit for a life on a man-o'-war. Yet I knew of no other man aboard who understood me. I had a world within me which did not require constant maintenance to keep upon its path, unlike that of the *Fancy* and the crew that manned her sails. My mind tossed, turned, and evoked endlessly within the non-physical. However, it wasn't simply that I constantly thought about how much my mind moved about. I came to recognize that I was embodying movement itself— constant movement of thought, of feeling, and attention. I had become movement. Movement was me. I mustn't ever stop moving, I thought to myself, even when I would be still. For if I did stop entirely, my insides would have imploded and I would have self-destructed. The road, the journey, the search possessed me, and I was indentured to her even as our boat came to a slow halt.

It was the first extended stop on land since Corunna. As a way to cope, I left the physical world for the refuge of the non-physical world in my mind, to escape the boredom of our outward journey from Spain to Bioko. I fluctuated back and forth between my surroundings and my imaginings. I'd pondered the past and the future to escape the present. The safest refuge from the world was a ship. The safest refuge from life was the mind. Neither evasions were to ever end. Chaoticism, my disposition, my diagnosis— did it harm me more than help me? Was I merely afraid of all adventure yet convinced myself to go on an adventure? Did life elude me because I evaded living by hiding in this head of mine? Is restlessness disorderly or does it serve a sufficient function? All I had were questions and more questions. This was the surest, truest way to live— to question it all— I told myself.

Captain Every and a few men took a tender, lowered by another few dusty sailors, to the beige sand. I saw a few natives escape the treeline to greet us. I'd never met an African before outside of England. Captain Every towered amongst his squadron of rowers on the tender. They reached shore, greeted the natives, and prepared for our careening. It surprised me that some of the natives remained this far west in Africa, even in the midst of the ever-expanding Dutch West India Company's and Royal African Company's slave trades. They spectated. Maybe they knew Captain Every, for it was rumoured he had been a slave trader in this area some years ago. Whether they did or didn't, we had work to do. Many ropes and spikes were brought ashore to prepare the layout and stations for beaching and careening. Captain Every didn't carry anything. I was more worried about the gnats than a disastrous failed careening or random ambush from the sea. We raised our sails again. Nearly all of us stayed aboard for the beaching. A man nearest the bowsprit heckled orders at us to drift the vessel slowly to the shore. We did. Thuds sounded from the bottom of our *Fancy* hitting the African sand. Then we took to the sand, for the heaving down of the *Fancy*, so we could clean her bottom and sharpen her.

I stood ashore, heaving down to careen, pulling a rope with force, hearing "heave" in my left ear. Toward the spike and the treeline, I pulled. The natives watched me. I pulled further then a pinch upon my leg distracted me. I held my right hand on the dirty rope, and with my left, I rubbed my thigh. None of the men beside me seemed to notice. Something like a hair tickled my leg. I swapped hands and slightly pulled down my britches. I saw the hairiest of Englishman legs as I looked at the dark, shadowy valley of my body beneath my clothing. I saw a small, pink blemish where my growingly itching sensation came from. The pinching had not left me yet. Something bit me. I hoped it was harmless.

A bit later, as the rope-suspended crew shaved and sliced the barnacles and crud from the tilted underbelly of the *Fancy,* laying careened and lifeless on her side in the sand, I felt a small throbbing on my thigh. I did not want to be a bothersome lad. I forgot about it, purposely.

The men hung onto ropes, cascading up and down the under-belly of the *Fancy*. They looked unified, singing jolly songs to-gether. Their machetes sliced away at barnacles and crud on the un-derbelly of our beached man-o'-war. And as we aimed to make the tilted vessel light, clean, and fast, their voices harmonised. Clancy

Williams' young voice sang, and the rest of the howling voices of our crew followed:

> *"Handsome young lad, as bright as a lady!*
> > *Blue eyes for the sea, served in the King's Navy!*
> *Gone off to a whorehouse, and never come home!*
> > *Now those ladies he serves, he's really makin' them moan!"*

> *"We drink and we whore, for we're hot-blooded sailors!*
> > *We sing and we roar, for we love the blue sea!*
> *Come sundown we're tired and a-ready for snorin'!*
> > *From sunrise to sunset, we're bound to be free!"*

> *"We raise up our flags, our grog, ale, and sails too!*
> > *Slaves to the wind, I tell ye that's true!*
> *For our blood and our hands remain holy at sea!*
> > *Whether Heaven or Hell, it be a good pyrate's dream!"*

> *"We drink and we whore, for we're hot-blooded sailors!*
> > *We sing and we roar, for we love the blue sea!*
> *Come sundown we're tired and a-ready for snorin'!*
> > *From sunrise to sunset, we're bound to be free!"*

By the shanty's end, the careening finished. After shaving the boat and raising her back up when the tide returned to regular strength, the throbbing on my thigh became the only sensation I felt. Later on, when the carpenter, James Fulton, and his mates all managed the removal of the poop deck and other elements of our superstructures, I knew something was terribly wrong as the throbbing didn't go away. After we razeed the boat to improve her speed, my mind had entirely abandoned my Chaoticism search. A limbic phenomenon, formed from the bite, consumed all of my attention.

It is hard to be an occupied thinker when one is tending to a whining wound.

I felt lightheaded standing aboard the ship. Life and the warm African sun were an afterthought to me. The leg was now swollen and I was painfully aware that I could no longer distract myself with my duties. My insatiable scratching had likely infected me. I was no doctor, but I was instinctive. It did not take a doctor to realise I had been poisoned by some bloody, slimy spider. I bet he was brown and ugly. I felt like a rag doll as my body slowly descended to the wooden deck.

As I flitted in and out of awareness, I found myself being dragged across the deck and into the sickbay of Preston Fitzgerald's surgeon's quarters, the infirmary. My left leg betrayed me and my head was light. All of the world around me began to spin, but I locked my eyes on the area above me. The wood ceiling in the ship became my best friend. It was stabilising and always there for me. Surgeon Fitzgerald and a few sailors stood over me. Then Captain Every came into the room. Whenever a man was about to die, especially at port, we all knew Captain Every would be deeply bothered. He was a man's man, without a doubt, but he did have a tender heart for his crew, as all honourable captains should. Surgeon Fitzgerald spoke and his bifocals carried his sweat.

"Cole. Is it— it was likely a recluse spider. Ye can tell by the bite. But that's not important right now."

"Get on with it. What's important then?" Captain Every intervened.

Surgeon Fitzgerald looked at Captain Every with self-depreciation, then back at me, wanting to prove himself and save me in that moment. Luckily for me, Surgeon Fitzgerald cared less about impressing the crew than saving them for he was a true physician. And with Captain Every in that room, he had no choice but to follow through and execute on his skills.

"Right, sir. Well, the bite is infected. And it is in yer bloodstream. I'd set ye aside for a few days, but nothing'd change, especially at this point. Yer body must heal itself. We have some primrose oil, turmeric, and Sudan gum. But no guarantees. And there is one more thing..."

"What?" I asked.

"We have to cut yer leg open first, son, and get some of the pus out."

"Oh, hell no. Nobody is cutting me. I'd rather not take the chance. I'd rather die from a goddamn spider."

"Cole, we have rum. Ye can drink plenty and it'll dull the cut," Surgeon Fitzgerald instructed.

One of my shipmates stepped in. He moved toward me, up close and personal, encroaching upon my ears, looking as sincere as a greedy prostitute.

"Listen Cole, ye're no bloody use to us dead or one-legged. Captains can earn the wood-peg but ye have to man up and keep yer goddamn leg. Drink the rum 'til ye pass out."

"I won't do it. Ye won't cut into me damn leg. Just let me get rid of the damn thing. Who the hell cares? Beach me here. Plenty of African women looking for a gentle Englishman. Let it take my leg. I can't do this venom-pain anymore. Or let it get rid of me," I wailed out as Surgeon Fitzgerald stepped forward.

"Cole, ye can keep yer leg if we're lucky, but ye need to drink and we need to cut. We're going to cut," Surgeon Fitzgerald said as he gestured to one of the sailors. "Get some rum for the lad. The rest of ye, hold him down." They followed his order and pressed me against the table, even Captain Every.

"Hell no, Mr. Fitz. I can't drink rum. My throat's made of velvet, softer than a woman. Give Captain or one of the lads the rum, they probably have throats made of stone. No offence," I pleaded.

Plenty of grimy hands pressed me against the prison of a table. My face was feverish and my mind was compromised. I wasn't as brave as I thought.

"Here, drink this lad. Don't be lily-livered," Surgeon Fitzgerald said.

"Just cut the fuckin' leg off, or let the bite take her. Fuck the rum. Just let me go. It won't work. I'll vomit the fuckin' rum."

I could handle pain, but the bite took me too bloody far and I was speaking in circles.

"Oh, shut the hell up." Captain Every said, as he shoved the bottle of rum to my mouth, forcing the drink down my throat. He then pulled it away before I drowned and, exercising further brute liberties, swung his arm and punched me with a right-hook on my temple. I fell unconscious from the strike of Captain's steel fist.

<u>*Chapter IV*</u>

THE STALLINGS

I woke up with a fresh bandage on my leg. The spider had been defeated and all of my limbs remained. Soon the scar would turn into a memory. I turned to the other man lying in sickbay beside Surgeon Fitzgerald and I.

"Spiders can't kill sailors, especially when a sailors' on the water. 'Tis a law of nature," I said to the lad, making a joke of my earlier spectacle.

"Shut up, Cole. Everyone heard about yer mollycoddling in here. Ye're lucky Every takes a shining to ye. Captains don't usually have room to mercy a coward," he said.

"Blanchard, right?" I asked the man, as recognition approached me.

"Yes. Ye want to know how I knew ye were Cole?" Blanchard spoke back to me.

"How's that? I'm the only other man in sickbay," I said.

"Good eye," he tried to intimidate me, "ye have the face of a wannabe."

"Really. I served in the King & Queen's Navy, Blanch. And when I helped take the *Fancy* the first night, I didn't see ye anywhere bein' a real pyrate."

"I was as much a part of that mutiny as ye were, boy."

"Do yerself a favour, don't call me boy, boy."

Surgeon Fitzgerald turned back around.

"Shut the hell up, lads. Cole, ye should be happy as a kite ye're alive. And ye, Blanchard...." he said staring at the sailor, "just bug off when ye're in my sickbay." Surgeon Fitzgerald showed his fangs, putting Blanchard in his place.

"How long have I been out, Mr. Fitzgerald?" I asked.

"Days. Doesn't matter. Infection's gone down. We brought some natives aboard. One shoved everyone out of the way. He brought a medicine with 'em. Couldn't tell ye the name of it but it worked. Barely spoke, the fella. Must be some sort of healer. He repeatedly said some foreign word to all of the men he shoved aside on his way to ye. I think it was 'move' in some native tongue. It affected Cap'n, when we were unsure if ye'd live, lad."

"Are we still in Bioko waters?" I asked as Blanchard turned away to himself, ignoring me and my new conversation partner.

"Far from it," Surgeon Fitzgerald said. "We've got ourselves the fastest ship in the Atlantic now. And we've taken two Dutch privateers along with their ivory, gold, and some fresh crew on the way." He laughed to himself. "Damned Dutch have been unlucky."

"Right. Where are we?" I asked sternly.

"I don't know, lad."

I felt I had been out longer than Surgeon Fitzgerald told me. None of it made sense. I would have awoken had we fought two ships. Then again, we were in West African waters. Little made sense to me in those foreign seas. I rested my leg, upon Surgeon Fitzgerald's orders, for the next few weeks. The thought of the poppy flooded my mind, likely trying to pull me away from my struggle, but the mirage turned out to only be a fleeting desire once I had awoken and shaken it off a day later. Life is a matter of acting, surrendering, and knowing when to do which. And it was my time to surrender, to observe the actions of our *Fancy*, to stop my hand from squeezing hold of a vice. The time aside replenished me. I was in a place of becoming and unbecoming, of being and inaction. I believed the crutches and infirmary bed, my newest friends, were where I belonged then, despite my endless reservoir of youthful vitality. But I knew I must keep my eyes open, and return to duty eventually. Probably sooner than I had expected.

That day came as we trekked further south and came across two strange ships travelling as a single unit in the heat of midday. It was my first day back and off the crutches, feeling resurrected and prepared to reclaim my manhood. I'd shed some weight, shed some fat off of my soul. I was happy to be back, happy to have rested the sword and more than prepared to serve my purpose again. The saga from Corunna to that point was all a great big stalling. I remembered how our lookout yelled, and knew the wind had changed.

"Two ships ahead, must be pyrates," the lad said.

How he arrived at that conclusion, I did not know. Their vessels portrayed French names but no French flags. A dark blue, obsidian-like flag and an array of cannons on each ship was signal enough that those men weren't fishermen. Captain Every stepped up in my view before we sped up at full tilt. We were approaching close enough to engage the strange ships.

"Men. We have the supplies, we have the numbers, we have the spirit, we have the speed. Now we must have the infamy. Take no mercy. But take prisoners if they look strong," Captain Every said and we closed the anticipatory distance.

Nothing quite like a speech to fire up anti-establishment swashbucklers. We were seasoned thieves, but novice pirates. That day, fates changed. In an act of boldness nearing lunacy, Captain Every dictated a gamble of a manoeuvre.

Both of the ships tried to sail away in escape, but could not flee as our speed was too much for them to quit. We gave and succeeded in chase. In the beginning, they did not intend to fight us, but we were an unrelenting foe who aimed to fight them, regardless of the two-against-one odds. We approached the closer of the two ships from behind, a small corvette titled *Renarde*. The other vessel, a frigate titled *Marie*, remained a ways off, speeding away from the little corvette. We were splitting them, closing in upon the starboard side of the *Renarde*, and to the far, rear, port side of the *Marie*. There must have been confusion on the corvette, as they lagged behind the frigate. If we could see our attack through, we could have both ships in a single manoeuvre. But the risk was great. We could catch ourselves in a devastating crossfire, however, it seemed to be the boldest way to assure neither ship escaped. So, we weaved into the middle of their paths, exposing ourselves to triumph and destruction.

We gained on the corvette, implementing our newly gained speed to engage in a cannon fight to dismantle their masts. I saw the enemy gathering around their armaments and yelling in foreign tongue. We could see their faces increasing in size as our distance decreased. Their first few shots missed far in front of our bow, and our first few fell short of their stern. As we approached and volleyed most of our port side cannons, they returned fire from their starboard side, firing up toward us, aiming to dismantle our masts. They also fired low, damaging and rupturing our hull, attempting to put holes into our keel to sink us. The *Fancy* was armoured strong and took the hits. I was glad, as I'd rather risk the sinking than take a 12-pounder to the sternum. More and more the cannon fire ripped off, bringing fiery, smoky, iron life to the valley between our warring vessels. We were thrashing them in the battle, and little by little, their morale died. The gunning crew to my left ripped off a bar or chain shot and demolished their target, rupturing the enemy corvette's mizzenmast. The base of their mast split into shreds and the structure tumbled swiftly down to their deck, inspiring a chorus of yelling. The falling mast crushed their helmsman. Our master gunner, Hardy, roared a "Yea." His voice was muffled greatly, dulled out by the exploding gunpowder from both ships. It smelled of war.

Their speed slowed, as the two vessels continued exchanging cannon fire. Since their mizzenmast and helmsman had been retired, the helm itself was flattened 'neath the fallen pole. The wheel must have been crushed moving left as their rudder was pushed to a sharp angle and the corvette began tailing off toward port, splitting off from our previously parallel trajectory. We followed them along and continued blasting relentlessly, preventing their escape. Our crews took light hits, but many, as the enemy was firing up at our superior height. It only served to blister our morale. The body of our vessel bore the brunt of the damage, as did our rails. We had greater speed, higher ground, and more hunger. At the centre of their main deck, there was a gaping hole in front of their mainmast from where we tried to bludgeon the bloody tower. The immense amounts of smoke in our faces from the repeated, heavy cannon fire obstructed our view, rendering our line of sight hazy. I imagined each of our gunning crews volleyed off five to seven times each before all three of the enemy's masts were crippled and grounded.

Looking at their desolated deck, with fallen masts and holes abound, I heard the frantic yelling of the enemy's French. I gathered that water was being taken on in their lowest deck, as many of their men disappeared down below. I imagined several cannonballs had pierced through the same places, ripping a gaping hole in their vessel bottom exposed to the water. The rest of the combatants manning their cannons were slowly being obliterated. They were no longer inspired when they managed to cause us any significant damage. I heard a loud 'gong' sound from one of their cannonballs crashing into one of our cannons. It rebounded and devastated a few of our men, wounding them into submission. It was not a fair fight, but we did not stop until their vessel limped along the sea. The smell of the gunpowder aroused me into the violence. Aggression served as armour, the only protection from being killed out on the ocean.

"The second one is on our starboard," I heard our master gunner yell.

To our disadvantage and horror, I looked to see the far-off frigate was upon us. We were nearing the end of our engagement with the corvette, but they still continued to volley back toward us. Whether it was by their design or some other cause, the frigate was dancing upon us. We had no choice but to risk being thrashed from our port side by the decaying corvette. We shifted our focus and placements from the dispatched cannons on the port side and ran toward our starboard guns. The *Fancy*'s wounded sailors clamoured and their voices became increasingly audible. I tore my hard gaze from the fierce action with the corvette and joined my brethren running toward the naked cannons on our right. Having come upon us with furled sails, the frigate let them down again as it sped alongside us after letting us catch up. The corvette remained frozen behind while the new skirmishing pair sped away briskly. I was in the wicked storm of the clash when I heard Captain Every's voice give the men new life.

"Move to starboard an' send 'em down, lads. This's it," Captain yelled, rallying us to kill or die.

While the frigate had tried to take advantage of our engagement with the corvette, our ballsy manoeuvre proved intelligent. Our starboard side was perfectly undamaged. The second ship's delay to join the battle, despite their attempted escape, proved too long, and we got into firing positions. Men returned from below with more munitions and powder to arm ourselves. Our sails and masts remained operational with light to moderate cavities. The halyards and some of the shrouds swung about, blown from their masters.

We streamed next to the frigate and smoke went up on both vessels. All of the yelling had been muted in my ears by the blasting and the sound of Hardy's commands of loading, wadding, ramming, aiming, firing, sponging, and reloading the cannon. We all knew what to do, French and English vessels alike. It was a saturation of far-off faces, oncoming shrapnel, aggressive cannonballs, exploding wood, and ducking for cover. Cannonballs and metal shards were sent both ways. I hadn't heard men scream and screech in agony like that since I was in the Navy. We received the battering we had dodged from the corvette earlier. Wood-chips sought to split me open, but I found myself lucky and untouched. We fired round after round of cannon, devastating the centre-stage of their vessel and exploding the bases of their masts, thus clipping their wings.

Captain Every then cut the foe off by sailing in front of this second stalled vessel, forcing them to disengage and slow to a near stop. Our damaged foremast was largely chipped and began to lean.

My blood boiled, but I did not want to die for two pirate ships, likely empty handed. We turned our vicious *Fancy* back around, making an about-face to approach on the starboard side of their ship to seize the opportunity with our own starboard side. It was a dangerous but intelligent manoeuvre, effectively using the frigate to block any late cannon fire from the disabled corvette. I looked over toward that first ship, the meek enemy craft, and saw three tenders filled to the teeth with men and small arms approaching. They rowed closer, little by little. I tapped Hardy on the shoulder and pointed toward the incoming reinforcements. He looked at them and shot me a gaze of overwhelm.

As we finished our rounding, approaching the crux of the stalled frigate, our rails nearly kissed theirs as we furled our sails. Cannon fire became the last priority. The next phase of our dangerous attack commenced. Captain Every unsheathed his sword, and all of us followed suit in unison. It was time for the boarding. In the headrush of an overmatched battle, I saw Captain Every point his open hand to the loins of the wooden enemy. We readied our grappling hooks, swords, and instincts. Some men carried pistols or muskets. I jumped over the edges and onto the starboard side of the crippled second ship. I screamed in violence, fear, and aggression, losing all thought, becoming one with the moment and my own sword.

"Pour *La Marie*," I heard a seaman of their vessel yell.

As our *Fancy* slowed to a halt next to their stationary ship, floating in the water at barely a crawl, dozens of us leaped onto the ship, using hooks and ropes or long-planks to cross over. Some fell into the water on the way over, and may have been crushed between the two boats. I would not dare prove incompetent at that critical moment. Gunpowder and gunshots sounded off beside my ears and in front of my eyes. A lone Frenchman stood in front of me, wearing dark coloured garments. Fixation and pure rapture took me over. We locked eyes and squared up, neither of us with a pistol or musket. Good. He charged me.

The French foe in front of me came alive, lurching forward with a large bound. His sword arched wide in an overhead swinging attack, which I deflected. After the parry, he advanced on me, thrusting forth a haymaker, which skimmed my brow despite my effort to dodge it. I repelled a follow-up thrust of his sabre. He continued sternly with another unavoidable punch to my liver, shooting his clenched fist into my stomach and stealing my breath away. As I clutched over after the blow, I looked up and spat in his face, discombobulating him for a moment. As both of us were disoriented, I dragged my unused sword across his stomach up to the bottom of his chin, surprising him with a rapid, upward slingshot of the blade. No more Frenchman, plenty of blood. He groaned in agony, dropped his blade, and put his arms across his torso as he fell to the deck and slowly faded away. I no longer knew myself. Killing was not in my heart, but it was in my body. It was my instinct, my survival. With every man I ended or saw ended, I drifted further from who I was and more toward a self-serving animal. He was not the first enemy I'd killed, but my first as a pirate and an outlaw. My first as a free man. My first up close with a blade. The first I touched.

"Nous abandonnons. Nous abandonnons," I heard a Frenchman echo.

"They've surrendered," a man of ours translated as I was still hunched over on one knee, trying to recover my breath from the gut-punch.

Their French captain had died, but his second in command, likely their quartermaster, must have ordered the stand down action for both of their vessels. The hand-to-hand battle ended quickly as we rushed and outnumbered them, despite both of our crews being rocked by casualties and fallen men. The incoming reinforcements from the corvette did not have a chance to face us pistol-to-pistol.

It ended and we reflected briefly. Damage was done, and serious repairs were needed for our fractured masts, punctured sails, blistered rails, and the small holes in our lower decks. We dominated two French pirate ships, killed many men, and fractured some masts that day. The battle lasted what felt like moments. What took hours were the repairs and Surgeon Fitzgerald's tall order of wounded to tend to. Their French doctor assisted him. Our casualties were incalculable, but undoubtedly less than the *Renarde*'s and the *Marie*'s. We took their supplies, recruited all of their willing survivors, and sailed away from their tarnished vessels. The French pirates had to join by necessity, not force. Defeat makes a pirate submissive. They were second-class, foreign-speaking pirates. Battles aren't quick when you're in the Navy. Battles with 'honour' last days. Battles with pirates often last moments or they never end. Advantage always takes the victory, but in the Royal Navy, the battle is more strategic, especially considering the larger numbers and forces involved in the conflict. I'd been yearning for swordplay and hot-blooded combat since joining up as a privateer. It was something I hadn't experienced in traditional naval warfare. That day I got it. And it took a lot out of me.

If only the sailing went as fast as the battles came and went. We were a ways off from the Cape and my hungers turned toward our destination, having been satiated with earlier danger. Each good-hearted lad has a monster in him, even if it remains buried. My mean streak was always close to the surface, cloaking itself as my quiet judgement. The judgement that no other man saw. Captain Every had a serious look and he was likely a madman at heart like I. All madmen are an asset when on your side, but are demons if not. At times, I wondered if the crew couldn't tell which side I was on, whether I liked or disliked them. It gave me an edge over a lot of the men on the ship, most of whom barely spoke to me. I liked it that way. It is better to be despised for retaining individuality than to lose oneself in accepting companies. The crew later respected and hated me, but I believed Captain Every admired me. And that was all I needed.

Later that evening, I did not hold my tongue. And it was the night I changed from a useful outcast into a marked man. I was on watch with a few other sailors as we anchored for the night. The golden hot lanterns and blackness of the night surrounded our squadron of men, huddled around the ember of a fire. About half a dozen of us huddled around the fiery metal bowl in conversation. A few others drifted around, and several watchmen patrolled on the corners of the ship and the crow's nest. We were alone on the open sea, and there was no need to take guard duty seriously unless the Captain came strolling around. In front of the men I fiddled with my unsheathed cutlass, retaining the dried blood of the slain Frenchman upon its blade. The mates talked about maidens and the world, as men often do on the sea. Most of the men sitting around the fire with me were nearly old enough to be my father. They were older lads who never grew up, following what was between their legs instead of something more. I counted myself out of that pack. I was a seaman and pirate for its freedom, not its gold or port-side ladies.

I decided to speak my mind, despite heavy hesitation. I was often chastised for my different perspectives, however it was high time to speak some substance into the night. Despite the persecution I'd faced for speaking of things so foreign to these men time and time again, I did it once more in reckless abandon. That evening, though, the stakes were different. There were Dutchmen and Frenchmen around from our recent conquests. Maybe they possessed more cultured, open minds than the washed-up Englishmen who mostly spoke nonsense and ripped me for aiming to talk sense. The ones who speak the most think themselves the toughest and the wisest. Fools. It is the quiet ones you should be wary of. The silent sword, not the loud battle axe. I was a bloody cutlass, and I never named my sabre, ever. My silent blade received full backlash in the conversation.

The lads were talking while squatting on barrels and crates on the deck. Our boys were making peace with the Frenchmen who joined us, in a fraternal league.

"It is a poor thing that we had to battle with ye gentlemen. 'Tis a dirty shame that many of yer boys didn't make it, same as our boys. Ye ain't half bad," a floppy old sailor, Warren Van Bailey, said to one of the Frenchmen, Jean.

"It is the nature of the sea, is it not?" Jean said with his accent.

"How does he mean?" Van Bailey looked around at the rest of us and asked.

"He's sayin' battling is an innate part of piracy," another sailor, Lee Armstrong said.

"Is he, now? Should we feel bad about it then?" Van Bailey asked.

"On the contrary," I interjected.

"What do ye know, Cole. Ye've never been in a battle before, have ye?" Van Bailey said.

"I have, old man."

"Oh, really then. Why shouldn't we have remorse for their brethren?" Van Bailey asked.

"Jean said it, mate. 'Tis nature. War is war. Battle is battle. Any man who enters the conflict accepts the consequences. But it is over now, so let us move on," I said.

"Aye, but he doesn't mean killin' is a remorseless act. Ye'll understand the older ye get and the more ye see," Van Bailey said.

"Aye, maybe. Any man who doesn't lay down his sword before the *Fancy* deserves to die if they clog our way. There are no trials on the Atlantic. What makes ye think anything in this blue foam, other than pillaging them and protectin' ourselves, keeps us from caving in on ourselves? We need war. We need the kill or die, and if someone who loses should survive, they're a loyal dog to their new master. There is no other way. Why do ye think the defeated party bribes on their knees for freedom or the joining up?"

Van Bailey chuckled. I continued:

"It makes no difference to me who is in our way. If they obstruct, send 'em down. It's us or them, Van Bailey. Don't ye understand, in all yer years of action?"

"Ye're some murderer, Cole, and murder ain't the same as killing," Van Bailey said, parading a half-sincere smile.

"Ye jealous that I killed a man today and ye didn't get a notch, Bailey?" Armstrong jested before Van Bailey then continued.

"Not me, no. I am not jealous, ye sick fool. We're brawlin' the *Marie* for all of five heartbeats and this boy over here managed to slice a man's stomach open. I think he likes it, the sick lad." Van Bailey looked back at me. "Must not fancy the Frenchmen, do ye, Cole?"

I looked at my crewmates keeping a watchful eye on our French crewmates for their reaction, yet these newcomers did not stir.

"It's kill or be killed, and we were ordered to attack. Why ye yellow-bellying, Bailey? Can't handle yer sword anymore? Is it drooping down and too far to the left? It doesn't rise up too straight nowadays, does it?" I said and knew this would grind him up, for he was easily angered.

"Maybe, Cole. Maybe I be a yellow-belly, but ye're a heartless lot. An inhumane," Van Bailey claimed.

Van Bailey and I looked at each other with satisfaction. Strange, perverse territorial satisfaction. Maybe I was as heartless as he said. I didn't think so.

"Ye'll do anything it takes to bring me down, Van Bailey. Anything. Call me soft, young, and weak or call me sickenin' and murderous. I wonder why ye feel threatened by me. We all know here if push comes to shove, Captain Every'd find me more useful than ye— a washed up one vs. a dangerous, bright, and brimmin' one— we know how fate would spell that duel. Is that what ye want? A duel? That'd make me a two-timing murderer on the same day. That wouldn't be fair to Davy Jones. Souls pilin' up, the blood on my sword thickenin', and the notches on my leather'd keep on extending. The locker-men and gatekeepers'd get overwhelmed, olde man." Tough talk for myself, a lad of contemplation.

I never got that angry from the men's charades. But I was angry then and there was no backing down.

"Say, boy, ye're a complicated one. Ye better watch yer back and sleep with one eye open," Van Bailey said as he pointed his shrivelled finger at me and walked away, going below, likely to his hammock.

The rest of the men looked at me in some shock. It felt to be an ugly exchange but I got the better of him with my threat. He left for the evening.

"I don't like talking like that. But this is the Atlantic and being a pyrate, it hath a price," I said, looking toward the departing Van Bailey as some of the men laughed at my audacious statement and Van Bailey's flee.

"Don't speak like ye have weight on yer shoulders, Cole. Why d'ye look to stir up trouble on the boat? Are ye mutineer for Every or mutineer for mutiny's sake?" Armstrong, the wise one, butted back in.

"I don't have peerage or superior rank. I only have my mind, body, and soul. There's no room in my heart for passivity, Armstrong, and I won't let that lad walk all over me," I defended. "Ye know better than most, a man's got to stick up for himself or else he is food for the sharks. And what we did was justified."

"This is a way of life, not a bloody game. Tell me— why'd ye mutiny with us?" Armstrong said coolly.

"I took part in the mutiny 'cause Captain Every is the best of us. Can we not all agree? I won't put my sword away now that he's captain. Not for bloody Frenchmen, that olde dog Warren Van Bailey, not for convenience, not for anyone. The blood stays on the blade and the blade stays sharp. I stay ready, always."

I yelled, Armstrong spoke softly, and we quarrelled with our voices instead of fighting. Squabble was an action Van Bailey was incapable of, for he could only insult and talk and sleep. I did not know why he backed down so easily beforehand. Armstrong was a different animal, though, closer to me than Van Bailey, in essence. He duelled me with his words.

"Ye sharpen yer sword to strike yer own crew, Cole? Ye don't deserve to be on this ship if that be true, ye coward. Where do yer bloody loyalties lie?" Armstrong asked emotionlessly.

"To what is *true*. To salvation and whatever may be necessary to realise it. To the good of the moment, not the good of all mankind. What is true for ye all…" I pointed to the gathered onlookers, "… may be too false for me to agree to."

I clamoured for my respect, knowing I never should have let it go that far and never should have revealed my inner workings to this extent. Armstrong quietly stared at me with eyes piercing through the dark.

"Ye're out of yer element and out of yer mind. Don't approach anywhere near me. I don't trust ye," Armstrong said slowly, having reached his final ultimatum.

"A bunch of boys ye two are," I said then pointed toward Van Bailey's departed direction.

"Coming from the one who can't grow a beard?" Armstrong said laughing.

The lads around me laughed with Armstrong. I was defeated. As I opened my mouth and struggled to find some angry, defensive words for the quarrel, I saw Captain Every come into my peripheral via the men's eyes looking away from me. They silenced immediately. My pointing arm, held up, froze and I looked at Captain Every. Captain approached slowly, mastering the spaces of the ship, staring at me. He did not look down or at anyone else but me. It was displeasure I sensed, utter disappointment, as he neared me.

"Captain Ever—" Armstrong tried to address him.

"Not a word," Captain Every cut Lee off. "I heard enough… now all of ye put out the scuttlebutt and man the watch."

The men scattered. Armstrong, Captain Every, and I all looked at each other, awaiting the next moment in the chronicle as three figures in the newly abandoned concourse.

"We should maroon him, Cap'n. Take a vote from the crew. I'm sure of it. We don't want or need this boy," Armstrong said.

"As if that is up to the crew to decide?" Captain Every said to Armstrong, putting him back into his place. "That's up to the captain. Now, ye're dismissed, Mr. Armstrong."

Armstrong walked away with his tail between his legs in resentful shame. I feared our meeting wouldn't be the last of our rivalry, or my rivalry with Van Bailey. Captain Every kept looking where Lee's head was moments ago as I waited for a lashing or flogging.

"Ye talk too loud, boy. I heard ye down below," Captain Every said to me, as he turned to look at my face.

"Sorry, sir. I was heated like a kettle and it got away from me."

Captain Every stepped closer to me, then turned square to me.

"That is fine. But not again." Captain leaned toward me. "Ye're a useful sailor, and a courageous, young lad. But as a man, I cannot judge ye. I don't know ye and I should let ye go off at a port somewhere to avoid some civil war on my young ship, but ye've proved valiant and talented for this line of work." He paused, lowering his head, and peered at me with his eyes beneath his brow. "But ye've been warned, Cole— control yer tongue."

I looked at him, in my silent dishonour.

"Killing is what we do. And it is irrefutable ye're a low murderer. A talented one at that too," Captain Every said finally, upbeat, as he smirked then turned away, and departed.

Was he playing a game with me? What a sly dog with a sick sense of humour. He said the words and walked away, continuing his round of inspections then likely returned to his quarters. I did not know Captain Every had room for humour in his heart or his responsibilities nor could I tell how serious he was. Whether he was mad or humouring me, I didn't expect him to meet me at my depths with wit. Did he truly agree with me? I smiled and looked out at nothing, proud of whatever the hell had happened. It felt good to be a madman, sometimes, when in like-minded company. But good lord, Captain appeared to be crazy. By God, Captain Every was crazy enough for me to trust him. And I assumed it was vice versa, for I thought myself teetering off the deep end. And everyone henceforth knew it.

<u>*Chapter V*</u>

’ROUND THE ROUND

Rumour was we entered the New Year of our Lord 1695. We did not hold a celebration of the new year, so I couldn’t be sure. We received word from a mariner vessel, in passing, of the early 1695 date. Captain Every must have certainly abandoned the official keeping of the captain’s-log. The *Fancy*, Captain Every, and the combined crew of Englishmen, Dutchmen, and Frenchmen had crossed beyond the realm of the Crown, into true pirate waters we had ventured, where honour was non-existent, and only its twisted variation reflected itself upon the crew. There were no prisoners taken en route to the Cape, only shipping lanes, sea thieves, slave traders, bargaining chips, and Dutch & English East India Company captains who played by their own rules. We were past the western side of the Cape of Good Hope, heading toward the ingress of the Pirate Round where the Indian Ocean began. The waters there were saltier, and the smell was reviving. It smelled of the waters near home, but it was no calm paradise. Being a sailor meant the destinations never ended. You’re always on the move. ’Tis a reflection of life. ’Tis a reflection of Chaoticism. Chaoticism is a sailor’s life, in essence.

Our new destination was Saint-Augustin, Madagascar, a bay for supplies and tropical fruit. It was quite a journey thus far. I had ventured into the depths of myself, letting the crevices I’d usually kept secret start to show themselves. I had no more concern for, or interest in, the cold of the Channel. Fear of the Spanish Watch in Corunna left me entirely. Absent was the concern for slave trader ships in the waters of Bioko. Strength had consumed fear. I had two able, healthy legs and a fickle mind, both of them ready to fend off opponents or my own crewmen.

It is said you must lose yourself to find yourself. Furthermore, I say you must earn yourself. The boredom, longing, and tenuous journey made me a stranger to myself. Possessing true grips of oneself is a long campaign, not a slogan to be realised in a single moment. I had been clawing and crawling my way back to who I was, carving my path toward who I was meant to be. The depths, as the *Fancy* ventured further and further south, were my sanctuary and my purgatory. Retreating within was what I'd do when waiting for direction and required a sacred hiding place. I wanted to live my philosophy, my Chaoticism. My philosophy, my mind, and my behaviour were interconnected. My Chaoticism was a decision, a motive, and an action. I aimed to solidify them all together. It was high time to keep moving forward in all domains.

After I had spent some time sitting on the bow of the boat, picturing the cleansed hull and feeding my self-obsession with a spiral of thoughts, my concentration was disrupted by the sight of land. It was a beige blot dead ahead enveloped by a few tenders, some small lodgings, and a world of green above it. It was beautiful, paradise-like. It was Africa, but not her desert. This was the Bay of Saint-Augustin of western Madagascar. I imagined nobody on the *Fancy* except for Captain Every had known of this bay, but I had no idea. We resupplied quickly and spared no time drinking, bamboozling, or carousing with women on the island. We stayed our course.

There were plenty of Portuguese in those waters. Even if they were our national allies, 'twas best beware and best be hungry. They had a reputation for being dangerous pirates, yet were known to be well-stocked. They represented a source of opportunity and hazard around there. We kept sailing north and scaled further up the western coast of Madagascar. A lookout spotted a pair of sloops, moving ahead about half our speed. He, as well as the rest of our crew, watched them sail directly onto the surf then the sand of an island, in a direct line. It was a most mysterious sight to see a pair of ships intentionally run aground together. Maybe it was out of fear of our big, bad man-o'-war.

We furled our sails near the island to inspect, slowed, and tried to spot their crew from a distance. There was nobody aboard, only a big pair of black decked nothings. A ghost ship? I'd heard legends of phantom vessels near the Cape of Good Hope before, but those were tall seamen's tales. Captain Every and a few volunteers, myself included, took a tender to go investigate the island. We sat on the small boat, looking to the shore and the chaos of the trees beyond the sand. Did they wait for us behind said treeline to take our captain, our vessel, and our lives? No, I thought. Phantom tales. Phantom tales. Shrug the fear off, I told myself as we rowed.

"Cap'n, why not even a dozen of us? If both their crews wait to ambush us ashore, we'd be doomed," I raised the issue, already a lost cause, as we were rowing on our merry way.

I should have spoken up sooner.

"And what do ye suggest, Cole? We bombard the island? Send half the crew to inspect and leave the other half to get ambushed at anchor?" Captain Every said.

"Aye, Captain. We'd best be on guard. Two phantom sloops—we're sure to have a good story or good wounds to tell this tale," I said.

Our tender was bombarded by the sea spray, relieving us of the heat. We hit land. Captain Every's boots touched the sand first, then mine. Like lightning, we barreled across the beach and surrounded their dark, double-masted vessels. I saw two unknown flags on both ships, neither of a European nation. I assumed these were pirate ships. One named the *Ability* and the other *Moura Encantada*. An English name and a Spanish name. These weren't East Indiaman ships. They were certainly pirates.

"Cap'n, look at their flags." I pointed to their cloths as some of our men boarded the empty vessels.

"Aye, Cole. Be on guard. These aren't Portuguese," Captain said as I watched our ten men grab the hilts of their sabres and inspect the vessels carefully.

All ships look tall when grounded, but the sloops were specks compared to our mighty *Fancy*. If we were to be ruined by those two little things and their crews, we deserved it. As we split our attention between the ships and the nearby wood, still fearing the Pandora's Box of these ships, a group of men appeared from the treeline adorned with much facial hair and an air of suspicion. The strangers were barbarian-like. They walked a few paces from the cover of the trees and stopped, staring at us in silence. None of their hands were gripping weapons. We inspected each other, on edge, before either party could think to say anything. Their head honcho, probably some admiral, commander, or captain, approached. All of their men dressed raggedy, and I could smell them from a distance— undeniable signs of a pirate crew. Shortly after their leader distinguished himself from their crew, Captain Every mirrored him and approached the empty space in the centre between us, meeting in the middle. They stood close enough to attack one another before either crew could engage, but far enough for the other lad to react.

"Hello," Captain Every said to the man.

"Are ye English?" their skipper asked with an elegant accent— Spanish.

"Most of us," Captain Every said cryptically.

"Do ye serve the English Crown?" the Spaniard asked.

"Not anymore," Captain Every said.

"Whose flag do ye fly? That red and white is like the English. And ye speak English."

"Our own. A skull and crossbones of white in a sea of red. And chevrons amongst crimson. These are our flags, as we don't take mercy. We're not fond of takin' prisoners either," Captain Every said.

The shepherd must always frighten the wolves to protect his flock. Sometimes bending the truth, especially with new sheep, is necessary to keep things in line.

"We thought ye were English coming to hunt us down. Ye are pyrates hunting other pyrates?" the Spaniard asked.

"What's it worth to take ye're two little ships down, Spaniard? What is yer use, hiding behind those trees in cowardice?"

"We can be crew— loyal and dependable. I am Captain Manuel Sanna of the *Moura Encantada*, and we took the *Ability* as our own. Who are ye?"

"I am Captain Henry Every of the *Fancy*, the most nimble, dangerous ship in the water, with a crew of English, Dutch, and French. Ye Spaniards'd make great additions. Any of yer English can find kinsmen here." He loosened up, addressing the Spanish Captain and all of his men, about sixty, who slowly moved out of the trees.

Their men murmured to one another.

"I'd be pleased to have ye all a part of our crew now," Captain yelled out to the cowering men.

John Durnburn, our boatswain, shuffled toward me. Durnburn had about 55 years to him and had plenty of raucousness that came from dangling with every vice and substance available to him throughout his years. But he was cleaned up, naturally peaceful, satiated with the wildness of life, and primarily concerned himself with the work of the crew, his wife, and a damn good laugh. Earlength light brown hair cascaded out of his coyote-like, wakeful face, up and behind his ears, beginning at his subtle widow's peak. His face had blemishes and little craters which often come from a life of seaworthiness and pipe-smoking. With many other sailors, pipe-smoking seemed quite like an effort to fit in, especially as an older sailor, as it was an impractical practice. But it fitted Durnburn's persona properly. He would walk away to smoke alone in private, not blow smoke in our faces. A small gap between his two front teeth painted his distinct voice with a slight lisp. Unending profanity dominated his speech, as he cursed approximately every other sentence. A trimmed forest of grey and black facial hair surrounded his mouth. His arms were youth-like and always at the ready, as he was an able one despite his age. Durnburn was the type of man who made a good companion to anybody, as he didn't give a damn about where a man came from. Our bos'n only cared for your spirit, willingness to put up a fight, or jump into the cordage at the drop of a feather. He was as fitting as furniture to the ship. I liked him. He was a sailor's sailor, through and through. He didn't like Captain Every, but obeyed him. The two would bicker over details from time to time but it never got in the way of the job. Durnburn was a guide to all of the men long before he became a dissident under command of the younger, more polished captain. Durnburn stood next to me and whispered— something he had never done before.

"Remember this. Keep an eye out for these men, ye must know yer enemy. And know the bloody wind," Durnburn said, giving me a command as one would a servant of his own private quarter, away from the captain's jurisdiction.

It confused me, considering the French were more of a national enemy, therefore more of a natural enemy, than the Spanish on the sea. Maybe he simply didn't like Spaniards.

"What are ye afraid of?" I asked, shaking my head at my superior.

"Keep an eye, Cole," Durnburn said, then walked away from me.

We sacked the sloops of their supplies and taxied our new shipmates back to the *Fancy* with us. A melting pot of various nations made up the crew of our ship. True pirates come from all across the world, as piracy is a universally human act, not only to the English and Spanish. It is natural, as even animals take from one another. The two sloops would prove incapable of keeping up with our *Fancy*, by both measures of speed and firepower. But if we couldn't have them, we couldn't let any other pirates have them. We set fire to them and let the sloops reduce to dust.

The fresh meat came aboard and were rightly appointed to their new places— the lowest of ranks, the grimiest of duties, and cleaning of the deck. They'd become our prime swabbies, taking on the most dangerous and dirty of tasks. All of them were happy to be alive but soon became bitter at being struck down to the lowness. Some of these men must have had significant pull on either or both of their old sloops but it had gone to the wayside— all except for

Captain Sanna and a pair of his trusted sailors, for they were given some degree of privilege and authority aboard the *Fancy*. A bold gesture. And then there was Thomas Howard, the new man who had joined me and my fellow able-bodied sailors to work the rigging alongside us. Durnburn, the bos'n, was our chief seaman. I much preferred to stay off the upper parts of the masts, especially the apexes of the topsails, as I was deathly afraid of heights. I was happy to pass off any height duty to a newcomer.

Thomas must have been from the *Ability*. One can always tell an Englishman from a Spaniard by facial hair, manner, and, of course, name. By then, I had ditched my toddler-faced clean shave and sported a proud moustache. Thomas was clean shaven but not for long. We would unsharpen him, get him right and scary soon. A beard intimidates a foe and accentuates masculine features. Any advantage is necessary. Thomas was a healthy chap with a pale complexion and dark hair. Darkness sagged beneath his commoner's eyes. For each regiment of any man's strangeness and eccentricity, Thomas had three amounts less. He was a conventional man. But no less a useful man. Often, in order to run a ship, there must be followers and hierarchy-abiders who move certain mechanics along, both socially and aquatically. I met Thomas as I went back to my duties upon loading the retrieved supplies and munitions back onto the *Fancy*. I prepared to carry out Durnburn's orders. The young man, slightly older than I, walked directly over to Durnburn who was handling some cordage beside me.

"Are ye the bos'n, sir?" the new man asked with a voice deeper than I expected.

"I am." Durnburn pointed to me. "Help this foolish lad prepare the main and fore." Durnburn dismissed him.

I climbed some rope after releasing others to allow the sails to extend. I went up the mainmast, slow and as low to the ground as possible, to address the main sail and do the same at the foremast to ready the fore sail. In quite improper timing, as it was a frightening time to make relations, the fellow young man paused and reached out his hand quite abruptly.

"Thomas Howard," he said, introducing himself, and I reached my hand out in greeting.

"Rollins Cole. Welcome aboard," I said shortly and returned to my tall duties.

Thomas didn't say another word to me for a while. He caught on to my temperament— quite an astute lad.

<u>*Chapter VI*</u>

LIBERTALIA

We sailed around the Madagascan waters for some time, searching, hunting, and living. Some stops were made back in Saint-Augustin, Johanna in the Comoros Islands, and the French settlement of Bourbon. Throughout, our Captain Henry Every and our 175-man *Fancy* had met and made an alliance with other pirate captains. We pacted with Captain Thomas Tew of the *Amity*, Captain Richard Want of the *Dolphin*, and occasionally, Captain Joseph Faro of the *Portsmouth Adventure*. Captain Martin Bennetts led the raids for the Libertalian colony. We raided some ships here and there, as a quartet, until we found a place— a place for pirates. We found ourselves in a hooked crevice on the Northeast corner of Madagascar, in the crotch of the Bay of Antongila and the Bay of Tintingue, off of Saint Mary's Island.

The hardest part of a pirate's life is the mutiny and becoming a pirate. The next hardest part is conjuring direction after that fateful day. Pirates are often slaves to the whims of the wind, with no inner compass. Their crew and captain dictate life as he or she knows it. The life was freedom to the point of slavery. Growing up, sailing was furthest from my heart, for I belonged on land. But the problem with land is the people. This I learnt as I grew into a young man. I love some people, but disliked the majority. The furthest place away from the sprawling grips of people and their smothering ways is a ship on the ocean. Although one is trapped with up to 200 of the same lads, he's forced to adapt. That was why I joined the Royal Navy to begin with. It gave me direction until I inevitably lost my way, only to lead toward the metamorphosis of converting to sea thievery, living a different sort of freedom. Chaoticism is a trait which allowed me to do what I believed, giving loyalty only to the search itself— a truly piratical existence in action and in thought. As is the motto of a true Chaotic— what is next? A place near two bays, between two islands was next— a place where I hoped my freedom and Chaoticism would flourish.

Moments came and went quickly as the gangly crew of Europeans traversed invisible paths on our way to that promised land. When we finally arrived, the days and weeks passed as if they had no weight. If time passes one by speedily, one must be in some sense of a home, whether splendid or torturous or somewhere in between. There are no homes for pirates, only temporary refuges— a ship, a crew, a vice, a captain, a woman, maybe a port... but never a whole land. That place I mythologized was the final place for pirates. I felt it. I believed it.

This place which I call a place for pirates was a location and an idea one must know someone to discover. Captain Tew, our new friend, knew of the place, Libertalia, and also the nearby gatekeeping settlement under Adam Baldridge on St. Mary's Island. She, our Libertalia, had little, pure houses scattered across her green grass belly, across her hilly chest, and on every bare place we trekked. The notorious Captain James Mission, a Germanic man with two spare plots of hair ranging out from underneath his hat on either side of his face and a long, horseshoe moustache, and the Priest, who was an olive-skinned Roman with shining black hair and white, bulging eyes, had begun the piratical colony before our *Fancy* arrived, some years earlier. Captain Want and Captain Faro did not stay in the haven with us, for they were to stay on the water, remaining in high piracy, to raid any of those around us who crossed into the eastern Madagascan waters. It was a privilege to have allies in a foreign land and protection on the sea at the same time.

Captain Every and Captain Tew seized the inhabitants' interests upon advent, evidenced by many of the peoples' stares. We landed at a village that was an unfinished, unfurnished product of desperation, full of potential by both the standards of untouched nature and desirous hands of oppressed men yearning for escape, coming from all corners of the world. And I could smell it in the air— Captain Every and Captain Tew wanted to take the place beyond its humble, hopeful origins, as opportunists leading a small society of optimists.

I caught sight of the large papers swapped in semi-private audiences between Captain Every, Captain Tew, and our carpenter. The etchings upon them lead me to believe our Captain would turn the free colony into a land of its own, a city, an independent civilisation of its own. The numerous drawings were of architectural layouts in the jungle. The centre of the pirate world, Libertalia, would bring the pirate hotspots of the New World to its knees, drawing hungry buccaneers away from the danger of the Americas and toward the natural fortress in the Indian Ocean, Madagascar. These prospective fantasies and powerful mirages captivated me, but I now see, years later, how much of it was speculation. I was blinded then.

Libertalia was a real settlement in the jungle, yet it was the substance of dreams. Although life was a series of contradictions and complexities, in Libertalia, we aimed to cut through that. Let the complexity of modern man and his civilisations fall away. Let man, primal man, dictate himself, in line with the simplicity of nature. We removed those unsure hands of humanness and let us beasts live together as beasts, self-governing. We put those hopeful patrons who started the colony under the command of us, an enterprising group of pirates who understood the laws of the jungle much better than they did. Libertalia was a place of man and the inhumane, and we let the inhumane run us men, ungoverned and untouched. We yearned for freedom as pirates, but did we deserve to be cast out for it by law? Maybe modern man was too afraid to ask for what we pirates found and took in Madagascar. Society and the collective were imitations of beauty. But humanity itself, in mass, simply got in its own way.

I recall one event in Libertalia that proved to me how serene this separateness from the world was. I walked into town one day, looking around and seeing people everywhere. I had been alone for some time, remaining in my quarters and doing my duties. But fate compelled me to go loaf around, to see people. When I looked at the populace, I could sense that they were excited to see me. They did not see the pirate before them, but another creature, one of them. I couldn't know what exactly they were thinking. Without the law, people around them telling them how to see me, and without any need for me to decide their character before meeting them, we could both meet, any fair stranger and I, on neutral territory. I remember the faces, the anxious eyes. They were eyes not of fear, but of excitement, seeing deeper into me than my occupation. My interactions that day were brief and monumental. I went about the different shops and experienced our own market. Needing new boots, I asked around and was directed. We were all equals. There was no political distrust between us, pirates and civilians. I found my way into the boot shop— a lone man, some leather, some tools, and footwear about. He straightened me up well. I felt no need to chat him up, no desire to run out of that room. Our interaction was pure. Let fly away, our need to define and separate from one another. We were simply men amongst men. Nature shined forth, stripping all artifice. Silence was our language other than talk of the business exchange. The new boots fit me well like a new man in this new world.

Everything neutral or open-minded, however, is therefore corruptible. Human societies are neutral. Humans are capable of being gods, but often they end up worms. And the surest way to become a worm is through the mishandling of other people and other peoples' mishandling of you. Let the man be, give him a jungle to run free, stay your hands away from him, and watch the god emerge. In accordance with the natural laws of this complex and contradicting line of thought, I concluded both this place and humans themselves were worthy of high praise, but more deserved cruel judgement. Oh, what high hopes and strong musings I held for Libertalia. We were in a fruit-filled, green, unoccupied utopia where men were free to become gods. Then again, what are pirates? Dreamers. Roamers.

We sing our shanties, do our dances with our bottles, and stay on some bloody, wooden structure keeping us from the depths for years and lifetimes on end. Delusional. What beautiful delusions we have. I was a happy man of delusion. Did the jungle drive me mad? Was it making me soft?

As we entered and immersed ourselves in our new realm, tombstones were raised and scattered about the young colony, either covered with new codes or remaining naked, baking in the sun awaiting an engraving of simple, makeshift rules. They were etched with guidelines to protect the freedom and liberty of every man's volition, not box us in. I read "Article Seven" on a tombstone, stating "No man shall bar another man from speaking." It took archaic ballsiness to devote an entire law to preserving every man's speech, harkening back to those Greco-Roman times when men weren't driven to sea because their words and thoughts were so disliked or deemed dangerous. This law prevented the invasion of superior dialogue, the hand of a dictator ordering men out, or commanding men to death. Or at least that was how those great societies were taught to me.

We used to be cast out as demons if we spoke our mind, and then in Libertalia, disagreement was no longer worthy of torture, but welcomed. How far have men drifted from God? How close to Him were we aiming? God gave man free will but man took it away from himself. In Libertalia, we gave it back. People need not be executed or banished for speaking their mind. Then again, the best bar to a pathetic man's tongue is a solid blade. But that is not simply a bar to a man's speech, that is a cut directly into the soul of man. We would not allow any more cuts into the inner voice of man. Not in Libertalia. No more.

I came into the centre of Libertalia another day, exploring again. A disagreement took place. The same cobbler who worked new leather for me was also the butcher. I wondered why his shanty little shop smelled odd. I thought it was refined leather, but it was bare flesh.

"Shut up," said the cobbler.

"Ye will not speak to me that way, sir," a young man said to the aged cobbler and butcher.

"Aye, well my price is the price," the old butcher said.

"Well, I don't have money, I have food I can trade ye," the young man said.

"And what can I do with that?" the butcher said, pointing at the bundle of lemons in the young trader's hand.

"Ye can trade it for anything else ye'd like," he said.

"I trade things for coin. I can't get anything with lemons around here. The natives already have plenty."

"I can give ye juice of lemon. Surely that'll fetch ye a fine share of coin," the trader said.

"Why don't ye go and do it yerself then come back to me with the money," the butcher said, and sliced into a rib of beef.

"Ah. To Hell with ye," the young man said and walked off.

When left to sort themselves out, men can come to their own conclusions, and nature can run its course. When interfered with by authority, nature cannot dictate the market. Surely the purest way for a market to operate is by the mysterious laws of nature and the freedom of man. This freedom is kept in check by the vast array of options. The young trader could get his beef through many different methods, none requiring bullying or even haggling. The natives, the Libertalians, and us pirates made up a small economy of our own— a barter of the free man. And when I say man, I also speak of the other man— women. Libertalia was inhabited by ladies and children too. European women and Malagasy women. European children, Malagasy children, and mixed children. I hoped we would not ruin these free relations. All souls had a place in Libertalia. That was what I had been thinking to myself those days. I pondered in generalisations but lived in nuances. Such is the case with any sailor-philosopher.

We settled down nicely in the jungle. The speed of adventure was quelled by the calm of the earth. Due to Captain Tew's relationship with Captain Mission and a native Queen of some native tribe, in addition to Captain Every's firepower of the *Fancy*, his overwhelming charisma, and the security of our manpower, both of the captains had found themselves leaders of the realm along with Captain Mission mere weeks after we arrived. The civilians of Libertalia— men, women, and children from all corners of the globe— were subservient to our brute pirate faculties, even though we did not exercise those savage abilities. We knew we had power over the first inhabitants like unsolidified, merciful kings. A land is run either by kings and queens, force, or rules. This place was, in its nature, somewhere betwixt all three and absolutely beyond those systems of human governance. Nature itself ran it in perfect equilibrium. Libertalia was a promising enterprise, the First Pirate Kingdom, under 'King' Captain James Mission, its founder, until something better was destined to come along. It did.

Things moved at too slow a pace in Libertalia, maybe because of the women. Who is to say what the Libertalian men were capable of had they been on their own? When in the presence of women, I am certain us pirates are distracted. Our men stopped labouring to observe them and pursue them, ceased their high talk for discussion of the female form. Although it is natural, our progress was certainly obstructed. We needed our own place to roam, as pirate men, and be rough with our efforts, free from distracting pleasures, for no pleasure is greater than that of freedom. Trying to exclude them was an impossible and foolish errand, but the lads certainly needed to get it together somehow.

The people of Libertalia seemed to lack a strong leader that us pirate crews were governed by. To be a pirate, it is a necessity to work as one under a leader. The people of Libertalia were so separate, evidenced by their distant homes, disagreeable notions of how the market was run, and apparent separateness in nature. Sure, us pirates would infight, but that was the nature of brotherhood. We knew that to get along, we must engage in conflict then let it go. I hadn't seen that lemon trader in some time, and I feared he and the butcher were an example of a growing, larger, eventual problem of Libertalia— they couldn't get along without an authority. When

Captain Mission was absent, they fell into rivalry. It was the opportunity and the weakness of freedom. The natives were one by birth and custom, with a capable leader. Us pirates were one by trade and survival, led by a charismatic captain. The Libertalians were all over the bloody place.

"I think they're going to be a problem mixing with us," Thomas said to me, during a day of hunting.

"I know. It is becoming obvious they are too different from us. We can overrun the Libertalians in a single effort if there should be any issue. Although we've meshed well with them thus far, I fear that we have come too late to be one with them. We are surely too brutish for them and they are too feeble," I said, keeping my eyes on the lookout for a boar on our hunt.

"Ye don't think we can balance 'em out? They have good intentions and character, but we have the manpower and experience," Thomas said.

"I know nothing of how to manage people, Thomas. My guess is only that our differing ways of life and prospect of surviving together will prove too polarising to maintain."

"Aye. I fear ye could be right. If only we could let go of our ways as pyrates," Thomas said.

"Our pyrate ways are not the issue, for our abilities are necessary and serve us out here," I said.

"Well then, if only both of us were more adaptable," Thomas said.

"If only, friend," I replied and we were interrupted by a darting boar, which we hunted and later killed.

Our conversation was relevant, but not for some time. The time did eventually come. There was a new, separate colony we carved out for ourselves, organised by Captain Every and the carpenter, Fulton. It was called "New Devon", named after where the captain grew up, Devonshire. It is also my birthplace and Captain Tew's supposed birthplace, although he was brought up in the American Colonies. In the large wooden hall of Libertalia, the first building the settlers constructed and where we ate most of our meals and held celebrations, Captain Every stood up and erected the plan and realisation of New Devon, out of thin air, imagination, and good old-fashioned hubris. Captain Mission was absent that night. Captain Every stood up, with his red coat serving as a beacon of attention to all inhabitants and patrons.

"Hark. Boys of the *Fancy*. We have an idea. Us... sailors, masters, of this place..."

The Libertalians observed silently and the pirate men laughed with Captain Every even though he, Captain Tew, and Captain Mission "ran" Libertalia as unofficial leaders of the free land, and the articles on the tombstones guided the people. And even as those quasi-rulers and physical articles co-existed, everyone did whatever the hell they desired— true independence and individualism. It was messy and full of boyhood ideals. Freedom was all I yearned for, away from the world's larger collective reality. And while I preferred a solid single captain to guide as opposed to a collective of a society, individual self-governance was the finest system over any other option of governance. For nature within and without is the most infinitely intelligent sovereign. People obstruct nature's directives. Improper rules, leaders, and groups tarnish her inevitable, equalising force.

Captain Tew interrupted my thoughts, the laughter, and the chatter. Captain Tew was an innocent, pale-faced man, whose innocence certainly did not match his temperament. His coat was a measure too short on his sleeves, and his gait suggested obedience to me. Thin, wiry hair fell beside his ears and a small brown freckle championed his right cheekbone. He looked like a simple lad, out of his element as a captain. But beware, there was a feisty, treacherous thief beneath his innocent, youthful mask. The three captains and the articles were more symbolic than anything else, for, as I said, everyone did whatever they wanted. It was in everyone's best interest to contribute to the overall wellbeing of the entire colony. Captain Every did what he wanted that night when he made his speech to the people.

"Ah, just get to it Henry." Captain Tew was the only man I knew who could address Captain Every as "Henry" and survive.

"Alright, alright, calm ye arses. This is my bloody moment, Thomas. Shut up." He turned back to us, the Libertalian and pirate mass. "There is another place in these jungles where we shall go— New Devon. It is a place which I and Thomas shall lead, in some fashion, some steps away from Libertalia. Libertalia is a place, a mother to us now, a mother to New Devon— a free place. But it is Captain Mission's to lead, as he birthed her... that's a lot of birthing."

I laughed. The rest of the Libertalians, mostly non-pirates, watched with quiet amusement. Did Captain Every talk to anyone about New Devon before striking it into eternity? Maybe those blueprint plans shared between the carpenter and Captain Tew I spotted were of New Devon and not of Libertalia. Could I be certain? Not entirely. It was beyond me. My hunch told me that Captain made this decision as our leader on the spot after thinking about it privately for some time. Those designs were originally for Libertalia until he decided to reserve their potential for only his men and himself. I doubted he would speak of this decision to anyone other than himself before acting it out. I would have done the same— the bigger the idea, the more careful one must be in realising its execution.

In a word, the designs and power dynamics of Libertalia I ramble about occurred not in such a grand, direct, physical, organised moment, but appeared to me in the form of numerous small interactions between various peoples, and the feelings I felt in my stomach when thinking back upon them. Events such as the trader-butcher disagreement, another occasion where they stole food from the natives, and worst of all, the strange reverence they held for their colony's founders, Captain Mission and the Priest. I did not understand seeing groups of men and women bowing to the admired pair. It was as if they had forged this separate colony, dedicated to the freedom of every person and yet they were carrying about in a similar manner as any man would back home in the presence of a king. It wasn't a bow of love that I saw from time to time, or an obedience to a capable captain which we maintained. Their bow was a bow of complete submission. And it bothered me. How could people of a free colony so far away from the civilised world bow their heads to two king-like figures? Bow?

Twenty hesitant men of the *Fancy* were captivated enough by the ideals and appeals of Libertalia, thus electing to remain behind and settle down in Libertalia, abandoning life as pirates for good. I think it was the women that appealed to them and blinded them. I was close to joining but decided to stay with Captain. Even though the settlement calmed my soul, the joy of continuous adventure was irreplaceable. The peace provided by a village accepting of pirates proved appealing and overpowering for some. When New Devon came about after many weeks living in Libertalia, this emerging Second Pirate Kingdom undoubtedly had plenty of men to operate and occupy her, despite twenty seamen refusing to migrate any further. And I felt we had a better chance of maintaining our lifestyle in our own realm rather than dangerously meshing with the Libertalians. We may have become weakened by them had we stayed.

The pirate articles that most pirate crews have are simple. I find most of them unnecessary. The articles that the Libertalians erected proved they could not rule themselves. Besides the seventh article regarding free speech, they later enacted rules stating "No man shall do trade with a native unless a witness is present", "A person's role will be dictated by the necessity determined by Captain Mission or Priest", and "One cannot couple with another unless they both reside reside in Libertalia." The last rule I found to be the most ridiculous, however, all of their rules, evermore growing in numbers, proved to me that they couldn't rule themselves and they truly cared not for freedom. At first, I could not grasp why the coupling rule was put in place, until I recognized that the consolidation of resources, constant increase of population, and maintenance of a family-oriented environment were premier foundations and tenets for the survival of a prosperous, secluded society. Natives were allowed in, so long as they stayed for good. As I observed from a distance their growing number of laws, I feared Libertalia was not anymore the free colony we arrived at before. In contrast, pirates don't need rules, we only need freedom to roam.

Competent, self-reliant men can lead themselves despite the dangers of anarchy. Hence why we created no tombstones or written rules in New Devon. But incompetence and over-dependency forces any people to act as a mob, enslave themselves to a king, or resort to establishing invasive rules. New Devon, the Second Pirate Kingdom, was made up of a fat bunch of squabblers, grimey ones, criminal saints, and noble sinners. We were not scum of the earth and need not be defined that way. We simply needed our own world.

The captains, there at our land of New Devon, were not kings but they were still king-like. We did not need to bow or submit, nor was the captains' authority solidified when we were off of our boat. Captain Every was superior to and far more charismatic than Captain Tew. Thus, some true seers of these two men were privy to Captain Every's true title— The King of Pirates. There can only be one King of Pirates. Long live the King. The King who ruled no man. The King who only ruled himself and guided other men, guiding the collective. That is the truest of kings. That was Captain Every and his role in New Devon.

What was once the three-headed conglomeration of Libertalia, composed of Captain Every, Captain Tew, and Captain Mission, split into Libertalia under the lead of Mission, and then New Devon, led by the King of Pirates, Captain Every, and his right-hand-man, Captain Tew.

What was my ideal society? Truthfully, I did not know how to lead men. But I could lead myself. Or so I thought. The best citizens are the ones who can rely on themselves above all else. The ideal society is a land of people who rule themselves, not others. Those who don't need more than two articles. It was a paradox to call our grounds "kingdoms." Bloody, complexities were everywhere. That was New Devon. That was nature.

It had been a few weeks after that evening of conjuring where the idea of New Devon became an imminent reality. The golden sun of candles and their liquid wax, which usually lit up the large hall, were snatched for our own, new hall in New Devon. It was likely some day around March of 1695 that I arose in my bamboo home, awakened by the light of the sun poking through holes of my hut. I inspected an anomaly— some shrubberies, a stack of foliage apart from their roots, in my living quarters that were not there when I fell asleep the night before. I glanced at the door— it was closed. I thought I closed it behind me when I retired the night be-fore. I was certain I did not drag the shrubs into my quarter. Wind, maybe, brought those shrubs into my lodgings.

I stood up, heading off to my duties and free day. Most of our time was spent sourcing supplies to trade, growing food, general ca-rousing, drinking, building small houses, dancing, singing shanties, exploring, talking to natives, or trying to recruit women from Lib-ertalia to join our separate colony. Thomas Howard, my only con-versational companion on the face of the earth, was my roommate in the little hut. He had become my sounding board for theories and views on humanity and our realm via numberless conversations reaching from night into early hours of dawn. I discussed my con-cerns of the Libertalia-New Devon divide with Thomas numerous times in those half-drunken, half-asleep conversations. He was one of the only other lads I knew to be contemplative and able to with-stand my long-winded nature. Thomas was a rare conversationalist. He had a unique nature, far more interesting to me than when I first met the shy lad.

Thomas had been the only one of us thus far to convince a na-tive woman for a dance since the establishment of New Devon. No native women had looked our way and few dared to venture onto our settlement. God knows why. Libertalia had a better reputation than the young New Devon, as there were more women and chil-dren there, disarming any fears from the natives. The only girl, a dramatic Malagasy Queen, Captain Tew's lover, danced with Thomas Howard. She and her servants joined a few of their male guards at our festivities the night before. Captain Every and Captain Tew must have had some inside access to the language and relations with the Queen, considering she was Madagascar native royalty. Everyone sat on the chairs, tables, and plants which haphazardly dotted the open, dirt plain of our celebration.

That night marked one the most eventful moments on the island. It was an evening where the torches lit up the dark Madagascar oblivion. There were plenty of pirates, and a few native men of Madagascar joined us. There weren't any European women, but a few native women, all servants of the Queen, who stuck close to the monarch. The Queen was beautiful. She had dark skin, a strong smile which rarely showed itself, and native clothing that I'd never seen before. I looked at her as I sat with Thomas, trying to stay awake through the long night of dancing and carousing with our shipmates.

"Say, Thomas, ye think we could find a way to snag a pair of the Queen's servants?" I asked, sitting on the clay, holding my half-full beaker.

"Rollins, ye're one horny bloke, aren't ye?" he jested.

"I haven't touched a lass in years, friend. What do ye expect?"

"I expect ye not to settle for a servant."

"Oh, ye suggest I steal some Libertalian lady? They're all used and taken, Thomas," I dropped my voice to a whisper. "Plus, the damned ladies cower at the sight of us."

The Queen, her retinue, and a few of her guards followed Captain Every and Captain Tew as they walked into the half-constructed New Devon hall, where the stolen candles of Libertalia remained planted in brass candelabras. The construction was halfway built and similar in design to the Libertalia hall. They were talking business or engaging in endless pillow talk. It made no difference to me. They walked away from our gathering in the open toward the partially enclosed hall.

"No, that one." Thomas pointed to the Queen, far away from our grasp, walking ahead of her parade of retinue and guards, following the captains.

I burst out in laughter. I couldn't wrap my head around my conversation with the dreamer.

"Stop, Thomas. Stop. She's royalty..." I said.

"I'm serious." He did look it.

"Oh, so ye want me to go into the hall and steal a Queen? We both know I am a poor enchanter."

"No, I want ye to philosophise with her. That's how ye get a native to sleep with ye. Ye're good at shootin' the high-minded blarney. Aim it toward her," he said.

I laughed even more. Then I directed my stare of death toward my friend for making a jest at my analytical nature.

"Thomas, ye know the only women I've been with, I've paid for... either with money or a hangover. I don't quite pick them up like that."

"I do," Thomas responded with dead seriousness.

"The lass is with Cap'n Tew whenever she isn't protected by spears and slaves. For God's sake, get a grip, sailor. She kissed the man tonight, Thomas. Their dalliance got us into Libertalia, now quit yer joshin'."

"I don't care that Tew hath a son with her. Or that he's known her longer than I have known of her."

"A son?" I got stirred up and tried to stop him.

"Oh, yes, she is a native, but she sailed with Tew on their last cruise to Madagascar a year or two ago. Heard it from one of his crew. That boy of theirs will someday rule this land. Her name is Antavaratra. She knows some English. I traded a fella some rum for this information and I want her. Bastard ripped me off because he knew I'd been looking at her. I've been watching her a lot. And she's been watching me. Ye can tell when a lass is unhappy with her lad. It's the reactions and things she does without being able to think fast enough to cover it up, Rollins. Those eyes. A woman can't deceive a trickster," Thomas said to me, revealing just how much his crotch could jeopardise our relations with the natives.

All I could do was look to the hall and nod, not sure what to make of it. Pirates are liars and sometimes lovers, but I did not think either of these things of Thomas, let alone both. The captains, guards, retinue, and Queen walked back from the hall some time later to the main square, where we were carousing. The guards and servants all left as she dismissed them.

Clancy Williams started to sing, and some more men joined him. It was shanty time, drunk time, as all of the audience and women had left. Drink and song go well together. The rhythm of deep, grotesque voices soothed me enough to close my eyes. I began to doze off. It felt as close to mock paradise as possible— Clancy sang and the men followed in disordered unison:

> *"Welcome lasses, ye look pretty!*
> *We promise we'll make yer time merry!*
> *Lads, get a fair one ye'd love to hold!*
> *Some flower with whom ye will grow old!"*

> *"Dance an hour!"*
> *"And play with me!"*
> *"Dance an hour!"*
> *"Hold onto my hand!"*
> *"Dance an hour!"*
> *"And be merry!"*
> *"Then dance an hour!"*
> *"Come and dance again!"*

> *"Welcome lasses, ye look pretty!*
> *Out of the land of kings and queens!*
> *On the edge of Earth, we love to roam!*
> *As long as we do not die alone!"*

"Dance an hour!"
　　"And play with me!"
"Dance an hour!"
　　"Hold onto my hand!"
"Dance an hour!"
　　"And be merry!"
"Then dance an hour!"
　　"Come and dance again!"

"Welcome lasses, ye look pretty!
　　Let's get off the bellowin', wicked sea!
Is there ocean left for us to sail!?
　　So long as we got love and a tankard of ale!"

"Dance an hour!"
　　"And play with me!"
"Dance an hour!"
　　"Hold onto my hand!"
"Dance an hour!"
　　"And be merry!"
"Then dance an hour!"
　　"Come and dance again!"

Sea shanties, and, henceforth, land shanties, were the closest thing to the voices of monks or God we could hear in Madagascar. Pirates are sinners but we found hymns within our beloved shanties. After the singing voices died down, a pair of lads pulled out instruments. The out of tune violin and accordion made jig music for our night.

The men began to dance like mad in the centre of our world. In Madagascar, I'd seen men dance to music one couldn't hear. I woke up beside Thomas, who was sitting on the dirt, watching the spectacle. The captains of New Devon and the Malagasy Queen sat across the way from the lads. Our group of men called out to her, the native Queen, and invited her to join them in their raucous dance. She was the only woman in sight. And she was doomed. The buffoons took some stellar joy in the presence of the moonlight and a woman of the island. The pirate men, predominantly from Europe, along with the woman from Madagascar, danced with drink spilling left and right. The Malagasy Queen joined in well and moved about to the sounds of our boisterous instrumentation.

Thomas stood up. He approached the small crowd, no longer the centre of attention. He made his way to the centre with the Queen and danced beside her. Thomas was just another sailor to her, it appeared, with Captain Every and Captain Tew's potent eyes half-watching. Eventually, I saw the dozen or so dancing men slowly dwindle away, leaving only one sailor, Thomas, and a native Queen together. Their rhythm slowed until the two were together, dancing as one in front of Captain Tew. Unsure whether this act was harmless or an apparent death sentence that Thomas Howard, my dear friend, had just invited upon himself, I did nothing but witness what occurred in front of me.

Thomas danced for all of us— for all of the lonely men there, looking for a lady's affection, whether it came at the price of her will, some shillings, or it be organic. In desperation, anything could be sacrificed for a single drop of that feminine tenderness. Mothers became an old myth to us. Lovers' and wives' touches were history. I thought fearfully of women, but realised how desperately the men were deprived of them. Thomas fondly danced with the woman. It was innocent, it seemed, by the look on the face of Captain Tew, her man. But underneath him, I feared his territorial viciousness lurked, fantasising his revenge on Thomas and plotting to straighten him out with severity.

The pair had one long dance and it was for us all. At least that was how I chose to see it in my observations and illusions. I hoped Captain Tew did not feel upstaged, for if he was, he certainly was an immature fool to be so easily provoked. That Malagasy Queen would certainly leave him one day, for she belonged to Madagascar, not the Rhode Island Pirate.

It was foolish to think the woman would dance with Thomas Howard without a deeper attachment developing between them as a result. One doesn't simply dance with a woman like he did and call it quits. As their dance ended, Thomas whispered to her before both parted the centre of the open dirt expanse. He said something that only those two would ever know. She returned to Captain Tew and sat down next to him without saying a word. Thomas left the festivities, walking away from the evening's gathering. I didn't know where he went.

Later that night, the one before I awoke the next day to the mound of leaves and branches in my quarters, I heard sounds of feet and something stealthy in the trees close by before drifting off to sleep in my drunken stupor. I figured if it was a predator, my door was closed, so I didn't bother panicking or inspecting. I ignored it and fell asleep. I assumed Thomas Howard, my friend, brought the Malagasy Queen into or near our quarters in some continuation of their special night. Hearsay maybe, as only a fool would bring her around me, a witness to their hypothetical infidelity. Then again, the wind would not blow a single, suspect shrub or leaf into our quarters like it did, had they not kicked it into our quarters in the middle of the night. Thomas wouldn't kick up shrubs in his lonesome. That mysterious green foliage led me to this grand conclusion as I sat up in my quarters putting it all together that following morning. I had my gleeful suspicions the man stole Captain Tew's woman not only for a dance, but for a few more private moments that night. If true, it was enough to warrant death from Captain Tew. And that was if Captain Tew were to ever find out. He wouldn't.

During the day, sporting a hangover in the hot sun of Southeast Africa, I walked into the rainforest with Thomas to look for some prosperous trees to chop down with our axes. I took the lead and purposely walked us further into the rainforest than need be. I turned around to face Thomas when I was certain the density of the trunks would muffle the sound of our voices.

"Ye did it. Didn't ye?" I asked.

"Did what?"

"A Madagascar Queen and an English pyrate have a child to-gether. Then another English pyrate takes her away for a dance and a swooning night. He safely returns her without a trace. And a lovely little language barrier is all the cover he'll ever need," I said, going out on a limb to confirm my hunch.

Thomas looked at me, smiled, and looked down. He couldn't lie to me, the poor lad. All I could do was smile and shake my head at him, the lover-fool. We had no women around there to speak with as we liked, let alone fully English-speaking women besides the ladies of Libertalia some distance away. I didn't blame him, the gambler. We all had a demon-beast within us that wanted to have a woman almost as much as we wanted to breathe. I was surprised the servants had been left untouched by our men's hands thus far. Men get desperately lustful in the jungle.

"This stays between us," he said, trying to establish some sense of dominance over me, as I was then privy to his secret.

"I hold an axe too, mate," I said, matching his authority as I lifted the axe to my chest. "And I don't know what the hell ye're talking about. I was asleep last night," I said, winking at him.

I turned back around and kept walking into the forest. I could sense Thomas smile a few paces behind me. We chopped trees down and didn't say more than three words to each other for the rest of the day. I guess there is harmony in the sound of trees being chopped to their knees. I felt softness in my belly, and I knew my friend had gotten away with a beautiful theft.

We hadn't seen anything of Captain Mission or the Priest in New Devon. When we entered the realm of Libertalia, we had crossed paths with Adam Baldridge and his formidable settlement on the nearby St. Mary's Island on the way in. It was a hidden fort, which could devastate a passing ship before they could sail away. Captain Tew was our liaison, for a previous journey to Libertalia some years ago familiarised him with Baldridge, Mission, the Priest, and therefore the native Queen. We'd had no contact with Baldridge since arriving. Captain Mission supposedly vacated

Baldridge's settlement years ago, as he was once a member of that original colony, in order to form his own— Libertalia. When Mission started his new settlement, the Priest left his position in Rome and vacated himself to Captain Mission's command, formally excommunicating himself from the faith to join the new cause. He wasn't a priest anymore, but everyone called him that. He had a reputation of undoubtable reverence for all beings, despite his discardment of a religious order. The Priest helped deliver this haven.

We were thriving in our land, thus I could imagine spending the rest of my life in Madagascar. It was easy to think life stopped once a beautiful haven was reached. But that is the terrible beauty of life— everything ends eventually, be it great pleasures or dreadful horrors. Happiness is found and something else then takes its place. Like my Chaoticism, once something is found and grasped, something else is searched for. Most people do not have a say when their life stops. But I was sure I would live my life intensely until it was over, following every deep whim I wanted to.

It was an assumption to think I was safe there, to live and waste away in the rainforest colony for the remaining years and decades of my life. It was an assumption to think my life would not follow the Chaoticism of my mind, to think permanent settlement was a remote possibility for me. It was an assumption to think we had mastered society, happiness, freedom, and self-governance in our safe little Madagascar kingdom-anarchy. All bold assumptions. I sensed how deeply these thoughts had taken root amongst the men. They lost their edge, drank more than ever, and languished in the fields. I knew it wouldn't last. Pirates will most always be pirates.

Chapter VII

SPACE BETWEEN THE RANKS

Following another day axing down timber with Thomas, we took leave to the shore and fished. I never caught a fish before. Thomas' company brought me poor luck. Every fish we'd acquire was a catch of his. I heard a voice from the coast call out to me.

"Oy, Cole. Captain Every wants to see ye," some nameless, faceless pirate yelled to me as I stood up in a skiff next to the seated Thomas.

Thomas and I looked at each other in curiosity. I set my pole down and we rowed back to the sand. I made my way toward the large opening in the centre of town, and then into the nearly complete hall where Captain Every and Captain Tew held court. The hall was an upside-down ship, appearing similar to a church. Paintings of the two captains hung beside constant candlelight. I walked into the hall and further into one of the two secluded rooms at the far end of the building, to Captain Every's kingly quarters.

"Close the door behind ye, Rollins," Captain Every said.

I shut the doors and sat down. My hands stayed at the ready on the arms of the chairs. I wanted to sit tall, look serious and competent. I felt nervous for some reason, then I thought of the drama regarding Thomas Howard and the Queen. For a moment, I feared for my friend's life and thought I would have to choose between Captain Tew's good side or my loyalty to Thomas, in the conversation.

"D'ye know Captain Martin Bennetts?" he asked and the unrelated subject calmed me down, relinquishing my attention from Thomas.

"Yes, yes I do, sir."

"Do ye know what Cap'n Bennetts does?" Captain Every asked.

"Aye. In some form or another, he is the last remaining of us Libertalians and New Devoners to stay off the land. I was told he's in charge of Libertalia's raids. Ye can take men away from pyracy but it seems ye can't take pyracy out of the men, I guess," I said.

"And d'ye know what he pyrates?" Captain chuckled and asked me.

"Not exactly. Methinks the only viable options are East India Company trading ships or Portuguese that pass through these waters."

"Yes, East India Company vessels. These East Indiamen are fierce and there are no prisoners to be taken among them unless they join Libertalia. It worries me that men formerly of the East India Company can live in a community run and populated by the same pyrates who held swords at their necks for their supplies and killed their disobedient friends just hours beforehand. I sincerely doubt the presence of familial women and children in Libertalia can truly pacify hot-blooded feuds and quell a prisoner's fury. None of these captured traders find their way to New Devon. And that is how I prefer it. That is my rule. The wind must be in our favour even on land and the only way a ship could sink is if water gets in the boat. D'ye follow?" Captain Every said.

"Aye, Cap'n."

"We allow prisoners to join our crew at sea because they have nothing left. But if they come to Madagascar as defeated men, they threaten her security, especially as their numbers grow and they see the women. I fear they'll get possessive," Captain Every said.

"I guess ye could take men away from the hostility but ye can't take the hostility out of the man," I said.

"Aye."

"Are they causing a resistance in Libertalia?" I asked, prying and poking my limits as a nobody in the crew.

Captain Every looked at me without speaking. He knew I was pushing my privileges and knowledge. I knew it too, asking the question.

"I don't know," he said. "That is why I've called you here."

"Why, sir?"

"It is becoming harder and harder to see who is who here. Keeping track is a problem, especially with those in Libertalia. *Fancy*-men are becoming confused with the men of Captain Tew and even more are becoming confused with the Libertalians. It bothers me, for I can't risk letting temporarily calmed prisoners into New Devon. Therefore, I need something from ye."

"What is it, Captain?" I asked.

"First— secrecy and confidence. Do ye guarantee me our conversation remains in this room?" he asked me and I felt the tide shift in the conversation.

"On my honour, sir."

"Cole, ye're a smart lad, I hear. And ye've been one of Durnburn's most able bodies since the beginning. I trust the men of my higher ranks, but I do not know where the hearts of the rest of our men remain."

"Do ye need me to spy, sir?" I asked and hoped he wouldn't request this task from me.

A man who spies on his crewmen is not an honourable man, nor a true friend.

"No. The booty from Cap'n Bennetts' raids are given to Libertalia and New Devon alike. But he hath become disillusioned with Captain Mission. The supplies and gold he takes are syphoned to us in far greater proportion than to the Libertalians. Captain Tew, Captain Bennetts, and I have been thieving from Libertalia without their knowledge. I fear it will not last much longer without their notice. Although Baldridge does, Captain Mission doesn't know we have an arrangement with Captain Want and Captain Faro, who trade with us. They're slowly uncovering both of these arrangements. We have no loyalty to those Libertalia folk anymore— something they've missed with our splitting up. Piracy is about self-preservation, Cole, not being everybody's ally. They shouldn't let the trade we conduct fool 'em," Captain said.

"Sir, I still do not know what you need from me," I said.

"Cole— every man must be accountable for himself. We must tend the land and must tend to our crewmen. Libertalia is crumbling slowly, for they don't abide by our standards or have the competence to even consider matching them. They cannot handle themselves out here. It is not only due to the hostility of these captured men of the E.I.C. That is one part of their plague. I need ye to be someone I can trust. Libertalia is too open and their strength is fading. Soon they shall be lost. And New Devon could carry on, but I fear not for much longer, if our ol' neighbours decay into mayhem from their threat within. I need a regular crewmember, as smart and trustworthy as ye, on my side. I shall have ye around when handling major business, as ye need to be in on this if ye're to understand what goes on here. But be the eyes and ears of our crew, will ye?" Captain asked, thus making me an unofficial quartermaster or midshipman.

"Captain... what do y—"

"Cole, I need ye to watch our goddamn back. Not only from men in New Devon, but outsiders. I can't lead us here or lead us out of here if danger comes to me before seeing it upon its approach. Keep yer bloody eyes out for any threat, son. And stay close to Cap'n Tew and I."

After I left the meeting in confusion, I returned to my daily work with Thomas. I could sense equal parts inquisitiveness and envy coming from him. By the time of my return, he held a sack full of fish to trade.

Thomas and I went southwest, to find the nearby native village. We brought swords and daggers, of course, for the jungle can still scare a seaman. The path to Libertalia was explicit, yet rarely travelled upon anymore. As our autonomy increased, trade between us dwindled. The path to and from the native village, however nonexistent, was traversed frequently, for we traded more and more with the natives. In comparison to fellow Europeans living in Madagascar but outside of Libertalia and New Devon, we had stronger relations with the natives than all other missionaries, ports, or settlements. 'Twas the rumour. We didn't trade in slaves, however, other European settlements in Madagascar did, those non-pirates. This strained their relationships with the natives.

Thomas and I found the village. Upon arrival, we met with Masovolana, one of the Malagasy men we frequently traded with. He was the main native whom Thomas Howard and I corresponded with. He was a quiet, bright man, older than both of us. He was dark, with wild hair and a calm face. I'd never seen Masovolana carry a weapon. I lacked an intimate understanding of Malagasy ways, but I wagered it was unorthodox for a Malagasy man to remain weaponless around two white men. The tribe-pirate relations had come a long way since before Libertalia and it must have been a new practice. But beyond the utility of the practice, as Masovolana had probably learnt, those who live by the sword die by the sword. His actions breathed wisdom into me and I respected the courage he displayed, regardless of our language barrier.

The Malagasy village was home to a tribe called the Betsimisaraka. I think the village was part of a larger tribe, as each time I ventured there, more and more new faces appeared. We were in the latter part of their rice farming season, maybe March, though dates were formed from speculation and the sun's position rather than a calendar. They did not have much rice to trade with us at that time. We didn't trade the stream crocodiles we killed, for they worshipped the predators, and it caused a rift on the one, early occasion Thomas and I brought one to Masovolana. The same went for the eel we captured. We were comparable fishermen to the local tribe, having adapted to the waters quite well. We more often exchanged rarely caught shrimp, crabs, and stingrays than common fish. The cattle and boar we hunted were quite valuable in trade as well. While we were still learning how, the natives already grew limes, mangoes, lemons, vanilla, sweet potatoes, bananas, and oranges. My favourite was the mango. It could taste quite like the dirt of earth itself, at times. But when it was sweet, nothing beat it. The most important thing the Betsimisaraka village cultivated for trade was their rum. They made some profit from the men's hunting, gathering, and building skills, as well as from the maidens farming and cooking, but the most valuable thing to these people was their rum. The average pirate would sell anything— an arm and a leg, for a desperate swig— and the Betsimisaraka knew this. They abused it for profit.

Masovolana took us through his village. We walked past many people from his tribe. We found ourselves in a plant house where Thomas dropped the sack of fish and Masovolana grabbed some rice for us to swap, measuring out the rice by a weight comparable to that of our fish-sack. I carried the rice back. It usually went like this for Thomas, Masovolana, and I. A simple walk, greeting, drop, measurement, grab, and go. We made our way back through the village full of dozens of huts. They were a busy people. It captivated me to sometimes stop and watch the collection of sentient minds and bodies moving about, performing their various tasks. I did the same back at sea sometimes on the *Fancy* when the crew, all separate but working as one, were focused on accomplishing something. One greater mind, composed of many smaller minds. If something caused a distraction, a few looked, a few helped, and a few disregarded the event. But everyone was always up to something. Humans amazed me, native or European. And yet they bothered me immensely.

Most days, we worked on what we wanted to and traded what we had for what we wanted. Currency was long gone. It was something of the past, of the Old World. We would take what we had and barter for whatever we had access to via the Malagasy locals or Captain Want and Captain Faro. We'd also resupply from Captain Bennetts' piracy endeavours. The happiness we possessed didn't come from what we had, but from how we used what we had. We didn't have much in terms of scale or variety of resources, but we had everything we wanted, and we didn't have anything unnecessary. Besides women, of course, for the native lasses were desired by the men.

Some of the men secretly had relations with native women from the local village. Then again, one could see a lot of the men, like me, harness desire into something different and remain focused. One would think with all of the time alone without the great distraction of women, a bunch of men together would spell ridiculous disaster and heightened aggression. In truth, it proved otherwise. There was an order. I saw men taking energy and putting it back into our community, not wasting it. That was my utopia. The world that required women for its beauty, its birthing, and everything else I couldn't begin to list, was undoubtedly different from the world of a pirate. A pirate's world is much like that of a rebellious monk's, associated with impermanence and a lack of permanent attachments. All booty, female or golden, was discarded. Captain Every was satisfied with the New Devon we'd already seen. But I'd have taken the New Devon I felt was on the horizon. The realm, consisting of these men, could autonomously reach something higher, something usually only a good woman could bring to a man— balance. It didn't last long.

There were no written rules about the lack of women in New Devon, but the men simply did not bring them around to stay. As time went on, they channelled their energy toward building our village, hunting, farming, trading, exploring, drinking, and dancing. Women don't corrupt men, but their presence invites a pirate to corrupt himself. And while it is common for a woman to disarm a man, it didn't happen in New Devon. I imagined the 20 sailors who abandoned us to stay in Libertalia were no longer fit to live the lives we lived. They were freed. But the rest of us needed freedom beyond that. We needed freedom to the point of absurdity. Preserving our strength was much more seductive than the appeals of sexuality, it seemed. Or maybe we were simply masochists too afraid to let go of our rambling ways. Maybe we all fooled ourselves. Maybe we were only boys, and boys cannot be one with women. Only men can.

A woman's touch would bring us into a different realm, but without our abstinence, solitude, and constitution, we wouldn't have progressed as far as we did to begin with. I found myself taking longer and longer strolls in the native village with Thomas when trading with Masovolana. I think it was the presence of those appealing women— I'd stare blatantly at them and I was attracted to their innocence. At a distance, I could appreciate those Malagasy women in a different light than I had ever appreciated any European maiden before. The women in the village— it could have been a great number of things that drew me more and more to that village, but I look back and know it was those foreign appeals. I never followed through on my desires, but instead returned my focus back to the pirate haven we were building and perfecting.

My emotions had always been a more accurate reflection of myself than my thoughts. My thoughts were often governed by what the world wanted me to be and my contention with it. But I yearned for what I wanted to be, not what others wanted me to be. The mind is but a tool. Long ago, I'd have never been a utopian, or a pessimist about the civilised world. Ever. My imagination was a realm rarely visited. Was that who I was, a practical man, or was that the person I had tried to be to gain the world's acceptance? Did the world only want me to speak well of its markets and rules? Was I never meant to consider what an experiment like New Devon, even a failed experiment, could merit other than the continuation of norms and the world I was born into? What was I? It all got confusing.

I could never understand why anyone in this great, blue world wouldn't choose piracy as a profession. It baffled me, but I was younger then and my ideals reflected it— especially that sentimentalisation. Preference exists in all spheres, but when it comes to freedom, why would someone realistically choose another life over the freedom of piracy? Should one take to the seas and renounce their country, they'd have freedom beyond belief, and the world would be their open oyster. But most refuse. Is there any price not worth paying for freedom? I do not know. I do not understand. I had friends, I had a crew. Who needed countrymen and country-women? These commodities were something to be understood and cherished as I aged, I presumed. Or maybe I was onto something there, despite the overwhelming sense I was engaging in improper thinking as I traversed through my Chaotic reflections. Is it not the glory of a young man's open mind, to think improperly?

I was no superstitious man. But I saw the wind change with my own eyes. I witnessed the wind changing drastically on a passing Malagasy fishing boat, and I had to ask myself whether I was truly superstitious. A few Malagasy, with their wild hair and superbly re-laxed faces, all messed about some distance from the shore, where I was sitting on the sand and thinking those reckless thoughts. They had a single strip of red cloth waving from a tall stick stretching up from the boat. Usually when the wind changed, it was sudden and volleyed back the opposite direction. But when I saw the wind shift slowly and continue on this path steadfastly, my entire being paused, inside and outside. Life is a series of split-moment decisions and slow patterned movements. This wind made a slow shift and continued along by a constant movement— 'twas an Easterly Wind. I darted my eyes from the little flag to the sun and the direc-tion was confirmed— the only East Wind I'd ever seen. God forbid this, I thought. I was only a man of God when I thought I was about to meet my end and meet Him. I was only a superstitious man when I acknowledged an out-of-body, otherworldly feeling in my chest. I only had one place to go after seeing the wind change— back to New Devon, away from the native shore, to the Captain who dis-patched me to beware of these mysteries.

I trekked through the jungle, convinced by a bloody myth of the wind, sprinting. Convinced a hunch like that would be useful to Captain Every, risking concrete heresy. Captain spoke to me of the wind that day, in his quarter, metaphorically but I received it directly. The wind. The bloody wind. A seaman looks at wind as a poet looks at inspiration. And our muse may have been mad. The gods of the wind must have given me a hint. I made it back to our realm. I ran to the large hall, and burst into his quarters. His lodgings were filled with numerous books he must have somehow traded for.

"Captain Every," I yelled, likely looking young and stupid.

"'Tis it boy?" he asked.

"Now Captain... I ain't a superstitious man but..." I said, sweating and trying to catch my breath. "But I've seen somethin' unseeable."

"And?"

"Ye said to keep my eyes out... aye?" I asked.

"Yes, lad, get on with it."

"The wind hath changed direction. I saw it on a Malagasy fishing boat."

"Malagasy have flags on their skiffs?" Captain said rhetorically. "They don't sail. They wouldn't know what an ensign is, sailor."

"They have a banner. A red one. Not a flag. One piece of cloth, acting as a telltale or symbol."

"What exactly happened, boy?"

"Easterly Wind," I said. "The wind hath changed drastically and unmistakably. Ye told me to mind the wind, sir."

He stopped. He looked at me and saw how serious I was. I expected a smile, a laugh, and a dismissal, just as I would have gotten from my father every time I told him I would boast in a boyish prospect. And yet, I later defied my father, following through on my sailing bent. Then, before me stood a man who invoked in me similar notions and dynamics.

"This sure is turning into some adventure," Captain said to himself.

"What?"

"Young Cole, the stuff of East Wind... Of the—the Bible, it isn't to be taken lightly, just as the Bible isn't. But it is a tale. Moreover, we have more pressing issues here in New Devon than myths of wind direction."

"Sir, the wind is a signal, not a guide— of monsoons, storms, danger. It is an omen now that we aren't sailors anymore. Have ye forgotten her importance?"

Every looked at me gravely and said, "Hey. Cole. Don't ever say that. We are *always* sailors. But I cannot do anything based on hunches of the wind. Now grow up, lad."

I walked out of his quarters with my head down and shoulders hunched. Sure, he didn't listen to me. Nobody harks to someone who fancies himself a sailor-philosopher. And it shall always come back to bite those deaf ears and blind eyes who do so, even the older and wiser like Captain or King Every. In my tantrum, I thought he was a tyrant-fool, a blind and deaf Every. Maybe those Libertalians he'd been stealing from did naturally deserve to behead the man. Only those who can hear well and see closely should lead men. I beheaded my deep reverence for my captain.

Chapter VIII

THE GIFT OF A FLINTLOCK

"Dawson, this is my new cabin boy. Ye'll respect him and let 'im into my quarters without question. Understood?" Captain Every said.

"Aye, Cap'n. He a bit too old to be a cabin boy, i'nt he?" the quartermaster, Dawson, asked.

"Cole, ye're the youngest one we've got, aye?" Captain asked me as I leaned against the wall in his office quarters.

"Aye, I believe so, Captain."

"See, he's qualified," Captain said to Dawson, who I could sense was becoming defensive.

"Aye," Dawson said, sharply and emotionlessly.

"Now, Cole, don't be botherin' with Pretty Al about yer duties as cabin boy. Ye're with me and me only. I don't want ye bein' a cook's bitch," Captain said.

"Aye, very good sir," I said and smiled.

I walked away, leaving his office after some further discussion. Nothing of interest. I caught up with Thomas, sitting in our quarters. It was early and I stormed in.

"Guess who is the new cabin boy of New Devon."

"What? Did we abduct a boy from the tribes?" Thomas asked.

"No. Ye're lookin' at him," I said and put my hands on my hips. Thomas laughed.

"What? I'll be in his quarters whenever need be. I'll know what is to happen before the rest of the crew hears a word."

"But ye're a man, not a boy," Thomas said.

"Aye, but I am the youngest man."

"Aye, the youngest runs the errands— that's how it goes. Very fitting. How ye gonna hear of things when ye're busy running errands?" Thomas said, hand on a cup.

"I don't know. I don't think he'll have me running too many errands."

"Sounds like Cap'n bent the rules to make ye an unofficial officer without pissing off the rest of the crew," Thomas said.

"I am qualified," I said.

"Ye're qualified enough to be hated by the officers now, despite his slitherin'."

"Maybe."

"Don't ye think Captain doesn't like ye? After that whole Easterly Wind business? Maybe he wants to make the rest of the officers yer enemies, as ye've already distanced yerself from the rest of the crew. I'd be careful of the Cap'n," Thomas said and I became wary of his disagreeable tone.

"I think 'tis simpler than that."

"Aye. How so?" Thomas asked.

"I think he sees somethin' in me and takes me seriously. This was the only way for him and I to have a constant audience without breaking the integrity of rank. He trusts me more than many."

"Interesting," Thomas said and looked away, struck by the thought.

"Don't worry, I'll tell ye of the news," I said, letting Thomas into the captain's quarters, in a way.

I knew I would only share with him logistics and general affairs, not the major developments. I would not betray the Captain's confidence, for he was in charge, and needed help to maintain order if any danger should rear its head to strike at us. Despite our equality at New Devon, Captain Every found himself assuming the role as knight of our realm. The old title he held as captain on the *Fancy* did not die off entirely. I'd seen Captain Tew plenty of times and the Malagasy Queen even more during the talks I sat in on— discussions of Malagasy relations, pirate shipments stolen from nearby waters, freed slaves joining the Libertalia colony. There were plenty of moving parts in our settlement. I'd heard the population numbers in Libertalia seemed to dwarf the number of men we had in New Devon. It only alarmed Captain Every and additionally Captain Bennetts, who was set to meet with Captain Every and Captain Tew. I was to sit in. I was a quiet, invisible man in those meetings. I did not ever speak in the meetings, instead I tended to drift into my imagination more and more when serious matters were discussed, mostly through choice and spite. I found it a privilege to share in the passing of valuable information, but not since my own input about the wind wasn't taken seriously. Not when I was only there for the advantage of others rather than based on the merits of my own contributions.

Captain Bennetts walked in that day looking scared. But he tried masking it from us *Fancy*-men. I saw beneath his disguise. Captain Bennetts was an East India Company dissenter who became a Libertalian. What was likely once a clean-shaven, English-looking man, had become a grown out, dusty pirate with sooty, wild, receding hair and the beard of an immoral beggar. I couldn't tell his age, as he sat anywhere between forty and sixty. Captain Bennetts sat down in one of the three chairs. I stood. I always stood, having not earned the privilege to sit at those meetings in Captain's quarters.

"Ahoy," Captain Bennetts said as he sat like a good dog. "Methinks I found something, lads."

"Tell me something good, Cap'n," Captain Every said, sitting in another seat behind a bullying desk.

"I heard of somethin'— maybe a rumour. There's a convoy coming some ways north of here— a Mughal fleet. Maybe fifty ships full of slaves, women, gold, expensive goods, supplies, and plenty of weaponry, but well-guarded," Captain Bennetts said.

"Where'd ye hear this from?" Captain Every asked in a sceptical tone.

"Some slave boy on the last raid we had. He was sold from a Mughal owner to a French settler that we pyrated. He spake of it," Captain Bennetts replied.

"What else did he say?" Captain Tew said.

"That's it."

"Are rumours the currency of kings?" Captain Every spoke more to himself than the rest of the room, as he stared up at the ceiling.

"It appears so," I said.

My satirical comment unexpectedly burst forth from the abyss, turning heads. Captain Every looked at me with confusion, disapproval, and dismissal.

"Captain, why would a slave lie? A freed slave. He is on our side now, living in Libertalia on his own accord," Captain Bennetts said, resuming the conversation.

"On our side? Libertalia and New Devon are not the same. They are only a liability to us. And methinks that it be my fault they will catch on to our devices," said Captain Every.

"Well, there's a stir, Captain. Captain Mission and the Priest are likely to be deposed from their high chairs. The men and women of Libertalia are unhappy, violently unhappy with their leaders," Captain Bennetts said.

"What is the cause?" Captain Every enquired.

"I can tell ye that, but what of the Mughal convoy, Cap'n? The slave wouldn't lie. Sure, he would embellish, as a child often does dramatise a bit, but— I don't see why it isn't worth going after. In the worst of cases, we go hunting for the score and nothing comes of it on the way, but we take a few slave ships or some Portuguese on our way back. There's plunder in this venture. There's always plunder in the Indian Ocean," Captain Bennetts said.

"And what if the boy is right? What if there are more than fifty ships? We don't have that kind of strength to withstand such a battle," said the cautious Captain Tew.

"Who else heard about this, Bennetts?" Captain Every asked.

"Only..." he looked around the room, turning his head in a few directions, "us four. The boy told me directly, trying to make some conversation. I can't promise ye he didn't say it to anyone else before or in Libertalia, but on the boat, I enquired meself, alone," Captain Bennetts said.

"Or maybe this didn't happen, it was never such a thing, and ye only want us to leave our settlement? D'ye want Libertalia to return to its roots and eradicate us New Devon rebels, Captain Bennetts? Ye don't have any witnesses now, do ye?" Captain Every made a forward joust.

"Cap'n, excuse me?" Captain Bennetts became red-faced, beyond the alcohol infused red visage many English pirates have.

"'Tis the perfect false flag— luring us *Fancy*-men out of our Madagascar haven with the prospect of booty, invade, and take our land. Isn't it a rather amateur strategy, wouldn't ye say? And all of the pyrate raids ye'd no longer split between two realms, as ye'd profit more for yerself, taking what used to be given to us. Seems like a worthwhile endeavour to kick us out," Captain Every continued rather forwardly.

"Captain... that is not true. And if I wanted more, who is to say I couldn't already do it without this rumour?"

"So 'tis a rumour?" Captain Every sat forward, piercing his eyes through Captain Bennetts.

"No, sir," Captain Bennetts squealed, dumbfounded.

"Who else did ye bloody tell about this?" Captain Every asked.

"Nobody," said Captain Bennetts.

"Aye," Captain Every said and arose.

Captain Every stood there, with his hands on his hips, nodding like he was aware something was being hidden from him, and knew of something Bennetts didn't. Captain intimidated the fool, twisting and testing Bennetts' mind. I didn't think Bennetts was lying about or hiding anything, but rather the contrary.

"Cap'n... Captain Mission and the Priest strongly suspect ye've been stealing from our raids. They came down on me hard after I came to the settlement following the last raid. They demanded to see the divisions of the shares, and forced me to count everything myself three times over. The Priest was more furious than Mission, for he cannot fathom a pyrate's ways, yet Mission can," said Captain Bennetts to the two captains.

"I find that hard to believe, Bennetts. The Priest is a Roman. Was he blind to the decadence of the Eternal City?" Every interjected.

"I cannot speak for that, Captain. Alls I know is they might already have a plan in place to attack New Devon. Or maybe their designs are simple— to kill both of ye."

"Might? Well, then there is only one thing left to do," Captain Every said, staring to the far side of the room, looking out of the window.

Captain Every slowly walked around the desk, toward Captain Bennetts. In one motion, he unsheathed and swung his sword, lodging it into Bennetts' neck in a failed attempt to decapitate the man. I watched with my arms crossed as I leaned against the wall. Inside, I was horrified. Outside, I acted like the savagery was necessary, desensitised by its 'justification.' Captain Every stared at the blood spray on the ceiling and shocked face on the head which gazed upward with dying eyes. The corpse sat leaning back, motionless, spouting blood across the room— so much blood. My heartbeat was unfathomably rapid.

"Either he was conspiring against us or Libertalia would eventually turn him against us. If it's real, that Mughal convoy could be too valuable of a score to let others get to it first. Then again, he may have already betrayed us if 'twas a lie," Captain Every said, still staring down at the nearly headless body.

Captain Tew and I listened to him justify the act. I remained confused at the series of events and his judgements throughout them. Captain Tew, seated with much blood on his garb and face, casually removed a cloth from his person and wiped himself clean.

"Aye," Captain Tew said to Captain Every.

I was the only silent one left in the room besides the dead man. That was how loyalties were shown— when men start getting beheaded, you either agree or keep your mouth shut. Best be smart or more heads shall roll.

"Sometimes ye must act off the tales of the wind," I said, looking at what was left of Captain Bennetts, making a poetic remark yet not saying whether I agreed in totality with the gruesome killing.

Captain Every raised his eyes underneath his eyebrows and looked at me, testing my faith and gauging my fear like a predator. He moved his whole head, his whole being, to face me with sword in hand.

"Aye," he said to me and I felt in that moment I had replaced his quartermaster, Dawson, as his trusted right-hand-man, for I had not seen Dawson in a long time.

"Gather all of the men," Captain Every said to Captain Tew and I as he dislodged his sword from Captain Bennett's spine, removing it like an axe from a tree trunk. He cleaned the blade.

We galloped to and then around New Devon to summon the crews. Then we headed back toward the centre of town. Thomas Howard was nowhere to be found. The men grouped together in a crowd, a large circle. They watched Captain Every and Captain Tew at the forefront.

"Men. We live good here. We don't have everything. And we certainly don't have many threats... Or so we thought," Captain Every said as he walked around in the circle of surrounding men who grumbled in a low murmur. "And now I am going to ask ye boys something I don't want to— something terrible of ye. I am asking ye to join me, to leave New Devon. I now leave Libertalia, I leave Madagascar, and return to the sea."

The men appeared confused. Heads looked around and grimaces pierced the revered Captain-King.

"Gentlemen, there is a fleet coming through the Indian Ocean— a big one, a golden one. I am the shepherd to this flock of free New Devoners, and I've done my best to guide ye, even if ye're yer own men to guide. 'Tis a captain's duty, so they say. Aye?"

"Aye," the many men responded, proud, and with heightened morale. They listened intently.

"Libertalia, our friends and cross-town mates, aye?" he asked again.

"Aye," the men replied.

"They want to take New Devon as their own. They want to murder Captain Tew and meself, leaving ye all without a captain and enslave ye all— expose ye. Now, I know ye boys sure can handle all that would come with those troubles, but no matter who they replace as quasi-leaders of New Devon, they would surely replace us with some despot who wouldn't have yer best interests in mind." Captain Every said as he paced around. "I fear ye would be tools to them, not free to them as brethren, but slaves."

"He's speakin' as a politician," a sailor mumbled to me out of the side of his mouth.

"Rollins Cole," Captain Every summoned me with a holler.

After hesitating, I walked forward to make myself seen by all. Captain placed one arm around my shoulder and held out the other toward the crew.

"Cole is a witness to these two prospects— the purse and the plot." Captain said to the men then looked at me. "Now, is what I say true, Cole?" Captain Every asked.

"Aye," I said, with my arms crossed.

"Aye. Aye," Captain Every said, nodding with enthusiasm, examining his men and Captain Tew's men, feeling for any distrust amongst the ranks.

"Poor men we are, poor, poor sailors. We became pyrates, aye? We had our sanctuary to get away from it all, aye? Well, I'm tired of being poor... 'tis why I turned to pyracy in the first place. I want to take, not merely be satisfied with nothing in the jungle, even if other men envy what little we do have," Captain Every said.

The crowd's silent eyes and attention were consumed by him.

"We had our sanctuary and it became a haven to all those that want what is ours. Should we fight for it?" he asked.

The men did not answer the question.

"We can. Or we can leave and take a Mughal fleet. We can take a fleet and use gold to make the rest of the world our sanctuary. No more nibbling for rice in a Malagasy village. No more farming and scavenging. No more pyrates confined to a hidden place not worth its weight in piss. We can fight the world to defend what little we have. Or we can let the rest of the world take what we had and grab hold of even more for ourselves, for our own good, and forever. There is more out there, lads." With that, Captain Every staked his captainship, and all he had, on the gamble of a slave's report.

I was not sure whether to merit this desperate act as trustworthy or twisted. A potential fifty-ship convoy? All the gold in the world isn't worth it if one dies for it.

"And if Cole be lying? What if this is a hoax?" a sailor stepped forward and challenged.

I remembered my father telling me when I was young that a man who lies shall never have any friends, for they shall not trust him. Then again, if a man wouldn't lie to protect his friends, can he call himself a true friend? Is he to be trusted either? Is his pride too great for his brotherhood?

"Believe me or not, ye must do what ye have to do, lad. I am going. And ye can join me. Ye'll learn things are not always as they seem," Captain Every said, deflecting.

Captain walked toward me and I knew he was about to further include me in this debacle, a scenario not to my liking.

"All ye lads wanted to kill Mr. Cole back when we took the French ship. Ye were a mob and he was yer prey, for ye all declared him yer enemy that evening. I did not allow him to be marooned." Captain Every said, volleying his eyes between the crew and myself. "Cole recently saw something. He saw something that threatened our way of life in New Devon and he brought it to my attention. The young lad protects and cares for all of ye, whether or not ye give a good golly damn about him. Ye all thought the man had not a heart after killing Frenchmen in battle, and yet he would speak up when the winds came to harm all of ye now, here, the lot of ye who once wanted him sliced? It is not what it seems, nor what any of ye could have predicted. Things are not what they appear. A man can be vengeful like a Libertalian. A man can be great like a New

Devoner. A man can be many things... but Cole is a man who is honest— a man who is a protector of our realm. Is everything I say true, Cole?" he asked me again.

"Well, not everything, Captain, but close enough. It all happened," I said.

"And shall there be a vote?" Captain Every asked the mass.

No man made any gesture for they were unlike common pirates, who put up a vote for everything. Captain Every had us all in his grips by then. The King of Pirates didn't need a democracy or even his council of trusted officers anymore. He only needed the hands of his trusted crew under his sanctified domain. His rhetoric was as swift as a sword.

"Aye. We shall go, then. Gentlemen, come with me. Let us return to our adventures and the chase, the true home of a pyrate. Let it be our Indian Ocean. All of the plunder I've promised ye, I shall finally deliver on. A Grand Mughal fleet awaits us now, so let us burn this all and leave nothing for the Libertalians. There shall be civil war if we do not, for they are imploding yonder across the jungle with madness and envy as its catalyst. They shall hunt us as they do hunt each other. D'ye want to be here when the chickens come home to roost? Ye're not expendable. Now act like it. This is a voluntary decision to be made. But if it is to be made, make it with all yer damn haste, lads," Captain Every made his closing argument.

I did not know how in the Holy Hell that could convince an anarchy of pirates to leave their free, untouched, untrampled kingdom. But they did. Fear is the prime motivator for movement. And charisma can convince a crew of sailors to do almost anything. If our providence was to meet great luck, we would take that Grand Mughal fleet and cherish the man who brought it to us. We needed our captain as much as he needed us. We would not envy or resent he who kept us free from the vulnerability of a Libertalia-New Devon civil war, attack, enslavement, or death. There'd be no need to kill him and let a usurping weakling take his place for Captain Every was strong and decisive. His decision, our move, protected

Captain Every from his crew and protected the neighbouring settlement's instability from caving in on us. However, he had to come through as he had come through before. Necessity would have to reward the captain a real pirate prize this time around— heavy treasure.

Ultimately, even among us self-reliant men, there was a communal aspect present in our utopia and a hierarchy had formed amidst the anarchy, albeit a discreet one, no matter how hard we'd tried avoiding it. Men dictated what they would do every day, without the hand of a Captain-King ordering them to do so, yet every man did something for the greater good without realising— it was marvellous. "Which direction to cut into the forest?" or "What supplies do we need out here most urgently, Captain?" They would ask, he'd answer, they'd abide. He had complete authority but had no control over the men. It was perfectly balanced. Then eventually Captain wasn't around as much and the men chose for themselves. But still, even when free to choose as a man pleased, men always returned to the carpenter or the Captain for guidance and direction on what to do next, always returning to ask about the greater good. What did we need to do? How could we sculpt this ideal? What manner of crew were we, to be so free to disobey even a captain or a carpenter yet nobody disobeyed them? Maybe it was the wilderness of Madagascar with its plentiful fields that caused each man to cling to his unwritten superior, in fear of the unorthodox environment. Eventually they got over the need for guidance in the Captain's random absence, thus causing us to be further self-reliant.

No nation is impervious to the suffocating laws and mob-like nature of people. Sooner or later, the men would have stopped talking to Captain Every or the carpenter entirely before deciding to build, to work, to trade, or anything, completely separating from him. Our crew would have had a catastrophic schism, for clans would have broken out in our freedom. If a servant has no need for a master, even if the servant likes the master, he would eventually go his own way and forge a new master— and it started happening. It was no wonder Captain Every needed me to watch his back— he wasn't there. The Captain's vulnerability was caused by his distance from the men, which cracked the solid foundations of brotherhood, trusted authority, and sea-fatherliness.

I doubt it was the thievery after all which motivated Captain Mission and the Priest to murder Captain Every. Maybe the portrait our Captain painted of Libertalia, its leaders, and its population was accurate. It appeared that a different monster had crept in slowly throughout Libertalia like a plague. It would spread to New Devon soon after, and lead both realms into mass destruction. The rugged utopias we so yearned for during all of the years on our ships, were hellish upon their Madagascan implementation and did not last long. Ideals of promise were buttressed by hidden monsters that lurked within us all. The world was far too appealing to abandon and too difficult of a beautiful imperfection to recreate anew, to recreate better, to escape from.

I recall one episode when I traded some gold with a Libertalian. He made a comment that stuck with me ever since. He said, upon completion of our transaction, "Aye, ye boys just do whatever the fucking hell ye want, abandoning us." In that moment, my instincts made me grab my blade, both in anger and worry. I walked away without responding. They'd felt we abandoned them? Maybe. But maybe the comment evinced something deeper— resent. We could have the freedom that they could not. It wasn't the bloody women as I had believed. I couldn't say what caused New Devon to be an enviable settlement for a Libertalian, if it even truly was. I sensed it in that man's voice, clear as day, that it was clear resentment. The Captain was right. We would someday need to defend ourselves after having abandoned our weak, dying Libertalia parentage, for they'd later come to our doorstep demanding satisfaction, help, or favours. The freedom we had in our Second Pirate Kingdom did not come without a price or unretired obligation. The Libertalian I spoke to must have thought we abandoned them, and thus cast us out of his heart. Is it foolish to believe he was one of many Libertalians who'd felt this way? It all felt ugly to consider.

Captain Every was an alpha-like ape. Those citizens we'd left behind to rot on the bottom of the totem pole, Libertalians, could not stand to see him and his New Devon reach heights beyond their capability. We flourished with the natives and within ourselves. How could a creator see his creation exceed him and not grow angry about it? They wanted to murder the man who had outdone them. Why else would they call for his head, if not out of envy of his progress? I was envious of Captain Every too, but it turned into an admiring tenor. I took my natural resentment and turned it into a sentiment of growth as a man. Captain possessed things I did not, characteristics I might develop one day. The Libertalians, in contrast, must have let envy give way to more aggressive notions. For the man's majesty and competence were too far above their abilities to subdue their growing frustration, I presumed. And they needed a target for their frustration. According to the rumours, the Libertalian people were tremendously riled up. It was not only the piracy we conducted against Libertalia that caused their supposed plans to take Captain Every's life, it was also their envy of the moral grandness of New Devon that inspired their desire to depose and enslave us. Our captain and our realm exceeded Libertalia and Baldridge's little colony by far.

Envy was a crude parasite that swept through their little utopia. Their people envied their leaders and their leaders envied our leaders— envy, unharnessed. Envy makes men turn on each other, abandon untouched havens for more gold that a captain would have had all to himself, or makes a man steal another man's Queen lover. Envy sinks ships. Our ships were bridges between the common world and our own world. Too far in either direction, submitting to the world or rebelling and fleeing to a hidden utopia proved to be foolish for a pirate. But somewhere in the middle, if he sails there, he'd be free to oscillate. That was where we would escape any envy or condemnation.

The citizen-sailor crews of the *Fancy* and the *Amity* all sailed for one reason— to leave the Old World behind. However, there in New Devon, we had gone too far with our great sailor-land-social paradise in the last few months. Hearing rumours of both the chaos in Libertalia and their apparent desire to kill our leaders, we saw what our pirate ways, our freedom, could do to a neighbouring people. Anarchy is appetising up until an entree of lawlessness approaches on her silver platter. So before we could allow ourselves to become like the Libertalians or suffer at their hand, we left. Intuitively, I knew that if we had fought in an eventual war against Libertalia, the victors would inevitably collapse into a civil war only months later, for a utopia cannot self-sustain. I thought Libertalia's instability meant we New Devoners were superior— New Devon would have fallen anyway, but a long overdue migration was in order, thus, a tragedy was wholly avoided. But in truth, they were a bit further along the same economical and social trajectory as us. Captain Every's hunt for the convoy was all that was needed to spark the fire of exodus under our crew's arses. We needed to go back to where we came from, yet be smarter about it. Keeping the balance between being a part of the world and operating outside of its rules was to be our equilibrium.

Eventually, I feared even the men of New Devon would have absolutely given in to the destructive temptation of envy and called for the head of our King Every and his loyalists in a frenzy. I saw it coming. Captain Every did too. What else would a group of ambitious men do if they were unrestrained and ungoverned in a jungle? The pirate crews of the *Fancy* and *Amity* would have eventually grown irredeemably resentful of our great Captain-King. Freedom without a responsible leader and its required obedience is self-destructive. Luckily, the venom of envy was captured early, and was drained out. When the lands are in the hands of all, it withers away. When the lands are in the dominion of great men, it flourishes. Our King Every's hands had delivered us.

The fiery destruction of our realm painted smiles on our faces as we were destroying it. It surprised me. Why would they enjoy the destruction of something pure, something we had created ourselves? We were going on another adventure. So much potential and promise was obliterated by the men running around with torches, nearly causing the forest to burn. Thomas Howard mysteriously appeared from the forest, finally making his way to our quarters as we sabotaged the huts. I had to fill him in on the spectacle of the day. I imagined he was sneaking about with the Queen, earnestly, that salty dog. Watching Thomas join in on destroying our hut, I spoke to him about what had happened

"Why the hell are we leaving?" he kept asking me.

"There are a lot of reasons. Are ye taking that Malagasy Queen with us?" I asked.

"I don't know what the hell ye're talking about."

"Aye," I said. "Did ye ever have any problems with a person from Libertalia the past few months?" I asked him.

"No, why?"

"They were not so fond of Captain Every anymore. That's why we're leaving. And I think they didn't appreciate our abandonment in the first place."

"I was just there today," Thomas said.

"What? Libertalia?" I asked.

"Yes, I was there before, that's where I'm coming from. Everything seemed fine."

"They had a problem with me once. They had a problem with Captain Every. They had a problem with everything we're doing here," I said and Thomas then stood beside me watching our old quarters slowly burn.

"I don't know what ye're talking about, Rollins," Thomas said to me and I gave him a puzzled look.

"Captain Bennetts said the Libertalians got wind of our thievery and they wanted our Captain's head. I spoke to a man some time ago who was furious at us for creating our own place away from theirs."

"That's strange. Everyone knows the arrangement of local piracy being split between our two realms," Thomas said.

"Of Bennetts' stealing? I— How do ye know?" I asked.

"I. Was. There. Today," he said.

"Yes, but why do you believe they know what they know? Is it all a lie?" I asked.

"I spoke to one of Captain Bennetts' men," Thomas said and I shook my head.

"He wouldn't know of the real arrangement," I said.

"Maybe," Thomas said.

All of my questions were left unanswered then and I did not know if I could trust the stories of Captain Every, Captain Bennetts, or even Thomas. The crew seemed happy to leave for the most part but Thomas was confusing me in his confusion. Did he know something I didn't? What was the real story? Was it all a farce so the Captain could lead us to some booty? What was really happening in Libertalia? Was the drama with Bennetts staged and Captain Every had just cut a loose end? What was the real plan?

We left that utopia in burning ruins, destroying all of the homes in our once beautiful realm, and returned to our ships. We left before we were ruined. I think the men were only half-convinced of the reasons for our exodus but became blinded by the prospect of gold in our old stomping ground— the sea. Or maybe I only wanted to believe in our new direction because I was happy to return to the world. The ways of the world needed improvement. But so did we. The world has been self-correcting since the beginning of time. It was more advanced than our pirate realm experiment could have ever been, created in only a few months. Upon our return to society or its distant, remote seas, we were to stand on the shoulders of giants—– to honour all the great men that came before us, not leave them in the dust. We needed all of our past to remember, and all of our Chaoticism to grow. And so the fields of New Devon were put to rest while all of our ships started moving once again. There was plenty of death and plenty of life.

Individualism and prime self-centredness have their merits, but inevitably, weaker humans let envy give way to destruction instead of being motivated by it. Envy can make a man great, make him see all that he could possibly achieve, even if this vision frustrates him at first. Or envy can make a man cynical, corrupt, and antagonistic.

The weak want to see great men like Captain Every fall. Our own utopia, and the inferior Libertalia, proved to us that no matter how close one gets, an individualistic kingdom-anarchy, standing superbly anti-collective despite boasting with members demonstrating grand care for their fellow men, is too complex and impossible a feat to realise. Even in Madagascar.

How did I once think I could settle down nicely in the great jungle? How could I aim to settle down if I had yet to experience the excitement of my soul, through a ravishing adventure on the seas? It was only natural for us youthful souls to be on the move again. Were we bound from the start of our venture into Libertalia to leave, and leave in disarrayed disunion? Why else would we smile at our burning exodus unless it was in our nature to leave? It was nature itself that dictated our behaviour during our stay at New Devon in the first place.

To conclude, and say it in plain words, we can only master ourselves, not the world and not our own human nature. Yet we try. Humans always try. The truest pirate utopia, the truest anarchy, is in the heart of every true pirate. It is an unseen kingdom-anarchy. Half of a man's nature is ruled and dominated by his own accord. The other half is free and ungovernable, to the point of animal-like mania. And this pendulum voyage between control and liberation in a man's life must be captained by each man in himself. Each man must sail in the greater ocean of society, as he navigates his own inner waters of existence. The day we left New Devon marked the return to greater lands, back to the world at large, back to society. We'd try to conquer the world around us, the world we could never escape from. Bloody fools we were. Bloody, boyish fools.

We left at dawn without passing through Libertalia. We went around. I had felt such peace the previous few months at land, and yet, I was always confused. When I was at sea, I felt I was always at war with myself. But I am in touch with my Chaoticism, riding the ebbs and flows of the ocean and my mind— no confusion, just freedom to be whatever I wanted. Chaos is natural. The search for order and something solid in this life can make a bastard of anyone.

I'd been both bored and wild. I'd been a searcher and a thinker my whole life, two seemingly similar concepts with vastly different implications. Being in a maze and being wholly confused are entirely separate experiences. Pirates shall be pirates, for we belong to the sea, or else we'd go mad— all of us knew it. Too many of the men thought they were becoming just like their forefathers when we stayed on land. We found ourselves living the same simple, small, predictable existence. Although we started to love it, deep down we hated it. Who would have thought? Us tough and rugged pirates becoming hardened farmers in Madagascar, and then leaving the pristine jungle for the sea once again. The clash between the men's enthusiasm for returning to their habitat and their grief over leaving Madagascar was sure to twist them. And I was in the same boat, equally conflicted by this change.

I set my foot on the wood of the *Fancy* once again, on the main deck. I felt oddly grounded. The sails and sheets had missed us, and we had missed them. Chaoticism is a fine line between boredom and angst. Chaoticism is the path of the maze. A man-o'-war was the perfect vessel to traverse that path— speed, strength, character, hardiness, and the oh-so-demanding industry to maintain such a vessel. Any man who left that hell-of-a-ship beached and unused deserved a long sentence in the Locker. I was glad we came back around because I felt back at home on the sea. I made everywhere I went in my life a faux home, but the *Fancy* was meant to be my home long before my time. I could get so sentimental about that gargantuan tub. My attitude toward most things I came across was always changing. Chaoticism was my philosophy that mirrored a sailor's life— active, changing, and always on the move.

We set sail a ways away from there, escaping the island without any quarrel. We slogged together loudly, but once the course had been set, it became eerily quiet on the ship as we lost sight of ol' Madagascar. I wondered what the temperaments of the men were like aboard the nearby *Amity*. It seemed strange that the May sunbeams, shining with glory, had been stripped of all of their green

Madagascar tree shadings. The crew— young and old men alike— were back where we belonged.

There was a demon in me I had hidden from myself and my crew members. I couldn't bring myself to speak of it or even think of it. I must have forgotten because I could not withstand the thoughts in my own head at the time. However, the more I rejected the desire inside of me, the larger, more crooked, and more haunting this phenomenon became— even if I didn't see it. I was on land for months with sweet fruits, native women, and a jungle surrounding me. I physically sunk my teeth into and satiated myself with only one of those three delights. Yet those fruits were gone henceforth. And the women whom I avoided along with the jungle, were left behind too. It was not the sweet fruit we'd left untouched or the forbidden fruit which I'd declined to court which grew to haunt me.

It was the thought of and insatiable curiosity for the smoothest, most euphoric, forgotten sweet, that, for some brief moments, hankered my teeth and tongue— opium. I know why it was this, above all other pleasures, that made me vulnerable to pawning my will— the euphoria, forgetting, oblivion, losing myself, and feelings I acquired faster and more potently than I could have if I had sought them through a more sincere, sober effort. A shortcut is more seductive than the real thing. It's quicker and prevents any second thought.

I looked at men and saw their dark passions, vices, and cruel yearnings pulling at them. I was such a hypocritical judge. I doubted anyone saw my demons. For I buried them and they went away for a while. I also observed the undeniable nobility and divine actions which ran men. But I couldn't tell whether my shipmates saw the best or worst in me either. After the first time I enjoyed opium in Corunna, before our turn to piracy, my desire for it went away. But during the episode when Pretty Al rejected my vice after we'd left Corunna, I was hooked on the thought of poppy, of acquiring and eating it, and of harping on the satisfaction of it again and again until I was obliterated into sweet nothingness. My curious urge went away by default as I tamed and quelled these thoughts into dull submission throughout our adventures and time in Madagascar. I wondered why the thought of opium's insights only came crashing upon me when I was at sea, especially at port. Nevertheless, it appeared again. Once one has been touched by the sinister fingers of the poppy, one cannot be untouched. I can only stand up to it, knowing permanent victory over her would never be attained. Its siren call could never be silenced. I can only muffle the call. I can only persist against and in spite of it. But fail.

The sea is a violent, intoxicating frontier. I understand now, looking back, that I used the opium to fight this intoxicating, beautiful ocean, to provide myself some perverse sense of control. How could I have expected the crew to have seen my inner affliction if I had nearly forgotten about the opium for a time? Being on land brings me solace. But I loved the sea, too.

New Devon, like the *Fancy* over the past few months, was another place where opium was not available, as far as I knew. But since we were venturing back into the world of seafaring and pirating, I feared I would confront my demon in the physical arena, not only the invisible theatre of my mind. I was once again confronting the vulnerable, scary, treacherous journey of being a pirate on the open sea, and resisting opium's pull at the same time. Opium was how I fought my oceanic fear. I did not know if I was ready to face the prospects of the ocean again, for my muffled desire for opium superseded my carnal control. As we ventured further into the heart of the East, further into the Indian Ocean toward Asia and away from the New World, I would have a showdown with the monster once more. I did not have a choice.

There was one notable night in Libertalia, before we erected the second realm and moved to our New Devon. I had nearly forgotten about its occurrence, probably to shelter myself from myself— as how opium lets me slip away from myself and receive insight, how I hid my desire for opium within myself. That drunken night, the sea was on my mind harshly and ceaselessly. I was craving its adventure. And along with the ocean, I missed the poppy— it was the cure, I believed, which could aid me of whatever moody ailments came over me and open my eyes to superior understanding. The secret of opium that no sailor ever speaks of is that for a rare few it can give rise to visions of the future. I was not one to dream at night and think I was predicting the unpredictable, however, I did believe that visions and sensations, much like the occasional omen, were deeper signals than mere fantasy. And opium gave me signals that I knew something others did not when I ingested it.

That was where my mind was that night which I revisited, in memory, after stepping back upon the *Fancy*. In the jungle, anger of a crying baby came over me as I hopelessly longed for opium or anything else that could quell my mysteriously overwhelming feelings— it was excruciating. An episode of anger had come over me. A bout of sadness, memories, loneliness, and angst. I left my quarters because I did not want Thomas Howard to see me for the weakling I was that night, at my lowest of lows. If my heart were to give out, for it felt to be dying, I would rather have dealt with it alone. I gave myself over to my inner chaos when I drank the rum a-plenty. I recklessly went into the night of the jungle, entering the predators' grounds against all instincts of survival. I couldn't cry, but I wanted to. I feared a walk would beget my hunting by a fossa, but a walk would undoubtedly calm me down if I survived my reckless stroll.

I shuffled around for a bit, grasping my hair and putting my hand on my forehead, as all men who've gone mad had done at dark moments. I walked myself into a spider's web, which covered my face and caused a havoc-filled fit of arm-flailing. I ran away from the pair of tree branches which nested the web and cause of my fit, away from the little eight-legged creatures I so despised. I ran alongside more trees in the green darkness. I thought about how lucky I was, honestly. Lucky and fortunate I was more sensitive to intoxicating substances than anyone else I had ever met. I was harshly vulnerable to the poppy's effects and terribly susceptible to withdrawals. What was usually a stroke of luck was then demanding a hefty price tag for the first time in months. I craved it.

My sensitivity appeared not only in my heart, but in substance. I hated the taste of drink, of rum, but when I got beyond that and had some swigs of the Devil's juice, I was quite prone to its effects. It affected me at a faster rate and with less consumption than it did most men who drank in greater quantities and in less time. The same went for the poppy. I would only take small doses, as even one-third of a serving could send me places most men only dreamt of. I was a jackrabbit, touched by poison, whilst most men were elephants in this regard— slow and impervious. And as a jackrabbit, I lived, felt, and thought in the same fashion— intensely, rapidly.

After I had rushed off that evening and felt some sense of relief in the maniacal misery, I came across a pair of natives, a man and a woman, near the sound of the coast. The woman saw me and became frightened to the extreme of hiding behind her lad. Why wouldn't she cower from the sounds of the jungle in the night? She'd looked as if she'd seen the devil. The man turned around and said something to her, then she ran away from both of us. This rather confused me— while I may have displayed an utmost intense face, I was in no regards an intimidating figure. I guessed the chaos of my entire being exhibited by my face and manner could be read entirely by, and give fright to, a woman after all. The man looked back at me and changed his posture from surprise to fear. He must have felt the hair on his neck stand up. It was a full moon and I did not immediately back away, to avoid hostility, as I always did.

Something came over me worse than anything I'd felt before. Worse than all that had happened that entire night and in all of my other episodes of angst, drunken or not. I felt powerless against it and my actions took over themselves, shoving my volition into the background. Caused by a thousand resentments of myself, an infinity of frustrations, and eternities of an all-being-encompassing anger, I yelled. I shot my anger toward the man like a thousand nations' cannons. I screamed, grunted, clawed, and choked the man. I mangled him violently. All I saw in the darkness was red. The fury of two-hundred demons leapt from me. In the end, I harmed him plenty, temporarily, however I harmed myself much more permanently. I ran off from him, as he lay there in pain and fright, trying to recover his breath. He likely lived but I did not know for certain. I never saw the man before that night nor did I see him after. I lost it on him, releasing all of my vexation on the native and made him bleed. He fought for his life and I only let him go once I had all of the control a man could ever want over another. The demon became me then left me before I could kill the man.

Dignity did not prevail that inebriated night but I wish it did. I tried my best to forget about that evening. I hoped I would never see myself punished for the act of insanity or allow despair to drive me toward such a level of inhumanity again. I hoped I would never see that man and hoped he was still alive. The memory resurfaced for me as we departed Madagascar, as the threat of retribution no longer pressed into me and the fear of my own lack of restraint and brutishness slowly faded away. The memory resurfaced as thoughts of the poppy resurfaced due to being on the sea, I supposed. Maybe it happened that night before I saw the shrubs in my quarters, the night of Thomas' dance with the Malagasy Queen. Maybe those shrubs were from the flee after I swung upon the man. Maybe I forgot about my nightmare actions.

"Cole," I was interrupted and hauled out of my musings, my memories, thus re-entering the *Fancy* on exodus from Madagascar.

"Yes, Captain?" I responded to the voice of my captain who called me and tapped on my shoulder where I sat atop the rail beside the bowsprit.

I was staring into our unknown heading, straight into the horizon, and then the man joined me.

"Thank ye for trusting me," Captain Every said to me.

"Trustin' ye how, Cap'n?"

"Trusting me enough to join me, leaving New Devon. Trusting me for all of the past months."

"Aye, Captain," I said, then looked away from him, gazing back out toward the horizon and downward to watch our *Fancy* shred its way through the sea.

"I've brought ye somethin'," the Captain said, and I looked back to him, beside me.

I looked in his eyes then down to his closed hands. A dark wood-handled and steel flintlock pistol was in his grasp. It looked used. He extended his occupied hand over to me and, by reflex, I put my hand beneath the barrel of the pistol pointed in my direction, to receive it from his possession. I felt the power of the weapon in my hands, and a longing gratefulness in my heart. I looked at him then back to inspect the weapon of trust.

"Thank ye, Captain," I said, unsure of what to make of the gesture.

He smiled, nodded, darted his eyes to the ocean, then walked away, leaving me to the pistol and the horizon.

<u>*Chapter IX*</u>

RUMOURS

"To Johanna. We must stop at Johanna in the Comoros," Captain Every said aloud.

"Johanna? Why Johanna?" I asked as I found myself once again leaning up against the wall of Captain Every's captain quarters in the *Fancy*, challenging the old idol.

"Ye'll see," he said.

It appeared we had no other viable options, letting Caesar take the helm with the crew following behind. We needed no other pilot. Such was the case with many great men— the flawed maverick and his passion lead the way, leaving the crowd and its demand for rationality to follow afterwards. 'Twas much like a harpoon— with its spearhead forefronting the way and the rest of its body in line to follow. And they say pirates know nothing of whalin'.

The *Fancy*'s governance wasn't a democracy, anarchy, or even populism to begin with, but the Captain used to hold audiences for major announcements. Those days of having large crew conferences to hear the voice of the masses were over on the *Fancy*. The ship and the crew take on the character of the captain. Such should be the way those two entities are interwoven and dictated. Captain Every, the ol' bloke, was a Commander at heart, and the ship would be sailed according to his commands. The bold one led and the rest followed.

He kept his bloody plans in his head, the captain. Yet, he had not failed us thus far. From the mutiny to the journey toward the Cape to Madagascar to then sailing toward Johanna. He seemed to gamble everything on fate and he had beaten the house thus far. But

I began to wonder— when would the house take it all back?— for the house always wins. We'd see if he could pull this thievery off. He had kept us all in the bidding this long.

We sailed to and arrived in Johanna, with our squadron from the Madagascar waters behind us— the *Amity, Dolphin,* and *Portsmouth Adventure.* They knew their place. We made brisk time and discovered we were not the only European ship in port. Whenever that happened, when a galley of our fellow heritage shared a port, a pirate best beware. It looked to be an English East India trading ship. They were such pretty and capable ships, English made. On our way into port, our convoy lowered our flags to conceal our identities and not alarm the East Indiaman. We passed the ship with ease, without conflict, and anchored away.

We were anchoring, rowing, docking, and walking onto land again. I had lost my appetite for land, yet I went with Captain Every and the few other men onto the dock and port along with some representatives of the *Amity,* including their captains. The captains and men of the *Dolphin* and *Portsmouth Adventure* remained where they were anchored. I wanted the action and the importance despite my enjoyment of the sea again. We walked past some people in the market, as Captain Every and Captain Tew led the charge. So many islanders were around us, yet the English and Dutch had an obvious influence there— trading and piracy dominated those waters, which were the effects of those two nations' ventures. Rumour was their Sultan was quite fond of pirates— pirates who didn't steal from him or complicate any of his interests and claims, of course. The leader must not have had much of a choice, considering he lacked a navy. It was neutral territory there, and yet we could all see the writing on the wall— be careful on that land. While there wasn't a Royal Navy, privateer, or Johanna Sultan ship to hunt us down should we flee to the open sea, it was impossible to know what dangers lurked inland among the populace. About a dozen of us, including Captain Every, moved about carefully. We approached an inn.

"Wait outside, lads," Captain Tew said, as he and Captain Every entered.

I peeked into the tavern to see European-looking men having a rowdy time next to prostitute-looking women. Most of our lads outside had a go at some grumbling. I preferred to stay away from that sort of thing and keep to myself. I walked away and looked around at the landscape and horizon. The sightseeing quickly led me to conclude that the oyster of the Indian Ocean had some beautiful scenery pearls to show for her. They were hidden, these islands, so secretively privileged to that realm. The captains reappeared after some time.

"C'mon, lads. Let's find ourselves a mapmaker," Captain Tew said.

The crew looked around at one another confusedly. Captain Tew noticed, stopping in his movements and brushed off an islander making his way into the inn.

"Why a mapmaker?" I asked, exercising curious dissent and privilege as Captain Every's cabin boy, his eyes and ears.

"He shall know of the Mughal convoy. He knows these waters much better than any of us do, young lad. I know the trader, whom I corresponded with in Madagascar— before yer time. He is here. He is the mapmaker," Captain Tew said, displaying plenty of hot bloodedness to me and my questioning ways.

"Aye, Captain Tew. Can't handle pressure from me cabin boy?" Captain Every jested, defending me.

If a man can't handle questioning by his crew, especially by a young and able pirate, he shouldn't be captain. Captain Every knew this. We walked halfway across the island, where town nearly ended and nature once again began. We walked to a little shack fit for a hermit with a little, faded painted sign on the windowsill reading *Maps & Trades*. Captain Tew, Captain Every, a man of Captain Tew's crew, and I walked into the wooden, creaking place. It smelled faintly of rats and manure.

"What kind of backwood, low-down, dogged shanty-man is this, Thomas?" Captain Every said.

"What? Who be comin' in unannounced?" the voice with a Scottish accent screeched, and a bearded middle-aged man, red-faced as all hell, blundered in, puffing a smoking pipe.

"Duff bloody Hendrickson," Captain Tew familiarised with the stranger.

"Aye, who goes?" Hendrickson said, pointing the pipe like a blunderbuss toward us.

"Thomas Tew. Remember me? St. Mary's? One of Baldridge's olde mates," Captain Tew said.

Hendrickson relaxed and his face shined with affability, starkly contrasting the look directed at us earlier when we entered the dark, grey hole of his abode. We took seats at a table in the next room over. The captains sat at the table with our host, while the other two of us distanced ourselves and sat behind them. The chairs were splintery— the prestige and privilege of being a captain's cabin boy. It beat the hell out of the dirt the rest of the boys were probably sitting on outside of the shack, however.

"How've ye been, Duff? I haven't seen ye in... what? It's been some time," Captain Tew said.

"Aye, better here than Madagascar, Thomas. Baldridge is a cheeky bastard. Too cheeky for my taste. There are plenty of customers here for me... and a lot less of ye damn pyrates," Hendrickson said.

"Aye. Lots of pyrates in both places, but less here. Aye, we've come to Johanna and come into yer place with a reason, my olde friend," Captain Tew said, shooting a quick look at Captain Every before putting his attention back on the Scot.

"What is it?" Hendrickson asked.

"Have ye heard anything of the Mughal Empire of India sailing a convoy through these waters?" Captain Tew asked.

"Nay, sir," Hendrickson replied.

"Are they making any significant way in the Red that ye know of?" Captain Tew asked.

"No, I am not one to know of the Mughals... I don't sell anything to them folk," Hendrickson said and we looked at each other dumbfoundedly.

"Oh, come on Duffy... I haven't been in the Red for over a year. I know ye haven't been to Madagascar for a year, but I know ye sell plenty of maps to anyone passing through these waters. I want one. A detailed one. And I want ye to tell me what rumours ye've heard of the Mughals."

"Or what? And at what price?" Hendrickson demanded and the tempers of all three men at the table flared up.

"Well, because ye're my friend, I'll pay for the map. And I'll pay ye for the information too, Duff," Captain Tew said.

My attention was honed onto the exchange at the table, but then I surveyed the room— the man had a pistol lying about on a ledge behind him, but the captains could slice and blast the man to Hell twenty times over before he could get to it.

"Aye. I got a map for ye. The maps of the Red Sea are what I've got. But I haven't heard much of nothin' about the Mughals," Hendrickson said.

"Ye haven't heard anything of the Muslims?" Captain Tew said.

"Aye. I've heard something sizable about them. And it's something I won't charge ye for, as it's common knowledge," Hendrickson said, with a big, fat, laughing smile on his face.

"What?" Captain Tew stopped.

"The Muslims... they're—" Hendrickson got cut off.

"Spit it out Hendrickson, c'mon. The Mughals *are* Muslims. The Muslims are the Mughal Empire. Ye're a mapmaker for Heaven's sake, and ye don't know that?" Captain Every blurted out.

Pirates are poor at controlling their emotions or restraining their tempers. Captain Every usually was the contrary, but the fool seemed to be gettin' to all of us.

"Oh, they haven't bought any maps from me or anyone in quite a while, ye ol' bitch. The Muslims sail the same way every year,"

Hendrickson said, eyeing Captain Every. Captain Tew stood up and mulled over the conversation.

"Alright, alright. They sail every year the same way? Why? What the hell are they doin'? Just for trade?" Captain Tew asked.

"Oh, lads, ye're Indian Ocean pyrates, ye should know this. C'mon," Hendrickson said with his rough Scottish accent, mocking Captain Every. "They're Muslims. They go on pilgrimage in the next few months. Usually, twenty or thirty ships in the convoy at a time, my boy. Every year. They travel into the heart of the Red Sea— India to Mecca. I thought ye used to sail the Red, Thomas. I didn't know they were called Mughals. I thought them Indians or just Muslims," Hendrickson said.

"Duff. I want the most detailed map of the Southern Red Sea ye've got. Every river, stream, port. All of it. D'ye know when they sail the convoy?" Captain Tew asked.

"I can get ye one, Thomas, no problem... I've already got a few maps to pick from, but they're expensive. And no, lad, I don't know exactly when they sail, but the convoy I know of should be sailin' sometime in the next few months."

The captains paid the man for the map, the information, and the troubles. Quite a reunion. Pirates aren't too good with people, unless these people are pirates. The captains walked out of the shack with a pair of maps in their hands and Captain Tew's man followed. I stuck around for a moment and looked at the Scot, who looked far out of his home territory.

"How did he find yerself here, Hendrickson?" I asked.

"A ship," he said and cut me down to my low rank.

"Aye. If ye know the Indian Ocean, tell me, what's that East Indiaman doin' in port? D'ye know what they haul?" I asked.

"Spices, opium— usual for most trade to Asia in this water," Hendrickson responded.

I sunk fathoms downward. My soul descended into my depths while demons clambered their way up. All objectives of Hendrickson, Captain, wealth, freedom, and life transferred to the imaginary insides of that East Indiaman's hold. And I thought of sneaking away from the prestige as Captain Every's trusted crew member in order to hold up the trade ship for one taste of the poppy. It was such a powerful curiosity, having done it only once, yet it reappeared from its hidden dormancy, taking centre-stage. I thought of the more probable outcome in which Captain Every would commandeer the ship's valuable goods, including the lion portion of opium, and eventually me thieving it for myself then hanging for it. I feared I must face the poppy demon alone, or worse, in front of the entire crew, one way or another.

"Besides the spices, opium's the only good, pricy thing the English want that the Chinese or Mughals—" Hendrickson continued.

"—Thank ye, Hendrickson," I said, cutting the conversation short and then left the room.

We walked away from the shack, the town, and then we rowed back to our boats, sitting pretty on the port's calm waters beside that English trading ship. The house of all of my hauntings remained inside that trader ship. I no longer saw the pretty and able boat I viewed on my way into port. On the other side of its walls hid a marvel.

Releasing the sails, lifting anchor, and making some way out of the port, we came to a stop far behind our three fellow pirate vessels, who surged ahead into the Indian Ocean. We went up alongside the East Indiaman vessel. I read the yellow painted name on the ship's navy blue nameplate— *Retriever*. We moved via plank across the watery void between our ships and onto their mostly empty deck. They looked so young— the sparse lads— and too soft to be sailing in those waters. The rest of the men, likely the able and intimidating lads of their crew, were presumably staying at the tavern, keeping the prostitutes company. Captain Every made himself appear large by stepping in between our two ships with a pistol in one hand and holding onto the shrouds with the other. He stood on the rail above every bloke on their deck and shouted out to the frightened English merchantmen.

"Where is yer captain?"

The men all looked around. Our crew infested their ship, spreading within and around all of their men. I held my sword tightly, with palms full of uneasiness despite the quiet commandeering, letting tensions of a fight and shivers of poppy desire consume me. I looked around for any promising lads who may be of use to us, or who may be a threat. A man appeared from below deck, with a few other men behind him. He was a fool for not being scared and prepared enough when a forty-six-gun man-o'-war rested in the same port with lowered flags and no ensign. Joining his captured watchmen, their captain, likely inexperienced, walked about and up to Captain Every, almost fearlessly and unflinchingly.

"I am the captain of this vessel. Do ye wish to do business?" the captain asked, with a most serious face and intention.

I inspected the lad. He had an English face, worldly manner, and wore the proper attire. Brown hair hid 'neath his hat but other than this, he appeared to have no secrets or interesting features.

Captain Every smiled and looked around, in a look of disbelief toward the forward lad. He laughed and the older men on our ship looked at him, joining in the laughter.

"I'll make a transaction of ye and yer boat, good sir," Captain Every said, still standing above the man, nodding in between words.

"What do ye want? We did not put up a fight, I'd suggest ye spare my men... unless ye want the bad luck of Davy Jones' Easterly Wind on yer side," their captain said.

His mentioning of Easterly Wind dispatched a chill up my spine. The captain spoke so nonchalantly of that sensitive omen Captain Every and I had come across just before leaving New Devon. Maybe in that moment Captain Every realised I had greater insight than most of those mortal men. Captain Every looked as if the momentum had been ripped out of him, scared as a boy afraid of the dark. How could he be so intimidated by a satirical captain? In that moment, Captain Every, a gruesome and immoral pirate, was turned into a schoolboy by some harmless merchantman. I'd assumed he disregarded our Easterly Wind discussion. I was wrong.

"What do ye got? Captainnnn—?" Captain Every said.

"Captain Benjamin Bridgeman, I am. We've got silver and some opium. Nothing more, nothing less," the captain said calmly.

The merchant shed no concern for the cargo, the goods that paid him and his men. I thought he must have either been mad or he'd spent his entire life at sea and was jaded. He was too young to be on his last voyage though, which usually gives weight to some careless effect in many captains, not wanting to face the end of their line and the end of their tenure in the deep blue sea. Or he simply concerned himself with more of the important things in a seafaring life like the adventure rather than the silver. He compelled me, this man of poise amongst peril, as he compelled Captain Every.

"And what of yer men? Are any as apathetic as ye, Cap'n Bridgeman?" Captain Every remarked, looking about the merchant crew on deck. "Any lads here wish to join our divine cause for freedom? We're sailing into more gold than any of ye could possibly have as merchants, and unshackling ye to pillage as ye please. Nothing less."

After some timid movements, a handful of us *Fancy*-men breached into the lower levels of their ship, finding our way to their hold to pillage all of their worthy loot. It was best not to take all of it, only the most shiny prizes. Considering we were already a well-armed man-o'-war, and yet heavily reduced to be the fastest ship in the Indian Ocean, it was best not to weigh ourselves down before a most pertinent, potentially bluff, speedy raid. We only took a portion of the cargo.

There were no spices as Hendrickson had guessed, only the silver which we took some of and a few opium crates we hauled back to the *Fancy*. We replenished ourselves with their food, munitions, and provisions as well. It was the best of luck to be well stocked before a raid. Then again, I'd always felt that a raid conducted on the last measures of supplies gave us the best chance, as the crew had nothing to lose— materially speaking— thus causing a dire willingness to succeed and a hunger which cannot exhaust the will. Thinking of Captain Bridgeman there, watching his supplies get looted, I found that I was one in a million— a non-materialistic pirate. I only cared for what the materials gave a man— freedom, security. I cared for the adventures of a pirate and the steam in my belly from the life I lived. Forget the loot, I thought to myself.

I avoided carrying any of the wooden opium crates back to our hold. I dreaded the idea of sailing with any of that cargo, and the weight it would put upon my chest. I accompanied Captain Every into Captain Bridgeman's quarters. There was no proper reason a pirate should enter the looted ship's captain's quarters, especially during a peaceful raid. No reason. Too dangerous and vulnerable for my taste to enter the lion's den. Captain Every, Quartermaster Dawson, Bos'n Durnburn, and I— the infamously unknown cabin boy— entered the quarters with their captain and a pair of his sailors. Captain Every stowed his pistol and walked about the ship as if he was familiar with it. Familiar with the decorum and manners of an English trader. It is what he truly was, more or less, on the other side of the law. We stood on opposite sides of the wooden, eloquent desk. Captain Every stretched his right hand out, the red sleeve of his coat hiding his arm. I had no clue of his appearance under that coat— tattoos, scars, memories, or a blandness of skin such as mine. I had little knowledge of Captain Every's history and secrets. It felt quite strange for me to know so little of a man I held in such high regard throughout our long journey. He pointed to a stack of papers on the desk belonging to the other captain. Captain Bridgeman sat behind his desk, likely ready to remove a blade or pistol from one of the drawers in a martyr's effort. I was aptly prepared to cut the man down had he made a fast manoeuvre or signalled to any of his lackeys.

"Cap'n Bridgeman. Ye're going to write a letter for me," Captain Every ordered the man.

The merchant captain agreed, reluctantly swabbing his quill pen with ink and collecting a paper from the pile. Captain Bridgeman looked earnestly at the pirate who held his life in his hands.

"And Bridgeman... do this or yer precious, fellow English boys across the Indian Ocean that we find won't receive the same tenderness as yer crew did," Captain Every said, tightening his grasp on Captain Bridgeman's attention.

Captain Every looked out through the back windows of the captain's cabin, composing the letter which encompassed the nature of fierce pirates on the hunt for gold, adventure, and the great, insurmountable unknown.

"To any and every English Commander, merchant ship, and Naval vessel in the great Indian Ocean: Us, the satisfied captain and crew of the *Fancy*, a forty-six-gun, 150-men crew, formerly known as the *Charles II* of the ol' Spanish Expedition at Corunna... are to be watched for. We have no quarrel with any traders or Naval vessels of England, though we have taken some small cargo of the *Retriever*, peacefully. This is a warning to all ye operating within this Indian Ocean, that so long as I command this vessel, ye shall not be harmed if ye reveal yerselves and ball yer flag up to be hoisted high. We outsail and out-cannon any. We shall not harm any Commander or crew who performs this signalling toward us, I say. I give my word," Captain Every dictated this proclamation to Captain Bridgeman as if the word of a pirate or a liar was useful to good Englishmen.

"I run my boat, but my crew operates her. I am a friend to the Englishman, but I cannot guarantee my crew of many denominations holds ye in similar esteem. So, reveal yerselves. I have not attacked any English vessel, nor shall I. There is a 160-man French ship in the Bay of Saint Mary's Island, Madagascar, near a pyrate settlement, who's crew I knows is out to harm all ye English at any opportunity they be gettin'. Take care of yerselves," Captain Every said. "And what is the month?" Captain Every asked Bridgeman.

"June, 1695," Captain Bridgeman responded.

"Aye, write 'Johanna, June, 1695. From Captain Henry Every,'" Captain Every concluded.

"That's it?" Captain Bridgeman asked.

"Aye. Go to yer nearest, fattest East India trading port. Bring this letter to the highest man in charge and have it dispatched to all East India Company and merchant captains. It is for yer own good," Captain Every said, trying to appear caring. "Will ye do this for me and yer countrymen, Bridgeman?"

"I shall sir. Not because of ye, but for my fellow men of the East India Company," Captain Bridgeman said.

We stormed out of the captain's quarters, leaving Captain Bridgeman where he sat, letter in hand. Captain Every led our walk out onto the main deck.

"I shall remember that feisty Bridgeman," Captain Every said to us and smiled.

"What is the purpose of that letter, Cap'n? The ships ye've lied about that we raided have probably all given word to their masters that it was the *Fancy* who raided them," Quartermaster Dawson contested.

"We must make some sense of peace or try to. If we pull off this raid, the only thing we have to fear in this ocean are the cannons of an East Indiaman. We can outsail and outgun any other. But those ships, when they cluster, can be too taught and tough," Captain Every said.

"And what of the French Madagascar ship, Captain? Surely that'll bring danger to these waters and our olde Libertalia. Is that a true ship?" I asked.

"Call it New Devon's revenge, Mr. Cole. Libertalia is sure to falter after our raid, for some ships will hunt down any trace of us or a supposed French pyrate ship in Madagascar. It is the art of mis-direction, lad, and they shall take the bait. The East Indiamen shall surely sail and investigate this supposed ship in the Bay of Saint Mary's Island purely on the merit of the letter, and they shall find Libertalia. Anything we didn't burn to the ground in Madagascar shall be scavenged and sold by the Company. 'Tis what Libertalia deserves for running us out of Madagascar," Captain Every said.

We walked onto the main deck, across the planks, and back onto our ship, fleeing into the open sea once more and later caught up to the three other ships. I wondered, did Captain play at the game of piracy as one calculates in the game of chess, or had he mastered the grand game of improvisation, making chaos a part of the plan as he went along? Was he the greatest, most subtle tactician?

We were on our way, off to the hasty raid. It was our intent to go north, beyond where any good-boy Englishman went. Into the territory of the Southern Red Sea, where internal alarm bells were a constant, and man was both predator and prey. A backstaff guides seamen, but instinct guides pirates and seamen that survive the Red Sea. Without instinct, one is as good as dead. Or so sailing wisdom says.

Chapter X

VOLCANIC GROUPING

August, 1695. I did not know whether we'd missed the Mughal fleet or not. We sailed through a strait called "the gate of tears" in order to make safe and speedy passage toward the island of Perim, some volcano-like land home to nothing that interested me. We did not go onto the terrain, instead staying on our ships, at the ready. Captain Tew and his _Amity_; along with the _Dolphin_ lead by tall, bearded Captain Richard Want; and the _Portsmouth Adventure_ lead by shaggy Captain Joseph Faro, our three comrade vessels, beat us there by a single day. Word must have gotten out about the Muslim pilgrimage. This was a demonstration that either pirates thought alike or Captain Tew knew how to communicate across seas, since a few more vessels and their captains joined our little flotilla on the surprise side of Perim Island. The gentlemanly, grey-haired Captain William Maze, another former patron of the Libertalia realm with his beloved _Pearl_, and a new, notorious face joined us— the bald Captain Thomas Wake and his _Susanna_. The other five ships beside our _Fancy_ reportedly all left their beloved Newport at the same time. The six of us, with varying masts, crew sizes, capabilities, and ships, arrived together within the span of a week. Therefore, it was safe to assume we didn't yet witness the passing of the Mughal fleet. I wagered that no six pirate vessels are that coincidentally late, nor arrive at the same time in failure.

On our journey from Johanna to there, we came across only one adversary, a French privateer, and we managed to dodge her. 'Twas best to avoid any quarrel before we took on a big one, which, in essence, disproved the old pirate adage— 'the only difference between pirates and everyone else is that pirates simply don't yield.'

I met Thomas on the quarterdeck, in leisure.

"Say, d'ya think we have control over ourselves?" I asked my friend.

"What are ye goin' on about now?" he laughed at my absurd remark.

"'Tis a simple idea— I feel that there are forces within me that dictate what I do. And that I do not have agency over myself, or what I want," I said as Thomas leaned up off of the rail, somewhat intrigued.

"No matter what ye think or what anyone says, ye have responsibility for what ye say and do. Ye're not a prisoner," he replied.

I heard him well and believed he did not grasp what I was saying, for Thomas truly was a man of the crowd, compelled by desires to fit in that certainly did not belong to him. In terms of intellectual discussion, Thomas thought in terms of the group, not from his own deep judgement— this posed a contradiction to me, contrasting with his roguishness toward and radical self-interest with Captain Tew's woman. Nevertheless, like many men in our way of life, he was complicated.

"Aye, maybe. But I cannot control what I think or want, only what I do, Thomas," I said.

"Nonsense. This is yer life and ye live it how ye please."

I knew he did not have the discipline within himself to control his desires. How could he fathom a man opposing the legions of forces constantly attempting to control and subdue himself?

"I don't think we have control. Sometimes we do. But it is an ebb and flow between the scale of controlling force on one end and easing surrender on the other. And it always moves. I do not think this movement belongs to us, we but rent this body and these forces in us simply go wherever they go, leading us in all sorts of different directions," I said.

"So which is it? Are ye a prisoner, thus controlled by forces in ye? Or are ye in power, thus subduing these forces? Which is it? Sounds backward to me," Thomas said.

"Ye've got me. Inside, we have no control. But on the outside, we can attempt to jockey the wild horses within us—"

"And how is that coming along for ye?" he interrupted.

"I don't know. I find it liberating to not be in power over some aspects of my life, to be a Chaotic on the inside. But as for the world around me... it is hard to navigate, my friend," I confessed.

"Loosen up. Drink something for God's sake. If ye constrict yerself too much, ye'll suffocate," he said.

"Then am I not free anywhere I want to be? Can I never gain control over my own ebbs and flows and resistances and fights?" I asked.

"In yer belief, I doubt it. But the way I view, ye always have self-control and responsibilities. Life is cause and effect, my friend, not a matter of randomness," he said.

For a moment I felt relieved he disagreed with me, for then I had reason to stop talking about the subject. The world within me acted of its own accord. It was not mine to handle and dismantle whenever I pleased. What I feel is a civilisation of its own, and I, an outsider, am a tenant of the world around me, so different from the one within. Could I be understood or agreed with? I've tried to distance my thoughts from the feelings within me by sleeping, in hopes that the escape to the world of dreams would distract me from the unremitting rogue inside.

The time had come to convene and plan— sunrise, first light of an August day. It confused me that sailors focused more upon the sun, basing their lives around its movements and effects, when the moon seemed to govern our seas and behaviours more significantly. Men appeared to focus on the apparent and visible— the sun— more than the secretive entity darkly influencing the tides and current— the moon. People operate more on longer tides than they do on shorter rises and falls. Yet they fail to acknowledge this. Then again, it is rare to find people reverent of the moon who not only acknowledge her superior influence, but furthermore operate according to her behaviour as one would act toward a teacher's guidance. Everywhere one looks, one can see a man or woman of the sun— those folk who busy their talk with daily occurrences. The quiet guide of the tides, silent light, and subtle darkness appear and disappear on a different, more discreet calendar— this is the moon. And I was a rare man of the moon. I comprehended that without the sun there was no light, therefore cause and effect were real, and I knew I was composed of both. Yet I knew each of their respective places. And I recognized which was supreme— tides and trends, not immediate rises and falls.

Thomas thinks life is simple and direct, like the rise and fall of the sun. I think life is an uncontrollable path we must sail on and adapt to, like the tides and subtle shifts of the moon. Surely we have some control on our vessels, but as for the whole of life, we are the servants and observers of the tide, not the masters of the day. And in my own language, when I asked any of the crew, all of them, one of them, Thomas included, 'what of the moon, the tides, and constant climbs as opposed to shifty ups and downs?'— they suddenly became deaf and blind.

If I had asked a crew member or fellow conversationalist about this philosophy of phases, currents, and long patterns, rather than immediate ups, downs, direct causes and effects, I was dismissed, and likely looked at as delusional, or even worse, in their own minds— deemed a woman. I sensed this with Thomas, which frustrated me and caused me to think myself wiser than him. The sun had blinded him. The sun blinded them. The brightness of the immediate moment made it impossible for them to see beyond the rays. Life is not that simple. Life is a constant struggle against forces beyond our vision. The lads could not operate in true darkness, for they knew nothing of darkness, and were unaware there was more beyond the daily grime of work or cause and effect.

How could a man accept there was an entity beyond his control that runs him and remains beyond his plans, schemes, vision, and actions?— shove and hide it away, as many men do. They knew nothing of the sole light which emanated the land of darkness and was mother to their whole apparent world. Can they fathom anything more than what they desire? Do they know why they desire what they desire? Could my crewmates see a larger pattern that caused whatever cause and effect they were privy to? These men and maidens of the sun— they're nothing but a lantern, a flicker, as life is. Men of the sun have no depth, no darkness to them, no mystique. They know not of the other world, for they are asleep when it shows itself. People speak so much, so loudly, that they cannot hear a subtle voice. They know nothing of their own blindness. When the world goes to sleep, they lay with it. When the world is dreaming, they do not operate. And they are, were, and shall always be... half a people, half human. But I am one of something else. I am a man of the moon, bound by utility to learn the ways of the sun— the ways of the world, work, cause, effect, and its known entities. Or am I a man of the sun— practicality— bound to learn the ways of the moon, this other way around, in all of my confusing attempts to perceive reality? Whatever the answer is, I must end all enquiries on a question mark. Or should I?

When light hit the horizon, and some time had passed, I went to the port side rail to gaze upon the other ships in our convoy, all bobbing about. Captain Every planned to host the captains of the other ships aboard the *Fancy*. I wanted to see the way those men acted when they thought nobody was watching, such as leaving their quarters and their precious ships to meet the big captain. One could learn much about a man by watching him in the subtler moments. People hide everything in their private movements. Words are easier to deceive with and can often be twisted, omitted, or simply falsified. But movement cannot so easily be faked. A man's actions can be restrained, but never fully faked, especially the movement of his eyes.

I watched all of the captains approach our man-o'-war in their tenders. They all approached near where I stood on the port side, watching them from the tall *Fancy*. Each of them were rowed gently along, and, upon arrival, their escorts stayed behind to man the little vessels as the captains boarded ours. The leaders were all different men. Some captains looked around at the world as they taxied to our ship, some kept their eyes and heads steadily fixed on the destination where I stood, some looked down, and some alternated between all three. None of them closed their eyes in transit. I wondered, were all of the captains tense and stirred up? Did any of them have experience with mighty raids? I found myself closing my eyes from time to time when I had the relaxing leisure of men rowing for me, which was rare.

I felt trust toward those other captains. United in our venture, us utterly untrustworthy pirates were on a mission where the goal, the desire, was a common one. Common goals unite men more than any other uniting measure. I had no fear, then, calm as ever on what was the eve of our raid. It was not strange for me to be tranquil that day. I'd often felt peaceful before engaging in something rather dangerous and deadly. I felt confident in our venture. I observed none of the captains had asked for a hand when climbing the ladders up onto our vessel. Little did I despise more in this world than self-important, weak, incompetent, overly reliant leaders. Little. And that simple, oh-so-simple, absence of a gesture showed me the captains were humble captains. I was optimistic about the mettle of our captains that night.

I watched them all ascend onto our ship, then I followed the last to arrive, noticeable by the shine on his bald head, Captain Thomas Wake, onto the lower deck and toward the officer's mess. All of them entered alone, without any retinue to follow. I came in last, and closed the doors behind me, unsure of my role as crewman counsel or a simple servant. I was somewhere in between. The captains arrayed themselves around the table, where Captain Every sat at the head chair. Two remaining empty seats awaited Captain Wake and if there was to be another knight of the roundtable who I had yet to meet. I felt the captains' eyes, all looking at me, confused about my presence and emanating a degree of envy at my young but favoured position in the room. I waited tensely, preparing myself against any embarrassment, for Captain Every to tell me to vacate, for I was only a lowly sailor. He didn't. I was a witness to the table of the men whose hands my life rested in, those men who would handle the helms of our venture, a lifetime, in the coming hours, days, weeks, and potentially months. I had no idea when the Mughals would come to pass, nor from which direction. It could have been between that day and a few months later. And while I looked forward to the skirmish and its challenges, I knew that evening may well have been my last supper. That night, I was amongst kings.

"Gentlemen," Captain Every said, implying more with the manners than was true, for pirates are not gentlemen. "A pleasure."

Two of the new captains replied with a neutral mutter.

"I was once a family man, a humble seafarer who sent most of my wages home. Home... what home?" Captain Every began.

I looked at the captains side-eyeing one another.

"This could be the biggest raid we'll ever face. But it could be a total miss. Heaven or Hell awaits us, whenever the ships go by. Many captains do not give their lookouts and men of the crow's nests much merit, but these sailors shall be the genesis of this operation, and they are to be valued evangelically this time around. I'm putting my best men up top and I recommend ye all do the same. Now, back to the subject of which way this raid shall go— we must move to elect a leader of the flotilla," Captain Every said.

"Is there a better option than Captain Tew? He is the most experienced captain. He'll surely see this through to the gold," Captain Faro chimed.

"Captain Tew is no simple lad but Captain Every does have the superior vessel and largest crew," Captain Wake replied.

"Slow and steady we must go about this attack," Captain Tew said cautiously.

"I do have the superior ship by speed and ferocity. And experience may not be the prime virtue for this raid, gentlemen, for experience lets a man believe he knows when he truly doesn't. Experience sets a captain in his ways and this is a raid no one hath ever seen the likes of before," Captain Every said.

"I lack the experience of a twenty-to-thirty-ship convoy raid, lads," Captain Tew said with humility.

"What difference does it make who leads this? We need only make the decision and follow him. And as long as we take out the masts of their most appetising vessels, surely those in the rear, for their treasure loads shall slow them, the catch is ours. Unless of course, the Mughals are intelligent as wolves, letting the slow ships lead the pace in the front, and protecting with the vicious from the rear. Either way, we are a convoy ourselves. I hazard that we go on pace together, to overwhelm them with speed, flanking, swarming, and surrounding. Together," Captain Every said.

"Whosoever leads the charge, surely at the vanguard, shall take the most damage and require the most resolve. Methinks that is Captain Every's vessel," Captain Want said.

"Then the matter is settled, Captain Every shall captain us captains?" Captain Maze asked softly, courteously.

Had the bloody men been emasculated? Or were they simply practical men to the point of weakness? To have a man "captain us captains?" It was the comment of a man too afraid of the fight. I'd concluded it was better to have Captain Every lead, for if the venture was not hoisting a man of fury at the forefront, it may well have been no more than a timid suicide. Timidness leads to more death and destruction than hubris. A man of fury possesses daring, and if we were to take the bright prizes of a twenty-to-thirty-ship convoy, we needed to dare.

"There is nothing else here for me besides my ship, my crew, the gold, and the triumph, lads. I accept the challenge," Captain Every said.

There was no shortage of bravado in the room, and yet in Captain Every remained the guts of these other five men combined. The other five men offered the caution which Captain Every lacked. The meeting concluded after some simple planning and a meal.. I returned to the main deck, to the port side rail, and leaned over with my arms crossed, looking out at the sea.

With each thought and each fleeting moment, with every single image in my head, I couldn't help but let my mind gravitate to the materials resting decks below me in our hold— crates of opium. Nature is neither friend nor foe, but ambiguously hosts both poisons and pleasantries. For the same flower that heals is the one that can harm. Man can corrupt anything. I drifted somewhere else in thought before walking. I was overtaken, reduced to a mere passenger to this other side of myself and its curious desires. I walked, covertly, down until I was in a dark hold, with wood, crates, barrels, bags, and a lantern around me. No people. I reflected on a memory of being a boy where my mother and father brought me to the theatre once. I thought of being with them, accompanying them to an evening concocted by them but for me. As I returned my attention to the ship, I knew then I would not ever be a boy again, but I would feel the elation of boyhood shortly, even if it came at a grave price.

I felt that nobody saw the dangers of the drink, especially seamen. I was a part of some secret society, someone who saw the drama, peoples' behaviour, and knew it was a game of appearances and half-sincere gestures. Wherever the rest of the crowd and its actors, who were roughly one and the same, went, I did not go. I saw the thespians and the story for what it was— men could not handle reality and men cannot handle themselves. And most men, or women, for one way or another they drink their share as well, wanted to feel what it was to be a boy or girl once more, without filters, inhibitions, or resistances. Life is too crude a stage for people to dance upon, so they drink. They want a safe womb. Those days and euphorias are gone. But peoples' denial was strong, and the desire to bring those good old dreams back, even through synthetic means, grows more haunting the further time moves on from childhood days.

The divide between who one was, who one was becoming, and who one wanted to become could reach a point of sadness within the soul. I think I was there, thinking of how far I'd drifted from my boyhood virtues. How could I think of that sensation if I had not experienced it at that moment? I aimed to consolidate my weaknesses, looking at the crates as I pondered. The crates contained a consolation. How could I call myself different from the people I criticised and condescended in my ramblings if I was not truly different after all?

My desires were less about drink, opium, or any vice that I spoke of for that matter, as they are the same message being delivered through different bottles. Rapture in that hold stared at me in my ashamed face. I was aware of the prices and payoffs of everything I did in my life. Or so I thought. 'Twas a blessing and a curse, I supposed. But most cursed of all was that I spoke of myself as a man with self-imposed will, yet was truly guided by dominions beyond my observation. I met one which commandeered my volition. The poppy, called me, cried for me, and wanted me just as much as I wanted it. It was a bitch. I believe I truly did not know myself or lead myself as I had once thought I did.

To the crates. One less dose wouldn't hurt the riches of Captain Every and the crew. I wouldn't be marooned for the act. I would only maroon who I truly was within myself. Whatever I was to do in the hold, alone, and whatever I was to feel, I believed would encrust my soul and emplace rust upon my heart. I didn't care anymore. Nobody spoke of the dangers, harms, and sadnesses of opium or the drink. I was aware of them though, all too aware and fine with knowing things others did not yet consider. Such awareness gave me power. Powers of perception that were about to be accelerated by tears of my majesty, the poppy.

For as much as I thought myself a cool lad, impervious to the shakes before any battles, I must not have been as invincible as I thought. I could die in our raid. But I must have one last go at the poppy. What a coward I was. The calm before the storm was not so calm after all. I shredded the top of a sealed crate with the help of my dagger and some wild force to pry it open. Was that what I had been waiting for? I cleared obstructions out of my way when I wanted something. I ripped through the hay shredding and looked upon a small row of what looked like cannonballs covered in flower petals. I did not know how I knew the crate was opium-filled, but I uncovered it in my first attempt.

I snagged a sole, rounded, opium sphere, shaped like a cannonball. I stuffed it into my shirt, that cloth which carried my familiar scent, for a sailor only washes with salt water once in a while. The smell of my body upon the Atlantic and Indian Oceans never left me.

I bustled around the hold, pacing back and forth, swaying my arms and hands about like a mad-man. Nobody ever saw me like that. I only experienced this part of myself when I was alone. It was my maskless self, whether on the opium or not, talking to myself and jumping around as a monkey. My boyhood excitement had not been lost on me yet, but the world was encroaching fast and strong, and thus my boy would be taken by the world unless I protected him. Is opium, or drink, or whatever one whores oneself off to, even a whore herself, the proper, adult way to preserve the rhapsody of childhood? If so, are these strong, seductive vices so common because of this aim? Yes? Then, therefore, was the poppy the manly way to handle it? I did not believe it was ideal. There was no substance substitute for the freedom of a child, his righteous ideas, awe, or proper actions. What was about to occur in that hold was merely an animal urge for pleasure with a philosophical attempt to account for it and protect it. I had considered us humans superior to animals. In contrast, we had little self-control and the little we did have was feeble at best. We are all hypocrites, as am I.

I hid, running to the far side of the hold and crouched behind the crates and barrels. Opium was accepted amongst pirates, but I did not want to be seen stealing from the ship in my weakness. Flogging, the potential penalty, was not a particular pastime of mine either.

Crouched, I unsheathed my dagger again and examined the blade's sharpness. The handle's dull wood was a chestnut colour. Although a common, mistakeable dagger, the blade was unique, meant only for me, and right then was meant only for the opium. I knew I was about to see and know new things. Things which no other dagger would bear witness to in that hold

After placing it into my hand, I tore the dull petals from the sphere, revealing a dark, brown cannonball-like, clay-like substance. Opium at last. I cut— vertically from the top of the ball and down toward myself, carving out a small piece slicing along an arc-shaped path. The promise of sensation appeared. I saw myself and my future in the dark mass. I ingested my portion, knowing I would likely vomit it back out later. The black paste reposed in my mouth like half-melted chocolate and with the seduction of molasses. There was no stopping once I started chewing it. The texture corrupted my mouth and I tasted its disgusting foulness, yet I did not stop— that goes for any vice and any intrusion into where the vice brings one— it is a flame which never goes out, but is only sometimes dimmed. And after sitting for some time, this light of mine turned back on, bursting its flame into a blinding brightness.

I sliced again and ate more, crouching over the dark orb. I beheld my numb body, numb face, and desperate tongue attempting to numb itself from the foul odour. The vice had a twisted taste. I put the gob of mania back into its folded petal covering and returned the shrunken ball back to its place, placing it in the compartment on the tray and returning the hay back into the box. Then, using the butt of my dagger's handle, I hammered the nails of the lid back atop the crate, sealing it closed.

First was the numbness, then came the rush and sensations. Oddly, I felt my crotch tingle. I was the only man I knew to experience the poppy like that, rather strangely. I looked around, sweeping the environment, searching for something, for nothing, in the dense air. I could relax if I tried, but I didn't believe it was the time. The lost skin and near-scabs on my fingers surrounding my fingernails began to rip and tear, repeatedly, as I used my nails to pry further into myself, under myself, in a frenzy. I itched only on the fingers, and I rubbed my crotch, lower belly, and face. Most people relax on opium but I grew excited. Sensation hit upon me every-where important to me, the head, the crotch, and the hands— limbs which a sailor guides and limbs that guide the sailor.

I laid down and forgot my body, immersing myself into the air around me. The ideas in my head danced around without a master. My mind had been liberated, and my thoughts were slaves no more. The reality of being a slave was a terrible thing and my gravest nightmare. Yet, there I was, lying beside a box full of enough opium to reach God. I was a slave to my curiosity. What is the difference between my knife, the poppy, God, and I? We were all useful and useless. We were all handled tools and controlling masters. Was I nothing more than a total slave? Was euphoria a feeling only slaves could know? I left my body and became subject to the experience in my mind.

It was not inspiration that I felt from her majesty, the opium— it was enlightenment. Then later I felt nausea and her bitter sway. Having consumed the poppy for the first time in many, many months, and the first time really alone, I felt deep awareness instead of blind, pleasurable sensation. I was not in control of my mind in that episode, but my eyes were indelibly opened. It was a tragedy to see me leave myself, but then again, all adventures require a vacation of some form, demanding something be left behind for the acquisi-tion of something new. All advancements entail a death and a re-birth. Death and rebirth in this life are ideas which Englishmen have no room for, as they are preoccupied with illusions of our one life, not visions of the many lives we lead within our solitary exist-ence. Death is wrong and taboo for Englishmen— unnatural and not of this earth. The concept of death is a sad one to them, those who were my countrymen. They believed the only good, true death, a divine death, was that of Christ. What they failed to realise is that we die every day. And to grow, we must have little deaths, for a flower doesn't remain in the soil or stay beneath the ground— it leaves and eventually it dies, having returned to the dust once more. And in its cessation, it serves to pollinate another. Life is begun by, made up of, and ends with death and rebirth. I felt reborn, laying on that floor. I felt like a flower would feel.

"Cole," a voice yelled down from the deck of shuffling feet above me.

I stared straight up to the ceiling, and I felt immense nervous laughter in my stomach. I tried my best to get up and look over the top of the crate to my right. I stood up and looked at a mirage of a man.

"Yeaaaah," I said, trying my best.

"We're looking all over for ye. Get up here." It was the voice of Daniel Smith.

"Aye," I yelled. Then "damn," I whispered to myself.

I walked back to the stairs of the hold. I walked up then kept going up, scanning through the crowds on each deck as I rose, until I reached the main deck. I looked around, curious at what summoned me from my alone time, looking to resent someone for this interruption.

"Swab the deck," John Durnburn, my only other master besides Captain Every, said to me in his uppity tone.

I turned around, and laid eyes on the man. He looked at me. I acted as if nothing out of the ordinary was happening within me. But I sensed he was onto me and my escapade. I roamed over to the group of men crouching on the quarterdeck, walking across the ship's body, out of my understanding, on pure instinct, toward the group. I squatted down and grabbed a sponge, filling it with water from the bucket. I began to scrub and brush back and forth to an untouchable rhythm. I stared at the sponge and the deck. I felt quite out of my element. Things began to slow down. Or I did. I reflected on the exact piece of wood I swabbed— it may not be there after the incoming raid. One lucky cannonball could put that sole piece of oak, or whatever timber it may be, out of commission. I could be put out of commission. I thought— 'I could die. Oh no, I didn't want to die. Not on opium. Not on a raid. Death is true and fine in theory, but horrifying in reality. No, no. Not for me. Not now, not then. No, no, no.'

I swabbed the deck for about an hour, migrating across the top of the ship with the group of swabbers. It was an unlucky day to be an able-bodied seaman, my formal role on the ship, and an unlucky day to be Captain Every's cabin boy, for I was not called in to sit in on any important business. I was not rescued and whisked away by privileges on that day. After the swabbing, I walked away from a group of the men, who were frolicking on the main deck around some spectacle. I returned down the three flights of stairs to the hold. What did the man say to Mr. Durnburn about my hiding? Was I suspected of stealing something from the hold? Was the hold off limits? Who knew. I was there and untouchable once again, hiding in the dark solitude for fun and in shame.

I stared at a piece of wood above me, similar to the one I first swabbed and contemplated on the quarterdeck. The journey had been a perilous one since the mutiny, since I was introduced to the true Captain Every. One doesn't know a man until one leaves port. I then knew the man. I'd seen plenty like him in the Navy and growing up in Devonshire. However, I never saw him in Devonshire. I didn't know what to make of Captain Every's future, let alone mine. I thought I would foresee the future on opium, but not that day. I did not have the frame of mind to forecast anything that day. I scraped along, passing time as I laid there alone in the hold, with the rest of the crew moving about on the decks above me.

I felt my heartbeat and my breathing, and felt so close to myself, so close to eternity. I did not make sense of what happened thereafter, as I kept escalating through different heightened sensations since the ingestion. I became someone else. I saw other things. I felt nauseous and threw up over my left side, a few paces away from where I laid. I still hadn't come all the way down. I kept going up— up, up and further beyond. I could not be bothered down there, in my lonesome. And I was kept company by visions of terror, visions of the future— visions of delight.

Chapter XI

BIG AND LITTLE FISH

Early September, 1695. My line was in the water before daylight. I was going through the motions the past month as we made preparations for the incoming raid. I salvaged some old Madagascar eel for use as bait from Pretty Al's kitchen on the second deck earlier that day— 'twas going rotten anyways. I heard the mackerel throughout those Indian Ocean waters was the best mackerel in the world. Fishing was not of any particular interest to me. I simply lacked the patience. However, when a raid was on the horizon and there was little to do but think of old wooden figurine trinkets and wait, fishing seemed mightily appealing. Anyhow, it gave me some calmness, I didn't need to talk to anyone but myself and concern myself with my line in the water.

I'd never caught a fish in my life. It must have been because whenever I'd fished, those five or six times with Thomas, I was more concerned with catching something rather than enjoying the act of fishing itself. The thought of mackerel, whatever it may look or taste like when caught, was more appealing to me because of my anticipation. As I waited, my line went wild, and for the first time I thought I might catch something. I did. I pulled and yanked for the thrill of it, having no interest in catching the thing anymore. I fished *to* fish, not *for* the prize of the fish. And that was why I had ultimately caught something, thus learning my lesson. My expectations had been permanently lowered since the first time I fished and caught nothing. I snagged a blue-grey flappy thing from the water, with some of the men howling at my triumph. It was slightly longer than my forearm. Maybe a mackerel. Maybe a youth, for I had seen much bigger sizes of mackerel. And looking at my fishing rod, made from scratch on the ship out of a thin wood stick, yarn, and a modified fork as the hook; I pulled the fish, a wild one, off from the grasps of my fork-hook. Then I set the pole down between the cannons and the rail, where it would remain for any further use.

I carried the flopping fish of clear, shiny eyes, and fine, beautiful scales down into Pretty Al's kitchen on the second deck. He wasn't around again, luckily, and I grabbed one of his long, thin-bladed knives. My dagger would probably massacre the thing. I'd seen men scrape and slice fish many times during my travels in the Royal Navy and piratical career. I'd always wanted to do it myself. I tucked the knife into the waist of my trousers, and grabbed two buckets— one empty and the other filled with water. I carried the mackerel and my instruments into the hold, alone.

I looked at a crate and set up my fishery shop. I threw the mackerel onto the crate. It was barely squirming. I placed my buckets on either side of the makeshift table and pulled the knife out, setting it beside the mackerel. I stopped for a moment and let everything pause. 'Don't mess this up'— I thought to myself. I looked at my prize, and began to slice. It flailed its last subtle flail then stopped moving. I scraped back and forth across the skin of the thing, shooting little scales everywhere. And after the scales were removed successfully, I lifted up his little fin-arms and cut off his head. Bloody thing. I then sliced his underbelly, removing the guts with my hand. I thought the stench would stay on me for some days. Maybe it would drown out my own harsh smell.

I dumped a splash of water on the crate, probably souring the goods within the crate, and cleansed the bloody guts from inside the fish, my catch. I threw the head, fins, and loins into the empty bucket. She was a blank canvas for me to slice a knife's masterpiece. I cut through the fish gently and courteously, from the original underbelly incision toward where the tailfin began. I flipped the mackerel over, revealing its whole sundered body. I mirrored my previous cut from the front of the fish to the tailfin, beginning on the top. It was all sorts of vulnerable. The two halves of the fish, soon to be my prized fillets, were eloquent, single, and flappable. I placed my hand where an accident could happen, on the side of the fish, flat. I pressed down gently, and began to repeat the cut atop the spine, further and further through the fish until the whole side of the mackerel was released. I chopped down on the beginning of the tailfin and released my first of the two fillets. I repeated this on the other side, until all that was left was the beautiful, near transparent tailfin, a spine, the meat between those bones, and the fillets. I tossed the skeleton and carcass into my bucket of waste, then rinsed my crate table once more.

I revealed my two fillets. I placed them skin down, and sliced diagonally away at their membrane, repeatedly, dismissing the red part of the pink meat. The knife felt to be a part of me, and I breathed it all in once more, taking uncanny delight in the smell. Henceforth, I understood the fisherman's delight. I understood him as much as I could. The fillets, with their pink insides and grey-blue skin on the other side, stared back at me. I put the long knife down. They were pearls. They were art. I felt like a master beginner.

A gunshot rang off. It was musket fire, either ceremonial or via combat, from the main deck up above. The feet on the deck above me began to shuffle fast and heavy. It was potentially a duel that was then resolved and a man was probably dead or wounded. Once again, the waiting around likely claimed the heart of another. We had been there before. Some men cannot adapt to the doldrum. I heard some activity on the other side of the walls of the hold, in the sea. Something metal, something dragging. Then the sound became louder and bumpy. This dragging occurred for some time, as I stood, frozen, trying to feel the ship and guess what was occurring. It was the anchor. We began sailing after the anchor was raised enough, and I nearly fell over from the jolt of sails catching wind. The gunshot was not from a duel. It was the commencement of the raid.

I wiped Pretty Al's thin-bladed knife on the edge of the crate, leaving behind dead fish residue, and then doused it in the water bucket. I poured the water bucket to clear off my cutting table. I tucked the beautiful blade into my waist once more, grabbed my two fillets in my left hand, and the buckets in my right. I walked out of the hold, ascending the stairs, less some bucket water.

I got to Pretty Al's kitchen on the second deck, still unoccupied, and left the knife in the cupboard where I found it. I hoped I could use it again. I left the empty water bucket, and carried the gut bucket up to the main deck with me. I went upward. The light barely cracked out beyond dawn, and I watched men moving about furiously 'neath the rising sun. I knew I looked like a tourist on our ship of competent men. I ran to the starboard rail, tossed the guts overboard, and dropped the last remaining bucket to roll around the deck with free will. I put my fillets against my stomach, creviced in by my tucked-in shirt. The raw fish stuck to my skin.

If Pretty Al had been in the kitchen, and if he had offered me opium, as he probably had stolen some too, I would have declined. But not because I could swindle it myself nor pay a shilling. Nay. I would have declined because I'd moved on. I only liked to do it once in a while. I may have been hooked, but I was not a despairing weakling anymore. And fishing or filleting could prove to be better pastimes than my lovely opium.

With or without opium, I had awareness— that heightened intelligence so few and far between, which only caters to and occupies the rarest of people. I was a bridge, a great connector. Opium only made me realise it again before I forgot. Awareness, sometimes exhibiting itself as wisdom, or deep feelings, is nothing more than being sensitive to the world around you and yourself. I had no tolerance for weakness. Weakness and awareness are often confused, but only by the blind. A healthy, perceptive mind shall create good, beautiful experiences no matter what. A destructive, blind mind shall create turmoil and misery. Opium only exaggerates the awareness of the mind, letting it pour over into one's life more than the sober mind ever could allow. If a boat had good sails and an able crew, she would use the weather to her advantage without question. If the sails and crew possess a poor constitution, the wind would ruin them both, imminently. Awareness is the prelude to wisdom, vision, and competence, needed for both sailing and living. Poppy intensifies the mind. And one's mind is the vessel for which to travel through existence.

I looked, having thought a lifetime's thoughts in a moment, at Captain Every on the quarterdeck, observing over the port side rail with his brass spyglass. I peered in the same direction to see a few ships— it was the convoy we'd hoped for— all with sharp angled latin-rig sails. The vessels were Eastern, so Eastern. They were Ghanjah dhows.

"All along, men. This is what we've waited for," Captain Every yelled.

I grabbed the arm of a passing man running in front of me, to stop him. It was "Lucky" James Brayden.

"Who fired?" I asked him, forcefully.

"Captain Every shot after the lookout gave word the convoy was passing to alert the other ships in our flotilla. It's on. We're all going," Lucky Brayden said, mirroring my zeal.

"Aye," I said, excited as all hell, and let go of him.

"To general quarters, lads. 'Tis time for battle," Captain Every yelled out to the scattering crew.

Brayden kept running, and I looked for Durnburn, yearning for orders and the hunt. I scanned through seas of men on the ship, and spotted him facing adjacent from me, ordering some lad who was climbing up the mainmast. I began to run and the fillets flew out of my shirt, falling to the deck. I left them behind. There would always be another fish to catch, whether large or small.

I ran up to Durnburn, who was half bent over.

"Orders, sir?" I asked him.

The crew of the *Fancy* operated like the Navy. Although I could predict them, I asked Durnburn for orders because I trusted his judgement as the bos'n. Aside from Captain Every, he was the most masterful seaman and navigator aboard, more so than our navigator.

"Just get ready to fight, Rollins. General quarters," Durnburn said as he looked up the masts at his men, our crew, occupying the sails and sheets like spiders, handling ropes with vigour.

I disengaged from Durnburn and looked around the ship for men in a position similar to me— men ready to shed some blood. On the staircase there was a grouping of lads, and some carried muskets. The gunner's mates must have been well prepared if they could spare some men to shoot and board the dhows. I sprinted over to the boarding party, where I was standing with the mackerel before. I walked into the group passing a flagon of grog around. It was about a dozen men— rough, gritty, and mean. They looked ready for a fight. Hopefully we had advantageous numbers against our foe. A twenty-five-ship convoy to a six-ship flotilla presented unfavourable odds. However, it appeared only two of their dhows were in our closest sight, as they had fallen behind from the pack. If many more of the Mughals should turn around, the operation would likely be my last as we would surely be devastated. I grabbed the group-grog, nearly empty from community consumption. I took a swig. I rarely drank, but drinking before a serious battle could be considered essential. The Mughal raid conjured more anticipation than any other raid or fight besides the mutiny. It felt different. It was different.

We sailed feverishly from our position in the Bab-el-Mandeb Strait, where the Red Sea ends, into the Gulf of Aden, where the Indian Ocean opened. We had to take one of their ships, and hopefully the heavier one which lagged behind. Maybe they lagged behind because their hold nestled the heaviest of prizes.

The distant Mughal convoy seemed to be scattering as I looked over the front of the bow and handed the grog to another *Fancy*-warrior. The ships, slowly in sail, dispersed. The distance stunted the two dhows in the rear— a large ship, likely a merchant vessel, and a small, speedy sloop, likely her escort. We were far off, having nearly missed the convoy. I watched their wooden fortress on the water move forward with haste alongside its little guardian. We were a pack of wolves chasing a scattering flock of sheep. And providence declared we would catch our two laggards.

The *Fancy* reached out ahead of our convoy, while the *Dolphin*, as I looked back over the stern to where we had laid anchor moments ago, was in the rearmost of our pack. Captain Every noticed too, for when I looked toward his direction at the helm, he yelled relevant instructions.

"Furl it all. Durnburn, wrap 'em up now," Captain Every yelled.

"Aye, sir," Durnburn replied without question.

Durnburn ordered and the men followed. We brought our sails up and tight, to slow down. It was confusing at first, having reduced our speed nearly to nil. I wondered why it did not cause Durnburn to question the captain upon setting our eyes on the escaping fleet. Surely if one did not see the lagging *Dolphin*, one would think Captain was acting cowardly or mad. We were the flagship, the head of our near 450-man flotilla of six ships. And we were slowing to bring our flotilla's flank ship upon us.

The other ships in our flotilla caught up then passed by us— all but the *Dolphin*. She, in the rear, finally caught up, while our crew stood around on the deck and quarterdecks, baffled at the captain's manoeuvre. He yelled over to the *Dolphin*:

"Captain Want. Abandon ship. Let yer men join ours. We have the speed today," Captain Every said to the captain of the nearby *Dolphin*, some distance away from our port side, with furled sails as well.

We lost time while their men prepared to board our vessel. I didn't anticipate how crowded our vessel would become by the advent of our American colleagues. All captains but Captain Every and Captain Maze were from the Americas. Captain Every and Captain Maze are Englishmen. Captain Tew is from England but was an American.

After some time was wasted while the haggard men joined our vessel, we set the poor little *Dolphin* ablaze, leaving it to burn into oblivion. What a time to scuttle a ship. We then returned to full speed and proceeded, moving fast ahead, toward our flotilla and our prize. Our telltales were firm. We may have had the speediest ship, but they all had significant headway on us. I didn't see us catching up or even surpassing the rest of our flotilla, due to the *Dolphin* gesture.

We sailed on our passage ahead, further and further from the lap of land behind us. We were wooden dogs unleashed upon the sea of blue and grey. Never had I felt such speed from our *Fancy*. She flew like an eagle. The sailing continued. The Mughal ships failed to impress me. Our flotilla looked to be catching up to the dhows in the distance. And we looked to be catching up to the remainder of our flotilla little by little as we streaked along. The *Amity, Pearl, Portsmouth Adventure*, and *Susanna* all gave chase to the two stragglers. And they were gaining significant ground. The *Amity* and *Susanna* led the charge as our *Fancy* carried the rear with the crew of the scuttled *Dolphin*.

A few more men emerged from our lower deck with arms wrapped around collections of muskets. We were ready. I was a sharpshooter in a party of sharpshooters— 'twas not foreign to me. I had a good shot. Then again, I was the same man who found there are more heroics in a sabre fight. The men of the *Dolphin*, of the American Colonies, had brought plenty of muskets too. Every man aboard on the main deck looked to be holding a weapon, whether blunderbuss, pistol, or musket. We had powder and angst for a thousand skirmishes.

I ran to the quarterdeck, protected by a privileged relationship to Captain Every. I stood a few paces away from him, without having to tend to sails and sheets under Durnburn's hand. I stood there with my back against the rail, looking at Captain Every standing in front of the helm as he shoved the spyglass up to his right eye. It was a gesture I'd seen him conduct about ten times since we began giving chase.

"Look," Captain Every said as he pointed out with his left middle finger to a spectacle about a league away.

The closer and smaller of the two ships, the Mughal escort, sailed in a serpentine pattern, with our four ships, in varying positions, steadily gaining ground behind her. That dhow was sailing back and forth, rattling off cannon firings at our flotilla as she sailed side to side. On her opposing turns in which the dhow faced our convoy, they fired their broadsides. It was an unusual manoeuvre, one I had never before seen. They must sail differently on that Eastern side of the world. I wished I had a spyglass to see the details of their movements. The feisty sloop was likely providing cover for the larger merchant vessel's escape.

The *Susanna*, the only ship in our flotilla with bow cannons, fired back at the Mughal sloop at a slow rate. Their position still lagged far behind the Mughal sloop and the *Amity*, whom the sloop began to engage with. The *Susanna* could not keep speed, for she was one of the slower vessels who only capitalised on a good head start. This continued as some time passed before the *Amity* caught up to the Mughal sloop, which had straightened out course. They engaged side by side, with both firing their broadsides about. The shots ripped smoke trails through the horizon, beyond our reach up ahead. The firing continued for four or five relays, some time. Another of us went down. The *Amity*, with our old, beloved, and experienced Captain Tew, veered off hard to starboard, away from the action. Deserters. Cowards. A Mughal shot must have spooked the lads. Or they'd lacked the stomach to fight through the first challenge— a poor characteristic of a man or men. Maybe they'd mortally lost the firefight. Either way, we had to continue, even if the morale had slouched at seeing the experienced Captain Tew's vessel and crew flee the raid.

As the pace continued for a long time, the *Susanna* failed to keep up, trailing our small convoy with her lagging speed. Our *Fancy*, proving her superior speed despite an increase of crew and supplies, had caught up to the *Pearl* and *Portsmouth Adventure* as well. We sailed in line abreast, with the *Fancy* on the far starboard end. Eventually we took the middle and sailed in vee formation, leading the charge with the other three vessels by our side and then later behind our lead. All told, we'd lost two vessels and one crew in the first leg of our dhow hunt.

Hours passed as we sailed on. Those hours turned into a day, and then into multiple days giving chase to the menace, who was likely damaged from the cannon fight with the *Susanna*'s bow cannons. We were determined to get them, for the winds and the fates favoured us. I felt confident, despite our early losses.

After three or four short days of chase and anticipation, which felt like several lifetimes, we closed the gap and could faintly touch the escort vessel. The small dhow was fast, but the *Fancy* was faster. We caught up to the ship, with Arabic or Persian alphabet on its nameplate, rendering it unreadable to us Europeans. The rest of our flotilla fell far behind us. Thus, we assumed no camaraderie, leading the vanguard alone. Catching up to her broadsides, and getting in firing position at general quarters on her starboard, the enemy raised the white flag. Dozens of the Mughals aboard their dhow stood with arms up in surrender. No resistance, no cannon fire, no musket fire. We brought our ship beside theirs, and the flotilla caught up slowly but surely.

"We give them quarter, but we cannot allow prisoners upon our ship, lads," Captain Every ordered us with a soft voice before we were to walk aboard the Mughal vessel, which had claimed more than the *Amity*'s spirits days ago.

We got close enough to jump across the void of the long fall to the sea. I shouldered my musket by the strap and helped put some planks across the way to connect our two ships. Some men simply leapt or used grappling hooks and ropes to swing across like gentlemanly monkeys. I kept my musket loaded and at the ready in case the Mughals were putting on a trap. Captain Every went aboard first, before any of the *Fancy*'s crew or our colleagues from the American Colonies aboard could. He held his two pistols in his hands, and I couldn't help but think of how weak those Mughals were and how merciful they likely hoped Captain Every was. They found themselves in a position of ultimate disadvantage.

Although quick, manoeuvrable, and capable, the small escort dhow stood no chance against our even faster, more ferocious, out-numbering man-o'-war. Their crew, made up of men and boys all dressed in beige-tan garments and colourful threads, looked at us like stunned deer. We boarded then entered their vessel, and made it our own, searching holds, rooms, cabinets, everywhere for loot and necessary supplies. I went to the hold on their lowest deck, still looking over my shoulder to spot my vertical musket barrel and the occasional Mughal around me. Despite the enemy's surrender, I'd never been more on edge. Gold and ivory composed the heavy loot we found on the vessel. I carried a fair share and brought it back onto the *Fancy*. None of the supposed brave men of the American Colonies carried their weight, they only guarded us European *Fancy*-men whilst we did the heavy lifting and searching.

After about an hour of trafficking captured men, loot, and sup-plies, I found myself looking at their pile of Mughal muskets, pis-tols, sabres, and daggers flying into the water. We had effectively disarmed their small arms access, by putting it into the sea. As for the cannons, well, I did not know what we would do about that, but either way we had our other three ships coming upon our rear. We commandeered all of their gunpowder and armaments for our rearming and their further disarming. Any firefight with them would evidently result in the Mughals' swift demise. Mughals were smart enough to know when to surrender, and additionally smart enough to stay surrendered when it was advantageous to do so. We left them behind, acquiring no prisoners nor adopting any Mughal as crew, sparing all.

The loot made, so far, for a successful raid, but if we were to split it amongst our flotilla mates, it would not be considered, by any measures, a profitable raid, especially when accounting for the price of the raid's anticipation, planning, and damage. It was simple to calculate— there was little to be taken in the loot department, since we took more supplies, weaponry, and provisions than gold or ivory from them. Once all of our men returned to the *Fancy* and we left the Mughals to wallow in their defeated surrender, I noticed

Captain Every back at the helm once more, standing statue-like. No new orders were given yet. The men of our crew and those of the other ships in our flotilla all chattered amongst themselves and looked to our ship for direction, for the lead. I decided to step up.

"Captain Every, what was that ship? Why didn't they have any heavy loot?" I asked, knowing it was the escort already, only wanting to see his response.

"An escort. The ship they guard is far ahead, and much fatter," Captain Every said, turning his head around to look into my soul.

"Do we give chase... Captain?" I asked, stepping above my station and circumventing all of the higher ranks who I was supposed to receive orders from.

"Aye, Mr. Cole. We always be giving the chase. Today is another one of those days. There is not enough to vacate, for too much hath already been sacrificed to let the fight down, and there is still too much to gain," Captain Every said, in a moment of truth.

"How do we know about the other straggler vessel, Captain? How do we know it carries plunder?" I asked Captain Every.

"We don't, boy. But do or die, we shall bloody find out," Captain Every said, putting me in my place.

I retreated and stared ahead at nothing but the open sea. My auditing did more for the Captain's conviction just then than any challenge from an enemy ever could— I questioned his judgement. One must always tread carefully when questioning a captains' judgement, for it was a sensitive subject and their rank grants them the power to dismantle you. It was clear, after I disengaged from our banter, that the distinguished officers on our vessel looked at me with narrow gazes. I saw Captain Every for what he was more and more every day. He saw me too. He trusted me. I trusted him. But I felt a calling coming from my gut. An urge to abandon his service. He was my master and my most frustrating competitor. I was no Jonah nor Judas, but I was Rollins Cole, a man with no sea-father, no master, no captain. Freedom drew me to the ocean, but I found myself simply changing ownership, not liberating myself. I was a wanderer, a pirate, and declared myself nobody's boy but my own. At that moment, after challenging the captain, I decided I would no longer sail with the man after we reached a safe haven. It was time for me to sail my own sea-lane, even if it was for another captain. Maybe a better captain— a captain who knew I could take his place at any moment, who would provide me true rank and respect. I had been conditioned by Captain Every for some rank or ulterior purpose. Had he groomed me to surpass him, as all true masters and mentors must do, whether they realised or liked it or not? I was uncertain of his motives, but certain of what I needed to do.

Onward. We pushed forward, breaching ahead of our flotilla once more at the sprightliest of speeds. It was an honour to be the lead ship of the flotilla, but undoubtedly a death sentence awaits the head of a vanguard. I had waited all my life for that rush. I'd searched and rummaged through the eyes of every sailor and foe I came across during my naval, privateer, then piratical career for something like that. I did not see that fear in any man before. But I felt it at that moment. I'd imagined something like that moment for many days as a boy in Devonshire before I took to the Crown's Navy. I would soon transform my fearful vision into absolute reality, if we could only catch our prize, if we could catch our Mughal foe, if we could catch the big fish.

Chapter XII

TO RULE THE WORLD

We were like falcons on high, covering great distances. After a few more days of drawing closer and closer to the dangerous dhow, our flotilla had sporadically spread out and broke up into a single leader, a duo in the middle, and another soloist in the rear. The only land in sight was a gravely distant island bit, as we had escaped all coasts. The small bank, or cay, composed of sand, was no more than one-hundred paces long by fifty paces wide. Looking as far as the sights went, the *Susanna* had managed to fall further behind, effectively removing itself from the fight soon to come. We'd lost touch with them. We aimed to cut down the dhow before she could enter Mughal waters.

Meanwhile, in the time since vacating the waters of the escort vessel, the men's spirits on our vessel had remained in an anticipatory hue. There was determined silence. No more doubts. Even if we had lost another ship's aid because of the long, perilous cruise, it would not have fazed our crew. We knew not exactly what we pursued, but I thought it was blind faith and hope, above all things, that kept us on the journey. Hope that the raid would be different from all other raids. Hope that we would live to see the other side of the conflict. Hope that the matters of the escort ship did not slow us too much. Hope guides a man out of the ashes, out of the necessary depths life has cast him in. Hope that he shall one day change. Hope that he shall seize the opportunity of a lifetime when it appears. Hope, although dangerous, strengthens us when it's paired with action. Hope must be accompanied by steadfast movement toward an objective. For hope without action is a paralyser.

The *Portsmouth Adventure* and the *Pearl* had maintained their relative position during the pursuit together, bridging the distance between the *Susanna* in the rear and our *Fancy* at the front. Less all doubt, I saw the big, bullying figure of the Mughal prize ship. It started as imagination then became real. The ship contained all manner of contents I could only guess at. A ship which held a mystery was infinitely more seductive and attractive than a ship whose contents were known. There could be anything aboard such a vessel. But I was certain this big fish, with all of her prizes and personnel imminently within our reach, would come at a steep price during the incoming ferocious battle. I stood, leaning over the bowsprit and looked through a spare spyglass. The dhow was there. I did not think a Mughal ship with that many decks and levels had less than forty to fifty cannons. The greatest prizes often require the most vicious of fights to overcome, earn, and maintain her. Oh, it may be terrible.

We sailed and caught up, using a fortunate wind to showcase our great speed to the universe. The small cay was close by. We were much further toward Indian territory than we'd planned or hoped for. The danger fired us up, and I was more on edge than I'd been during the entire campaign. The terror of capture near their country spurred us on. Or at least that was my experience. Men's fearful hands spilled flagons of grog about, in tantrum-y shivers. Our back was against the wall and we could not hide in a canal once the raid was finished. We would have to flee altogether, as fast as possible, to avoid running the risk of meeting an Indian fleet.

Making our approach, the *Fancy* was alone to face our foe once again, as the flotilla fell far behind. As soon as we met the ghanjah dhow, and sailed next to her, the volleys began. Cannons from every which way fired all at once and without any trammel. Wood splinters and metal shards chaotically flying everywhere elicited more yelling from the men than any wounds could have caused them to screech out. Severed, wood slices of our *Fancy* chopped and lodged into my arms. It stung me and felt acutely painful. There was much blood, but I told myself I was lucky once more as I removed the splinters, in pain. Holes and shark bait were made of men on the unfortunate ends of cannonballs. The screams were of agony, ferocity, and pleasure, when they weren't screams of the wounded or dying. An oh-so-great release of discharging cannons was launched by our group of Europeans and men of the New World against the Mughals. Despite the overwhelming thoughts and heightened presence of neighbouring death, gratitude overcame me as I was replaced as a gunner by a member of our increased crew numbers, thus making me a rifleman. I did my best to take cover, holding my musket. I looked up and down her spine. I incited some marksman prayer upon her, hoping, asking her to be accurate and true. Asking a musket to protect me that day. The duel looked as if it would more likely result in my sword protecting me, or the pistol Captain Every gave me, for the close hand-to-hand action would be ferocious if they did not surrender. The loudest explosions went around from firing and damaging all in my sight. The cannon war was great and terrible.

We sailed side by side in stride, firing everything we had at each other. Volleys after volleys were sent off, as I sat, almost defecating my pants, sweating from the sun, and fearing the high chance I'd meet the Reaper. I kept firing my musket as fast as I could, remaining on the far side of the stairs at the stern of the vessel. I watched cannonballs of black trailing off and away beyond the other side of our ship into the sea, never to be fired or touched again, for they made craters into the water and plunged down to the depths. Plenty did not. Plenty of cannonballs hit man, boat, or both. The main deck of our *Fancy* was exploding, so I stayed under cover, only whisking my head and arms out to let off an occasional shot. I was glad to be an able-bodied sailor who had no bos'n's orders to heed. I followed only my own timing of aiming, firing, reloading, and covering. 'May God have mercy on me and if He were to take me, and he likely would, may He take me quickly', I thought. 'Take me swiftly as lightning could.'

I heard a roar and the sound of our men cheering over some little triumph in the firing. I peeked my head around the edge of my cover 'neath the stairs to see the Mughals' mainmast wholly punctured and tipping. There was no escape for them anymore. And as I looked at the big timber splitting and twisting and jerking then falling, an explosion went off directly below their main deck, halfway toward the bow from their centre. In their gunning, a cannon must have exploded from too many loaded charges. Or we must have fired the perfect shot at the perfect, incendiary moment. Regardless, an advantage. Their vessel likely had seventy cannons. They needed no escort. They were the bloody escort.

Our ships were sailing closer and closer. One would think the cannon firing would cause their entire vessel to combust. That would be an easy way out. Their men, who were coming into my closer view, must have dropped echoes lower in morale, even with their previous, obvious firepower advantages. A pair of blows like that, the mainmast and explosion, were sure to be a demoralising pair. The Mughals were in our grips. Captain Every did not hesitate— he took advantage of their stooping morale amidst the chaos of carnage by bringing us closer to their ship, and slowing to match their dwindling speed. Soon, both of our vessels were bobbing in the ocean at a halt. They had no escape.

We came up alongside her— the great, fat, tall Mughal vessel, waiting for us to decimate her. I looked at some of our other marksman parties coming back up from the lower deck stairs, ready to take the fight to the enemy. The mugs of grog were once again passed around. They gracefully flew up, around, and tilted, spilling their contents about, as if timed to music. I went over to the cluster and butted in. Cutting through the group, I got my hands on the grog and took a swig fit for a mammoth, then I belched and yelled.

"Attaaaaack," I screamed, full of berserk excitement.

The men looked at me with confusion and intensity. They were laughing at me, momentarily ignoring the violence of the day. It was not a jest for me, but to them, whatever I did was a jest. Naturally, I was a fool to all of my crewmates, as any fairly arrogant, aware, young man would be. But they were greater fools than I. I was aware of my deficiencies, but they were blind to their own, this crew. They sensed not my lack of seamanship nor my lack of sailing talents. Yet I should not have been a pirate or sailor by any standard measurement of innate seaman talent. Hell, I was an able-bodied sailor, and I was afraid of heights. My intensity as a fighter and skills as a marksman were not doubted, hence I was lucky to be entrusted with a musket. But nobody could possibly be blind to one of my most supreme strengths— I was a great learner. And the culmination of my entire life's experiences, including those of the past week giving chase, had caused me to learn much. I learnt to yell prematurely, especially as an outcast of the crew.

I had an epiphany within the Mughal-hunting party consisting of criminals, thieves, murderers, and learners— all of these pirates standing beside me— that it was the best moment of my life. It was the moment of truth. There, right before we boarded the vessel and found out what we were really made of, facing a most likely end, was right where I needed to be. I thought I may die a rich man one day, or die poor on that day and rot in the sea, or die poor some other day. I may even die that day with the most treasure I had ever laid eyes on, in my hands, on some unknown Mughal ship in the Indian Ocean. I may have never told the tale, I thought. But I would know, in my heart, that at the very least I was there. I was alive. I was free. I felt, right there, alive once more. There was life in every breath I took as I faced death and did the dance with the Reaper once more. To Heaven, to Hell, to Valhalla, to the Elysian Fields, to the Locker, to the void, wherever I would go, I'd go with fury and with no regrets, simultaneously leaving all of my future behind and no ounce of courage behind. I had truly lived.

As the cannons were slowly abandoned and their sounds dwindled into silence amidst the yelling, we finished our rounds of unspoken battle preparations and faced the ship out there in the sea pitted against ours. They were unable to escape, for their mainmast was toppled and they were left behind by their convoy. The gods watched us perform from above, around, and below. If there was a Kraken, let him come. I approached the space between our warring vessels, the middle, the great fall down to the sea between the two castles of boats touching wood. Their vessel's height was a whole man and a half or two taller than ours, therefore we all had to climb to board the tall dhow.

I prepared my musket to fire, loading the ball, powder, and charge, then approached the middle to fire my weapon. I aimed across. I looked up, my musket erect, and pointed forward across the sights to see a spotter in the crow's nest up high throwing explosives at us. I shifted my aim to him, directly toward his heart, and fired. She fired straight, my trusted musket, and the target fell, joining his rear where his boots stood a moment before. He slowly rolled over and fell from the heights and descended into a disappeared land on the Mughal dhow.

Instead of the once small crew of marksmen who would have led the front of the storming group of pirates, nearly all of the 155-man crew stormed at once. Eventually the fearful near sixty men of the *Dolphin* aboard joined us, after some hesitation. Grappling hooks, bombs, angled long-planks, and musket fire went up and spanned the distance to the Mughal ship. The foe looked to have hundreds of crew, armed and dangerous, likely more on the lower decks. I removed every measure of goodness from me and left it on the *Fancy*. We hopped the rails, landing our boots on the Mughal vessel, and many men were immediately pierced by the first crackling shots of muskets, effectively shot back onto the *Fancy* or left to fall to the water in between the ships. Many were sent back by musket fire and blades. Pikes and bayonets charged at my face from every direction. The cold iron threatened my existence from head to toe at every pace. I froze at first.

Going over the top was a bloodbath. My crewmates around me were losing their lives in the dozens. I saw men surrounding me being shot and stabbed and tackled from above, around, and below them. I could only tell the Mughals apart from us by the colours of their clothing, hats, and dark skin. I engaged with a pair of men in front of me, having made it onto the deck— one with a musket and the other only a sword. I threw my discharged musket at the man aiming his musket at me in order to discombobulate him, and then charged the swordsman. I jumped up, into, and through him, slicing my sabre clean to the other side of his torso. I watched the blood of my earlier wounds from the wood shards dripping down to my hand and the ground. The momentary distraction pulled me away for what felt like a lifetime. Then I turned to the man on my left, almost recovered from my throw who had a gash on his head bleeding from contact with the butt of my thrown musket. After a few parries to deflect his charging bayonet, I whipped my sword, putting a slash across his neck. He spun away as he fired above and past me, missing his post-mortem shot. It happened in ten full seconds. Both men were dead.

I looked around and saw men pulling others up from the ground, and equally, men being pulled down by the wounded with daggers and clubs. Men were being choked. I couldn't help them all, my crew and allies, and it crushed my heart into a pebble, as it had already hardened to survive. Blood and bodies were being slipped on. I tripped and felt a Mughal grab my ankle. I put my sword through his gullet, effectively letting some animal in me take control.

I screamed, clawed, and grasped at the men around me, only seeing red and seeing the brown skin of my enemy. Those were the only two colours I saw, red and brown. I was deaf to anything outside three paces from me. Cannons could make me deaf, as could musket fire and screams of agony. But my spatial awareness only let the closest of threats and stimuli be accounted for. Musket firing rates began to fade as the time available to reload shrunk smaller and smaller until, eventually, only blades and hands and heads and elbows and knees could be used to fight. The skin of my enemies, the skin of my allies, and the blood of all drowned my sight. God had drifted from the close action on the boat. He was furthest from there, at that moment, that hour.

My aggression, which then was a life of its own, took itself out on every Mughal soldier and sailor around me. The enemy must be killed or must surrender before we were to even think of treasure. I knew no faces in the fight, only those wearing the same pirate uniform as me or the enemy Mughal uniform against me. It was a binary fight and chaos surrounded me, distressing my forward progress.

I held both my dagger and sword in my hands, left and right respectively, and kept looking in circles, trying to find a target taking advantage of my shipmates, looking to save my colleagues. I saw a man, about to fire his musket, with a brown neck, and I ran up to him and thrust my dagger through his left shoulder and swung my sword across the back of his knees with one fell swoop. He fell and a *Fancy*-man or *Dolphin*-man caught his falling musket, aimed, and fired a round off next to my ear, deafening me, but eliminating a charging Mughal who I then turned around and saw was closing in behind me for the kill. As the Mughal fell and tumbled to the deck he slashed a cut across my shirt. I was not cut, but my loose and blood-stained shirt was torn. The ally sacrificed my hearing and shirt for my life, a worthwhile exchange. I was indebted.

I saw men asleep from death and succumbing to wounds. Some came back, having recuperated, to thrust daggers into men's boots and ankles, cutting them down. There were no rules, only us vs. them, on both sides of the fight— tribalism, on the boat. I did not see Captain Every or Durnburn or Captain Want or Thomas Howard or any man whose face I could ever forget. I was a nameless combatant and every other man I saw either had a friendly or enemy face. We were sailors and soldiers fighting, nothing more. Eyebrows, eyes, brows, hairs, mouths, noses, and throats— that was what I saw and aimed for when I was not cutting down knees and thighs or discharging blades into chests and abdomens. Severed arms laid on the deck around me and I found myself with the original man whose life I saved and who had saved me, back-to-back. We were covering one another from the hind, the only safe strategy that worked in the rabble of harsh combat. Part of me felt released and liberated during a conflict such as this, the long-winded, tiring, purely rush-filled conflict. I'd gotten my lifetime fill of valour that day.

Not only were our key men and ranked pirates nowhere in my sight, furthermore I did not see anything resembling a captain or officer among those Mughal threats being eliminated in triple the ratio as to our losses. I looked upon a Mughal below me as I stood over him. He put his hand up, pleading for mercy, and I thrust my sword into his head through his eye, putting him where he belonged. It was not worth the risk of leaving him alive so he could slice my crewmates' ankles. I reflected for a moment how different the two parts of me were— the vicious, savage, tribalistic warrior and the soft, sensitive, contemplative sailor. It was not Mughal territory anymore, as I saw less and less live Mughals, so I could let my guard down for a moment. But I gathered my focus again and continued on. Whipping my head around left to right thus seeing Europeans and men of the American Colonies, it became clear it was time to venture below deck, into the worst, most congested danger.

The smell of smoke overwhelmed the battle, and it was the ship on fire. I climbed over the sprawling mainmast to get to their staircase. I walked across bodies, aiding most of the men alongside me as we fought for our desires. I swung my sword across the occasional wounded Mughal. The fire and smoke came from the same area as the explosion that took out a few gunner squadrons before. It could have been an hour or three since our fight commenced, for I had lost all sense of time in the violent haze.

The *Pearl*, along with the honourable Captain Maze and his crew of nearly forty, finally arrived, dropped anchor, and stormed the Mughal vessel, providing ample reinforcements to clear the lower decks with us. As I ventured across the deck to descend upon the near defenceless lone wolf of a ship abandoned by its pack, Captain Maze's men scoured the ship in stride with us *Fancy*-men and Captain Want's men of the deceased *Dolphin*. I got to the stairs leading to the deck below, where I was behind the many venturing to clear out the ship and look at the damage, fire, cannons, and chaos below. I knew it would be a tight conflict. I looked ahead and spotted I was some fifteen paces behind the back of Captain Every's red jacket. He was at the front, engaging with Mughals who were slowly backing away and dying fast. Some of them succumbed to hopeless panic, focused more on dousing the fire rather than firing or slicing back at us, their charging enemy. They cowered behind cannons and swung their jackets in an attempt to smother the wicked flames. But they kept fighting.

We pushed further into the heart of their resistance on the second deck and in front of the captain's quarters we saw across the way. Men were coming out from every cabinet and quarter of that deck, surprising us and cutting some of us down as they rapidly delivered death. The tug of war melee went back and forth for a long time during our close quarter engagement, pushing fast and slow, back and forth, causing men to fall over cannons, cannonballs, and bodies. I slid my way from the back of our phalanx-like formation attack through to the frontline, beside Captain Every's lead, to protect the captain. But it was every man for himself, tribe against tribe. Every man's eyes were piercing and full of daze. The rush of combat was a violent dance with our enemy in the shadows of the vessel. All pirates are Chaotics in some way, doing everything in a dance, a frenzied search. The dance that day was a search for the Mughals' surrender, so none of us would have to die anymore. Above all, it was a search for treasure and also their officers, who held the keys to both of those bright end-goals.

I found myself grappling and choking Mughals who threw punches and wrestled with me in turn. I was sliced across my chest and my shoulder by a Mughal blade, but by some miracle I had survived the bloody wounds thus far. Many others weren't so lucky. We pushed on. As we eliminated a mountain of Mughal fighters and their bodies piled up around us, the path to their captain's quarters was lined with a mound of corpses. A band of us, including Captain Every and myself at the front leading various *Fancy*-men, *Dolphin*-men, and men of the *Pearl* behind, reached the door of the captain's quarters. The remaining pack of us hungry, malevolent wolves continued down the stairs to explore the lower decks for enemies and prospects. Luck, advantageous explosions, experience, and flat-out macho combat ferocity, on the hunt across lifetimes, seas, and a Mughal ship, led to our victory slowly coming to fruition. We had no drummers, no rhythm, like the Navy provided. It was the sounds of men, iron, and gunpowder that provided rhythm to the conflict.

At the door to the captain's room, we faced a locked entrance and aimed to overpower the blockage. The dozen or so of us, with the path finally cleared behind us, and more paths being cleared below us, pushed and heaved our shoulders like a united battering ram, trying to break through the doors, its barricades, and its hinges or swivels. We could feel the door straining, moments away from giving in.

"Heave men. Heave like the Devil's in ye," Captain Every yelled to edge us on.

We overcame and finally broke through, splitting open the doors and splintering the planks that were nailed across the doorway. It was boarded from the inside. Bursting into the room, I fell over forward along with a pair of other tumbling men. Kneeling on the ground, I looked ahead and saw a cabin containing a dead Mughal body with a big, bloody, split head. A smoking blunderbuss was in its hands. He looked like an officer, the corpse laying there. The room was vacant, following what must have been a desperate suicide. Wherever their captain was, he was either dead or had acted cowardly, for that was not the captain there. We got up fast and followed Captain Every down the stairs to rejoin the warfare.

I readied my gifted flintlock for any more surprises on the ship, loading her with powder and a musket ball. I kept the blood on my dagger then sheathed it in my boot. I was beyond being scared, having overcome fear, for action had removed my thought and worry. My attention was bottlenecked, and only instinct ran me. My fear was converted into terrifying, charge-filled hunger. As we further infiltrated their ship and descended another deck, filling it with life and death, we came across passengers and civilian Mughals forced into submission, not dressed like soldiers, but with weapons on their person.

"They've armed their passengers," Captain Every identified.

"And why do they carry passengers on the vessel? Why are there passengers on a ship of soldiers?" I asked Captain.

"They did not expect our convoy. These may be overflow passengers from other ships in their convoy," Captain Every said.

I wondered if the passengers or prisoners had armed themselves or were forced to. Regardless, I had no room in my heart for mercy at that time. Let fate do with those Mughal civilians as it would, I thought. I did not give a second thought to the terror they must have felt toward rage-filled, hungry pirates until later. Upon seeing us, the civilians dropped their weapons, we spared their lives, and we separated them from the pistols and swords.

We reached another room and once more our passage was barred by closed doors again. It looked to be a large room, not like the close quarter, small rooms scattered throughout the vessel. This one was different and we were not on the lowest of decks yet, where provisions, cargo, loot, the hold, and peasants still remained. I sensed men of importance remained hidden behind these doors, confirmed by the shared look Captain Every gave me as we neared the doors that halted us. Upon trying to open them with a single push, our intuition was confirmed. We grouped up once more, heaving as a team, and burst through the locked door. This time I kept my footing after barging through. Staggering into the new room, we saw a spectacle of sunlight piercing through large windows and illuminating the dark, shadowy ship.

A trio of slave girls with sheer garments barely covering them, held swords with pitifully uncoordinated hands. They trembled in fear, streaming tears, naive to what they'd been thrust into. They had been employed by their masters behind them for protection, but they shook without end in paranoid fear of death. Captain Every approached with his two pistols in his hands, swords holstered, and pointed the pistols at the Mughal slave girls. They dropped their swords immediately, screaming and crying in surrender. They faced the floor and prostrated themselves on the ground, knowing who their masters really were. Behind their prone, weakened bodies, was a dark man with a trimmed, black, and grey beard and pathetic eyes— the captain of the Mughal vessel, not worth sparing.

Captain Every did him right. The *boom* of Captain Every's firing pistol startled the women behind and in front of the captain. The Mughal captain was shot in the foot. While he did deserve a cowards' death for hiding behind slaves whilst his crew fought and died, we spared him for now— an intelligent decision by Captain Every. I heard the boot steps of more and more pirates behind me entering the eventful room. Behind the thin layer of the three, proned, unarmed slave girls and a wounded man who was foolishly once elected captain of that vessel, we saw women who looked to be royalty— a young, beautiful lady with a mature, competent disposition accompanied by two other women, likely her attendants. The leader was hard to lock eyes with, for if she felt you look, she'd look right back. It was a stand-off with the female. Her dark complexion contrasted with mine, and her Venus-like figure piqued all of our curiosity. Next to her stood the two beautiful, pure, bejewelled lady assistants, but their station was obviously below that of the central woman. They were not slaves, for their jewels, silk, and eloquent garments covered all three of their bodies with regality. The smell of their perfume overcame our inhibitions, intoxicating whatever values we'd somehow held on to, and we forked them further over to animal instinct and attraction. I sensed the worst brewing in myself and my fellow men at the fragrance and sight of those soft, tender-looking women.

"Do they speak Arabic or Persian?" Captain Every turned his head to the side, asking any of our crew for vital information.

"Mughals speak Persian," a voice yelled from our crowd behind.

The central woman spoke her foreign tongue, almost inaudibly, and asserted herself. She acted invincible and stepped forward in majesty. She must have thought she was untouchable and protected by her privileged position, which was foolish, for we were pirates not diplomats. She tried to challenge us with her words and confident manner. The lady talked briefly.

"The lass thinks there are laws here at sea," Captain Every jested and the crew laughed, after responding to her foreign Mughal words.

Those were the first laughs I'd heard since the hellish laughter on the main deck earlier, which could have been more than three hours ago. I thought I knew what would happen next for the woman and her assistants— either violated and killed, violated and spared, or spared altogether. I did not want to know. My heart may have grown cold from the murder and fight, but it was unbearable to think of doing something to a woman against her will. I left that to the sailor-pirates who lacked souls.

I turned around, vacating the room of three women and almost two dozen hungry, unsatisfied pirates. I did not want to see. 'Twas a waste if our men would terrorise them without second thought— the girls could have given us information on the ship's treasure. I thought, hopefully, Captain Every would utilise the situation and not waste it.

"She is more pleasing than jewels, lads," Captain Every said to his men about the royal girl, proving he was smitten or lustful, thus neither confirming nor denying my prediction of his actions as I walked away.

I continued to the stairs, away, and went down another deck to see law and order thoroughly executed on the passengers and prisoners. Our crew had already separated all of the women and children from the men, in order to isolate the strong threat of their able-bodied masculinity. Their brig was lined with their own prisoners and the adjacent deck was overflowing with scared passengers. The Mughals could not defend themselves. Any man or lady who looked like an imminent threat was cut down. Barely any unarmed were killed, but some of those who appeared to threaten a lottery of murder were. We cleared all the quarters and rooms, herding the passengers and the harmless into an observable mass until the fight was over. Their prisoners stayed in their cells in the brig. By then, the ships had stopped their minimal motion, both having dropped anchors by whichever of us pirates still remained above the decks.

I descended another deck to get to their vacant hold, the only important place left on the ship, beyond the clusters of passengers, prisoners, and royal prey. I was where Captain Every should have been. I would do what captains forget to do, as a venerable pirate would. Laying my eyes on the chests upon chests taking up the entirety of the dark hold, I saw the closest thing to the Holy Grail on the ship. I approached one of the dozens of identical chests and placed my hands on it. It was lockless, likely guarded until we arrived and slayed all of their guardians. Opening it, I feasted my eyes on gold and silver coins in the hundreds within the chest. There were likely tens of thousands of coins within the remainder of the hold saturating my proximity. Slivers of diamonds, gemstones, and ivory harkened my attention.

I retained no hopes of what sow we would reap from it, but a vision spontaneously entered my mind. The sight of those shiny jewels and coins vanished. What lay before my mind's eye was the vision of a man totally free from the firm grip of any other man's captainship ever again. I saw myself as a retired pirate, a privateer, or a man of high society, away from the freedom and pillaging on the seas. The means to those ends sat before me, all around me. It was my eureka. I loved my freedom as a pirate, but after that day I'd had enough. I knew I would have the means to retire from piracy and do whatever I wanted. Life on the run was not appetising anymore, nor was the threat of the hangman or the sword. The ultimate prize, the ideal that drove every pirate on the face of this earth, was ours. We reached El Dorado. I began to imagine a life beyond piracy when Captain Every then stumbled down the stairs. He set his eyes on the chest I squatted in front of, with its glimmering contents revealed to him. He looked around the room of booty.

"'Tis enough gold to rule the world," I said to Captain Every and he maintained his look of awe.

Chapter XIII

BEYOND PENANCE

What happens when the captain of a ship full of passengers acts cowardly in the face of a raid? Pirates overtake the vessel and treat the passengers the same way as their captain— for usefulness and for sport. Advantage, excessive liberties, and satisfaction are taken. Without a shepherd to guard or guide their flock, it is only natural for the sheep to be taken advantage of. Blood drips, tears run, tears dry, and people drown. This is what happens.

I stood as one man amidst a shepherdless Mughal flock subjugated by our pack of pirates. That day, on the evening of our great war, we rested shortly after loading the precious golden, silver, bejewelled, and ivory encrusted cargo into our exquisitely stocked hold — the pay of a lifetime, the pay of a century. It made all the carnage worth it, at least for the men who didn't kill for the fun of it, for they had already been gifted with satisfaction. The price was about thirty dead or dying *Fancy*-men, twenty dead *Dolphin*-men, dozens of wounded, and most importantly, our humanity. And after their hold was emptied of their sums of treasures, we put all of the prisoners of the raid war into the lowest deck. Their sailors, soldiers, men, women, and children were all stowed down below. I watched hundreds of people get paraded down the stairs like slaves to the king of the hill. And on the decks above, closer to the light and further from the depths, we would soon make further use of our Mughal subjects. In the brig, however, the Mughals' original prisoners were merely viewers to the spectacle, as we left them in their chains and cells. I stood by the wall between the cells and the open area, spectating the parade of Mughal prisoners, held against their will, being sent down to the bottommost of the dhow, stripped of treasure and dignity.

Upon walking to the second deck, where we had battled through the fire that raged hours beforehand, I viewed the royal girl walking into their captain's cabin, which once displayed a Mughal suicide as its primary furniture. Behind the girl was Captain Every, swinging his open hands at his side, dancing to this woman and her enterprising company. He entered his temporary quarters without a care in the world, undoubtedly mesmerised by her perfume. The door closed behind them, thus secluding their entanglement to privacy. Upon final glimpse of her before those doors shut, I could identify the regret and sluggish reluctance in her body. She did not seem remotely as excited as the captain about their likely dalliance.

Whilst Captain Every took leave in the room with the woman, most of the crew followed suit where they could. All except Durnburn and those spectating him. Durnburn was charged, as I could tell through simple observation, with torturing crew members, soldiers, and passengers over the whereabouts of the rest of their ship's hidden treasure, if there be any. Their hold was emptied and the rooms were searched, but a pirate left to his nature would sniff for more, for greed guides him. Durnburn started with their wounded captain, their false shepherd. Captain Every left us to manage ourselves. We stood around, loitering. It was only a matter of time until we took advantage of the Mughal flock. Their captain was incapacitated, mirroring our captain's example in a more painful, less fortunate way. Durnburn brought him from the room we found him in, his foot bleeding incessantly, and dragged him to the middle of the floor on the second deck. A band of us watched, but our captain occupied himself behind closed doors.

"Start by telling me what treasure ye had down below. Let us waste no more time counting," Durnburn said to their captain, holding the Mughal's lapels in his dirty hands, squatting and keeping the captain laying on his back.

Their captain would likely lose his foot since blood of his leg was funnelling out of its wound. The captain answered Durnburn in some Persian or Arabic confusion. The language barrier would not break our will, the will of Captain Every exercised through Durnburn. The language barrier would only bend our will. Durnburn, thinking fast as a good bos'n would, snapped his fingers at one of his able-bodied sailors standing by. Then he pointed back to the *Fancy*'s direction where it sat bobbing around on the other side of those wooden walls.

"Fetch me some gold coin," Durnburn said to one of the surrounding mates.

The lad ran off in haste while we waited. I leaned against the wall as usual, the position I took on when I'd curb my feelings into a blank countenance. My body rested up against a cannon of theirs that was settled quiet, no longer in use. The wait for the pirate to come back took too long for my comfort. Some of our group vacated the deck, venturing below to join other pirate activity. Some shifted above toward the main deck where the light was strongest. I stayed frozen, attached to the cannon.

The errand boy came back, holding some coins. Durnburn grabbed them from the lad and held them in his spare right hand whilst his left remained fastened to the Mughal captain's jacket. He held the coins up, pressing them in between his and the captain's line of sight. The captain's eyes followed every movement as Durnburn pointed the coins in every direction of the ship. Durnburn inquisitively cocked his head to the side, indicating to the wounded captain that he wanted to know where the rest of the coins on the ship were. Lord knows if the Mughal captain understood. He may or may not have followed, since he only shook his head with eyes open as wide as possible. Durnburn, his patience exhausted by the impossible conversation, jolted the man's lapels, and effectively his head and neck, to the floor, leaving the captain for the rats. Our bos'n walked away from the Mughal. We went below, following Durnburn to the next lowest deck, and looked for leads in the last open room of cannons. It was a lost cause for the language barriers proved insurmountable. I abandoned the hunt and made my way to where no cannons remained, departing the search party in efforts to find something more appealing to pique my interest.

I traversed down to the tertiary deck which contained the brig and many cabins, above the lowest deck where the many civilian, sailor, and soldier prisoners remained in an empty hold. The belly of the beast, the Mughal purgatory where I stood, had at least some features worth inspecting. I'd already seen the Devil in my captain begin to inspire the Devil in all of our crew. I did not want to be a part of this repulsive crowd. I walked to the brig where I had been some hours ago.

I ventured behind the wooden entrance door. There, the dirty and the grimy were revealed to me. The unwanted men who see more than many think. The people who know, but do not yet know how to conceal or contend with what they know. The objectionables. I approached the iron cells and the Mughals' own prisoners. Black cast iron enclosed the offenders. And hiding in the back, next to another Mughal prisoner, was a woman. The only lady in the brig. She was a dark Mughal and possessed a grimy, bewitching, menacing appearance. Her dark hair was strewn in front of her face. Her eyebrows disappeared into the forest of her black tresses. If ever there was a lady-prisoner I'd come across in my days, she looked like she'd been in the dirty prison for long.

Beside her was a man, likely her protector and only executor of her survival in the small cell, equally grimy but with a face and bright eyes that displayed no apparent sadness, remorse, or regret. His gaze was tranquil in the quite untranquil hell he occupied. The man was tall, light brown, and able-bodied, with an abundance of life in his eyes which suggested to me he'd seen another world away from this one. He looked as if he'd seen the whole of life yet had not lost his optimism. I immediately trusted him. It was a strange sentiment, meeting a person and immediately trusting him. I saw myself in him, beneath the bodies and masks that so separated us all. If I could have removed the personification, I was sure I'd see his spirit was kindred to mine.

When a person looks upon a pirate or a prisoner, two quite similar humans, it is often menacing fear and condescending morality that strikes first and hardest for pirates. The Mughal prisoner before me was a breath of fresh air. He looked like a child amongst coffins, a green-leaved oak posturing in a burnt forest. In the other men, and this rare woman, I saw darkness around the eyes, sadness in the gaze, and an exhausted spirit. This one prisoner was lively and unburdened. I sensed no barricades between us as we locked eyes after I assessed the woman beside him. I wanted to befriend him immediately and uncover what they'd both done to arrive there for they piqued my interest. He was potentially my only companion within a thousand leagues, besides wherever Thomas was, something told me. Something I could not explain told me this. I waved my hand to softly and kindly request his approach, as if he was not the sewage of society— likely how we were both looked upon by most strangers.

"Come here, lad," I said, acknowledging it was not the words he would understand, but the tone in which I said them— I was approaching as a companion and a hopeful ally.

The man grabbed his female companion's hand, shielding her from their forward path, and they walked toward the iron bars between us. The other prisoners abided and got out of the way with some slight difficulty. It dawned on me— even in a vessel which held all the gold we needed to make our wealthy way back into the world, back into honest commerce, I still found ways to interest myself elsewhere, appeased by that which gold could not buy. What had gotten into me?

I took another step closer toward the cell, more intimately, to the approaching couple. I got a better look at their faces. I was honoured by his presence, the man who protected the woman, albeit likely with some favours in exchange. Maybe not. Maybe they were true, pure companions. Maybe she was one of his many Mughal wives. I wasn't sure.

"So ye're a pyrate," the Mughal man said in a strange accent.

The surprise hit me with a rush. I did not predict this man would have multiple tongues.

"Ye speak English?" I asked him.

"Some. Enough," he said.

"And how do ye know this, sir?" I asked the older gentleman.

"My father and his father before him have learnt some of your European languages. They were merchants," he said.

"Oh, my," I said, shifting my posture and looking deeper into his eyes.

"Do you speak Persian or Arabic? My wife cannot join this conversation if we continue the English," the man said.

"No, sir, I do not. I am an Englishman, not a man of the world," I said. "What are yer names?"

"My wife is Zeenat and I am Jalal," he said, introducing his kin and himself.

"I am Rollins," I responded.

I stood there, with bars and lines between the Mughal pair and I, seemingly even further apart than our separate worlds had distanced us before our meeting. But the gap had been bridged. I heard many, many loud footsteps of pirate boots above heading down the stairs, on their way to the other side of the deck and down to the lowest deck. I paid it no mind. I lacked the interest and bothersome nature to join the ordeal they would inflict on whoever they brought back up, whether it be torture for speculated information or murder for sick pleasure. I was not a man fond of those forms. I thanked God for my innocence, being one of the youngest aboard, for it may have protected me from the imminent regret and tarnishing of the soul that follows those wrongdoings.

I looked into Jalal's eyes and could not determine whether or not he heard and fully comprehended what occurred some distance behind me, on the other side of the wooden wall. I hoped he was ignorant. The stairs, after being occupied and then emptied, had become loud and lively again, with more feet accompanied by the struggling screams of predominantly women and girls being dragged up the staircase to the deck or decks above. I knew what was to happen. Jalal certainly knew. I was not the only man, I hoped, of the *Fancy*'s, *Dolphin*'s, and *Pearl*'s crews who did not partake. But only Heaven knew. I did not want to go out there. I would rather be a man of the *Portsmouth Adventure*, still aboard their own vessel, away from the imminent madness.

"Tell me, sir, what got ye locked in here? I may be able to get ye and yer wife out of here, and maybe all of yer fellow prisoners free," I said, unknowingly establishing some authority in the room.

"Do you want to know what they say we are in here for, or do you wish to hear the true story of what we did which landed us here?" he said.

"Both."

"In the eyes of the Empire, we were once humble people on our way to Hajj, on this very boat as passengers. And now we return, as rotten prisoners. She— a heretic. And I... well... I was an architect."

"An architect of what?" I asked about the mystery.

"Let us not talk of those things. I am in no mood," Jalal said and shook his head.

"Talk of what? What mysteries have ye built?" I asked.

Jalal scoffed at my forward, curious nature.

"I have built mosques. I have built official buildings of the Empire. I have built homes. But these are not the creations which landed my person here. On more than one occasion, I was an architect of mandirs— Hindu temples, but disguised as simple compartments," Jalal said to me, superseding my knowledge, with sternness.

"I am no expert on the world of the Mughal, sir. I do not follow," I said.

"I've told you, I care not to discuss it," Jalal said sternly.

"And what is to come of yer fate? I suppose whatever sympathies ye and yer wife have toward yer work? They have brought ye here? What happens next?" I asked.

"We're going to be executed. An example will be made of us," he said.

In all of the humanness I could possibly muster, I looked deep, as deeply as I was capable of, into his eyes. I tried, without moving a hair nor my tongue, to express my sadness and condolences. His fate may be an ordered death, but I felt no surrender from the man's spirit. I did not look at his wife at that point, only at him, into him. I was carrying his burden in my own heart. And I could not let it down until it was settled. I'd feared the day, for many, many nights. I knew it would come. I'd always known it, but I did not know that which it brought would command me more than my own volition could. I feared I had become the pirate with a heart.

I began to walk away. Jalal reached his arm through the cell holes, brushing my arm in an attempt to grasp it.

"Where are you going?" he asked.

"I shall return, friend, fear not. The great pyrate, Rollins, does not desert a friend." I reassured with a small jest, unsure whether that statement was as true in reality as it was in humour.

I walked to the wooden wall concealing those cells. I turned my head around and watched Jalal and his wife walk back to the corner where I first saw them. I left the room, headed to where the hall of great damage and silent cannons remained, and walked to the stairs, empty once again. I heard crying and talking from the deck below. I wondered who guarded the Mughals, who kept them contained in the lowest of decks. Their whole convoy had abandoned them. But should they gain enough fortitude and boldness, and if we insufficiently guarded them, it was conceivable that our prisoners could overpower our numbers, even after the *Portsmouth Adventure* had later caught up to lay anchor with us. I feared there was a sleeping dragon in our captive cellar, composed of hundreds of heads.

I walked up the stairs two decks above, where the dead Mughal captain lay in the middle of the second deck. But what the deck contained, besides a dead captain, useless cannons, and the room of our captain, most importantly, were dozens of bodies strewn about. Our crew, Captain Want's crew, and some of Captain Maze's men terrorised the live bodies of others. The Mughal captain's corpse displayed a sword sticking erect, lodged in his dead, lifeless chest. But there was plenty of life around me.

I looked about the deck, appalled at the numbers of limp Mughal women, mostly stripped. Their private parts were used up and exposed for all to see as even more live Mughal women were being violated and beaten to a bloody pulp. The rumbling I heard coming from this deck, and the one below moments beforehand, was thus far concealed by the crying and agony of the lowest deck, where the prey were held before being taken to this terrible, free brothel I stood amongst.

I saw multitudes of men bending Mughal girls and women over cannons, their undergarments shredded and their skirts lifted to cover their faces. Oh, what their terrible faces must have looked like. I did not wish to see. Some women crawled through the ship's cannon gunports and slipped out into fresh air. A few fell through the holes, screaming their way down as they plummeted to the deep blue sea, seeking a drowning sanctuary less painful than whatever I could call what occurred there. They crawled out right in front of me. I could describe that deck as nothing other than 'one man's Hell is another man's Heaven.' I walked away, coolly forcing myself to accept that was the nature of my life— the work of these modern Vikings around me. Where had love gone, in these men's hearts? Where had conscience gone? I counted at least five Mughal men sitting on the floor with slashes and scars across their chests, leaning their defeated backs against the cannons with abdomens exposed while our men punched their cheeks and noses, and cut their flesh. All done presumably for information about their treasure, but more probably for the sheer sadistic release, cloaking their intentions under the widely accepted notion of 'hunting for hidden treasure.'

I was no saint. I had parts in me that were tempted to join the men. Join both parties— the raping or the beating. But I would not. And while I stood there in my boots, on the wood of a deck within the heart of the dhow, amongst many men and women, all strangers to me, I renounced this sentiment of piracy. I rejected this element of the profession and hobby which afforded me superior, infallible freedom. I rejected the darkness of the torture which comprised only a small sect of piracy, the same piracy which illuminated my light of curiosity, Chaoticism, and the exploratory life it all afforded me. I rejected the nature in my crew. I rejected the nature in myself. It was beyond shameful to witness this abuse, and yet I could not force myself to stop any of the ravishment.

I headed up the stairs toward the main deck, to see the sun and all of its exuding light consumed by the dark, inevitable horizon of twilight. I looked around the main deck to see similar notions and actions— Mughals being violated, Mughals being beaten, Mughals being tortured, Mughals being murdered. I wanted a Mughal girl for myself and yet I did not know if the stain of moral violation would ever leave me should I have proceeded with that action. I already had one occasional demon— my dear poppy. I did not want to be cursed, followed, or plagued by another, her cousin— lust. Lust and the control over a lass, even if it was a Mughal foreigner, against her own powers?— I could not. I thought of the women I grew up around. It was evil around me on the *Fancy*. But would my intervention be righteous either? I would be dispatched with words, arms, or swords as swiftly as any Mughal prisoner. Is that noble? To die protecting what is already dying, inside or outside? Was I a weak man or a practical man? I felt powerless and shaken by the ineptitude

I saw myself within every pirate thrusting his hips into a weakened woman and shooting his knife or fist into a defeated man. And I knew the terrible crew of mine could see themselves in me, later in their lives. But that would only be the case if they noticed me witnessing them. And I did not think they did— they were too preoccupied with their orgy of ravishment and violence to look around, to look at any man of their crew standing apart on the stairs, completely baffled and agonised yet not surprised at their actions in the slightest. I understood them. But I still chose not to join them. I could not expect any of them to understand me in my baulk. I felt coldly alone in the Indian Ocean's heat.

I once thought Thomas understood me— at least the Malagasy Queen affair was born of mutual passion, not one-sided foul play, as far as I could see. Maybe there was some shred of hope to be had for that friend of mine, whom I did not see anywhere, whom I rarely saw. Maybe the men who shared the same dismay I did remained off the Mughal ship. I could not imagine it was beyond any man's nature in the convoy to have taken a Mughal woman to their own ship, to their own quarters, for their own desires. I'd rather not have known. I didn't want to witness more of it should I have gone back to our *Fancy*.

So, I went back to the only refuge I had in the flotilla consisting of the *Fancy, Portsmouth Adventure, Pearl*, and the Mughal vessel with its unreadable foreign notation on the nameplate of her stern. The *Susanna* never made it. We lost them in the days of sailing chase for this Mughal vessel. I went back within the hub of the dogged madness, back to the brig, where Jalal stayed in chains with his wife. I could not go to the other ships in our convoy, for they were strangers to me, not my territory. I wouldn't dare go to the *Fancy* and chance an observing of any more terrors. And so, I went to an innocent stranger.

I descended down three flights of stairs and walked across a deck of empty rooms to the brig once more. I walked in, and paced toward my earlier place beside the wall of iron bars. I remembered I'd forgotten to make an effort to free them as I said I would. My friend and his wife were sitting where they were earlier. Most of the prisoners seemed to occupy their same positions. I lacked the patience to stand in one place for more than a few moments. But imprisonment must force someone to cultivate that skill.

"Friend, I want to talk about what happened to ye and yer wife. I wager it is more pleasant than what occurs on this ship as we speak," I said, directly to him.

Jalal rose, taking his wife, Zeenat, by the hand, and walked to me with regality.

"Do you really want to know what happened?" he asked me, testing me.

"How about this, my hesitant friend— ye tell me a story, and I tell ye a story. I could use a good story at our present junction," I proposed, tipping my head to the side, speaking the same unspoken language.

He looked at me. He shed a slight grin, and quickly squinted his light brown eyelids at me, seeing into me. His dark brown eyes darted to his wife's direction, then to the ground behind my back left flank, then returned to me. The man was calculating.

"Do you wish to know the story of my wife? Or of me?" he asked.

"I want—"

He interrupted:

"I shall tell you my story, if that is what you want, now. But if you wish to hear my wife's story, you must tell one first," he said in an unordinary exchange of vulnerabilities.

"I am talking to ye, and if what ye tell me is true of yer wife's language barrier, I am only talking to ye now. I want to hear the truth of yer story," I said.

"Very well," he said and took a deep breath. "I am an architect, as I said. I have done much work throughout Delhi, surrounding areas, and places as far from the capital as one can go within my country. My country is a Muslim nation, ruled by a harsh Muslim man. I am officially a Muslim. My wife is a Muslim... officially," he said, preluding to a conversation of religion I foresaw.

"Ye're not Muslim, are ye?" I asked.

"I care not for religion, Rollins. My wife does care, but not for that of Islam, not for the Hanafi, Sunni Islam, which our Emperor endorses with his violent and forceful decrees. No, it is my work which lands me here, not my wife's religion," Jalal continued.

"Did ye topple a building on a man? What did ye do?" I asked.

"I told you earlier. I was responsible for numerous projects of varying importance, which caused eyes to be cast on my subsequent actions. I was the primary architect for some of the Empire's government building projects and many more private, commercial buildings. I started designing structures with an enigma on the blueprint. Eyebrows were raised and people asked questions. The wrath of the Emperor's unforeseen royal whip was cracked when I, with my respect to humanity and Zeenat's religious beliefs, constructed buildings for customers of the Hindu religion. It is not a crime to design for a Hindu. But it is illegal to stow a hidden room for prayer within the architecture. They utilised the space privately, covertly, as a temple for their banned religious practice. I was foolish," Jalal said.

His wife, bored of standing and observing a foreign conversation, sat down next to him on the grimy, wood floor. She put her back against the iron cell, looking despairingly in the opposite way, away from me.

"I got away with it. Or so I thought. And I came here, during Hajj, to Mecca via this ship as a way to publicly demonstrate my loyalties to the Emperor's religious dictations and stances. I went to Mecca, did what I was supposed to do, and was to return home having, in some sense, cleared my name and played the part of a devout Muslim. But I was not cautious enough. I was once again privately in discussion with some powerful but secretly Hindu families of our destination's country to construct homes with secret rooms to serve as Hindu temples. It had been years since I last did any of the private temple constructions. I never should have gotten myself caught up in it. I wish these people would have kept their business to themselves. It was because of this recent attempted resurgence in Mecca that I was found out. I'd thought of leaving my country. And if we could travel to another nation, a denser Islamic country, maybe I'd still receive some offers of a similar nature, as I thought I had garnered a reputation by now. I did, unfortunately. Even though I turned down these projects, despite incredibly favourable payout offers, when we boarded this ship a second time, to return, she and I were arrested. Although I played the game, I was found out. My reputation as a Hindu sympathiser was affirmed and my reputation as a successful architect was destroyed. As my life itself shall be," Jalal said.

I found myself with my arms crossed and my hand on my chin, seeking some form of self-comfort in the gesture. I did not know what he may have made of my view on the subject, the poor fellow.

"Ye know, where I come from, Catholics and Protestants do the same thing to each other. It is all the same, friend, wherever ye go— two men with different views, yet seeing nearly the same thing, keep finding ways to kill and ruin one another. Everyone wants the same thing, Jalal— Heaven on Earth... But the path to that place, never-ending as it is, is littered with people murdering one another over the method to traverse it. I do not agree with what is happening. But it is universal, it is constant," I said. "But how did ye not only learn English, yet command and master it?" I asked, trying to change the subject.

"That is another story, my friend. I have already told you one. You must return the favour," Jalal said to me, kindly.

"Ah, yes. A story. What do ye know of the saints?" I asked him, beginning to divulge in my childhood Christian instruction.

"Saints of Christendom?" Jalal asked, shifting his weight.

"Yes," I said.

"Nothing sir, but I do not want to hear the story of another, I want to hear your story. I thought that was the arrangement," he said, maintaining the integrity of our minor deal.

"I shall."

"Good."

"So, my friend, I once knew of a young lad. He became a pyrate by circumstance as much as by choice. He sailed around the world and met many men and a few women. But only two lads ever compelled him— his captain and a fellow shipmate he'd met along the way. And over time, these two close companions, both from his own country, became shadows, distant relatives, instead of friends to live and jest with. These were not the young pyrate's hopes or futures that he had envisioned. But regardless, he kept on, for what else was he to do?" I began.

"Continue," Jalal interjected.

"The lad was full of hope. Surely two friends drifting was a small matter. Surely two doors slowly closing did not affect the thousands of other doors that could open. So, he continued and sought people out that interested him. For that is what provided him much excitement— finding friends in life. He wanted the profound, so he searched the world for it. One day a man struck this profundity. Although he was a different man, from a different walk of life, the sailor believed they shared remarkably similar maxims. The lad, although a pyrate, an often lowborn trade, was astute and cared more for learning and experience than much else. The man he met lived in squalor, in misfortune. And the young lad felt he was chosen, if there is such a thing, by God to rescue the man, to give the fellow a second chance at life. And so, the young lad set about his method of freeing the man... And methinks he freed the man," I said, then fell silent.

"You think? What will happen?" Jalal said.

"Well friend, ye told me a story of ye, and told me of what ye believe yer future holds. I told ye a story I know of, of me and what methinks my future holds. But neither of us know what destiny will provide for us," I said, speaking as a prophet for the time being.

"Rescue?" Jalal asked.

"That is another story, Jalal. We have made a deal here to share story-for-story. One-for-one," I said.

"Fair. You are sharp," Jalal said.

"As sharp as my sword. And I find ye to be wise as well, my friend. I shall be retiring now, for it is getting darker and darker. I'll find my way back to my ship. Stay sharp," I said, with a grin.

"And you do the same. Good luck, Rollins," Jalal said.

I nodded in mutual respect, and backed myself away from the cell, further and further from the prisoners, leaving the brig and walking away. I got to the stairs and ascended two decks to see the second deck nearly empty of our convoy-men. At its centre was still the dead Mughal captain and a sword in his chest, as erect as Excalibur. Around him lay some dead Mughal bodies, with a hefty stench. Blood puddles dotted the floor. I did not hear my crewmates exfiltration, although there were many less Mughals and pirates on the deck. I must have been too immersed in my conversation with Jalal. The room which Captain Every had entered earlier with the royal woman was vacant, and its doors stood wide open. I continued up and reached the main deck. I looked around. The night sky surrounded our convoy. The deck was devoid of any live Mughal, only those tied up and dead or dying. A few shipmates stood about and I began to walk across the deck. I walked to the rail, hopped over onto the walking plank, and set boots back again on the deck of the *Fancy*.

Albeit our boys and men tried to haggle information of hidden treasure out of the Mughals by means of molestation, torture, and murder, we did not find anything more. We had plentiful supplies and ample treasures, yet somehow believed the ridiculous notion that the fruitful vessel hid more ripe fruits for our harvest. We did take everything, believe there was more, and interrogate for more, exercising complete carnal liberty that day. And yet we walked away with nothing more than blood on our hands, stains on our souls, and material riches. Captain Every did not instruct us to do so. I had no knowledge of whether Durnburn was instructed to torture for information or not. But Captain Every did not stop us either. A crew shall always mimic the master. The flock shall always follow the shepherd. Greed, hunger, desire, and lust overtook him. He succumbed to his lower nature, and could not harness his desires into something higher. Then again, I did not know for sure what transpired behind those closed doors between him and the royal girl— maybe something of a more compliant nature, a congenial, mutual engagement. But the crew did not, by any means, have a lofty experience such as that. They did not inflict any actions upon the Mughals which those Mughals, in turn, would have found mutually beneficial.

Their jewels, their exotic clothing, their robes, their skirts, colourful garments, skin, eyes, and hair— it was all ruined. The images of the Mughal, who appeared so different to me before, were tarnished. What does the East bring to the hands of Western pirates? Beautiful and neutral means vulnerable to our corruption and our abysmal, carnaging desire.

I went to sleep then awoke the next day, rising from my hammock of despair to put on my boots, gather my blades, and stow my pistol on my person. I put myself back into some sense of duty and orderly preparation. My first and only objective was to find the keys to the Mughal brig, maybe on the dead captain. I doubted a musket ball could pierce through the cast iron cell locks. I walked away from my hammock and looked around at our crew's sleeping quarters to see I was one of the last to rise, as I had been one of the last to go to rest the previous night. I walked up to the main deck, blinded by bright morning light, and looked to see a near empty deck on our *Fancy*. Across and above, over to the towering Mughal vessel, I climbed.

The crowd of my shipmates and *Dolphin*-men were divided amongst the Mughal vessel. Mughal prisoners were being pushed around by the arguing pirates in the act of claiming slaves. Men and boys bickered and scuffled over their choice of private prostitutes and servants. I heard yellings of "aye, she's mine" and "no, he's mine" and so forth. It was the wildest of free-for-alls aboard the Mughal vessel. Captain Want stood, as I saw him once again after not seeing him for an entire day and evening, on one side of a small cluster of people. He towered over all, standing on the Mughal vessel guiding groups of slaves being enveloped and gathered for travel onto our *Fancy* in pairs and triads. Women, wearing barely enough to cover, and weak boys bruised and beaten, both obliged, ready to serve their new masters. There was much chaos and yelling in the crowds of our dominant crews. And silence hailed over the Mughals, omitting the yelling and screaming of families being torn apart in single transactions. Captain Every supervised the rough exchanges, standing tall upon the rail above the hysteria, grasping the shrouds. I could not see keys on his person. Durnburn may have had them. I impatiently watched the large spectacle for some time, as any effort to walk toward the heart of the lower decks through the horde of rowdy men and desolate prisoners on the Mughal vessel would likely yield no success and only cause frustrating blockages. I had to wait.

After spectating the prisoners and slaves being transported to our vessel, I saw Captain Every descend from his high position on the shrouds and encroach to directly handle the transport of some prisoners. There were four women coming his way, all young and primed, no older than I, stripped of all but slim undergarments. They were bound up in ropes. I was curious why the royal girl was not in the slave quartet. Surely Captain Every would not concern his hands in the direct transfer of four arbitrary slave girls onto our ship. He would leave that to the dirty fingers of the crew. He was not touching, but regardless, he was there, up close, managing them.

"Bring them to my cabin," I heard the captain order one of our lads who had his hand on another Mughal woman.

Captain pointed the way then walked them close to the edge, as they shuffled along, before they reached the plank between the Mughal vessel and down to our *Fancy*, where the wooden sides kissed, touched, caressed, and met. The appetite of the captain's eyes burned holes into the backs of the girls in front of him as they were then handed off to one of our lads. However, the lad only paid them a fraction of the attention Captain Every did, for he was occupied with his own Mughal booty. In a sweeping, unsupervised gesture, the four girls hobbled then skipped then ran away, still bound together in their ropes. They escaped up the ship, a few steps from the Mughal bow and beyond the grasps of any of our men. Four women, in white, leapt and fell to the sea.

In a four-woman unison, the Mughal slaves who were tied and likely to be further used for one-sided sexual pleasures or financial sale, jumped off into the Indian Ocean, together in a group suicide. The laughing, yelling, and heckling beside Captain Every fell silent. The erratic movements of the crew and the still postures of the two captains slowly fell to a deadly stop as all stood shocked in spectatorship of the hesitating captain. All of the boys and men froze. We watched the void where the four slave girls had stood a second ago, before they jumped and plummeted to the sea, to four fateful imminently drowning deaths. Horror paused every moving thing on the ship. Although victims had killed themselves the day before by sliding through the gunports, those four were an entirely different spectacle.

I did know, and yet did not know, what it signified, this omen. Yet their choice was practical and human. It was enough. The suicide spectacle, claiming four female lives more gracefully than the rest of their lives would have been aboard our *Fancy,* left their mark. Few men ventured onto the lower decks of the Mughal vessel after it had happened. Most of the men returned to their ships, their stations, vacating Mughal territory. The women jumped, falling like martyrs at the Tarpeian Rock. And we fled. How courageous of us. It made me wonder— is a man at some given point beyond penance? Beyond forgiveness? Beyond atonement? If so, were we stumbling upon that far-off point?

Captain Every believed he was not, and later exercised some fashion of penance. I was awestruck by the horror-spectacle. I felt I was one of the last remaining pirates on the vessel with remorse, as I took a seat and tried to collect myself while remaining on the main deck. Some men went below, but I was deeply bothered, and had to stop where I was. Under Captain's hand of direction, a drama was arranged shortly after— penance, in Captain Every's style. Having gathered the majority of the Mughals still alive onto their deck whilst surrounded by our venomous convoy of snakes, Captain Every delivered a speech. He stood above all peoples, holding onto the shrouds again, talking down to us all, wounded Mughal and hungry pirate alike. After gathering myself back up, I forced myself to suffer through his speech, despite the keys' returning monopolisation of my attention. I wished the fat crowd in front of me, constraining my path, would part like the Red Sea.

"Hear ye, hear ye, Mughals. We have elected to set ye all free. Set ye free from the weights and burdens of yer treasures. And we've let ye go onward to yer destination. Four young women died today and my heart is broken over this. No more innocent blood is to be spilt and we shall not take any of ye with us as prisoners," Captain Every said aloud.

I hoped Jalal could hear what a comedy that was from his brig cell down below, echoing through the timber walls and floors of the Mughal ship. I wished he was there to hear those pathetic words on the lips of a guilty, irredeemable man. Beyond Captain Every's care, Jalal would likely be one of the only Mughals who could understand such talk in our captain's English tongue. I was near foaming at the mouth to hunt those keys then liberate the man and his wife. But I waited for the speech to finish and the crowd to disperse.

"We have decided, eye for eye, to pay a price of four souls for the four we've taken," Captain Every belted with his voice.

I saw the benefit in the language barrier. If the Mughal men knew of his audacity, they would likely have abandoned all survival instincts to jump and attack Captain Every right then. Four lives? What difference does it make? We had taken dozens, a hundred innocents. The dignity of countless people. And four would set us straight in the casualties of this war? Nonsense.

"Four of yer own hated, dirty prisoners, we shall take off yer hands, and maroon them, making peace with God, yer Allah," Captain Every said.

I violently entered the crowded mass, aiming to pierce my way through the behemoth of moving bodies that beleaguered the stairs. I pushed through the beginnings of the crowd and feared the worst. Then my fears were confirmed. Members of our crew, emerging from the stairs, brought out a corresponding quartet of dishevelled, dainty, dirty prisoners from the lower deck brig after Captain's signal wave. My path was blocked and my view was mediocre. The prisoners stepped forward, behind and in front of a handful of our crewmen armed with multitudes of muskets and blades. I froze to get a glimpse at the prisoners' faces. I saw the Mughal heads— two unknown, faceless prisoners walked and behind them came Jalal and Zeenat, all bound in ropes together.

I ran back through the mob a short ways to Captain Every, both forgetting my place and honouring it, forgetting Durnburn, the dead Mughal captain, and the keys to the brig. I was met with the side of the captain's face after making my speedy way toward him.

I knew he saw or felt me approach him in his peripherals, as I stood below him and the shrouds he grasped onto.

"Captain," I said.

"Don't interrupt me, Cole," Captain Every said without looking at me.

"Captain, do not take those prisoners. The two in the back, the man and woman. Let them go," I urged him.

"Challenging me in front of my crew?" Captain Every tried to scare me off with his authority as he kept looking dead ahead.

"Captain, the man... he... he can be of use. I should have spoken earlier. He speaks many languages. Good English. He is an architect. He could join our crew and be a carpenter. He knows the Mughal waters. He can lead us to more ships. And, and, the woman... she can be of use too. We can certainly find a place for her as a nurse or cook or something until we sell her off," I said, trying not to shudder.

"We have a Carpenter in Fulton as good as any, and Pretty Al cooks like shit but it's warm," Captain said then spoke back to the crew. "Who of ye lads shall row to the cay, yonder?" Captain Every said, pointing to the little sandbar nearby. "Who shall bring the offerings to the sands?" Captain Every denied me aloud, and continued addressing our crew without sparing a single gaze for me.

Some crewmen stepped forth, raising hands, to take the job of bringing the sacrifice offering to the nearby cay. I had become an insect, a begging insect. And Captain had the face of a stranger, the gaze of a superior that paid no mind to a pest. It was lost, my cause.

"Sir, have God and practicality drifted from ye? We can use that man. We can use him," I said, destroying decorum, accepting that I could join the marooning or enter the brig myself for my exploits.

Captain Every turned to me, looking down from the rail where he stood holding onto the shrouds, resting one foot on a deadeye. He leaned his head in slowly and spoke without remorse.

"There is no God at sea... I am the one... I am God here," Captain Every said to me. "Now shut up and watch."

He pulled his head back. I fell stone cold silent, looking at the foreigner whom I addressed as my captain, then at the foreigner whose life would be lost. Jalal looked back at me, hearing what had just occurred and knew what would occur.

"I shall take the task, Captain," I said, challenging him one last time, despite his minute fury.

"Ah, yes, Cole. Be of use now... go along to the cay," Captain Every said sarcastically, containing an underbelly of rage, pointing his arm out toward my prisoner-friend. "On second thought, Cole, let us put a vote to it," Captain Every said, stopping me, surging one last beat of hope into my chest.

"Aye, Captain," I said properly.

"Lads of the *Fancy*— Mr. Cole here hath strong sympathies for the Mughals, especially Mughals who can speak English and plug holes. In light of our great deal, Cole thinks it worthy of tarnish by only taking two of their prisoners to the cay to be marooned... What shall we do, gentlemen and thieves? Spare two prisoners and debt us two more still to God? Or follow through and relieve our burdensome debt? Do we repay the Mughals four favours or only two?" Captain Every yelled, looking around the deck.

"He is an architect, he can make anything. He knows these waters. He can speak English and Arabic and Persian and French and Spanish. He is useful, that man. We can find two different prisoners for the offering," I said to my crew, pushing the envelope, lying to save a life, yelling for democracy.

The crew, measly as they were in their near 140-man totality, cast their votes. Only a few men raised their hands, maybe twenty including myself. It was a moment in which I painfully regretted my individuality, solitude, and honesty. For if I had been a better *Fancy*-man, more liked by all, away from my position as an outcast, I may have yielded the man's life to be spared by popular demand. I did not.

"There ye have it, Cole. The people have spoken," Captain Every said to me in his wager, thus proving gold reveals one's true character.

"Ask the Mughals. Ask the Mughals what they want, Captain. This is our debt to them. They should have final say," I said, continuing to plead. "The prisoner can speak to them for ye— one of his many talents and languages. He is a translator," I said.

"What brings ye so close to a mollycoddle for this prisoner, Cole. Are ye not a pyrate anymore? Have ye lost yer edge?" Captain Every asked me, speaking to me for once as a man.

"I am simply an opportunist, Captain. He can be of use," I said.

"No. This was yer opportunity to challenge me in front of my crew. I've been reasonable. Reasonable enough. Do ye want mutiny, cabin boy? Away with ye and yer trifles," Captain Every said to me, putting final touches on the failed deal as he looked back at Jalal and Zeenat's direction. "Alright lads, it is settled. Keep on. Maroon those four and let us erase our debt," Captain Every hollered.

The crew exclaimed with haughty jeering. I penetrated the crowd on the Mughal vessel, engaging with the horde and navigating toward the prisoners. I rushed through the chaos. Finally, I met my Mughal friend, who would meet his maker faster than he deserved, for I knew what happened in a marooning. I confronted his face and the face of his wife, as I stood before both of them in earnest.

"I am coming, Jalal. I will come with ye," I said.

The pirates who stepped forward to bring them to the cay joined me beside the prisoners. We loaded them down the Pilot Ladder and onto the tender. I said nothing to Jalal, nor did he speak to me. We entered the water then rowed slowly and truly to the cay some distance off, in plain sight of the anchored convoy. I felt powerless even as my arms moved the tender full of human cargo. I was one of the rowers, and I ensured I sat across from Jalal, who sat beside his hysterical wife as she could also identify what was occurring without knowing English. The prisoners remained within the bounded rope confines. The men in our tender's crew didn't bring up the spectacle between the Captain and I. They simply rowed.

"The future is uncertain... isn't it, Rollins?" Jalal said to me, astonishing the rowers' ears and eyes.

They turned to look upon his multilingual mouth, confirming I had some right to speak up earlier.

"Aye. Mine is. But I fear yers may not be so uncertain anymore," I said, making rowing the only priority at the moment and trying to distance myself from my new friend.

We returned to our silence. The view in my eyes, behind Jalal and his wife's back, was our familiar convoy. Behind me was a sandbar without trees, without seabirds, without vegetation, that I rowed towards. Jalal was the only prisoner who did not cry. His wife and the other two, a young man and a middle-aged man, wept. It was before midday, and I was to cut the ties of a man, his wife, and two strangers, thus leaving them all for a dry, sunny death. We made a moderate pace and beached our tender on the sand. The reality forcibly set in as my boots touched earth again.

While some of the crew exited the boat and guided the rope of our bound prisoners to pull them forward to walk toward the end, another seaman and I manned the rear as spectators. Water slowly seeped over my boots and I recalled the nights when my crew would haunt me for being heartless. Where were their supposed hearts? Who of us wasn't a murderer aboard the *Fancy* anymore? All pirates are heartless.

We walked the prisoners up a ways to the centre of the cay on its smooth, soft sand. The lead pirates turned them around until the only person facing the cay was me. I stood straight, facing the uninterrupted horizon, and turned my head around to look back at the convoy. I saw the limber boats with their tall masts and small specks of men on their decks watching us. I turned my head back to the prisoners. I looked directly into Zeenat's eyes, her brown, bloodshot, tearing eyes. I was doing my damndest to limit the tearing of my own eyes, forbidding any pathetic crying. Was a pirate allowed to cry around his shipmates? Was a pirate allowed to cry for a stranger? Crying wouldn't do anything for them. Zeenat, the woman who I'd met the day before, and I looked at each other without interruption. I felt that she had spoken to me. Her quiet message was too honest to bear. I was ashamed.

I then looked at Jalal, no longer a stranger, and he returned the gaze. The rest of the crew, who'd brought us out there, knew their place. They remained observant, still, and quiet, at last giving Jalal some sense of last respect after overlooking my admiration for the man. I felt that part of me would forever remain on that cay with him, even as I departed and headed back to our *Fancy* in the moments after. Jalal looked away, past me, to the convoy. He said one thing:

"I know, Rollins... I know," Jalal said, and on that cue I approached, along with my crew.

We sliced all of the binding rope free from their hands and arms, doing our job. One of the other prisoners, the younger man, tried to fight and swing upon our men until a pirate lad punched him in the gut, reducing the Mughal down to the sand.

"I don't know what to do. Maybe yer ships shall come back. Maybe they'll be better than us," I said, beseeching the fates.

"Let it go, Rollins," Jalal said to me, shouldering both of our burdens.

"I shall. But if I have the chance to return, or know of a way to send for ye and yer wife, I am seizing the opportunity," I said.

"Let it go," Jalal said, acknowledging finality.

I moved forward and shook the man's hand— the hand of the man who I did not know one day before. The same man who I would likely never know again. A strong part of me had been drawn to him, for just a day, for just a few conversations, on the most hellish of eves. And somehow, he had cast a perpetual hold on me.

"Take this. Catch some fish, look for sand crabs. Maybe yer ship will retrieve ye. Yer convoy should come back. Survive until another vessel nears, then wave like ye've never waved before," I said to him, as I released my hands and handed over my dagger to him, affording him a last tool for survival. Alarmed, my shipmates placed their hands upon their swords in response to the armament.

Finally, the crew and I walked away from the prisoners and their severed rope on the ground of the cay. We boarded the tender and pushed off from the land, entering the water completely. We rowed. I looked at the quartet on the cay getting smaller and smaller in the distance, becoming less of a moment and more of a memory with each passing row. And I asked myself, would I want to die that way, the same way as Jalal? Without a fight, without a question, without an argument, in the middle of nowhere? Jalal had said nothing to Captain Every, and he could have spoken up. But he didn't. Why? He did not renounce the horror, nor did he beg for life. One could call that heroism. He did not fight for the preservation of his wife's life either. I found it cowardly, to let fate make a person and his love out to be martyrs. How could such a coward earn that much of my respect? 'Tis too absurd. I could not understand. I could not think of it anymore.

They had no shade on that little island and the sun would likely claim their lives. We put the tender alongside the *Fancy* to be rigged and raised for stowing. After it was done and our crew of cay executioners re-entered the ship, it dawned on me that I had seen Captain Every's true colours. I'd never felt as alone on the man-o'-war as I was at that moment. A hue of me wanted to go overboard with those women. A shade of me wanted to be on that cay with Jalal. A tinge of me wished I had joined the men in the brutality the day before, without restraint, thus at least knowing for certain I was a worker of the Devil, having purged my soul, leaving no goodness remaining in me to feel guilty with. I wanted absolutes. My yearning would go unanswered, for I knew I had some good in me. And I knew nothing was simple anymore. Had I lost my soul because I did nothing? Did I lose all of the goodness in me by not taking advantage, nor preventing a stranger's life from the swift sentencing to the Locker? Captain Every was once my hero. But there are no heroes at sea. No more false idols, captains, heroes, or gods— they were all the same. And I would no longer be let down by them. I would no longer trust in fantasies.

As for Captain Every, I should have known it was in a scorpion's nature. And as for all of the men who had followed each other and their captain, following what was not truly them, having become mere slaves to the dictator and the crowd, they could go to

Hell. They were slaves with permanently haunted souls, who should be hunted by the dark guilts of their actions until the end of their time. At least I felt so. Maybe they were too far gone to have a conscience. And I, although somehow having managed to distinguish myself from the crowd and its molestation horrors, would be haunted too, with a different curse— the curse for being a passive observer.

Shortly, we reeled in anchors, unfurled sheets and sails, and left. I could not come back to Jalal unless I wanted to die on the cay with him. Our *Fancy* made headway southward, with the convoy behind us, and all of the loot in the safest hold— ours. The Mughal vessel, raided and liberated, shortly set off eastward.

We sailed further from the cay, and from a distance I looked back and watched the Mughal vessel pass the cay without stopping. I viewed the two male prisoners in the length trying to swim toward the Mughal vessel in open water. But it was too far away and they could have drowned. The naked Mughal ship departed the cay without receiving any more prisoners. It was clear our men had lost their souls on that ship, lost their souls for that ship. The Mughals must have lost their souls too— they did not rescue the prisoners on the cay. It had been a wonderful, fulfilling week for piracy. But a terrible, dreadful week for humanity.

I ran down to the second deck, to Pretty Al's kitchen, and grabbed a thin-bladed knife to arm myself again, replacing my absent dagger. And with this new knife I would never be found weak and wanting again. I would always have my advantage and the upper hand. If ever, it would be others who begged for mercy, not me. I mourned Jalal for less than an hour.

<u>*Chapter XIV*</u>

ESCAPE

Clancy Williams sang alone to us jolly wildmen, having seemingly forgotten what we'd done, only thinking of where we were going and what we'd captured:

> *"When the lanterns all run out, and me luck hath run*
> *down low,*
>> *Don't go tellin' mother I'm a-never comin' home!*
> *For Captain Smithby saved my life, and he's made me a*
> *rich lad!*
>> *When the gold is in my hands, I'll be a-merry and*
>> *oh so glad! "*

> *"Lads, don't let me be!*
>> *Don't let me sail too far!*
> *'Cuz when I got a ship o' mine,*
>> *I'll go a-sailin' to the stars!"*

> *"All around, those whaling boys and us pyrates, far and*
> *wide!*
>> *Those boys workin' those sheets, they've got their*
>> *endless pride!*
> *Sailing makes one a tough lad, for it ain't no flimsy job!*
>> *With the wind upon yer hardened face, ye die or*
>> *become strong!"*

> *"Lads, don't let me be!*

> *Don't let me sail too far!*
> *'Cuz when I got a ship o' mine,*
> *I'll go a-sailin' to the stars!"*

> *"When the sun hath jumped way high, and the darkness*
> *hath gone low!*
> *We struck good luck when the swells were shinin' a*
> *big, fat, amber glow!*
> *For the surf upon the shoreline had turned into a woman!*
> *And fortune runs unto ye boys when ye've found*
> *yerself some lovin'! "*

> *"Lads, don't let me be!*
> *Don't let me sail too far!*
> *'Cuz when I got a ship o' mine,*
> *I'll go a-sailin' to the stars!"*

It was a strange experience to run headstrong into a raid that afforded a pirate the ability to retire. And the most comical thing about it is once the loot is gathered, the mind goes everywhere but there. It is incredibly human— as soon as we get what we want, we forget about it entirely. Mans' appetites are infinite, yet his time is entirely finite.

The gold and other loot stayed in the *Fancy*'s hold, the safest of places, as we left the hot and dangerous realm of the Red Sea and Northern Indian Ocean. We met at some safe haven halfway toward Madagascan waters, at the islands of the Seychelles. It is an archipelago far enough to flee the dangerous waters, but close and fruitful enough to restock and take leave on land.

Only our *Fancy* and *Pearl* remained. Our pair sailed for the islands with haste. Since the *Portsmouth Adventure* arrived at our torture convoy after the battle, and missed all of the bloodshed and action, they deserved no prizes. They departed our convoy on a different journey, directly to Madagascar, potentially to Libertalia.

Since the very beginning of the raid, the *Susanna*, *Dolphin*, and *Amity* had been left behind and deserted, burnt and abandoned, or submitted and fled, respectively. There were only two of us remaining. And how Captain Maze let Captain Every secure all of the loot in our man-o'-war's hold en route to the Seychelles, undoubtedly dangerous waters, was beyond my understanding. I could not have foreseen him allowing this to happen smoothly, for Captain Every was not a man to trust in these sorts of post-raid dealings. If one belonged to the *Fancy*, Captain Every would have his back. But if one was an outsider to us, he would be treated as a useful stranger, no more. The elder Captain Maze of the *Pearl* had missed this and he would come to regret it.

It was days later, after the dispersion. I had filled my time since we left by tending to my roles as an able-bodied sailor, once more responding to Durnburn's orders of managing sails throughout our days. For every night we dropped anchor and rested in our hammocks, I was filled with repose, as the raid and carnage of the aftermath, although it never left my mind, was over. A pirate's life is often quiet and when an opportunity arises, his life becomes loud. All until it silences again and the cycle repeats. Yet the past few months since Libertalia had been an unusually, deafeningly loud saga. I wanted rest. I wanted reflection. I wanted to know who I was again. But I only got it for a day before rampant carousing began.

So I filled my days of transit with singing shanties alongside my brethren on the ship, the brethren sharing in the duties. The crew of Captain Want, his boys of the American Colonies, had become one amongst our own. All pirates are brothers, united in the case for freedom to the point of causticity. The sailor music of Europe and the American Colonies were one in the same, for the songs rhymed on the same sound with the same rhythm. My head was becoming, as the days went by and we got further from the Mughals and closer to the Seychelles, filled with the sounds of men's singing voices, not the old sounds of Mughal women's screams. Fortune was good, loosening the grip of that terrible toll on me over time. I was in better spirits after some time had passed. Crates of ale, those festive images in my head and in front of my eyes which consummated the pirate parties on our vessel when we did not operate the sails had replaced the sights of Mughal bodies and blood. It happened slowly and steadily, this transfusion of my view.

My life as a pirate was a before-and-after involving many events— the mutiny, Libertalia, and the Mughal raid— all major points in my sailing tenure. The shanties, banter, laughter, and bombastic carousing within these times remained the same throughout my short ageing and wild adventures. The voices may change, but the songs remain constant. As did the melancholy.

Old, drunk men talking to drunk, young lads was entertaining at best, and bothersome at worst. But it always happens. They whined about young lasses and lovely maidens we'd longed for between the shores and ports. Captain Every showed his face at random times then disappeared for days on end to hide in his captain's cabin. I had not been called upon to exercise my listening privileges with him. Were we all untouched by what had happened before? Did the treasure blind us to all of our doings? What's a pirate supposed to do with himself on the cruise to freedom? How is a young, boozing pirate to respond to the drunken senior? The drinking and dancing made us forget what we'd done. It didn't seem to bother anyone else. Did it bother any of them?

Night fell on one of the seemingly unrecounted, rhythmic days where we wasted resources on celebratory evenings. I found myself alongside Thomas during the festivities, sitting on a pair of barrels on the main deck with another twenty to forty men enjoying themselves at the pulpit of our pirate world. No other nation had likely heard of the raid other than the Mughals. We sailed upon, fought, stole, and sailed away with heroic haste. I felt a keen confidence we would become legend for our acts once word reached the masses. Us— legends dancing and yarning about with tales of mermaids and krakens? We were like anyone else. Mania, pure mania, engaged us in the dance with humming and drunken crowds of men, for we took no lady prisoners from the Mughals. The humming, shanties, rumbling bumping of boots on deck-wood, and yelling were enough music for us to dance to. It was alive, our fancy *Fancy*. How strange it was that what pure joys we had were brought about by such impure acts.

I knocked a full mug into Thomas'. We toasted to our good life, our rags to riches, and the reckless venture. The night's rare occasion warranted me a drink. The black of nighttime, gold of lantern flame, and brown of wood surrounded us hot-blooded, dancing men. Past rage had become fodder for cannons of euphoria. Grog and the promise of gold aboard our ship was enough reason to engage in dancing. I found myself hoping once again I would have a true friend in Thomas Howard, who sat beside me, in respectful camaraderie. He had disappeared from my mind and eyes for a while over the course of the *Fancy*'s raids and adventures. I must uncover why, for some reason, he once more sought out my conversations, I thought. He was a poor fool who would have been a great man, however he was too much a part of the crew to be his own man. His relatability was his consolation yet his restrainer. But in truth, Thomas, amongst my other mates aboard, consoled and restrained me too. The crew coveted my attention away from the singularity of solitude's repose. Yet when I abandoned my private course and joined in conversational league with my brethren, I restrained myself from drifting too far into the diversion of group companionship. As for women— well, I was married to the sea.

"What are ye going to tell folk when ye hand them over Mughal coin?" Thomas asked me, engaging in one more serious conversation before we lost ourselves to the drunken evening.

"I haven't thought that far yet. What about ye?" I asked.

"I'm going to tell people it was an inheritance. Going to find a way to rid meself of it if I can, but make 'em believe I got me some Arabic family up the line takin' good care of me if I can't," Thomas said, and I laughed at my friend, the character.

I walked away from Thomas and entered our crew's jolly revelry. Alas, a clown infiltrated our frolic— while engaged in the middle of a dance that I had joined in merrily, a lad, with a face unknown to me, stepped out from below the stairs. He entered our fray with boots on his outstretched arms and bare feet covered in an incredible amount of toe-jam and hair. He danced around, adding to the suspense of the night. When men should be sleeping, sailors are to be found dancing. If ladies want to find men who share similar temperaments yet different habits as them, look no further than pirates, for every true pirate has the heart of a woman, in essence. If not, how could we dance like that?

The bearded, boot-armed man stood in a T-shaped stance with his arms covered up to his elbows by boot and his many earrings obscured by long, black hair. He spun as a spindle through our cotton clan. Fun. It was an escape from the incessant chatter of my thoughts. I loved dwelling in my thoughts, but, boy, did I love the gist of dancing's joy quite the same. Some vices are stronger than others, but reclusiveness and all-around chaos are kindred twins to one another. The necessity of fun dictated we dance around the spinning, boot-armed man, the centrepiece to our grog-singing craze. I looked around, in the midst of the spinning and jumping and sweaty yelling, to the deck of the nearby *Pearl* anchored beside us. I saw only their watchmen, similar to our watchmen, going about their duties properly, and peering into the night water to protect us. No dancing aboard their dead deck, the poor fellows. They missed the goodness of pirate life that only came once in a full moon. We were wolves. Wild, wild wolves. And the *Pearl* was home to a pack of sorry omegas.

<u>*Chapter XV*</u>

COLUMBUS

It was the end of another day and we had recently anchored at the Seychelles, in betwixt one large, tall island and a small, short nub of an island. Both islands were covered in dark green and both of our ships, the *Fancy* and the *Pearl*, were resting. The exchanging and division of the loot was to begin upon arrival, as per unwritten pirate code, between our two sailor sovereignties. Yet, Captain Every managed to deny and delay Captain Maze and his crew aboard the *Pearl* the privilege of booty securing until the following day. It was night. We took tenders, carrying a few handfuls of men from each ship, to the port and docked to enter one of the main islands' pirate sanctuaries for debauchery and release. I drank my fill rather fast that evening and fell asleep before any other man in the tavern did. One moment I was at the end of the bar leaning upon nothing but my arm, talking to the bartender about the Indian Ocean, and the next moment I was asleep. Luckily, I was spared the abuse of my restful vulnerability at such an early hour of the night, as most men often took the opportunity to expose and exploit a man who dozed off in a tavern first. When I awoke, before the sleeping whores had left and the roosters had crowed, before light had fully reached the horizon, I was not at the inn, where all squabbles are created, the place where I had fallen asleep. I was back in a hammock on the *Fancy* sailing in open water the next morning. It was dark, but I had enough sleep to know the night had nearly passed.

I awoke from the sleeping lullaby by the creaking and settling wood ship which ached and squeaked at each swell and shift. The beautiful phenomenon of the wooden sounds becomes as familiar to a seaman's bearing as the sea legs he adapts. Yet when he reaches port, the sounds do not continue to deteriorate his ears like the sea legs do his balance.

I arose with my new dagger, sword, pistol, and boots still on my personage. Whichever lad had transported me from my rest at the tavern lacked the knowledge of the proper etiquette to relieve a man in the position I was in. My said carrier, whoever had brought me back to our ship, was supposed to remove a lad's blades from him, putting them atop his lap and underneath his hands for sleepy safe-keeping. I was quite lucky I had not punctured my hammock, or sliced myself with my blades. Returning to a sense of wakefulness, I walked about and made my way to the stairs when the stammering of too much rum grasped me. I managed to walk up onto the main deck, revealing the early morning's ocean to myself, devoid of moonlight or bright sunlight, with only lanterns lighting my way in the morning darkness.

Durnburn and a few of his mates, myself excluded as I was somehow still under Captain Every's privilege despite our disagreement over Jalal, worked the mainsails. They lounged, scattered about, away from the group of men on watch duty. Walking forward, I found a lad sitting alone, manning the watch away from any of the groups huddled around barrels and lanterns, likely swapping stories of maidens, wisdom, and fables. The watchman was Alan Edmund, a *Dolphin*-man. Or at least I thought his name was Edmund. He was incredibly olive-skinned for an Englishman, with a black, tight beard and short black hair, thicker than molasses. His left eye beamed at me with youthfulness but his right eye was always near shut. I never asked why. Ruggedness dominated both his appearance and manner, as he spoke fast and directly. I felt a sense of trust with him. He reminded me of a friend of my father's, and thus I could not unsee this sailor stranger as a familiar figure. He sat on a crate by the bow, holding a musket upright, where the butt of the rifle rested next to his boot bottoms.

"Where are we?" I asked Edmund, who wore a felt, brown hat, looking newly purchased from the Seychelles' port, and sported a smoking pipe in his mouth that altered the sound of his speech coming from his sun-tarred lips.

"The ocean, lad," Edmund said and laughed briefly, watching the void sea.

"We've left the islands?"

"We're sailing for Bourbon," Edmund said, referring to it with a tone that I should have known this information as plainly as fact.

"And why do we do that? Why sail in the dark before sunrise? Why does the *Pearl* not accompany us? Or does my vision betray me? I do not see that vessel around us."

"Yer vision's fine. Last night, Captain Every went to shore and left Durnburn to the *Fancy* while a couple of lads rowed him and meself to port. We came to the inn where he told us to grab all of ye boys and quietly return to the ship. I was at the inn with ye, Cole. I saw ye gettin' yer beauty rest, babblin' a whole bunch of nothing. Murmuring in the night, cold asleep, and we left with ye, carrying ye to the tender, we's did. Ye don't take to the inn too much, do ye?" Edmund turned as he spoke to me, laughing and miming the entire story with his eyebrows, lively eyes, and hands.

"What made Captain travel with such haste and stealth?" I asked.

The lad narrowed his left eye, his demeanour matching my seriousness.

"Wot?" Edmund asked me, confused.

"Why'd he tell ye lads to do that?" I asked, deliberately speaking plainly.

"We left the *Pearl* behind. Took off with the treasure ourselves. But rumour says Captain Want implored him not to. Rumour is lads of the *Pearl* tried swindlin' us, tried to exchange us clipped gold, they did. We gave 'em some of their treasure for repairs at port, at the exchange, but they tried to ruse us with trimmed coins. Captain Every got wind of the act and confirmed us pyrates were in conventional pyrate company. So he bid us return the favour. I went to the inn, picked ye and the rest of the crew up, gathered the remainders, went back to the *Fancy*, and we sailed off a few hours later when every man on the *Pearl* was fast asleep. Consider yerself lucky we got ye. All the gold is ours. There were no watchmen on the *Pearl* so we slipped away," Edmund said, proud of his adventure and judgements.

"Aye. Well, God save the *Fancy* then," I exclaimed, not knowing whether or not to believe the tale.

"Aye," he said and turned away.

I walked away from Edmund and went toward the stairs. I wondered about Captain Want and his New World crew aboard our Old World vessel, having heard of Captain Want's rumoured passivity. I turned back and walked over to Edmund again, watching him stand up as I got nearer.

"Aye, lad, what of Captain Want? Why's he yellowbelly about the scarpering?" I asked.

"I don't know, mate. It's only a rumour that Want was coward. Him and his crew are still aboard, still armed. They're with us, at least for the time bein'," Edmund said.

"Aye. I bid ye good mornin'," I said, terminating our conversation.

"Aye," he replied cordially as he nodded his head once and I walked away.

I ventured to the stairs, and descended down to return to sleep once more. Only on this turn to my hammock, I removed and rested my blades between my belly and hands for safekeeping, so as to not puncture myself.

After many more calm, watchful, conversation-filled nights like those, where the *Fancy* sailed alone, we eventually reached Port Saint-Denis on the island of Bourbon for the second time since we became pirates. The Port and surrounding island looked the same. There were equal numbered nights of raucous laughter, man-to-man conversations, stories of home, and tall tales. We were once in Bourbon ere the Libertalia days, ship hunting. But the second time around, after fleeing that Seychelles inn, was likely October or November, 1695.

There, in the privately anchored safety of calm water, we set about dividing the treasure gained some time ago. The crates, chests, pouches, and other containers held gold coins, silver coins, ivory, and some precious little gemstones of varying colours. Each man was given his share. The pouches many of the men used to store their shares were taken from the Mughal dhow. Every man who walked down the stairs in the line to the hold came walking away satisfied with his fill of treasure. Captain Every took his shares last, like a good captain. He used one of the Mughals' looted coin chests to carry his lion's share. I stood before him in the line with a pair of lads in between. I looked at him lift his chest away, and knew he'd acquired satisfaction. His determination would thus expand seventy-sevenfold. Once, the raid was only an imagination of Captain Every's and a rumour taken from a man he tried to behead. His vision had manifested into grandiose victory. Captain Every had become a true alchemist, if even for only a moment in eternity.

With all of the money, I had no more allegiance to the job. I was no longer reliant on a master. I could retire from the heartless gig and do what I wanted. It was my immediate plan to leave, however, if I jumped ship in the wild Indian Ocean, I would likely not survive or stay anonymous for long. I resolved to leave the *Fancy*, but only when I would reach safer waters. For what good is a promise kept to oneself if one dies or goes to prison shortly after? My feelings toward the Captain and his demanded duties did change however.

I noticed a similar attitude of apathy toward orders pouring over some of the lads in a slothful divide growing between the crew and our captain. Greater degrees of freedom entered the minds of the pirates who possessed more gold than they ever dreamt of having. And yet, despite our shared notions, I knew many of the lads would remain loyal despite their inclinations to leave the *Fancy*. Captain had performed a miracle once. Who was to say it could not be done again? Who would abandon a ship in the most vulnerable territory in the world? Who declined the directions of the man who brought us enough gold to dazzle the eyes, and enough Mughal women to satisfy their tempestuous desires, even at both of their respective prices? It was not the prospect of treasure that kept my or any other man's ankles tied to the *Fancy,* or Captain Every for the time being. It was the promise of adventure and survival— the passage to safer waters. The Indian Ocean was dangerous for us. We were all likely to have targets on our backs, and 'twas best to stick together until we found a place far, far from there, somewhere far from the Indian Ocean. The East India Company would surely set sail and employ privateer captains, crews, and soldiers aplenty to find us if it meant profit, if it meant taking back the monstrous plunder. For profit runs the world and the world runs on profit.

Chaoticism, the destination and the direction, was more ingrained in my actions rather than my thoughts at that point. I'd matured. Although thoughts guide actions, I was not so confused in the search for who I was, although that search never does finish. I was confident. I had money to operate with, something I had never held an excess of. I was a Chaotic in reference to exploring the world as an adventurer, but I embodied my created school of philosophy in a more grounded, actionable manner. I was more concerned with means and worldly matters, and less with my intangible inner identity. This was natural, as my philosophy had developed from my ever-advancing evolution in temperament. Another change appeared, which was all a part of the plan— I had become externalised.

We were once poor sailors, embittered sailors. We then became pirates and wanted autonomy, wanted control. Once we'd gotten that, we went even further, attempting to create our own utopia, our own society, but it became destructive and toppled out from under itself. Luckily, we fled before the fledgling house of cards damaged us too terribly. We then returned to the world, smarter, with a yearning to not escape the world anymore, but with plans to dominate it, as any mature boy wants to when he evolves into manhood. We had to go too far in an ignorant direction in order to find out how far we could go and reorient ourselves in the best direction possible. And then, with our Mughal profits, our treasured worldly currency, we were to master this universe. Or at the very least, I would try.

There was one issue— the shortcuts. To take shortcuts in the world is to risk both reward and safety. There is always a price for everything, especially when money was stolen, dishonestly earned. And for every one of these men who wished to conquer the world with gold, only a third had conquered themselves considerably enough, or were in the never-ending process of doing so, to counterbalance the aloofness that comes with the privilege of heaps of gold they'd earned. The other two thirds of our men would lose, would fall hard, as that is the nature of survival and the fate of those who take shortcuts. Only so few will get away with it and flourish in perpetuity. Pirates are great spenders, and horny ones at that. Thus, the two thirds I speak of would likely go on to blow their share. Fast.

Take the currency of the world or an industry away from a lad, whether it be money, talents, connections, power, or intelligence, and he would turn away from said world or industry in an attempt to escape from what he doesn't have yet he wants. But this escape is not a solution, it is a temporary fix. It is a necessary phase, for escape informs a man of what he could be, in ideal, and shelters him from the rejection which he despises, even if it be by measures of a thin veneer. Next, comes the restoration, the overcoming, the transcendence, and rebirth— he must return to the world he once departed. To do this, he must wake up, pick up where he left off, grow some teeth, and acquire the currency he dearly needs. With his eyes opened up, he aims to instil his ideals upon the real world, using his newly acquired currency. We were in the midst of that effort, having already been robbed of our pay, mutinied, escaped to Libertalia, and acquired our worldly means from the Mughals. It was thus time to assert and build with our resources. I wondered how it would proceed, for the laws of nature favoured us as did the laws of the sea. But the laws of society looked harshly down upon us shortcutting swindlers with keen disdain. We were pirates, criminals, and thieves. Shortcuts are ill-advised and illegal. We had to proceed with caution. It was one matter to steal the treasure from a small ship. It was quite another to plunder and violate the crown jewel of a rich convoy.

"Ye've been here before, Durnburn?" I asked my bos'n with his wealth of experience.

"Bourbon? Only once before. Last year with all of ye," he replied.

"D'ye know who hath been here? What lad would know people who know things on the island?"

"Aye. What kind of things are ye looking for?" he asked.

"Well..." I ended my lean against the rail of the *Fancy*, and joined him in moving crates about the deck, meeting his labour.

"Ahh, I know. Ye're looking for a good ways out, away from the *Fancy*, aren't ye? D'ye want to leave the pyrate's life?" he probed, seeing into me.

"Nay, sir. It hath crossed my mind, but I shall not retire. I am only looking for a blacksmith, or a locksmith," I said.

"Aye, Cole. Find Captain Every. He was mentioning his wantin' of a blacksmith a little while ago after we divided our shares."

"Where would I find him?" I asked.

"Well, the island of course, lad. Ye know... keep yer eye for his red jacket," he said, shooting me a satirical smile.

"Aye," I responded crudely, annoyed at his broad, scant advice.

I headed down the stairs and got to the second deck, searching for Pretty Al. I may have been delaying my efforts to inevitably leave the life of piracy, but the urge to ascend to a life where nobody told me what to do brought about a passionate impatience. I'd hated orders all my life. Optional directions and guidances were better. I hated bosses but I enjoyed leaders. I walked to the kitchen but did not see Pretty Al, or his bald head, at his station. I imagined he was on the island. He may be one of the only old-timers who knew much about the island of Bourbon besides Captain Every or Captain Want.

I returned to the main deck, and got on the next tender heading for land. Captain had been wary of docking at any port since our Corunna mutiny. Anchors or moorings were the safest options. We'd almost always anchored in a harbour and rowed to shore— 'twas easier to come and go should emergencies necessitate. In the tender I boarded were almost a dozen lads, *Fancy* and *Dolphin* crew alike. I'd wondered if the crew of Captain Want would depart us before we left the island. Or if we would depart them. They were overstaying their welcome, and needed a ship of their own.

We rowed to the dock and left a man there, keeping guard of our little boat. The rest of us set foot on the streets as one group then dispersed to fulfil our varying needs. I looked about each turn on the streets and around buildings for a reference or map of the island. As the lads were beginning to separate, I asked the question I should have asked earlier.

"Hey, any of ye know where Captain Every is, or where I'll find a forge or locksmith around here?" I hollered.

Most of the men shook their heads and kept walking away, unwilling or unable to refer me. One man pointed to the left at the street I originally began walking down, which hugged the barriers of the water. I saluted the lad, we both turned about-face, and we continued our separate ways.

I walked forth, following the guidance of my crewmate's pointed finger along the street of pirate haven shops and quasi-homes encompassing the landscape. Eventually, I heard the sound of iron striking iron from a distance. Blunt metal forging metal of potential. I heard the noise carried by the wind. I altered direction and accelerated my pace every time the sound of metal striking started and stopped, growing louder with each successive clank. I reached the source of the small collisions, emanating from some building ahead. It was a forge.

I opened the wood doors to reveal a dark cave of metal, tables, and lanterns cluttering the interior. Tough, sweaty fellows occupied the furniture and tables. I found the exact source of the pounding— a rough European, a bit older than I, striking an orange-hot sword with a hammer as he forged and moulded it. His hands were darkened with soot. I approached.

"Aye lad, ye speak English?" I asked.

"Yes," he said.

"D'ye know where I could find the best locksmith around here?"

"Aye, talk to our master. He'll help ye," he said, darting his eyes and head to my left, where a closed door sheltered another room, likely an office.

He returned to his striking. I walked my way yonder and heard talking and laughing on the other side of the wall. Wasting no time, I opened the door. Captain Every was off to the left, wearing his red coat and holding a beaker of some drink in his hand, lounging back in a chair and laughing. To the right was a different lad, leaning his back against a table with his hands resting on the tabletop, talking to Captain Every. He wore an ivory undershirt and an apron that matched the worker's, with dark stains covering it and sweat about his brow. His brown, curly hair shot off away from his head but his beard kept close despite its outgrowth. Green eyes swindled my attention, and his bent, rickety posture suggested hardened toughness to me. The men whipped their smiling heads toward me, the intruder upon their conversation and laughter.

"Ahoy, Rollins," Captain Every greeted me.

"Hello, Captain," I said, then turned to address the supposed master.

"Good day, what can I do for ye?" he asked, looking for business from a small chap such as I.

"I'm lookin' for the best locksmith on the island. D'ye know of him?" I asked quickly while he permitted my intrusion.

The man, with crossed arms, pivoted to look at Captain Every and then back at me.

"Well, I'm the man for that. We do the work of locksmiths on this island, not only metalworking. What are ye lookin' for?" he asked as his demeanour shifted away from apprehensive curiosity to the calmness of a businessman.

"I'm looking for a single-key lock. And a small chest I'm looking to buy with the lock on it. I've got me some cargo I want to store."

The master blacksmith smiled, shot a sharp look at Captain, and they both grinned ear to ear.

"Funny, lad. Yer captain here hath requested something similar. Don't good minds think alike?" the master blacksmith asked.

"Aye, yes they do," Captain said, providing me with a compliment, and allowing the comparison to stand.

"Well, I can do that for ye, we've got plenty of those here. What size are ye lookin' for?" the master blacksmith asked.

"Aye. No bigger than a flintlock's storage, sir," I said, then looked at Captain Every, who regarded me neutrally.

"Come here," the master blacksmith said and guided me back out of the doorway I stood in, across the sea of men and tools, to an area displaying a plethora of metalworks and hammers.

The master blacksmith kept going and opened a door to show me a closet-room with chests piled up. Some with eloquent ironwork and locks, others with simple design. I pointed to a small, ugly looking one for its look of cheapness. Expensive chests can undoubtedly be broken by the same tools as a cheap one. The master blacksmith went in and grabbed it. He was squatting down and looked back up at me, the customer.

"Ye sure about this one? Works just fine, but there are many others in here ye haven't seen. Better ones," he said.

"I'm sure, sir."

"Very well."

He carried the chest by the two handles and walked me over to a wall of hanging keys. He tossed the dark tan chest on the table, and exposed the bottom, revealing a small burnt etching in the wood— a small symbol. He looked at the wall of keys and found the one with a corresponding design on the metal head of the hanging black iron key. They matched, sharing an identical ideogram. He took it off the wall and inserted it into the chest, unlocking and opening it. He showed me the inside— empty and befitting of my needs.

"I'll take it. I bet ye make a lot of business from chests on this pyrate island," I said, returning to more casual conversation, removing serious business from the discussion.

"Aye, here and there," he said as he inspected the chest and key one last time.

I handed over a silver coin from my small, heavy purse. We exchanged the goods for silver and he returned to his office where Captain Every remained.

I watched him off and thanked him.

"Rollins. Come here," Captain Every's gruff, grave voice called from the other side of the shop, in the office.

I put my pouch into the chest. The key was held up by a twine lanyard which I then hung around my neck. Holding my chest at my side, I stowed the purse once tucked on my person securely. Hungry blacksmiths would surely find a way to take my prizes if I flaunted them around more than already necessary. It is not the sight of the purse that entices men, it is thoughts of the mysterious unknown within, which so strongly weighs on the purse, that invites hunger, the curiosity of what the purse may contain. I walked to the office and rejoined the two men, holding my chest with the stowed key 'neath my shirt.

"Aye, Captain," I responded.

"Sit down, have yerself a drink with us," Captain said. "I missed ye last time the both of us were at the Seychelles inn," he laughed.

Embarrassed, I obliged. I was not concerned my own captain would steal my loot, for we were both satisfied. And I sensed that if the master blacksmith tried to forge any operation for my prize, the captain would have my back. I took a seat on a stool, making a triangle of the three of us, and accepted a flagon from the master blacksmith that gave off a scent of rum. I put my chest on the floor beneath the front of my feet.

"So tell me, Captain, what are ye here for?" I asked.

"Looking to trade in my chest for a double lock and key chest. I stuck around after our business," Captain said, pointing back and forth between himself and the master blacksmith.

"Ye can never be too protective of the precious things. And ye can never be too close to a blacksmith. Because whenever ye're in a pinch, and need either of them, both yer valuables and a good blacksmith can save yer arse," the master blacksmith said.

I grinned, and took a swig, blending in.

"What can a blacksmith or locksmith do for a lad if he is in a pinch that precious things could also do?" I asked.

"He can get ye a good sword, a trusty dagger, or anything he can make. It isn't so much what he can do for ye, but what it is he makes that can do for ye. Ye follow? Good tools are as precious as what precious things can get ye. It's their utility," the master blacksmith said and I nodded in agreement.

"Ye gonna stash yer chest on the *Fancy*, Cole? Any lad who sees that chest, even if he is already happy with his golden lot, may want to get greedy," Captain Every said, warning me.

"'Twas the plan. Or not. Are ye gonna stash that large chest on the ship? That chest is more desirable than any purse of mine," I said to Captain Every.

"Touché, Rollins," Captain responded, and we took a drink.

"Excuse me for bringing up the *Fancy's* business in front of our blacksmith friend here, but to where do we sail next?" I asked, doing my best to avoid the already divulged golden, silver, gem scent of our crime.

"To Madagascar, lad. To Libertalia. All roads lead to Libertalia," Captain Every said.

It then dawned on me, my mistake— I shouldn't have asked. If the blacksmith lad had any incentive to trade our whereabouts or our identities for a hefty prize, once he learnt where we really had come from, he would. Any reasonable man would. And we'd just given our destination away, us men carrying heaps of gold and silver. Yet, it confused me, Libertalia. We high-tailed it out of there months ago. I did not understand why we planned to return after such thievery.

"Aye, lovely women there in Madagascar, don't ye think?" I asked Captain, trying to change the subject.

"Aye. Methinks yer lad Mr. Howard would agree about that," Captain responded.

I fell speechless. The master blacksmith had been nearly excluded from our veiled, private conversation.

"Say, fellas, is the silver ye gave me from that Libertalia ye speak of? It is untraditional," the master blacksmith interrupted.

Captain Every and I looked at one another quickly, then returned to the master blacksmith.

"We've found ourselves in a bit of a hole, ye see," Captain Every responded to the master blacksmith double fast.

"What kind?" he asked, failing to cloak his curiosity.

"The kind where we look to buy and sell slaves but alls we've got is this Madagascar silver, still worthwhile to trade," Captain Every lied, bringing up his old profession, slave trading.

I then knew the prospect of returning to Libertalia was a falsehood. The captain lied to cover up and protect us from anything this blacksmith could do. He was still hiding our true business with deception. I had to play along.

"We've traded in Madagascar, and we've got Madagascar silver. But we want to try our hand at buying some Bourbon slaves. D'ye know where we could find?" I continued the lie and covered for our *Fancy*.

"Ahh, yes, I see. Ye do find yerselves in a most precarious position," the master blacksmith said cordially, as he inspected the silver coin I'd given him.

He then pulled some more out of his pocket to inspect, presumably the coins of Arabic or Persian calligraphy that Captain Every exchanged with him. Captain slid his chair out away from the table by the window, and from under it he dislodged the large, purchased chest from the darkness.

"I heard from some Madagascar folk that it is best to buy slaves with odd coin, in order to trade them in for better gold. Then again... I've never seen this kinda silver before. I wouldn't know who else'd accept something as odd as this. I've never seen silver as this even from Madagascar," the master blacksmith advised and found himself befuddled.

"Aye. But ye do know where we could purchase some slaves from the island, do ye?" Captain Every asked, lifting his chest from the floor, and held it hanging as both of us stood up to depart.

"Well, out here, ye're sure as hell far enough away from the Royal African Company... it'll be a private venture, difficult to track down," the master blacksmith said.

"Aye. We understand," Captain Every concurred.

The master blacksmith advised us where to search for commissioned slave traders on the island. Both Captain and I took note, but we did not go immediately. I realised that in order to preserve the evidence of our crimes, all of our men would have to trade their foreign currency soon.

Later in the evening, when most of the ship's lads had returned to her, Captain Every ordered the men to gather around before any of them returned to port for a night of carousing. We all stood about the deck of the ship, in the darkness disrupted by lantern flame. Captain Every and a few surrounding lads towered over the mass of men on the quarterdeck.

"Lads. Ye all deserve to enjoy this island and her festive complements. However, as we are all thinking, we must keep moving. The time shall come to cover our tracks, for we are surely to become marked men. A raid like the one we've committed shall rock the boat of trade. They'll be looking for me. They'll be looking for us. We must leave within three days, and I advise all of ye to trade in yer coin for something to sell, so the Mughal silver and gold stays here, though we will vacate," Captain Every commanded our men and after a long silence he continued. "That is all, me boys. Enjoy the night," he said, sending us off to the evening.

As the mumbling between the men started, out of discussion instead of disagreement, a few lads on the deck stood apart, not moving away with the crowd of dispersing men. They stayed as frozen as statues, and looked at Captain Every. I noticed this out of my peripheral vision before I stopped to witness.

"Captain. Where do we go next?" a man standing in the centre of the clan asked.

It was Manuel Sanna who spoke, the Spaniard and former captain of one of those two beached vessels we frightened into joining us a year or years before.

"That's up to us to decide. I suggest we go to the Americas," Captain Every said.

"Aye, and shall we be flogged if we propose going separate ways to disband?" Sanna asked.

"No, lad, every man decides where he goes, with or without the ship. But the ship, I, and the obliging crew shall go one way. All else who wish not to, are free to go," Captain Every said.

This was news to me. I believed that although we were free men, it was unwritten pirate code that if you abandoned your captain and shipmates, you were targeted. This tenderness from our captain was unusual to me. But those were unusual times. Those were times to get away, no matter what.

All in all, we'd elected to go in the direction of Captain Every's suggestion— the New World, to New Providence, a haven for pirates on the other side of the world. It was an act of balance, our vessel's governing. Most ships were democratic. We'd been under a dictatorship, however, as time passed, our *Fancy*, like most vessels, became a hybrid. The captain needed his crew as much as they needed him. There was a group of about thirty dissenters, mostly Spanish and some of Captain Want's men, who'd decided to stay on Bourbon. They gathered their belongings and left their posts, no longer participating in our voyage. We bid them farewell and prepared to set sail for the Americas on the morning of the third day, bright and early.

We'd followed our lead to the slave trader, upon the master blacksmith's advice. Fortunately, we found them. Using a large aggregate of the crew's money pooled together, we purchased the sum of thirty slaves to cover our dissenters' labour and numbers, but also to cover our tracks and rid us of some Mughal currency. The plan was to sell the slaves later and redistribute the compensation, thus sourcing good gold from our previously deemed dangerous gold.

We set the slaves up in the hold, some in chains, and planned to allocate all of the grimiest duties to them. I wanted to trade the slaves again as fast as possible and get some good currency. I feared, even though severely outnumbered, the slaves posed a threat to the stability of our ship.

This new scenario only reassured the validity of my decision to have bought the chest. If our crew was caught stealing from a mate, he'd be punished, viciously. If a slave stole, he'd be sold or killed. Regardless, it was best to ward off either of those cases by hiding it in a chest and preventing any loss of money.

At midday, when most of the lads were on the main deck, I worked some boards loose on the floor near my hammock to hollow out a spot for hiding my small chest containing the gold, silver, and gem-filled pouch. I purposely put the stashed chest under planks near the wall, so I could inconspicuously cover the top of the shifting and squeaking wood with some other item— a crate, perhaps. I kept the key with its twine lanyard around my neck, resting the metal key against my hairless torso, and covered it with my shirt. Men may have seen me with a wooden chest, but they'd never know where I'd stowed it. Nor would they probably care. Some men slept with their pouches in their shirts, pockets, or in their hands— plain for all to glimpse. But fools placed their valuables in view for everyone to see. Wise men hide their treasure, even in plain sight. One day I observed Captain Every open and close his stashed chest which was placed within the latrine in his captain's cabin. It was brilliant, for no outsider would search the toilet for all of the captain's share of the raid. He showed me where he stashed it, amidst the paths of urine and waste, in case the time came where I needed to access it for him. It fit snugly into the latrine. I once saw him put one of the key's twine lanyards around his neck, however, I wasn't informed of the other key's location needed for his dual-lock chest. 'Twas likely hidden in his quarters somewhere where I would never be permitted to know its location, unless in an absolutely necessary life or death situation. Leaving Bourbon and setting off to the New World, I felt like a well protected wise man amongst a collection of vulnerable fools.

<u>*Chapter XVI*</u>

SHELLS AND SHALLOPS

What happened on the ship, in our lives, consisted of sporadic routine and duty. Since we'd acquired slaves, most duties had been delivered from our hands and backs. Once every few days, however, something unique would happen. Something that made all of the quiet sailing worth it. It was good enough in itself to be a sailor for a living, but the adventure and mania that came about at random truly multiplied my appreciation for the job, serving to exponentially grow the sense of inner fortune of experience accumulated from my line of work.

We'd been en route to New Providence from the Indian Ocean for maybe a few months. It was likely late 1695, or we had reached the New Year of our Lord, 1696. A day or two after vacating Bourbon, we came across Captain Faro and his *Portsmouth Adventure*, then all but a few piles of wood, ropes, and sails in the water. They'd been shipwrecked. We'd found the captain and about forty crew members on Mayotte, near Johanna, one of the Comoros islands we'd been raiding around before Libertalia had become our home amongst those waters some time ago. I wondered what had become of Libertalia, especially since bounty hunters supposedly hunted for our heads throughout the Indian Ocean. Especially after the East India Company took the letter Captain Every sent to them, via the opium merchant vessel, seriously. Captain Faro joined us, along with the greater part of his fifty-man crew after we rescued them from the island. It was a reunion, of sorts. Since then, we'd been hosting Captain Every, Captain Want, and Captain Faro, all on this ship composed of slaves, *Fancy*-men, *Dolphin*-men, and then *Portsmouth Adventure*-men. A person from any crevice of the world could find a place on our *Fancy*.

I found that while I had been serving here and there for Durnburn, returning to my role as an able-bodied sailor, and whilst sitting in on some evenings with the three captains as the cabin boy, I had plenty of time to think. Plenty of time to audit my place on the ship, in the world, and in history. The idea of telling or exaggerating my tales had occurred to me on several occasions, especially when I thought of being hunted for our treasure snatch. But if a pirate has a fruitful career, he will likely meet his end in a noose. And when the hangman is pictured time after time, a lad can't help but think of the means toward immortality. He can't help but think of what he can do before that time comes, to compensate for the time in his life lost after his premature demise.

What abilities did I have? I, along with Captain Every at the least, could read and write. I could swim. Not many men, especially on the ship, could say they were proficient in all three of those skills. I could use a sword with the average pirate, aim and fire along with the most accurate of riflemen. I could outwit any lad on the ship. I felt my talents were suited for more than piracy, the incredibly short-lasting undertaking, liberating as it may be. I wasn't yet twenty-five. I still thought of the future, I thought of what would become of my name after my life would end. I could not decide if these were worthwhile ponderings or melancholy ones. Did my talents exceed my station or was I merely overestimating myself? I felt blue, thinking of the end. Regardless, morosity serves the purpose of strengthening the powers of joy when it is later felt. Life as a pirate has plenty of the sullen and plenty of the gleeful to go around. A man becomes a pirate, conducts hefty adventures, kills, bleeds, finds his fill of treasure, and if he survives all of this, he spends a lot of time thinking about his life, unless of course he is too busy spending away his time and treasure. I'd say there was enough signal to begin my exodus from the profession. Was there not?

On that day, moving through currents and wind channels of the open ocean, my thinking, that wholesome activity which had at first accommodated for the lack of worldly adventure, had come to a halt. Adventures had been had, but then we spotted good land, thus pulling my attention back into reality— a small, triangle split of an island comprised of a few hills on one side and the middle. There was a large mountain on the end looming ahead of us. Navigations by the stars, maps, and general guesses had all suggested this was an island called Ascension Island, a place used by passing Portuguese ships. In broad daylight, we ventured close enough to the green-brown island to drop anchor and row to her sandy, barren shores. The rowing took forever and I couldn't wait to get my feet and fingers onto the island. I was leaving my ruminations at sea to once more set foot upon land.

When we eventually reached the shore, I stepped out of the boat, and took my boots off to let my bare, pale feet feel the sand. I lowered down on the beach and pushed my palms into the clay, digging until I could find some crabs in the depths. I found none. But I found a sense of joy being there, halfway around the world, possibly the furthest away from my home I had ever been in my entire life.

The rest of the men, off to inspect, explore, and look for some food, whether it be animal flesh or something from the soil, walked right by me where I crouched in the sand. My act of appreciation did not prove to be a communal experience, with the exception of a few lads who stopped and admired the foreign sand with me. A man who can stop his incessant actions and let a moment in life itself fill his loins is a rare lad. Among my fellow loafers and idlers, maybe numbering a half dozen of our over 200-man crew, was Thomas. I saw him sitting on the sand. I was happy to see he still shared a shred of commonality with me. I'd been under the assumption we were cut from the same cloth, but that theory had undergone much discernment, challenge, and scrutiny.

Further along the shore was a grouping of black rocks, numbering maybe fifty, on the sand. On the ground, where I was still bent on all fours, I looked to my left at the spectacle, squinting my eyes. Life made no sense to me anymore in my head, but when I saw what the rocks really were, I knew I did not need to try to understand life, I only needed to live it. Life just is. The rocks were moving. The rocks weren't rocks— they were sea turtles. Big ones. It was phenomenal. So natural. I had never seen them. Then again, I had never seen that side of the earth. Sea turtles storming about the sand. Life in a grain of sand.

I ran over to the turtles by myself, without a word, flying through the dunes. I streaked, likely attracting attention to the turtles. As I neared closer, I could hear the men, lifetimes behind me, talking of the spectacle and following me. I reached the turtles and stood to watch them as they all shuffled over the sand, travelling toward the land from the sea. They were all a bit larger than my torso and abdomen. Men joined in with me and when I heard the next voice, I remembered why we were on the island.

"Quick, lads, grab 'em," a pirate yelled.

Then, like hungry rats finding something to chew on, the men on shore descended upon the dark green turtles, maybe fifty or sixty, and snatched them up. The turtles were all about. Every man ripped a sea turtle from the sand or hunted for their eggs as the big fellas crept into their shells. I let one, walking right past my feet, keep going slowly while the world around him changed rapidly. I returned to the sand, kneeling down to watch him closer. He did not go into his shell like the rest of his brethren. Then again, he wasn't picked up and grabbed by a pirate's smelly mitts. Whether he was aware of his haywire environment or not, when the rest of his world around him was descending into chaos, he simply kept moving forward, kept persevering. I admired this turtle, this wise and oblivious creature. I picked him up and walked to my right, behind all of the lads scrambling to grab a turtle or two along with their eggs. I left the pack and went to where the sand ended and the brush began. I let the big sea turtle go free out of an odd respect. He never once hid in his shell. I guess he could sense I was friendly. I turned back around to return to my duty, the crew. I never saw the little thing again.

We ventured further onto the island, not uncovering any man or skeleton, but finding a trip of goats whom we captured and killed for the feast. Our meal of turtle stew and cooked mutton was what all the men spoke of when we took shade and refuge on Ascension Island that day. Pretty Al had his hands full with dozens of turtles and their eggs for the stew along with a heap of mutton for the cooking. Pretty Al had quite the expectation on his shoulders, yet, it is not easy to disappoint hungry seamen who have an appetite for turtles and goats. The meaty flesh itself would be tasty enough. All he needed to do was keep the bloody things somewhere between rawness and burning.

The seabirds surrounded us. The smell of stew invited the devil in all of them. They say the souls of dead sailors reside in the hearts of seagulls. I agreed with this theory, for no man enjoys turtle stew as much as a hungry sailor. And the gulls acted alike. Even though we spared as much mutton and turtle for the rest of our voyage as possible, the scent and seduction of these appetising items made the feast a royal one.

Pretty Al took his kitchen and supplies to the sand, joining where nearly all 230 of us lads and slaves were gathering. We claimed the sand as our own coliseum whilst the *Fancy* was vacated at anchor. Pretty Al and a few of his lads slogged around under the canopies we erected. The joking and arguing between lads brought us home. Halfway around the world, some things never changed— the pleasures were all the same. Food and laughter is treasured on either side of the globe.

The stew was good enough and the fire-cooked mutton was salted and fine. One man was dumb enough to feed a gull. The damn thing wouldn't leave him alone thereafter. We ostracised him, for the rest of the birds who chased him up and down the sand wanted more food he did not have. A fool. What kind of lad feeds turtles and goats to the seabirds? He deserved to be chased, for he obviously did not care for these tasty commodities' value which the other men cherished.

Captain Every walked into the mass of men sitting on sand, barrel, and crate. Holding his meal and plate like the rest of us, he made an announcement standing tall between two sitting, feasting Griffin brothers, Simon and Benjamin.

"Lads," he said and kept eating, taking another bite of his mutton share. "We're getting close to the Caribbean in the next few months. Anybody who hath been there before knows it is a city on water with many towns and boroughs. With many enterprises, and many threats. I suggest ye keep a low profile. Best be kept simple, keep track of yer shares, and don't blow your treasure. We shall finish exchanging our Mughal currency to cover our arses. We will face many ships like us— crews who fly one flag from a distance, and then show their true colours when close enough to fire. This is the Caribbean way. And believe me, buccaneers shall fire. The Mughals, and whoever's gold that was, shall likely put a bounty on our heads that trumps any price they'll pay for stringin' up any olde pyrates," Captain Every said.

It used to be a dialogue between crew and captain in the beginning. As time had gone on, it had become Captain Every simply talking at us. The words were valuable, but his delivery was not as enchanting as it used to be. Captain was becoming less of a leader and more of an old captain.

"And one more thing. I am under the alias of Captain Benjamin Bridgeman from now on. I wager the price for Captain Every shall be steeper than some pyrate called Captain Bridgeman," Captain said, then walked back to where Durnburn, the other captains, Want and Faro, and some other important elder lads were feasting.

We stayed on the island. While most men slept elsewhere, I remained on the sand, sleeping where I never slept, on the dunes. The next day we packed up camp and returned to the *Fancy* with our slaves, turtle and goat meat, provisions, and supplies. Nearly twenty men decided to and were allowed to remain on the island. We continued without them. I looked at the lads with respect for their choice to flee, but I thought they were mad. They wouldn't survive the month unless they found another passage away.

I thought of Captain Every's speech, and what awaited us after we left Ascension Island, continuing to New Providence. He renounced his name for the sake of self-preservation. Did he therefore renounce his family? His wife? There was no way, as of yet, to send his 'wages' to his family. Did he have room in his heart for them anymore? Does any greedy, strong captain have room in his heart for anyone but his crew, himself, treasure, and the honourable foe? The Devil takes as many men as the sea does. But fear claims the most men. And I wagered fear was starting to lay its claim on Captain Every, who was once a fearless buccaneer. When fear begins and its prey does not recognise or curb its influence, he shall be swallowed by it.

Was the captain's name change the most honest signal that he was ashamed and in hiding, no longer the bold, fearless man who had captured our hearts so long ago? Was he not the same man in name, stature, or manner? Maybe he got what he wanted and he had moved on to other desires, other priorities, other names. How does a man getting what he finally wants, what he had hungered and hunted for over years, simply change upon satisfaction? Does murder and forcing himself onto a woman thus change a man? I know not what that Mughal princess and he did. But my imagination filled in the blanks which all of my questions surrounding the mysteries of our captain opened up. It took me some time, but I was graced with second thoughts anytime I regarded my captain. He was from then on a different man.

The great storm, which began some days after our departure from Ascension Island, struck fear into every man as harshly as the lightning struck the rabid swells around us. Black was the night and terror was her sky. The tempest's twisting of the boat and of fate scarred all. In every seaman's life, he comes across many storms. There is always one storm, however— *the* storm. Where every lad without fealty to the good word suddenly becomes God-fearing and God-promising. If one managed to see more than a few paces ahead of himself, looking out onto the black and white sea that shifted vertically and horizontally faster than he could blink, he would think there is a school of mermaids laughing at him, and their siren calls urging him to beg mercy and jump overboard into their illusory embrace. I could not hear any siren. I could not see far beyond the *Fancy*. Nor did I become that desperate. It was a black void around us, with God screeching in the evening. I'd been to places in my soul that felt like this too many times to be as afraid as one experiencing the storm for the first time. I knew it would pass, yet I was undoubtedly frightened.

The sky was grey as powder and the eve, black as tar, controlled our wills. Men died. Several. And we could not go back for them. As we were shortening our jib and furling our mainsails, thinning the vessel under Durnburn's command, I knew any man who climbed the main or foremast risked death. We battened down the hatches, as every bos'n was born to say, and did everything Durnburn told us. I was not exempt from my duty under any privilege of Captain Every, or "Captain Bridgeman." No. I was on the deck along with my other mates and watchmen. We had to surrender and follow the waves. An anchorless night. It was the highest of highs and lowest of lows. I'd never heard more seasick pirates in my life than during that squall of all squalls.

We began tossing some crates, some cargo. All of the men who were not on the main deck saving the rest of the crew were ordered to form a line from the hold to the tertiary deck to the second deck to the main deck, effectively transporting crates of tradable goods up the stairs to be tossed from our rails to the sea in an attempt to lighten our vessel's load. With any luck, we could recover some cargo whenever the storm would end. But I did not cast any hopes on that likelihood. Unmarked crates of useless goods were transported then disposed of into the water, and I eventually saw through the wall of rain that there was a crate of the opium in my hands, deemed useless in the tempest. I threw it overboard. Even as the water was half blinding me on the main deck, I observed what the crate was, and I knew, even as we discarded all of the crates of opium, I would not see the end of that serpent's slithering. Maybe not for the rest of the journey to New Providence, if we should survive the night, but sometime after, it would return. But luckily I wouldn't be tempted again shortly, being on an opium-free ship.

I would call a storm an omen, but what I refer to was Hell itself, riding the back of Poseidon's trident on Hades' orders. Each swing of the wind was an omen. Neptune himself had abandoned all seamen for the evening, and let nature whip us around in our folly. The storm fluctuated between a gauntlet and roughly pushing us around. But she lasted all night. It claimed an unlucky seven men. The eternity of howling thunder, meandering lightning, incessant rain, and brutish waves demonised our vessel. But as all storms eventually do, this one ended. Davy Jones took seven to his Locker and was satisfied, so he spared the rest of us. And the slaves of our vessel had seven less crewmen to angst against. My caution continued to rise even after the clouds evaporated and the resurrection of the sun commenced.

Captain Every or "Captain Bridgeman" was nowhere to be found during the squall. Credit for our safe deliverance belonged to Durnburn's direction. He booted the pilot off of the helm and manned the helm himself. He had ordered all of the crew to empty our hold of non-essential cargo, owning the ship and crew for the conflict of the night. Was Captain Bridgeman scared? Drunk? Busy? I did not know. But he sure as hell was not where a captain should have been. I resented him for it. Me and my shipmates, who I usually did not give a lick about, had toiled and suffered to keep the *Fancy* alive. Keeping the crew above water without the help of our captain? Our captain. Our captain? It makes a man wonder, causes a man to think. When a lad thinks he's reached the end of his rope and looks for God, who isn't there, then looks for his captain, who isn't there, he dispenses of those near useless utilities thereafter. Gods and captains are quite different for God is not a person, and a captain is only a person. But it makes a man question whether he needs a God, a captain, or any other master if they are not there for him. Despite Durnburn, a man must lead himself through the abyss. His own character takes charge, not the God of our universe or the god of the ship. All it takes is a brief, fleeting thought for faith in those trusted, leading authorities to start slipping away.

Should the bos'n lead? These men, along with I, had been begging the question since we saw Durnburn behind the wheel, and the captain was nowhere in sight. Durnburn appeared to fit piloting the *Fancy*'s wheel, having dismissed the helmsman. Let me not forget he was with us since the beginning. The wheels had started turning. And that may not stop, I thought. I could not unsee Durnburn behind the helm. Although he was a washed-up lifer, maybe that is what the *Fancy* demanded. It is usually the same lads who are the best at gaining, who are also the worst at maintaining. Pirates need a strong, upstart captain like Every to lead them to the promised land, but an old, proven bos'n like Durnburn to ride the waves of glorious fortune.

When the sun finally broke through after the night's storm, ever clearer with beloved, renewed skies, the days of Captain Bridgeman's end felt closer at hand than the days of his ascension via mutiny. Why was this end felt?— throughout their feared reactions, the men had looked confidently toward Durnburn commanding them amidst the great storm— looks and expressions of great trust, like those accompanying the trust in a captain. We'd weathered the storm entirely without Captain Bridgeman. Kings rise and fall, often due to their own oblivious actions. They alienate themselves from their kingdoms and their own intelligence because of fear, thus allowing a hero or usurper to grasp the intoxicating power of leadership. Whether the captain was scared or drunk, he was no doubt intoxicated by something. And intoxication is quick to dull a king's character, dull his mind, and weaken his sword. Who would be our champion?

We neared, as weeks passed, closer to the Americas. Even the seabirds were different. They flew differently. They flew much closer to our viciously crowded ship. I stuck my arm out as we sailed swiftly under the scorching sun and a gull flew in close. My temporary companion. We were undergoing a metamorphosis that bid the question— did we require a new captain for the new realm? The spirits of the men were starting to fly, considering we were lucky to be alive after surviving the deadly storm. After the darkest storm, came the reemergence of high spirits. The inside of the ship and crew had changed dramatically. Must the outside leadership follow a similar transformation? A transformation of a captain's spirit via a new captain? Maybe a seaman was in higher demand than a master thief. A seaman who maintained a propitious momentum for a few weeks after the storm, up until we came across what the master thief had warned his lads about some months ago.

We were likely a few days or weeks out from Barbuda, losing sight of the beginning and hoping for an end to the long voyage, when we came across the only vessel we hadn't been able to avoid, nor did it attempt to avoid us— a long, skeletal-looking vessel sailed on our horizon, barely crossing paths with us. It could have been a galleon. They looked to be intersecting, going further along in the same direction. But they diverted course in broad daylight, moving toward but not directly at us. I immediately knew this would be one of our first tests of naval warfare in a long time, as they slowed and let the wind halt them, thus letting us catch up in our speed. We stayed on our committed course, for our speed and ferocity were unmatched. They turned so we could not see the rear of their vessel and their ship's name. We maintained our colours, evidently pirate colours, without shame or cover.

Their flag, first seen from the spyglass as Durnburn concurred with Captain Bridgeman, was raised for all to see. Men aboard their vessel looked to be scrambling about in the distance. No doubt they were trying to change their dress and manner in order to match their costumes to the false flag— an old, but late tactic, which Captain prophesied on Ascension Island. Their vessel raised a flag of the Royal Navy. While it confused some of the men, it brought up memories of home for others. But we all knew it was false. A fool would know. I sensed an alarming fog of uneasiness sweeping over us.

The gap closed, and empty distance quickly turned into hot, occupied hostility. Their bowsprit aimed directly at us as we both faced one another head-on. It was a most unusual manoeuvre since their vessel was a bit to our portside rail. Although their flag was that of a Royal Naval vessel, they must not have practised proper Royal Navy procedure, for they did not carry themselves accordingly, steering their ship oddly. A spyglass wasn't needed to spot the poor effort to deceive us. Before we got close enough to see the whites of their eyes, their bluff Royal flag was dropped from the sky, and their true colours were hoisted, for we were approaching aggressively and they likely knew we saw through their charade. Our cannons were readied. Their cannons were readied. They hoisted a black pirate's flag with yellow, broken shackles over top of a white skull— a flag I'd never seen or heard of. Captain's off-hand prophecy on Ascension Island came true.

Before our port rail matched the galleon's port rail, and the imminent cannon fight could commence, Captain Bridgeman gave an order that Durnburn delayed and outright disagreed with. To question a captain's direct order, especially during combat, is punishable by death aboard this *Fancy*, whether by death of hesitation and subsequent destruction, or by formal execution after the fight ends. Unless of course the captain felt lenient and allowed the best strategy to prevail, which usually involves hesitation, thinking. But it was not our way anymore, unfortunately. The best strategy no longer mattered, it was only Captain's plans which sufficed.

"Battle stations, gentlemen. General quarters now," Captain Bridgeman yelled, although most of us were already edging toward our posts with cannons, muskets, flintlocks, and sabres.

"Captain, we should furl the sails and slow her down. We will have the advantage of the broadside. Their bow faces our path and if we do not slow down, they shall match or even beat us to the broadside. We can blast them into dust before they get a single shot off, Captain," Durnburn yelled his advice.

"No. That is what they want us to do. Keep ahead, full speed. We have the wind. We must never relinquish the wind," Captain Bridgeman decreed.

"Captain, we need not be damaged. Be a seaman, for God's sake. Let us fire at their bow and remain untouched," Durnburn responded back most practically.

He stood on the quarterdeck beside Captain, yet remained a world away, trying to get to the bottom of what to order his loyal mates to do.

"No, Durnburn. Be a Bos'n, not a Captain. Follow my orders and keep her moving," Captain snapped back, looking straight at Durnburn's face, not as a leader, but a tyrant.

Durnburn shook his head and said nothing in reply, keeping the sails high to maintain our hasty stride, following orders. Captain wielded the helm without caution, and only with blind aggression. We got closer and closer, a ship away from brushing hulls, when we saw all of their marksmen revealed on their bow. We ducked in time and heard the shots ring off. Some men did not crouch fast enough. Musket balls chipped the wood rails. I'd dropped to the floor for cover, near my only two masters.

Durnburn couldn't cross Captain Bridgeman, although he surely wished to dismantle the ignorant captain. There was no turning back, for we were in the eye of the firestorm. As Captain turned the wheel, and we rounded the corner, he ordered Durnburn to have the men furl the sails into a near dead stop, as to stay in a volley line adjacent with our enemy's broadsides, side by side, instead of our broadside to their bow for we turned late. Some men could not reel in all of the sails, as the muskets cut our able-bodied sailors down. But we managed to halt and freeze in the water alongside the enemy. I took aim, still taking cover on the quarterdeck, firing an honest shot across the way. I was met with overwhelming cannon fire that pierced the rails and wood all about our ship.

We fired back, of course, engaging in cannon warfare as our vessel drifted to a halt beside the enemy's. As the seamanship was removed, it became a weapons war. Cannonballs ripped to and fro.

Captain abandoned the helm and snatched a musket from another marksman beside our hunting party on the quarterdeck. He ran behind us to the edge of the stern then ripped off a shot. I couldn't tell if either of our shots had hit their targets.

I assumed all of our lads who weren't getting shredded by the wood chippings of our vessel, who originally were to mount the enemy's vessel carrying sword and pistol, took cover and prepared for their time. Iron and wood flew everywhere around me and likely the rest of the boat. Medleys of cannon shots from both ships' decks ripped and sounded off. I thought of how Durnburn and Captain wanted the same result but through entirely different means. We were in a position of death and destruction. Durnburn advised Captain to put us in a stationary position of advantage, but that ship sailed. It was for naught. I hid and reloaded my musket for another chance at a shot, maybe to some hopeful avail. As I dropped another ball into the barrel of my musket and prepared my powder for another shot, shock tore my mind away from my body.

Chain shots ripped through the spaces and structures of our vessel. Our foremast, I saw, was badly damaged and began to lean over, almost broken— a short distance toward the middle and she would have been gone already. It was not the mast that startled me so. The shock came from looking back to the area beside the helm, devoid of Captain Bridgeman, and seeing with my very own eyes as a similar chain shot hit its target— a chain ripped through the waist of Durnburn, effectively severing his torso apart from his legs, and missing me by only a few steps. His authority over me vanished at that moment. Blood spewed everywhere. I was then apathetic about my death, having seen the worst carnage in life. After his lower half had been blown away onto the other side of the ship and into the water, another shot rang off and exploded onto the deck beside his upper half, effectively blowing him and the wood where his head had rested for a painful moment into a pulpy oblivion. The man was defiant, yet blown in half and evaporated by battle. The images seared into my mind.

He was nearly 20 years Captain Bridgeman's senior, and was gone. As was my concern over him or his chilling death. The action continued and I stifled my reaction. As I had to. The distance, although filled with cannon fire and musket fire, remained. A small tender of ours was loaded with a boarding party. As was theirs, already en route from their stern to ours. I peeked over the rail, reloaded swiftly, peeked again, and fired at the rowing crew slowly making their way to our ship. One of the men in their tender was struck from my shot and fell. The enemy looked European. The cannon fire continued as we stayed close enough to shoot and cover, but too far to board one another. An explosion went off beside me and wood chips pierced my right calf. Again, the wound spelled a quick visit to Surgeon Fitzgerald's infirmary when the fight was over. That was if I survived and resisted any mortal wounds, of course.

Gusts of wind cooled my hot-tempered shooting and frantic reloading. My ears were tender and almost numb from the sounds of cannons firing. There was carnage aboard our vessel. I'd never seen the *Fancy* torn up like that before. I saw our boarding party meeting the enemy's midway in open water, where they were squabbling with pistols and daggers and cutlasses. The enemy's boarding party was cut down in the quarrel that rocked both tenders, but ours prevailed.

The battle continued but slowly their ship shot less and less, until the lads throughout their decks waved white flags and threw their muskets and swords into the sea. Our boarding party was climbing about halfway up the back of their stern's balconies and windows. Their grappling hooks were deployed but unnecessary, as the firing stopped shortly after the enemy's white handkerchiefs and flags were raised. It was over.

We tended to the injured and fired a couple more shots, putting many wounded men out of their misery. Thirty-five of our men died across our three crews. Then we took to fixing up our foremast and other damages. It required two days to manage all of the repairs. Our boarding party, joined by Captain Bridgeman, composed of maybe twenty more, and I, entered their vessel. The galleon was full of a mixed lot— Europeans, Africans, Chinese, and everything in between. A diverse crew similar to ours. We filed through their vessel, scavenging for anything of worth. In their hold were slaves, about thirty, like ours. Their vessel read *Arcanum* on the nameplate, a lad of our original boarding party told me. They did not declare their captain, for he was supposedly dead. And the quartermaster, an Englishman, spoke for them.

"What plunder did ye hope for?" a man from our boarding party asked their quartermaster.

"It was for the slaves. I have no shame in telling ye all now, for we are defeated. Only those buying and selling slaves come this close to Barbuda. There is nothing else here of worth but them. Ye must have some, do ye not?" their quartermaster said.

"Aye, we do," Captain Bridgeman responded to the lad, shaken up.

"And ye work for Codrington?" the quartermaster asked.

"Who?" Captain Bridgeman responded.

"The Codrington sugar plantation. They run the island," the quartermaster said.

"Ye will take us to him, Quartermaster," Captain Bridgeman ordered.

We rounded up their slaves for capture into our hold, adding to our collection. By musket and threat of the sword, we forced our prisoners of war, those sailors of the *Arcanum,* to labour alongside our slaves in fixing up our ship, eventually allocating them as slaves on our vessel. The replacement of the mast took much time. All but their quartermaster and senior crew were put to work. Some men who resisted too harshly were executed and tossed into the Atlantic for shark bait.

After much time, when our ship was polished back up, we sank their vessel and about twenty-five excess men of their crew with it. The rest of their crew remained as our slaves, whilst the quartermaster and about fifty other crew, including their bos'n, were spared and integrated into our crew as men among us. We killed about forty of their men in combat, sunk or executed thirty more after the battle, enmeshed fifty into our crew, seized all of their weapons, gunpowder, and cannonballs, commandeered thirty of their slaves, and enslaved about thirty more of their men. It was a terrible day to be an *Arcanum*-man.

A few days, maybe a week, later, we sailed close to Barbuda to scout, then sailed around to the western side of the island. It was there, in a small inlet, where large vessels are prey to smaller ones, we saw a small shallop, with a furled single mast, rowing out to meet us. An older, lean man stood tall as he led a crew of rowing slaves. He waved, with his dark boot planted upon the front edge of the shallop, as a captain with showmanship. They must have seen us coming and wanted to intercept us. As for why they did not fire upon us or approach with arms, I did not know, for we had been flaunting our hoisted pirate colours the entire way.

"Why aren't they scared?" Captain Bridgeman asked the quartermaster.

"Ye're sailing slow and ye're not French," the man responded. "No ship could take this plantation, therefore, they fear nothing."

"And how does King Louis fare against everyone else?" Captain Bridgeman asked, as we drifted closer to the shallop, and he spoke of worldly matters.

"News of the war comes sparingly out here. Alls we know of it is that the Colonel there..." the quartermaster said, and pointed to the leader on the shallop. "... leads plenty of battles against the French around these islands. And he imports slaves which we pyrate."

"Aye. A Colonel, ye say?" Captain Bridgeman responded, intrigued.

We sailed forward and met the older, grey-haired man, probably in his fifties or sixties. He had a staunch voice and the accent of an Englishman who had faded into the New World. He smiled at us, happy to see Englishmen approaching. The fogy was lean and fit-looking for a man of his age. He wore a pewter justacorps coat, an ash long vest, a bone-coloured shirt, a tight, light tan pair of britches, and brown leather shoes. A straw hat placed atop his head shaded a European face. The man introduced himself as Colonel Codrington, the proprietor of his own town on the island of Barbuda, the town of Codrington. We dropped anchor shortly, prepared some tenders with as many men as we could fill, and joined him onto the land. The grand majority of our crew and all of our slaves stayed aboard the *Fancy*. Part of the landing party were Captain Bridgeman, Captain Faro, Captain Want, Thomas Howard, myself, the *Arcanum*'s Quartermaster, and some lads. The island was beautiful and plentiful, untouched and vast. I had proof of why they called it the New World— it was like the Garden of Eden cascaded out across a continent. Wherever the island held houses, they were beautiful and strong, but minute in comparison to the sweeping environment.

Our group joined our graceful host, who was surrounded by his slaves. The captains all joined the island colonel at the front, while the rest of us remained in the rear. I walked in unison with Thomas, who somehow managed to tag along for the venture despite any privilege. We went further onto the island and saw their plantation— it impressed me, a lad who cared not for these sorts of things. The three vast windmills, eloquent huts, and modest castle full of cannon defences conjured up my respect and admiration. The island, Codrington, and his design elicited my esteem.

"D'ye think Filch is gonna be our new master?" Thomas asked me.

Arthur Filch had been the Bos'n's Mate, Durnburn's right-hand man on the *Fancy* since the mutiny. Thomas likely did not know that history, but he was aware that by rank and by competence Filch would in all likelihood be occupying Durnburn's former role. Filch was about Captain Bridgeman's age. I knew nothing of his past. The open position was quite a pair of boots to fill.

"I don't know. Captain can fill the vacancy with whomever he likes," I responded, disregarding which way the wind blew on the *Fancy*.

"They didn't have a fucking funeral for Durnburn, for God's sake. No ceremony, and they didn't speak any words... nothing. It's outrageous," Thomas raised his voice in an outcry.

"Shut up and let it go, Thomas. There's nothing to be done about that now. D'ye really think Captain would honour the man who could've taken his place? Ye think talking so bloody loud about it is going to bring him back?" I put Thomas in his place.

"Aye. Well at least we have a true gentleman in our midst now," he responded, referring to Codrington.

"Colonel, gentleman, soldier, plantation owner— makes no difference to me. As long as he buys our slaves and doesn't swindle or kill us, he's useful. We'll never see him again," I said, trying to keep both of our heads on straight.

"Aye," Thomas acknowledged, knowing I stood amongst the grounds of truth for a moment.

We kept walking, levelling our heads. Codrington escorted us to the main villa while we acted as court to Captain Bridgeman, as outsiders to their conversations. The pair of leaders sat in separation from us. I overheard Codrington loudly bragging, repeatedly, that King William had made his son a man of the Grenadier Foot Guards due to his bravery and valour in battle. In silence, out of my ears' reach, I wagered they spoke of the sale of our slaves, and purchasing of supplies with our foreign currency to get both of these resources off of our hands. If the Captain did not discuss those two chief matters, he surely was a fool. Regardless of the slave and gold talk, it did not occur to me whether he informed Codrington of our battle against the other thieves of his island. The *Arcanum*-men that joined our ranks, including their quartermaster and bos'n, were safe. There was some speck of honour remaining in us thieves that day, as Captain classified their insurgence.

Later in the afternoon, Codrington sent numerous near-empty tenders to our *Fancy*, and returned with what looked to be all of our slaves in addition to the slaves of the slain *Arcanum*— all in all, numbering about ninety. He bought them. As for our crew's exchange of Mughal currency, there was no update and no sale. However, we did get a safe, shilling-filled chest for our shares of the slaves. We split the spoils and plunder quite handsomely, as Captain Bridgeman did not take the lion's share befitting a captain as designated by our agreement, but only a single share like the rest of us. I guess that was all of the humility and meekness he could muster up in respect to the grimy, dead Durnburn. 'Twas the furthest he could go in the direction of humbling himself before the spirit of the fallen bos'n, slow-rising tensions of a distrusting crew, and possible mutiny. But humility does not absolve a captain from mutiny, envy, or resentment. Competence, redemption, and direction absolve him. Then again, does humility play a genesis, medial, or terminal role in the birth of those three virtues?

After the slave sale and resupply, the captain shared an audience with Codrington again, and the achievements of Codrington's son were overheard once more. Our captain swapped stories of naval combat with Codrington, who relied immensely upon a walking stick. The men shared drinks of rum in his villa through the night. The next day, we departed Barbuda. Despite our numbers having been thinned from selling the slaves, we travelled heavily from gaining some men from the *Arcanum*, and those of the *Dolphin* and *Portsmouth Adventure*. The *Arcanum* and its Quartermaster were not spoken of, as the first had been destroyed and the latter, along with some of his men, became brothers among us. They were absolved for their combat. On a bright, apt day, we continued onward to New Providence, the heart of the Caribbean, the centre of the New World for pirates. We were furthest from the Old World realm that we'd ever been, finally entering the waters of second beginnings.

Chapter XVII

CORRUPTION

March, 1696. We got close to New Providence. Within a day's worth of sailing. At that point, we were exhausted, for the trip had brought us across the world, and yet it felt as if we had been transported through the entire universe, our entire endless selves. We dispensed with the raggedy Captain Faro and his remaining thirty crewmen, in addition to Captain Want and his remaining thirty-five crewmen. For the first time since we gave chase to the Mughal convoy, many months and lifetimes ago, our crew and captainship was restored to its most honest numbers of *Fancy*-men, 118 souls or so— English, Dutch, French, Spanish, Africans, and maybe some Irish, Scots, and Portuguese in there somewhere. We were a mobile mega-society hailing from the Old World. Keeping count of the vessel's numbers had been a job in itself and it required my attention. I had the time on my hands to keep track. More attention was paid to keeping track of our personnel than the days of the year. There was enough room again for every man to have a hammock as a bed. No more floor sleepers.

Captain Bridgeman penned a message in a letter. We anchored in a hook of some port harbour at Royal Island then sent a fully provisioned group of about a half dozen men to carry the message, and potentially our deliverance, to the governor of New Providence some thirteen leagues away, to Sir Nicholas Trott. I did not have the opportunity to read the letter. I couldn't say whether there was a shred of truth within the message nor what kind of message it was. Maybe a plea to allow us safe passage to the governor's island.

In the time since we left Barbuda, my idea and hard commitment to remain a member of the *Fancy*'s crew had faded away, as it had been fading for some time. The previous inclinations to cease sailing on a ship under this captain, other than the fear of ever-raising chances danger would take domain over me, had returned to me. Better to die trying to live free than survive in cowering fear behind oh-so-flammable curtains. I disregarded the danger of travelling as a lone wolf. Since we had reached the New World, I thought myself safe enough. The next best opportunity I came across, whether it involved the sea or not, I would seize it. I was afraid of falling into the trap of believing those were my 'glory days', which could keep me attached to the ship and captain. I was a young lad, but ageing made me want the growth that came from more adventures, more chances, elsewhere. I wanted freedom from the past. There was no more room in my heart for captivity on the *Fancy*.

Filch became the new bos'n, and he fit perfectly in that mould, as he was trustworthy and would maintain the status quo of Captain Bridgeman's ship. A bos'n should never overshadow a captain. Durnburn had it coming, by Neptune, unfortunately. He was a great challenger, a captain in his own right, a commander of his own lads. He should have been patient.

Although many things had changed on our ship, I faced the same inner plagues. There was a great hole in me that I could not seem to traverse my way into or through. I did not know who I was anymore. Was it good that I had changed and lost sight of who I was? Or was it an irremovable curse? A man could stumble upon the void, the twilight of all twilights, and in the nothingness confronting him, there is nowhere sensible to look for guidance or truth but from himself, into himself. In the same way a puddle or a lake is constituted, a man sees his own reflection and he finds himself. But I did not recognise what I saw. I was a blurred mirage despite once being clear. The void that comes after adventure makes heroes and villains of many men. But it makes strangers of all men to themselves. The void made me walk on both sides, back and forth between the known and unknown, swinging between safety and danger. It was the most unfathomable pendulum, this journey.

But going back to land, to civilisation in New Providence after the Governor permitted us entry, proved to be the lantern I needed for me to traverse my inner darkness. Our men returned with the great news and we made our way. Seeing Charles-Town for the first time upon our arrival brought colours into my life again, for most of what I'd seen the previous year was the blue of the sea, brown of the vessel, gold of the plunder, and red of my enemies. I needed a New World. A New World to make sense of things.

All men, upon arrival and settling into the nearly empty town which was being rebuilt, were required to pay a certain share of our bribe for Governor Trott. And we were also required to refer to the city of Charles-Town as Nassau from then on, as Governor Trott had rebuilt and renamed the town that was reduced to ash some years beforehand. We were the fiercest ship in the harbour, although there was not much competition. The bribe chest was carried by Captain Bridgeman onto the dock where all of our men returned to the earth. Shortly thereafter, Captain Bridgeman disappeared into the abyss of town, presumably to meet directly with Governor Trott for other matters. I never met Governor Trott. My privileges as cabin boy, or whatever one would call my position with Captain Bridgeman, became extinct. I wasn't dining with the upper ranks nor sitting in on important matters, for the crew had disbanded. I was back to being the able-bodied sailor I was before I'd made a powerful friend. And I liked this return to simplicity, devoid of drama and high duties.

Part of our deal for safe passage into New Providence, required us also to give up our *Fancy* and supplies for good, hence our disbanding. It was a more advantageous position, for the *Fancy* could be hunted by its name, stature, and notoriety. Our hold, full of everything we'd acquired on our journey, was the final price of admission into Trott's island. It was emptied. I didn't care anymore about trading. I'd had enough. My little chest was enough.

The return to the average able-bodied sailor had lasted from the departure of Barbuda to dropping anchor in Nassau Harbour, for we were sailors no more. Although Nassau was sparsely populated, I'd rather remain out of the eyes of an island under the Crown's jurisdiction for a while, even if the governance of the islands was corrupted in our favour. I decided to stay amongst the trees near the shore, alone, and out of the town. I wanted the danger of public freedom but the safety of private seclusion. When we left the *Fancy* for the last time, I quietly retrieved my personal plunder chest, removed from the floorboards near my hammock and wall of the retired *Fancy*. It worried me that I had no feelings over departing the *Fancy* in perpetuity. I sensed my exit was not the end of the road for our crew's allegiance to our old man-o'-war, our home. But that remained to be seen. I did not look forward to that day of final farewell, whenever it were to come.

A pair of months passed and news came that the world was looking for us, looking for Captain Henry Every. In the empty inns around town with only a half dozen whores every man but myself had tried, we grew paranoid again. I did not see Captain Bridgeman for two weeks. At first, I thought he was in correspondence with Governor Trott. Then I thought he'd fled us all. I was spending my time doing whatever I wanted whenever I wanted, and I could not be bothered by anything but fishing and living simply. The thought of beginning my second life was all that occupied my mind outside of whatever I was presently occupied with. Making something new of myself, most likely requiring a change of my name and identity, was my North Star. I reckoned I would wait and look within myself for the best guidance on how to move forward. The crew never knew what was best for me.

All I'd done my entire life was move as fast as possible and neglect the inner voice, downplaying its validity as mere Chaoticism, running to my mind with Chaoticism, to the water as a sailor, and to pleasures via vice. But with a heavy coffer and nothing to lose, I had become one thing I'd never been before— patient. My environment was quiet and slow. I did want to leave all of the past completely behind, but I would not squander my opportunity by being too hasty and quick to act in building my future. Throughout my time in New Providence, I kept returning to my chest of plunder, spending. I felt that the key around my neck grew dull from overuse. I was constantly looking in the chest and exchanging Mughal gold or silver whenever I could with whomever. I did not know what to do with my diamonds and ivory. Yet strangely I had faith in my slowly dwindling and still immensely pervading treasure's means of deliverance. I had faith in the outcome of the next few days, weeks, or months despite certainty that we were being hunted. I was not spent, although a portion of my loot was.

Chaoticism, the force which propels change in all things, could also be called the chaos principle, or the inborn inclination toward change. It is the image of life-force that prevails over and within everything that causes one to do all sorts of unidentifiable, unknown things. It is a mass of moving energy, compelling everything, forcing you to go here or there. And it forces you to continue further to other, more "heres" and "theres". Constant movement was the dominant law of my life. Then, I sought to abandon that strategy. But was that aim to change, or moreso, to stop changing so much, still in itself an act of chaos and constant wavering? Either or, contemplation was needed between leaving my old life and starting my new one.

Chapter XVIII

SAINT SEBASTIAN

I finally worked up the courage, or apathy in relation to moving along, to abandon Captain Bridgeman and the men of the *Fancy* once and for all. I was to permanently leave my life of piracy and any prospects of staying together. As the ship had left my life, all of the other foundations of that person I'd become had started to fall away. This island was my place of liminality in which I could continue to be the Rollins Cole I had been for the past two years or I could become the Rollins Cole, or whatever I would change my identity to, I was meant to become.

I was foolish enough to wait for a sign, to believe that a saviour was coming to my aid or provide me with all of the answers on how to proceed. Maybe everything I thought at that time was wrong. I thought being a man, and to some extent a pirate, had merely happened to me. But as much as I believed that, I realised the most important things in life were, in truth, things I must deliberately decide and walk into becoming. It was both manly and weak to be led by a captain, crew, and fate for the previous two years. I called my career voluntary, and yet, I could not have left the man-o'-war had I tried throughout. Being the man I wanted to be was a firm choice. I chose to move on, but I was curious as to how I would exactly.

In my mind, I envisioned two paths laid out on either side of me. The path to the right— curving rearward. And although it was not history, not the past, it looked awfully like the same path I had traversed before as a pirate. But the other path— a dark and mysterious one which appeared to go forward then disappear. A man should not choose to disregard a path forward simply because he does not see all of it. Progress requires trust, or at least, reckless abandon. Fear is necessary sometimes, but it is an inevitable experience on the path toward becoming. But this path, which did not curve and revert itself in the same fashion as the path of repeating the past, the path of Rollins Cole the past two years, called upon me stronger and more honestly. I knew I must enter a hidden, unknown future.

It was not the activities, unlike for most of the men I heard complaining, which I underwent the past few months that bored me. I loved fishing, my odd new hobby. I loved filleting fish. I enjoyed commanding my own vessel, even if she was a little shallop I bought myself, which I named *Mackerel*. I commanded her, fishing often with any willing friend or seaman on days and evenings. One mast and two sails were enough for me. A one-man captain and ever-changing one-man crew was all I needed. The thought or inclination of the taste of opium left me entirely. I knew I would never completely overcome the seduction of that serpent, as all tempting apples and forbidden fruit keep growing in the garden of life, and serpents keep finding their way into that bordered garden. But I felt fine.

The burdens and weights of being a sailor, the longing, had left me as well. For sailing was not a calling anymore, but a means, an old friend, and a path of experience once traversed. Sailing may be the last thing I must do, in a full circle, to leave the life which was decaying away. I may sail away from the crew and captain in New Providence. Upon the moments I mustered the guts to leave, not knowing exactly where I would go and not needing to know, I knew in my mind my liberation and moving on would be through the sale of my *Mackerel*, my lovely *Mackerel*, and taking the next available sloop out of those Bahamas, wherever it led.

On the same day I decided to take the leap of faith, pondering exodus, an old friend crossed my path. I was, by the work of God or something else, walking alongside the harbour of Nassau as I always did, where a ship, the *Irene*, had docked earlier that one day to do whatever business it was conducting. I looked upon the faces of a ship's new arrivals to the island whenever the chance presented itself. Upon looking at the *Irene*, I saw the fleeting shape of a man, a most dark man, removing his gangly, lanky self from the ship. He walked up the dock to my right as I turned to walk slowly away from the harbour and into town. After I faintly saw the distant figure and turned away, he called out to me.

"Rollins," the voice yelled.

The man's voice sounded familiar. I looked back. His face, as it approached, was that of a man who returned from the dead— Jalal. My jaw went down, and my heart went up, both travelling into my throat. My forgotten friend. He approached and I smiled. We embraced in a hug, a shocking, confusing hug. I hugged him forever. I recalled the cay. I imagined his anger, as I pressed my face into his shoulder, was superseded by his humanity. It must have been, for how could he hug the man who abandoned him?

"Ye were dead. Dead to me. I never sent for ye, I'm afraid. Ye must hate me for it," I said to him, forgetting my whereabouts, only concerned with the man in front of me.

"I do not blame you. Yes, my wife is dead but I survived. A ship was passing through and I was rescued. It was your blade that saved me and kept us fed," Jalal said as he showed me the old dagger, and put it back on his person, keeping it.

"And... and... ye're alive, but ye're here?" I asked and we started walking together slowly.

"Yes, I was the only survivor. Even if the English and the rest of the world cannot track you fellows down, an architect is smart enough to find a way to you," Jalal said and smiled.

"So it is true then... we are hunted?" I asked.

"Desperately," Jalal said, as I guided him to join my walk back toward the original direction I was travelling in.

"And how did ye find yer way here, on this *Irene*?" I asked, pointing to the ship.

"Faith," he said.

"Oh, my—" I began to respond.

Jalal stopped me and himself from our walking banter with an outstretched arm.

"I have something I must do. I did not return here to just find you, my olde friend. Is the captain still on the island as some say?" Jalal asked.

"Why do ye ask this of me? Do ye wish to compromise me or my olde captain?" I asked him, retaining a partial, if dying, allegiance to the captain and the life I decided to abandon earlier that day.

"I ask to see the man who tried to kill me. I want to look at the murderer and regain satisfaction for my wife, both of us knowing I survived and beat him," Jalal said and I could not refuse.

"He is holed up in town, in his own quarter, near the Governor. They apparently have some union together, *quid pro quo*," I responded, as a messenger.

"I know enough English but I do not know the phrase you speak," Jalal said.

"One of the men's hands washes the other man's hands. And vice versa. They are partners, likely in business," I responded, clarifying. "Captain scratches the Governor's back and the Governor repays his favour. Ye follow?"

"Yes. You shall take me to him," Jalal ordered me.

I escorted him into town. At the building where he was said to reside, the captain was either unresponsive or not around. Jalal and I decided to walk around for some time after looking for the captain, then sit on some steps. Where we sat atop the steps it was easy to see if Captain Bridgeman entered the supposed quarter. Jalal and I maintained silence for a brief moment until he chronicled what happened on the island after the Mughals and us pirates left them for dead. In the middle of his story, at the point where he was just losing his wife to starvation, and he was nearly succumbing to the sun, displaying terrible grief and miraculous overcoming, we saw Captain Bridgeman with Filch, the new and useless bos'n. They were at the bottom of the stairs and we were atop. No more was Captain Bridgeman a bearer of that notorious red coat, his dead giveaway. He dressed in neutral colours henceforth, of tans and greys, the much lighter garments helping him blend in. Finally, the Captain relieved himself of his oh-so-weather-inappropriate attire, and adopted practical, lighter clothing for the heat of the Caribbean.

The two men stopped at the bottom of the stairs and looked at us. Jalal rose up, and their stares left me. Jalal and the Captain found their gazes locked upon each other.

"Cole," Captain Bridgeman greeted me.

"Ahoy, Cap'n," I responded.

"Good day, sir," Captain Bridgeman addressed Jalal, not recognising him, and then Captain put his hand upon the handle of his own sword.

Captain was suspicious. He likely believed I had a man there who would aid me in turning him in for my own amnesty and a fatty prize. He must have been paranoid, as he would lightly look me in the eyes, and then look around the environment as much as possible without displaying his concern. His mind was scattered. It was interesting to watch him react to his own illusions, and drift further from the confident boulder of a man I had once looked up to. But beside me was not a man of the authorities, it was Jalal, an old friend nearly killed by the Captain ascending the stairs beside his new bos'n. Jalal stood next to me with a most eager look upon his face. His eyes did not leave Captain Bridgeman. I witnessed it all.

"I have made peace with Allah, but your debt shall never be paid, and you shall suffer forever for it," Jalal said to Captain Bridgeman, speaking in a moral riddle.

"And who are ye... a priest?" Captain Bridgeman volleyed back, feeling threatened and administering threat in return.

"I am the man who hath lost a wife to you. A man who swore vengeance on you when I saw the life leave her eyes," Jalal said, as the two men kept ascending the stairs slowly and I backed away from the confrontation.

"I've dispatched many men and many women before, lad. I don't know ye," Captain Bridgeman said.

"But you didn't kill me. And I shall not kill you, for you are the lowest of the earth. The wind will take you, and the rivers shall take you, for your blood you've shed already fills the streams of the world. You are too low of a human to strike down. Guilt is your curse and evil lives with you as your burden. You will never know any good. That is vengeance enough, and I have not the life left in me anymore to fight you, you ugly thing," Jalal said, as a prophet from another world.

"Then shall ye know death? Is that yer wish?" Captain Bridgeman asked Jalal, as they stood face to face.

Jalal did not answer. All he did was stare at Captain, stare into him, intimidating him, making him feel weak and out of control.

"What does yer dog want, Cole?" Captain asked me, laughing in the remark and looking to his bos'n for an answering smile.

Captain and Filch were both clearly uncomfortable at the incessant staring. Captain looked at me, and I kept a straight gaze, shaking my head in the unknown. Jalal continued staring at Captain. He just kept bloody staring.

"And has yer mission been completed, speaking to me like some priest and holding empty hands like a coward?" Captain asked of Jalal.

"I don't need to fight you," Jalal said, staring and smiling at Captain.

In Captain's true nature, he couldn't resist an honest fight, even if it was one-sided. Captain punched Jalal in the gut, who then fell to the stairs. Captain grabbed a pistol from his person, and beat Jalal's guts with the butt of it. I stepped in after two or three blows to break it up. If I was not there, Captain likely would have killed Jalal. Captain and Filch continued walking past us, releasing the suspicion of any theoretical betrayal I was believed to be participating in. And as he was nearly gone, Captain turned around and spoke to me.

"Cole, the bounty hunters and whomever wants us shall arrive in days, Trott told me. We must leave the island, if ye are still a man of my crew," Captain said, holstering his pistol, and walked away.

After he recuperated, Jalal and I spent the day out of town. I took him fishing with me on my *Mackerel*. He took some time to recover and then finished his story about his survival and arrival. Then we took turns philosophising and talking of our past. His grief was buried. The fishing was fulfilling and the fruit of the island was sweet. Fish and fruit were the only things I ate anymore.

"I shall be going to a place called Port Royal, Rollins. I look forward to seeing you there if you find a way," Jalal remarked to me, sitting on the white sand.

"Aye. Maybe," I said.

"I will be leaving tomorrow afternoon and you should come with me, friend, before you meet the hangman," Jalal said to me, and then I looked to the sandy spot beneath a crooked tree where I buried my chest of plunder in the earth.

Jalal stayed in my camp for the evening, then departed, disappearing into town for he was to leave with the *Irene* that next day. I came to my own private conclusion to sell my *Mackerel* and buy passage to Port Royal alongside him, aboard the vessel. That next day I dug up my stashed chest and met with a baker on the island in the early morning. I paid him heavily, watching him carefully conduct the job I had tasked him with. He was a reserved lad, so I dared to trust him. I employed him to bake a loaf of bread stashed with my remaining unearthed gold, silver, jewels, and ivory within the dough— the safest place to hide loot. I made my exit plan up as I went along. I had bought a pouch to put only necessary, non-foreign coins within, which I would keep readily available for safe usage. I was on my way to the harbourmaster, bright and early, to see about selling my *Mackerel* shallop as fast as possible that day and get some money back. I carried my pouch on my person and in my arm I carried my *bread*, wrapped in cloth. The streets never saw a more concealed, rich man. It was on that bright, sunny day some twenty paces from the harbourmaster's office I was walking toward to sell my old boat and ditch the past, when I saw Captain Bridgeman frantically running in my direction holding his dangling, heavy chest. He was pistol-less, sword-less, and potentially dagger-less. Something was wrong. I'd never seen my old captain run frantically before. Nor had I ever seen him disarmed unless he was in his quarters alone.

"They're here, Cole. They know where we are. A dozen men captured. I know not where the crew goes," Captain Bridgeman said to me underneath a yell, looking behind him as he sprinted toward me.

"Lord," I said, shaking my head, and continuing with him, running away from the harbourmaster, from town, and returning to the outskirts where I came from, toward my camp in the woods and away from the *Irene*.

All thoughts of the *Irene* departed my mind, and I thought the worst— thought of the noose, firing line, and authorities. I thought I would not see life beyond New Providence. But those thoughts left me, and all I did was run out ahead of Captain Bridgeman, guiding him for once, toward my camp.

We ran like the gales of Poseidon into the wilderness, the scenic route to my *puerto pequeño*. We got to my camp and I glanced at the tent and table nearby. I grabbed some of my food and threw it in a sack. I did not dare toss my cloth-wrapped *bread* into the sack of provisions containing fruit, fish, gunpowder, water, grog, musket balls, and a compass. I concealed the loaf of *bread* within my shirt, as I had done with the first fish I ever caught and filleted months ago.

"Tell me ye've got a plan, Cole," Captain yelled at me, as I stood next to my table and he stood panting, hands on his hips.

"Ye're the captain for Heaven's sake," I fired back and began to move toward the watery coast, where the trees ended, sand relaxed, and my shallop stood land-anchored.

"The *Mackerel*?" Captain Bridgeman yelled. "Ye named this thing the *Mackerel*?"

"Ye're damn right," I said to him, defending my honour and taste in ship naming.

We both entered the shallop where I was captain, in my territory. My sack of provisions and Captain's heavy chest both thudded on the wood when we placed them down. We released the anchor and used the oars to move along, off and away from my camp. We sailed with haste to the northeast, along the skin edge of the New Providence coast until it was visible no more. After passing Potter's Cay we headed further northward toward what looked to be an inlet along and within Hog Island, the island across the harbour, north of Montagu Bay. We got as far from the partly-constructed fort of western New Providence as possible.

We effectively sailed the *Mackerel*, Captain and I, to the other side of Nassau Harbour in our flight. Nearing our destination, we lowered the mainsail and rowed the shallop into the little harbour and land-anchored it again. We escaped capture by slim margins. But we had only bought ourselves time, as this was not a true escape, only a temporary get away. Captain exited the shallop with his treasure chest and I exited with the provision sack.

"Let's take these to the treeline," I said.

We moved along, out of the shore's sight, to drop our valuables— the chest and sack— just beyond a pair of palm trees to hide them. Captain and I walked back onto the sand and sat down. We looked to the other side of the small harbour and the *Mackerel* in between. I double-checked that my pouch of coins and cloth-wrapped *bread* were still on my person. The time was silent and my thoughts drifted from escape, moving toward the silent captain beside me.

"D'ye know where yer goin' next?" I asked Captain.

He didn't respond. Deafening silence. Then I looked over to him, staring to the other side of the inlet. He shook his head 'no' then looked down.

"Do ye?" He mumbled.

"A ship leaves Nassau for Port Royal today. I intend to be on it one way or another," I said.

"What kind of ship?" Captain asked me.

"I don't know. I just know the best option is to strap meself to her mast and let fate do what it must," I said.

"Any man who straps himself to the mainmast is a madman," Captain said, laughing, sharing a moment of humour with me.

"Any Englishman who goes to Nassau is a madman," I said.

"Where ye from, Cole?" Captain Bridgeman asked me.

"I'm from Newton Ferrers, from Devonshire. Same as ye," I said.

"Oye, ye didn't tell me," Captain said.

"Aye, aye," I said and the conversation fell silent once more.

We spent much time on the little shore of the Hog Island cove discussing plans for escape from the Nassau authorities. Captain repeatedly mentioned his fear of being recognised. The man was so afraid, so tenderised by panic. After we cooled off and the prospect of being caught was reduced, I took some fruit out of the sack of provisions then went south to where the inlet ended and the Nassau Harbour began, in order to spot the *Irene* on its departure, whenever that would be. I peeled and ate an orange.

Captain lent me a small spyglass of his, but upon first examination, I could not tell if the *Irene* had left the port yet or not. I felt certain, also, that the captain would join me in sailing and buying our way onto the *Irene*, in the middle of the open harbour if necessary. It felt to be our last chance, other than hiding on Hog Island beyond that day. The Hog Island prospect was utterly undesirable, and so was the likely prospect the authorities would find us there if we remained. We elected to risk buying passage onto a vessel that was potentially hunting us.

After some time as morning turned into afternoon, but with evening still remaining far away, Captain brought our sack of provisions and his chest of treasure to sit beside me, so as to keep the valuables within easy reach. The *bread* stayed in my shirt. We kept watch in the direction of the Nassau port, waiting, looking through the piercing glare of the sun's reflection on the water. I thought the *Irene* had been halted, or had departed the harbour unorthodoxly to the west, instead of our eastern direction. The waiting panged me as I stared at the big island to my right, and I began falling into a boiling pit of doubt.

Did Jalal lie to me? Was he embittered about his ordeal and thus tried to get both his attempted murderer and his bystander old friend caught and killed? Was every moment he and I shared the night in my camp before as friends simply part of a conniving plan, a small procedure in a grand scheme of revenge? Did the authorities come to Nassau on the *Irene* itself? Is the *Irene* in the port of Nassau for many days beyond today? Where was Jalal?

I did not know and I could not know for certain the answers to any of my burning questions, but when I spotted an approaching ship on the horizon bearing a similar appearance to that of the *Irene* from my brief memory of her, I knew we had to take our chances. We moved quickly to load our short, slow boat with the chest and sack within the hollow footing area in front of the tiller, and climbed into our respective positions on the shallop ourselves. Removing it from my shirt, I hid my wrapped loaf of *good bread* in the sack of provisions, and ordered myself to remember its place.

We released the anchor and rowed our way out of the little harbour near the island's end until our mainsail took over the task. There was more than enough time to meet in a collision course, undoubtedly fear-filled, for our little ship was aimed to cut into the frontward path of the far off, incoming, large ship. This was our chance. The wind felt to be generous and fate had returned into my favour for the moment. We neared closer, heading strongly southward, as the ship approached from the west. With each glance at her, I felt more secure in my gamble that this was the *Irene*.

"D'ye know Cole, every man I come across thinks of us pyrates as good fellows. We've earned the lot's admiration," Captain Bridgeman said, looking off in the distance as an obliviously arrogant man on a vessel captained and steered by his former trusted crewmate behind him and facing him.

"Only those who don't know what happened to the Mughals. Only those who don't know of what we did say that," I said.

"Yer wrong, Cole. It is not just pyrates who the people love, it is I. If the people could speak, they'd have me welcomed as their hero, not the criminal," Captain said.

We were almost halfway to our desired position on the water.

"And what would the Mughal want to become of ye?" I asked.

"The King of Pyrates. Same as the Libertalians," Captain said.

"Yer mad," I said, laughing and shaking my head, noticing his smile out of the corner of my eye as I removed my gaze from the distant, incoming vessel.

I turned my head to the back and right, looking at the wood stern of my vessel, her tiller, and rudder. Instantaneously, I felt the *Mackerel* shift weight. I glanced back over toward the front of the vessel and Captain as he stood up then moved reasonably closer to me as I was working the tiller. Then, he got too close and the *Mackerel* rocked sharply. The unarmed Bridgeman lunged toward me with his right hand, grabbing the handle of my sword on my left hip, attempting to remove it from my scabbard. I grabbed the wrist of his lunging arm with my left hand, freezing the sword in the scabbard and his grasp on the handle.

"What are ye doing?" I yelled at him.

He took his other hand, his left hand, and charged it into my neck, to choke me and suffocate me. My right hand abandoned the tiller to let the rudder do what she wanted, speedily trying to rip his fingers from its deadly grip upon my neck. I had no breath, no sight, and was being pushed back nearly over the rear-port side of my *Mackerel*, my rocking *Mackerel*. His indestructible hand closed my throat and my neck was pressured toward fatality. My instinct then took over in my confusion.

I disallowed him to fully extract the half-removed sabre from my scabbard, and before the closing, devilish hand could snap my choking gullet, I released my right hand from his gauntlet then pulled my knife out from behind my waist, out of his sight, and plunged the fish-dagger-blade into where his abdomen met his back, on the left side of his torso. I fiercely twisted the blade, lodging it into him and disarming him. The rage on his face turned to shock. I had to pry the loosening grip from my neck, regaining my breath and control. It happened within a moment.

His grasp upon the handle of my sword, almost completely unsheathed, loosened, and I let go of his wrist. Bridgeman fell down and my sword fell back into its scabbard, making a subtle clank sound. I gasped loudly, trying to force air back into my throat. The *Mackerel* rocked again as his dead weight fell to the floor of the shallop, jolting her. I stood up over him at his feet, diagonally resting atop the bench. His body remained in the crease between the shallop's two rearward benches. His eyebrows pointed inward and upward, and his brow grew incredibly furrowed. It happened too fast for me to comprehend.

"*Phstneaugh. Huoughhtt,*" he grunted in imperceptible pain.

I moved closer but kept my distance. Captain was not dead, and retained my knife in the most painful of bodily holsters. I ducked to look under the sail and see over the bow's starboard side, to determine whether the approaching ship was too far away to view what had happened unless she looked with a spyglass. We were hidden, covered by the sail. It was far enough. I looked back down at Captain, whose face was manic and becoming ever paler. He continued making grunting sounds in angst. I could not feel anything, and I noticed my heart beating intensely. My animal protected my life. I looked in his face, darting my eyes upon his wound and back toward his eyes.

"Why? Why did ye make me do that?" I yelled, crying as I lowered myself down to move my face near his.

His face, along with mine, was all wrinkled and wrought. Mine was full of energy and sadness, whereas his was full of white and struggle.

"Ye... *pshnoughuh*... ye wanted my treasure. Ye were gonna sell me out. I knew it. Ye and yer friend were turning me in," Bridgeman said.

"Ye're mad... Yer reason is lost," I yelled.

"I... I... have... what ye wanted," Bridgeman responded, unwaveringly denying any humanity in either of us.

"I never wanted yer bloody treasure. Is it in yer nature to strike the friend who lends ye a hand? I wanted to save both of us, not betray ye," I responded.

I looked at our heading, tailing too far starboard, off path.

"I knew ye only brought me here... for my chest and the bounty," Bridgeman said.

I moved away to the next compartment to create distance.

"Ye slither in my trust, my honest trust. And ye—ye lurk as a serpent of Satan. I—I—," I said but could not finish my sentence, unsure of what to say.

I was full of confusion and heavy emotions as I looked at Bridgeman descending slowly into near lifelessness, from a few steps in front of him where he couldn't see my face.

"I know yer plot," Bridgeman said.

"No," I returned and remained beside myself.

"Ye... ye said it then... I'm a pyrate.—It...—I—I guess it is... my nature," Bridgeman said, then drifted. "Put me out of my misery... ye fool," Bridgeman gave me one last order.

I took my eyes off the stabbed Bridgeman, turned around, and went one compartment further toward the bow of my *Mackerel* to remove a musket ball and powder from the provision sack. I loaded my flintlock after looking backward at his body near the stern of the vessel, cocked the flintlock, then returned to stand near the tiller and aim the weapon at his head. I stood, aiming and aiming, then lowered the flintlock to move closer to his side again. I knelt beside my old captain and put the pistol up against his wrinkled forehead. He stared up at the barrel then at me, menacingly. I pointed the pistol at the man who gave it to me a long time ago.

"Do it, Cole," Bridgeman said and nodded once sharply.

I held the flintlock to his head, above his temple, and clutched onto his grey jacket. I remained in this position for an eternity, looking into his eyes. Every question came upon me, and I was lost.

I got back up to stand on my feet, and kept the flintlock pointed at him from a distance. I lowered the pistol, turning away to hide my face from him, and yearned for absolution. I silently yelled within up to the heavens, screaming in a whispering agony at the betrayal. With a broken heart I looked and searched for God. But He was not there, and He did not put His gentle, guiding hand upon my shoulder that day. So I got to thinking. I stood frozen, captive in my *Mackerel*, and cried. I begrudged the saviour, Jesus Christ, for never having to hold this pistol in his hands, for never facing the dilemma and ability of killing a man he once looked up to. And then, I understood. I understood all too well in my great folly, my flawed thinking and wicked justifications.

I raised up the pistol once more. This was where boys become men. And my heart cried for deliverance, screaming quietly for whatever God could bring me. I did not know what the answer was. I darted my eyes to see we were far off course from our deliverance. The pistol rattled in my hand, and it then rattled no more as I squeezed then fired a shot. The loudest bang echoed through the air and my soul, jolting me in shock as it usually did, even when I knew the sound was coming. I was calm, and Bridgeman remained alive, as I had fired the musket ball into the water of the Nassau Harbour beside him.

"I can't." I embarrassingly let out.

I looked at him, into Bridgeman's eyes, his angry eyes. I did not give him satisfaction. I did not make him a legend or a martyr, nor did I make myself a masochist or murderer for that matter. I dropped the pistol and charged toward my old captain, an old god, a new Judas, to grab the key and twine lanyard from his neck. I searched about his person, his pockets, and, in his pocket, found the second key to his double-locked heavy chest. He remained speechless and watched me, perplexed, as I was possessed by something I had never felt before, something I shudder in thought of. Then with both keys in my possession, I moved near the sack of provisions to the chest, and opened it up. There was an extraordinary amount of treasure— the absolute lion's share.

I threw his discharged flintlock, the one that was meant to be in my hands only until that moment, into the chest filled heavy with gold, silver, gemstones, and bright ivory. I trusted the odds of buying my way onto the incoming ship without a pistol. I slammed the chest shut, superiorly confident in myself, without taking a single coin of his. I ripped the end of the twine lanyard, put the twine lanyard through the second key, tied it again, and placed the two keys for his treasure chest around my neck and underneath my shirt. If Bridgeman were ever to hunt me down for revenge, if he survived, these keys would provide insurance for keeping me alive. They filled the empty area on my torso where my treasure chest's key twine lanyard once was. I rummaged through the sack of provisions to grab my *holy loaf of bread*, removing it from the bag of mysteries, and then left all of the other food and supplies in the provision sack on the shallop with Bridgeman. I then summoned all of my strength and willpower to lift his heavy treasure and gun-filled chest to the rail of the *Mackerel*, my *Mackerel*, resting one of the sides on the bench and the other over the open water.

"What—what are ye doing?" Bridgeman clamoured, looking at his chest and I out of his peripherals.

I said nothing, ignoring him, and kicked the heavy chest full of gold, jewels, rubies, and a discharged pistol to descend into the bottom of Nassau Harbour, sending it plummeting to the ocean floor.

I looked into his eyes as I discarded and forgot the supposed prize, viewing his contorted face, his guilt ridden eyes shedding tears. His head looked down. He never before cried in my presence, but I dared not cry in his.

I swung the tiller to redirect the rudder chaotically away from the direction of the incoming ship, putting the *Mackerel* onto some random path. Then I unsheathed my sword and sliced the mainsail apart, rendering the boat dysfunctional and leading the boat wherever the wind would take it, far away and off the path of our incoming vessel. My *Mackerel* was free. Then I grasped the wrapped *loaf of bread*, nestled it into the safe harmony of my arm, walked away from Bridgeman toward the bow, and jumped into the water of Nassau Harbour. Abandon ship. I didn't look back at first, but then decided to steal a last glance. I swam toward the direction of the incoming ship, no longer waiting for deliverance, instead moving forward, toward it, taking the initiative as a captain should. I swam for a lifetime. The tears I cried, upon my one-armed swim directly west, relayed from my eyes to my cheeks to the ocean. I did my best to keep the *bread* above the water. I felt the twine lanyard keys banging against my chest along my swim. The sun shone brightly and warmly upon me from above. And I was washed clean by the harbour of Nassau, the waters where I left my days of piracy behind, swimming toward an unknown ship.

Christmas Day, 1696. Skerries, Ireland. I live here, beside my native island, not as Rollins Cole. I go by Henry Bridgeman among the locals. I am a fisherman. The ship that approached me on that April day in the Nassau Harbour was not the *Irene*. It was a privateer vessel titled the *Jackal*. After swimming close enough to the vessel's path, I was spotted, and brought aboard. I paid their captain and crew the entire non-foreign, gold and silver filled pouch of mine to bring me along toward their destination, Tortuga. Upon arrival, I ripped open my near-soggy *bread* and went to a proper blacksmith for the smelting of my Mughal gold and silver. I used the ivory to trade for and buy a new dagger and a Holy Bible, respectively. I ripped the Bible apart with my dagger, making a hidden compartment in the pages for my gold, silver, and gemstones. I removed the twin key lanyard from my neck and tied it around the book, closing it. All it took was patience, dear patience. Tortuga is the land of pirates, where everyone is a thief. And the only place pirates won't enter in Tortuga is the House of God. Nor did they act with patience. So I hid everything in the best, safest place— the Good Book.

I then bought passage upon a thin-crewed vessel called the *Rubicon*, and had finally arrived alive in Port Royal to conduct my search for Jalal. I was in Port Royal for a few weeks and could not find Jalal anywhere I went, nor did any Every or Bridgeman come knocking on my door, demanding keys to some chest at the bottom of a harbour. I even looked for my old mate, Thomas Howard, who was rumoured to have fled New Providence for Port Royal, but I found nothing to prove the rumour true. The port was a booming pirate sprawl, even after an earthquake had ravaged the land some years before. Captain Joseph Faro later came to the island of Port Royal and I found myself reunited in the company of his crew one night, which privileged me the opportunity to recount the valour of our great thievery. They allowed me to sail with them on the *Sea Flower* to Ireland in July.

Captain Faro's lads frequently asked what became of Captain Every, or Captain Bridgeman. I did not speak of the last time I saw him. I told them I did not know of his fate, claiming I was ignorant of the matter. I truly was. Aboard, we all adopted new, different names with forged documents to get into Ireland. Who would look for the most wanted pirates in England's own backyard? I was the only one who kept any resemblance to the names of old. Who would think the most wanted man on the face of the earth would keep any part of his real name or alias? I told the crew of the *Sea Flower* that the name I adopted, Henry Bridgeman, the two halves of both his Christian name and his alias, was a risky effort in order to draw attention away from him, wherever the captain was, and possibly misdirect it toward me. That name was the safest moniker I could conceivably forge. And adopting it was one of the most foolish things I've ever done. I don't understand why I did it.

Maybe I would be proven mad and my door could be busted down any day by the old captain or by the King's soldiers. But keeping his name somewhat somewhere on record could prolong his legend, maintaining it within the minds of the people and even my progeny. Or so I told myself. That decision comprised my endmost duty to my old captain and it ensured I'd never forget all that had happened. I would remember what my expired idol had become, and what I had done to move on, who I became.

Upon arrival in Ireland, I did not know where I would go, nor did I travel further with any of the crew, but I found my way alone to a place the locals called the "Hill of Tara", where the Irish *Stone of Destiny* remained. I buried the old captain's twin keys in the dirt beside the place where all of the High Kings of Ireland were once coronated. I got what I wanted, what I never had, and what I thought was lost to a time before mine. The King of Pirates is dead. Long live the King.

ACKNOWLEDGEMENTS

To Wendy Leigh, thank you for believing in me, encouraging my gifts, and inspiring me to make the impossible possible. Your generous listening and occasional wake up calls allowed both the book and I to find our way. Without you and your intuition, this book would not exist, and I never would have gone sailing on this exhilarating journey. You have my gratitude for inspiring the life of these characters and keeping their integrity intact. To collaborating on one great story and to many more— cheers.

To Kerry Patrick McCarthy, thank you for teaching me how to be honest as a writer and a human being. I am forever indebted to you and forever grateful for the experiences I had in your classroom. I cherish the inspiration and passion for literature that was born in me because of you and those days.

To Zachary Low Reyna of The Editing Cooperative, thank you for your direct and precise feedback. You were the first professional to read the manuscript, and were incredibly helpful in its refinement. I greatly appreciate how gentle, academic, and sincere your critiques were. Your observations helped clarify the big picture of what this book is supposed to be, and greatly matured me as an author.

To Gary Smailes of BubbleCow and Ben Espach, thank you for bringing Rollins and I both out of our internal milieu and into life. Gary, your esteem of the book meant the world to me. I am incredibly thankful to have met your standards, not only as an author, but as an American who wrote about Englishmen and wrote from an Englishman's perspective.

To Dennis Moritz, thank you for being the first writer to impress artistic advice upon me, and for keeping my manuscript safe. On many occasions, both purposefully and unintentionally, you gifted me lessons on how to take a group of words and lift them into poetry. I am lucky to be your "fellow traveller."

To Robert Craig Baum, thank you for firing on all cylinders and setting a fire in my belly. The enthusiasm you have is wonderfully contagious. You have always challenged me to tell the truth, in both real world and fictional settings, setting flames to any firewood that I may have.

To Avram Dorfman, thank you for taking me sailing and granting me the hospitality of a true friend. I treasure our adventures and their lessons. Even if a sailor gets queasy or vomits, he's still a sailor.

ABOUT THE AUTHOR

WILL RITTWEGER is an actor, writer, director, and filmmaker from New Jersey. He has contributed articles to *New Jersey Digest* and *dosage Magazine*; acted on stage with avant-garde theatre group, *N1 Theatre*; and is the producer, co-writer, and lead actor of period-piece feature film *Man Freed*.

Will aims to move people deeply by telling stories and playing characters, whether communicated through the written word, moving image, or human instrument. When he isn't writing or working on a project, his favorite hobbies include hiking, camping, cooking, and playing baseball.

www.ingramcontent.com/pod-product-compliance
Lightning Source LLC
Chambersburg PA
CBHW022110310726
48972CB00007B/1975